MW01141923

For Mar...
thanks for
reading +
coming to support
me!

Reconcilable
DIFFERENCES

Enjoy the journey

Mary Ann

Copyright © 2016 by: Mary Ann F Clarke Scott
ISBN: 978-0-9949507-1-0

ALL RIGHTS RESERVED. No part of this publication may be reproduced, distributed, or transmitted in any form or by any means, including photocopying, recording, or other electronic or mechanical methods, without the prior permission of the publisher.

This is a work of fiction. Any resemblance of characters to actual persons, living or dead, is purely coincidental. M A Clarke Scott holds exclusive rights to this work. Unauthorized duplication is prohibited.

You can sign up to follow M A Clarke Scott's blog & website at www.maryannclarkescott.com to get release dates, discounts, giveaways and contests.

Library and Archives Canada Cataloguing in Publication

Clarke Scott, M. A., author
        Reconcilable differences / M.A. Clarke Scott.
(A having it all novel)
Issued in print and electronic formats.
ISBN 978-0-9949507-0-3 (paperback).
--
ISBN 978-0-9949507-1-0 (ebook)
I. Title.
PS8605.L372R43 2016   C813'.6
        C2016-905642-2
        C2016-905643-0

Reconcilable
DIFFERENCES

M A CLARKE SCOTT

For Pindy

Because you always knew I was a closet shrink.
And because you've been there since the beginning.

one

Kate O'Day checked her watch, eager to begin, but they were still missing two important players. Today marked the beginning of a brand new mediation. She scribbled the date in bold strokes at the top of the page of her case notes.

She sat back and observed the woman across from her, the immaculately well-groomed and chic D'arcy Duchamp, her client. D'arcy stared sightlessly out the window at the grey haze that blanketed downtown Vancouver's urban skyline, patently ignoring her mother's chosen counsel, Sharon Beckett. Not surprisingly, top dollar.

The sound of the door opening caught their attention and the young receptionist stepped in. "Excuse me, Ms. Beckett? Lynda from Goode & Broadbent just called to say, Mr. Broadbent was suddenly called to judge's chambers and won't be able to attend. But they are sending a replacement."

Their host, Sharon Beckett, sat beside Kate, her tightly coifed flaxen head bent over her smart phone, jabbing it forcefully with her fingertip. "I didn't get any message about this, Carrie."

Carrie cleared her throat daintily. "Um. No, apparently it was quite unexpected. They sent their apologies."

"Well they'd better not keep us waiting. Who's coming instead?"

"Someone named, uh…" she referred to a paper in her hand, "Simon… Sharpe?"

Kate gasped, her body stiffening like she'd been hit with a Taser right there in her chair.

"Oh, really? All right, then," Sharon crooned. "Thank you, Carrie. Let us know when he arrives."

Kate's hand jerked up to cover her mouth, her pulse kicking into high gear at the sound of his name.

"Oh well, these things happen. I'd forgotten he'd recently changed firms. I haven't been in touch with him much lately." Sharon lifted her head, a small frown creasing her brow. "I assume, Kate, that you informed Eli of today's meeting. He won't know about this change."

Kate had worked with Sharon before and was familiar with her reputation. She was a darn good lawyer, but she was rigid, repressed, and confrontational. Right now, she couldn't think of a response. Her thoughts were suddenly scrambled. Had she heard correctly? She swallowed. "Who did you say?"

Sharon made Kate uncomfortable. Sharon reserved a special tone of voice for her colleagues. Tolerance, iced with a hint of disapproval, as though she couldn't be sure you were worthy. With her crisp taupe suit and primly buttoned sage green blouse, she reminded Kate of a tiny, tightly wound army sergeant ready to pounce on wayward recruits. One could never fault her. She was always correct, strictly business, though one came away feeling abused, somehow. "Eli?"

"No, I mean–" She couldn't bring herself to say his name aloud. Simon. Simon Sharpe. Kate's breath became as shallow as a gentle breeze ruffling the surface of a calm lake, upsetting the glass-smooth surface, tossing a leaf or two into the air like the harbinger of an as-yet unseen storm. A storm that would soon heave the water of the lake upside down, churning its muddy, murky bottom into a roiling stew pot of reluctant rememberings. If she stopped breathing, maybe she could prevent the storm from coming.

"*I* left him a message, Sharon," D'arcy cut in, a knowing smirk on her glossy ruby lips, like the self-possessed cherubs that Kate had seen in the Baroque paintings of Rubens.

"Good." Sharon offered D'arcy a patronizing smile that stopped short of her icy blue eyes. "Well, well. So we'll be working with the charming Simon Sharpe."

She had heard correctly. But there must be some mistake. Or maybe it was someone else with the same name. That was possible, wasn't it? The thought of him walking into the room any moment caused Kate's stomach to clench into a hard, heavy knot of dread.

"You know him?" D'arcy asked, examining the perfect claret tips of her soft white hands.

Do I ever! He'd touched her body and soul.

"I was in law school with his wife. We're good friends," Sharon replied.

His wife. Of course, he would have a wife. Why wouldn't he? Kate hadn't seen him in –her mind spun back in time, calculating, counting the years– fourteen? Fifteen? Since her third year at university.

D'arcy shrugged and reached for her small Louis Vuitton handbag, retrieved a nail file, made a minor correction to her manicure and put it back. She tossed the bag onto an empty chair.

As if from a distance, Kate observed the way her hands fluttered about like doves in a cote, in direct contrast with her serene countenance. She was a strange mix of cool confidence and nervous energy. And now so was Kate, aware that she felt breathless, her pulse racing. Adrenaline flushed her body, her head and chest suddenly hot, sweat breaking out on her face.

Kate frowned, taking in the cool, glossy black lacquer table, the spare modern leather and chrome chairs and stark white walls. A too-loud hum emanated from a grill vent in the ceiling and the view from the eighteenth floor window was flat and faded by cloud covering the sky. She had a sudden image of herself fleeing, flying out the window like a bird and disappearing into that soft, concealing grey. The ostentatious board room of Flannigan, Searle, Meacham & Beckett, Barristers & Solicitors, was as cold as a surgical theatre and too impersonal for Kate's liking. As soon as she'd won her clients' trust, she'd suggest a move to her own, more homey, studio.

Her muscles tightened again. But she couldn't have him there, in her space.

D'arcy cleared her throat and spoke in that peculiar accent that was uniquely Montreal-bilingual, neither the lilting cadence of a Quebecois Francophone nor CBC-Radio English, but something in between. "I'm dying for a cigarette."

"Are you nervous, D'arcy?" Kate asked, distracted. "Today will be just an informal introduction. Nothing too serious, yet." Not for D'arcy, anyway.

D'arcy rolled her khol-rimmed round eyes toward the ceiling. "No. I'm just in nicotine withdrawal. I'm quitting." She was glamorous in a silent-movie-siren sort of way, but dark circles under her eyes betrayed an otherwise cool, well-contained façade. "I *have* quit."

"That's an excellent decision, D'arcy, dear. Your mother will be pleased to hear it," Sharon said, glancing up from her phone.

D'arcy's lip twitched, barely suppressing a sneer. "I suppose you'll be discussing that with her, too? Would you like to know what I ate for lunch?"

Sharon clucked her tongue and went back to her phone, her teeth clicking. "What's taking them so long? We can't wait all day."

Kate pulled herself together and bent over her notebook to jot down a few impressions while they were fresh. She wasn't known for following the norm — such as meeting clients individually prior to the first group session — and she had chosen not to this time as well. Her unconventional style involved feeling her way through based on the people and their raw reactions, affording her a glimpse into their inner nature. She glanced up, her eye drawn to the sweeping arc of a red umbrella in an impressionistic Mediterranean landscape on the wall opposite her. The gash of red against blue sky provided the only spots of color in the sterile room.

Today's introductory session was just that, an opportunity for her to get to know her clients, D'arcy and Eli. And, unfortunately, their lawyers. Kate had to stay calm and keep her wits about her. Focus on the clients. Right. Just ignore the lawyers. Both of them. As if she could ever ignore Simon Sharpe.

Sharon pulled a notebook and pen out of her briefcase and silently made notes. Kate tried to smile at D'arcy, who offered a weak smile of her own.

"When did you last speak with Eli?" Kate asked her.

Her face sullen, D'arcy searched around with an exaggerated air. "A couple of weeks ago, maybe."

Sharon flipped a few pages in her notebook. "It was September seventeenth. The night of the..." her lip lifted in a sneer, "... party."

D'arcy's eyes turned glassy, and Kate fervently wished she could do her work without the interference of lawyers.

Clients came to her because they hoped for a resolution to their conflict that was as congenial as possible, usually in the context of a complete communication breakdown. She looked up, pushed a loose strand of hair behind her ear. Success for her was nothing short of reconciliation, healing broken relationships.

The better she understood their strengths, failings, and fears, the more effectively she could help them.

Her cell phone jangled in her bag. Damn, she forgot to turn it off. "Excuse me." She picked up the phone and squinted at the screen, her irritation rising at the interruption as she silenced the ringing.

Jay. The last person she wanted to hear from right now.

Guilt swamped her, her finger hovering over the "busy" button, recalling her last conversation with him. Her phone buzzed in her hand. A text.

Hey, Angel. How about dinner tonight?

She thumbed a quick response. *In client mtg.*

Another text buzzed.

She clenched her jaw and put her phone away without looking at it. She was going to need to call Alexa tonight, if she made it through this afternoon, not Jay.

She knew what he wanted and she didn't want to deal with it. Jay had been the perfect companion. Their two year relationship was a record for her. He was gorgeous, talented, fun, sexy, easy-going and lacked the capacity for self-examination. In other words, he was a long, long way from thinking about commitment. Or so she'd thought. Lately he'd begun hinting about the future, spoiling everything.

Kate studied the shell-shocked D'arcy, trying to imagine what a couple as young as she and Eli were thinking, getting married in their early twenties. No wonder they were having trouble. On the other hand, she thought with sympathy, they must have been wildly in love. Perhaps they still were. She remembered what that felt like.

Now all Kate's relationship skills went toward helping her clients sort out their problems and providing them with happy-ever-afters. That was enough for her, since she wasn't ever going to get her own.

Most people needed a prod to their self-awareness, and help clarifying their goals. Unlike Kate, who, through counseling, already knew herself far too well. If Jay knew everything there was to know about her, he wouldn't want to push for more.

There were too many ghosts in her past that made intimacy hard, if not impossible. And yet, nothing less than true intimacy could induce her to spend the rest of her life with one man. There had been only one man that had made her feel that way. She closed her eyes for a moment, feeling numb. Apparently he was about to enter the room.

The truth was she didn't need the complication of a man in her life at all. Jay distracted her from her work and somehow made her feel guilty for devoting herself to what she loved most. Except... at thirty-five, she did, in theory, want to settle down and have a family, too.

The three women sat in silence, fidgeting and avoiding eye contact, the minutes dragging, until the annoying whine of the HVAC system began to grate on their nerves. D'arcy rolled her eyes to the ceiling with a huff.

What was taking them so long? It was like waiting on death row. Kate just wanted to get it over with now.

She cleared her throat. "I understand you went to McGill, D'arcy. Did you like it?"

"What's not to like? It was my hometown, you know. All the local kids went there who didn't have a plan." D'arcy lifted one round shoulder. "I did figure out what I wanted, eventually."

"Political science, wasn't it?" pressed Kate gently.

"Yes. And history. Daddy thought I should study journalism. Maybe work at one of his magazines until I met Mr. Right." She pulled her mouth tight. "But it wasn't my thing. I organize people better than words."

"Sharon mentioned you worked as a campaign manager for a while," Kate said, nodding. "What happened? Did you enjoy it?"

"I loved it!" D'arcy paused, considering her hands again, while a wistful expression stole over her features. "Eli happened, I guess. When he came along, it was obvious he needed me more than Minister Bradley ever could." A breathy laugh escaped her lips. She paused, gazing past Kate. "Anyway, I fell hard." One side of her full lips quirked up.

She knew what that felt like. Interesting, Kate thought. So, D'arcy was one for causes, including the struggling artist Eli.

"Looks like you should have stayed in Montreal." Sharon said with a drawl. "Where are Eli and Simon, I wonder? It's nearly two."

As if on cue, the door opened again, and Carrie entered. Kate's pulse kicked up again, her eyes locked on the door, feeling an irrational but powerful urge to leap out of her chair and run like hell.

"Mr. Benjamin is here," she said with a flicker of a smile, then slipped back out the door. Kate let out her breath. Not him. Not yet. A young man entered and scanned the room through narrowed eyes. He made a point of not looking at D'arcy. Flopping himself into the chair to Kate's right, he draped his agile frame over it like a blanket. Ignoring both his wife and her lawyer, he settled back and assessed Kate from under hooded lids, while she studied him in return. She could feel the tension vibrate between husband and wife like a plucked cable, though they didn't acknowledge each other.

"Hello," Kate said, realizing the others weren't acknowledging him.

"Hey. Nice to meet you, Kathryn O'Day," he said, tossing her a careless smile, his dark espresso eyes smoldering. Ebony waves grazed the shoulders of a weathered brown leather jacket. He emanated sexual heat.

A bad boy? She held her face as neutral as she could to conceal her reaction, piercing him with her x-ray stare. "You can call me Kate. Good morning, Mr. Benjamin."

He sat up a little straighter in his chair, a veil of boredom descending, the 'come hither' expression vanishing. He yawned.

"Call me Eli. Please."

"Eli." She nodded. She quickly explained the change of council to him. "He should arrive shortly. We're overdue to begin." She glanced at her watch. "I hope you're okay with the change."

"He won't care," D'arcy said. "Eli's not one for legal matters."

"Au contraire, ma chere. I fired my last lawyer, Kate," he said pointedly, turning to her. "We didn't see eye to eye," Eli elegant dark brows furrowed. "And I really was looking forward to working with David Broadbent. He's a great guy."

"Don't worry, Eli. You'll like Simon just as well," Sharon said. "I've known him for years, and he's a fine lawyer."

Kate's skin tingled, and she suppressed a shiver of mixed anticipation and dread. Just then, she heard footsteps in the hall outside, and they turned as one to face the door like spectators at a tennis match. She straightened her spine, pulled back her shoulders and took the deep, calming *Pranayama* breaths she'd learned in yoga class. Shanti-mukti-shanti-mukti.

Eli frowned as the door opened, his eyes scanning the man who entered.

Kate's gaze locked on him, her breath frozen in her throat. There was no mistake. Simon Sharpe had hardly changed at all. Her mouth moved, but no sound emerged.

The tall blond man slid into the room. He shook the raindrops from himself and shrugged out of his wet, wrinkled raincoat, revealing a light grey suit that was hardly better. With a world-weary air, he grinned and looked around, taking everyone in. His startling bright eyes settled first on Sharon, nodding his acknowledgment while her eyes glinted like an eagle sighting prey.

He assessed D'arcy for a moment. Then his gaze rested on Eli, his brows lifted, and finally on Kate herself, where it froze, a look of bewilderment appearing, as if he found himself suddenly in the ladies room and wondered how he'd got there.

Simon Sharpe! Kate's breath stuck and her heart pounded in her tight chest. An explosion of disparate thoughts and feelings crashed around in her head, a chorus of dissonant voices. She darted an anxious glance at the others in the room, but no. They didn't know, they couldn't know who he was. To her. *Pull yourself together, Kate.*

"...em..."

Simon Sharpe! Simon! No. Her stomach lurched. Perspiration blossomed on her brow, upper lip, palms — everywhere. She tensed against the hard leather seat of her chair, wishing she could run and hide.

Kate heard Sharon speaking, circumventing Eli, who was already half out of his chair. She grinned at Simon like a Cheshire cat. "–pleasant surprise," she cooed.

He lifted one side of his mouth and his left eyebrow, an unruly wing, the only elements of asymmetry in an otherwise even and striking face and addressed the room. "Simon Sharpe. How do you do?"

"Did David—?" blurted Eli.

Simon faced Eli, rested a hand on his shoulder and took Eli's hand, almost more a caress than a handshake. "I'm sorry to catch you off guard, Mr. Benjamin. My colleague, David Broadbent," he explained to the room at large, "was suddenly called away, and asked me to step in this morning. We tried to reach you without success. I've been fully briefed."

"Hey, dude." Eli shook his hand, shrugged and flopped back into his chair.

"Simon, delightful," Sharon said. "You've met Eli. And this is D'arcy Duchamp, my client, and Kathryn O'Day, our mediator." Simon Sharpe visibly flinched. His eyes darted around to acknowledge Sharon's introductions, then sprang back. His gaze locked on Kate's face, curious, squinting. *"You're* the mediator?" She was staring. Kate took a deep ragged breath and discretely wiped her damp palms on the legs of her trousers, forced herself to rise from her chair with an outer appearance of calm and control that she didn't feel. Like an automaton, she turned and took two stiff steps toward him as he approached. Her mind whirled. *I have to take the offensive. He's late. He's unexpected. He's making me uncomfortable. What do I say to him?* She raised her gaze to his chin, attempting to swallow the cotton stuffed into her dry throat.

"Yes. Mr. Sharpe... at last." She took another reluctant step as though she were trudging to the electric chair. Should she pretend they'd never met or acknowledge that they knew each other? Play it down, then own up later? "How... nice to... meet you... again. Please take a seat. We'd like to begin." Gathering her courage, she forced herself to meet his penetrating blue eyes with her own, revealing nothing, she hoped, of her inner turmoil. She almost succeeded. Her heart thumped violently in her chest as she gaped at his familiar face. That beloved face.

"Kate?" he said, his voice a strangled whisper. He didn't move toward a chair.

"You know each other?" Sharon asked.

Did they ever. "Yes. We knew each other... as students... years ago," Kate said with a flip of her hand, as though it were nothing.

He peered at her, his face devoid of expression, his eyes searching her features.

"Isn't that right? Or am I mistaken?" Kate said, tucking a strand of hair behind her ear.

"Yes, that's true. Excuse my rudeness. I'm surprised to see you after all these years." He dropped his eyes, scanning down to her feet and up again. "Kate."

She'd seen his expression metamorphose from bewilderment to a cool blank stare, but not before she saw a flicker of annoyance there. That was no surprise. She was likely the last person on earth he wanted to see, let alone work with. However passionate their youthful affair had been, he clearly remembered, as she did, its sordid ending.

Her ribs tightened like a clamp around her lungs, squeezing. Warning. Stop it!

He couldn't possibly know how he'd broken her fragile heart when he dumped her, or that her unrequited love for him had grown into a malignant obsession that was nearly her undoing. That was her dirty little secret.

What the hell am I going to do? She reached out her trembling hand, petrified at the effect his touch would have on her. "Likewise," she murmured.

He inclined his head and gave her hand a gentle but masculine shake. Did his grip linger overlong, or had time slowed down? All her nerve endings zinged with the electrical knowledge of him, his skin touching her skin, and she could not take her eyes off their joined hands or form another coherent thought. A great weight on her chest seemed to be crushing the air out of her. She lifted her shoulders up and swallowed through a throat that seemed to be closing up, stiffening, as though she'd swallowed a bag of rocks. She recognized all the familiar signs of a panic attack, but it had been years. She'd been fine. *This can't be happening to me.*

He squinted at her, a subtle smile curving the taut bow of his lips and she jerked her hand away as though she'd been burnt. *He's laughing at me!* She was ridiculous, getting all worked up now. This shouldn't matter. But it did. It did.

It was happening again. The anxiety. She couldn't trust her own reaction to him. Looking at him made her instantly realize he had the same effect, unwittingly triggering painful memories of her trauma, tangling up her reactions to him. Attraction, obsession and repulsion. She'd thought those days were long past, all of her skeletons buried.

Simon sat next to Eli.

Kate sat down and picked up her fountain pen, noticed her hand trembling, and set it down again. She clenched her fists to stop her fingertips from tingling. How could she take notes now? She tried slow Pranayama breathing, *shanti-mukti-shanti-mukti*, smoothing her brow with nervous fingers while she stared blindly at her notes. She had to find a way to carry on as though the earth hadn't fallen out from under her.

"Shall we g-get started?" she smiled around the table, trying to meet everyone's eyes. The smile on her face was so tight she was sure it would crack. When she reached Simon, her gaze flitted past. Trickles of moisture tickled her breastbone as they slid down. How could she feel anxious and phony? It's not right. This was her arena. It was impossible to muster her usual sincerity or enthusiasm when starting a new case. Focus! Be strong! *Remember why you're here.* She adored her work as a mediator. She was able to share her insight and experience with people she could truly help.

Each new case was an adventure that she relished, just like a crisp, new romance novel; she knew what to expect. She would crack the front cover and meet the principal characters—her clients—in a story that involved misunderstandings, hurt feelings, secrets, and revelations, perhaps even a villain or two to hinder progress. But then there would be love, hopefully enough to pull them through to the happily-ever-after ending that Kate believed everyone deserved. *If* they were willing to do the work.

Looking down, she loosened her tight fist, frowning at the red arcs her fingernails had inscribed on the palm of her hand, barely registering the pain. *Breath.*

She understood how damaged people were. How this led them to hurt themselves and the ones they loved. She had been that way herself, once.

This time, D'arcy had filed for divorce, while Eli refused to consider it. Attempts to negotiate at first escalated and then broken down entirely. Neither the lawyers nor the family were getting anywhere, and emotions were incendiary. To Kate, this sounded like a classic case of people not saying what they really wanted to say, or asking for what they wanted. A perfect storm of hurt and betrayal.

This case, in particular, was special. Nearly ten years had passed since Kate had become a mediator and made a name for herself as a specialist in reconciliation. To commemorate her career accomplishments, the Mediation Roster Society was presenting her with a special award at the annual meeting and banquet early in the new year. The board had asked her to give a presentation when accepting the award, and since this would be her fiftieth case, she'd chosen to make a special study of it. Kate was flattered by the award, but even more proud to be able to share the details of her methods with colleagues. She planned to take careful notes, and in particular, record her own emotional responses and strategies. If she could focus. How could she do it now? She had to remember her goal.

His being here would *not* interfere with her job. She took a deep, determined breath and hardened her mind, shutting out all awareness of Simon Sharpe.

"First of all, thank you all for coming. D'arcy and Eli, I know how difficult this must be for you. I want to commend you both on your courage in embarking on a new and different approach to resolving your differences. From conversations I've had with D'arcy and Sharon, I understand that your hope is to sort out your current stalemate regarding a possible reconciliation, versus divorce."

She met first D'arcy's eyes and then Eli's. D'arcy appeared wary, her pupil's dilated, poised for fight or flight. Eli compulsively scratched lines on a notepad in front of him. His art a kind of personal armour.

"Before we go there, I'd like to get to know both of you and your history, and try to apply my expertise to your communication challenges. Our goal here is to get you both on the same page. I am absolutely confident you will be rewarded for your efforts and leave here feeling better about yourselves and each other, whatever you decide is right for you." She intercepted Simon sharing a small smirk and raised eyebrows with Sharon, and scowled. It was bad enough having Sharon to contend with. She'd have to confront them immediately before they poisoned the atmosphere. *Damned lawyers.*

Kate much preferred working without them. They tended to make her job as mediator harder. While some showed compassion and professional integrity, others, like Sharon Beckett, balked at the very idea of mediation. Kate shuddered. With luck it would only be for this first session. For so many reasons.

"Sharon, Mr. Sharpe—"

"Simon."

Her breath caught. "Simon. Thank you. I'm sure attending mediation sessions offers you a more passive role than you're used to, but I appreciate your willingness to participate today according to your clients' wishes." Kate lifted her hands, palms out, in a welcoming gesture to the couple in question, consciously keeping her elbows close to her hot, damp body.

"I want to remind you that you've chosen mediation because of your conflicting objectives. D'arcy, at the moment, still wants a divorce, whereas Eli does not. You two have come here with a goal of seeing if it is possible to reconcile your relationship.

Rather than wasting time and money, and making everyone miserable, we're here to get to the bottom of what you both want and why, so you can move forward with consensus."

She felt like a rookie on her first day, mentally following the protocol in her textbook. "My goal as a mediator is to help you explore your issues and see if it is possible for us to come up with an agreement where we lay out new ways that the two of you will interact. You could think of it as a type of marriage counseling."

"Now," Kate met Sharon's gaze first, hoping from previous experience that these words would disarm her. "We need to have a mutually agreed upon set of goals. I'm not talking about material ones, which might be the usual stuff of divorce settlements. This is couple's mediation. It's meant to be different. The way I do it, it's more structured than open-ended marriage counseling."

Kate scanned the room to check her audience. Simon was leaning back in his chair, elbows on the arms, fingers steepled, watching her intently, an expression on his face that could only signify arrogant disdain. *What on earth is he thinking?* She tried to ignore a sudden pinch in her ribcage, reminding herself to breath.

Not a man for rules and schedules, Eli squirmed in his chair. She reeled him back in, remembering that her first responsibility was to put her clients at ease. "How does that sound to you, Eli?"

Eli's gaze questioned her. "S'okay with me," he replied, shrugging.

Sharon smirked, her eyes darting to D'arcy, but D'arcy avoided eye contact, remained reserved and placid, seemingly oblivious to all the undercurrents in the room. She instead regarded Kate, awaiting her next comment.

"Before we go any further, I want to address the purpose of mediation," Kate said, warming to her familiar script. "My role as a mediator is to help you to *talk* to each *other.* I am completely neutral and I can't impose a solution on you. I want to help you to find your *own* solutions. I am not a judge in a courtroom." Struggling to swallow with a parched throat, she offered a reassuring smile, glancing at Sharon and Simon. "My job is to work *with* you to improve a situation that has become *un*-workable."

Sharon cleared her throat, and Kate glanced at her. "Yes?"

"Nothing," she replied, her face pinched.

"Any negotiation must involve the discussion of substantive

issues, of course. But r-relationship issues are at least as important, and until we settle those, we cannot hope to agree on the
substantive ones. So we will begin there."

"Seems to me you're making a big assumption that reconciliation is both possible and advisable for our clients, Kate," interjected Simon quietly.

Eli's head shot up.

"There are divorce proceedings underway already," Simon
added.

She heard the challenge in his voice, saw the contemptuous
smile lurking below the surface. She blinked at him. Another
sharp pain shot through her ribcage and she sucked in a long
slow deep breath while waiting for the aftershock to abate, willing the anxiety attack under control.

Kate stiffened her spine, raised her brows and continued,
"D'arcy and Eli agreed to come to me, Simon. However, I was
about to say, you should be aware that my background is crisis
counseling and psychology, not the law. My bent, therefore, if
you will, is to examine the underlying..." she swallowed, " ...
causes of the problem. I am unabashedly a therapeutic or reconciliation mediator. And an optimist." She smiled. "That is my
explicit bias."

"That's fairly unusual, isn't it?" Simon asked.

She shrugged, again outstretching her hands. "If in the end
both parties wish to divorce, that is their choice." She swallowed
the thickness in her throat. "At least keep an open mind, for your
client's sake."

"As I trust *you* will, Kate."

She responded with a tight smile and a hard glare. *What's up
with him?* How dare he challenge her?

"I have complete confidence in your *objectivity*," Simon
continued.

Was that sarcasm? "Excellent!" She turned away. "Eli," she
said, looking directly into his dark eyes, mirroring his grave
expression "You and I haven't met before today. You weren't
involved in my selection. If you have any concerns, please tell
me now. You feel that your interests are protected." She saw his
gaze waver toward Simon, as though tugged away by magnets.
Two strangers.

Simon's eyes narrowed, advertising his suspicion.

Then Eli's eyes returned to hers, and she felt her magic take effect. So many mediators forgot to be empathetic and warm. He relaxed, a weak smile flickering across his face. She could feel his hopefulness as he nodded almost imperceptibly. She turned her gaze on D'arcy, head inclined, until she nodded too. She was alarmed to see her words had the opposite effect on Simon, who tutted and tossed down his pen with a dismissive and cynical air. Why was he being so contentious? Did he have that much contempt for her still? Who did he think he was coming in here and trying to undermine her credibility? Well, she'd show him. What did he know, anyway, about mediation? About relationships? About her?

Increasingly flustered, Kate was relieved to hand out consent forms and wait quietly while everyone reviewed and signed them. She hesitated, biting her lip. Conflict of interest was kind of an issue here. Strictly speaking, she had an ethical responsibility to acknowledge any current or previous relationship with the disputants *or,* she supposed, their lawyers.

She squinted in Simon's direction, pondering the problem. Fifteen years was a long time. His features, tranquil while he scanned the form, were even more handsome than they had been at nineteen. She felt her pulse race wildly as the memory of him then, how he had made her feel, all that he'd meant to her, invaded her mind, and body, like a creeping virus.

He glanced up and studied her just as carefully over the bent heads of the others. Her gaze locked briefly with his, and one corner of his sensuous bow-shaped mouth crept upward in secret acknowledgment, as if daring her to tell her clients that they'd in fact been lovers. She panicked, glancing down at her notes, her heartbeat like thunder. Was he mocking her with that sardonic smile? Her breath wouldn't come, and she struggled to draw more air.

She couldn't do it. She just couldn't make herself do it. She could send them to another mediator, but... so much was riding on this for her. Another perfect case study like this wouldn't come her way before the end of the year. Would it affect her performance? Her objectivity? She prayed not, but she was in such a flustered state. If neither of them said anything, who would know? Was that wrong? She'd think it over. There'd be time later. Maybe she could get rid of him some other way. Maybe David Broadbent would come back. She grasped at the threads of her thoughts. *What was I saying?* She stood up and paced the length of the table and back.

"I--I can assure you all that--that, though I may at times appear to be meandering in my questioning, I am quite purposeful in my methods. We are going on a journey of discovery together, and I *do* have a map." Kate paused, conscious she was reciting her script too quickly, hoping for a serene countenance to conceal her distress. She'd never felt so lost at sea in her life. Well. Almost never. But she wasn't going there again. She'd gotten over him long ago. There was nothing to worry about.

She gathered the forms and tapped them briskly on the table, resuming her seat. "I can also assure you that, if you play by my rules, you will both leave here satisfied. *Both* of you." She looked from D'arcy to Eli and back again. D'arcy's crisp brow creased with a tiny frown. She couldn't fail to notice Simon's lip curl in disbelief. Annoying man.

She leveled her gaze at both lawyers, trying to suppress her feelings of skepticism. From past experience, Kate knew she'd have some trouble with Sharon as things got going. Simon's game plan was a complete mystery. What kind of a lawyer had he become, anyway? Was he the cynical, embittered, arrogant man he seemed? They'd better not mess this up for her. It was too important. She would simply have to handle them, like she handled all difficult people. His eyes followed her as she moved.

She felt so exposed -- so naked under his scrutiny. She folded an arm across her churning middle and fingered the silver eternal knot pendant that hung at her neck - a reminder of the inter-relatedness of all phenomena - and drew a deep breath, using it to calm herself. Was there a reason Simon had walked back into her life today? What lesson was she supposed to take from this?

His eyes were very expressive, very watchful, cerulean blue, though his face was impassive. What thoughts swirled in that gorgeous head? His hair was still blond with a slight wave, but cut much shorter than she remembered. It looked darker than she remembered, too, almost brown at the nape. But it still shone with golden highlights and looked windblown, inviting touch. His nose was long and ever-so-slightly kinked to the right, his jaw still lean and strong though his face was much fuller than it had been when he was nineteen: less scrawny-boy, more chis-eled-man, with more than a hint of shadowed worry. She wet her lips as her eyes followed the slope of his jaw up to Pan-like ears that made him seem... *What am I doing?* She had a meeting to run.

A job to do. She pushed on.

"So. Um. If I have everyone's agreement... have I?" she glanced around again, and everyone nodded.

"You have my complete commitment, Kate," Sharon said. For some reason, her tone only increased Kate's doubts and worries.

"Of course I respect your methods, Kate," Simon's warm tenor carried a hint of private amusement. "If what you are looking for is cooperation, you have it. But I can't be expected to commit to agree to a settlement I haven't seen, or a process, for that matter, that is not in my client's best interests, can I?" He raised his sandy eyebrows expectantly. Eli, who had been industriously doodling with his fountain pen, sat up straighter and glanced at Simon with a hint of concern on his handsome face.

"You do understand me, Simon. I am looking for full participation, not an arbitrary substantive agreement," Kate clarified in a voice intended to reassure Eli. *Play along.* She forced a smile onto her face.

Over the next half hour, Kate reviewed confidentiality policies, then went over the step-by-step procedures. She reviewed the rules about handling emotions. And finally she talked to them about the written agreement that would be the important end result of the process.

"Good. Now about our timetable, we should commit to continue until, say, mid-to-late November, though I am optimistic that we can come to a resolution before then. I prefer to meet once a week, if possible. After the first session, it won't be necessary for Sharon and Simon to attend." Could she simply get rid of both of them? Dared she hope?

"I'm afraid it is," Sharon said. "I've been requested to attend every session by Madame Duchamp, who is paying your bill."

Kate drew in a breath, held it and let it go. *Nicely done, Sharon.* "Of course. For some people it can be cost prohibitive."

D'arcy's gaze rested on the ceiling, making Kate wonder who was calling the shots. Sharon pursed her lips and looked at Kate, chin raised in a challenge.

"If she's here, Simon is too." Eli glared at Sharon while still avoiding eye contact with D'arcy. "You'll stay, right Simon?"

Simon nodded. "If that's what you want, Eli."

Damn. She was stuck with him, as long as she kept this case. And she very much wanted this case for her presentation. "Okay. But remember you're not here to stir up trouble. Your schedules everyone?" Kate said, flipping open her calendar. Her head was buzzing, and dark spots danced at the periphery of her vision. She rested her head in her hand, trying to gain control. She wouldn't faint, but bile was definitely fighting its way up her gullet. *How am I going to do this?*

Sharon scanned her agenda, while Simon reached into his briefcase in search of his. "I'm pretty flexible, Kate," she said. "I'm at an advantage, since I have no travel time. I'll defer to Simon, of course." She blinked rapidly at him. It was a peculiarly feminine gesture at odds with her rigid bearing that made Kate cringe and wondered how well she knew him, or wanted to. Against all logic, a twist of jealousy tightened her jaw.

She imagined the young idealistic Simon growing up, growing older. What had his life been like to make him so hard, when he had been such a gentle soul? Who was he now? And why should she care? She's gotten over him long ago. She'd been through therapy; she understood how her memory of trauma had transferred to Simon. She shouldn't be falling apart now. Nevertheless, a surge of nausea washed over her and her vision darkened.

Simon found what he was looking for, flipped through the pages, frowning. "I can meet Tuesday or Thursday mornings, with my current caseload, or possibly Friday afternoons but no later than 4:30." He looked up, his brows raised in question.

Kate peered at Simon as though down a long tunnel.

She felt a wave of dizziness, swaying in her chair.

"Are you okay, Kate?" D'arcy asked, reaching out a hand.

"Um. Yes. Yes, fine. Thanks." An upsurge of nausea overwhelmed her. Cold sweat chilled her crawling skin. "F-Friday afternoons are no good. Bad time— bad time of the day *and* week. Everyone's energy is at its lowest. Let's say Tuesdays. Nine o'clock. D'arcy... Eli? Are you all right with that time?"

"Not before ten, ple-ease," Eli begged. D'arcy twitched, glowering at Eli.

"Is there a problem, Eli?" Kate asked through her teeth. *Please!* She was feeling so dizzy and sick, she couldn't tamp it down anymore. *I have to get out of here.*

"I need my shut-eye, that's all," he replied. "I'm not an early riser. I paint at night, and sometimes-- "

"Hah!" barked D'arcy. "More like paint *the* night. Who are you fooling, Eli?" she snarled. It was the first time she had looked at him or addressed him directly. They glared at each other.

Please don't start now!

"Oh, so you are speaking to me after all," Eli snarked. "*I* don't schedule openings and receptions." He jabbed himself in the chest. "They expect me to show up." He curbed his tone at the end, glaring at her, his eyes sliding over to Kate, patches of color rising on his cheeks.

"Well, then," Kate chirped, barely holding on, speaking in a quick staccato. "We'll start at ten a.m., on Tuesdays. Emotions can run high if people are hungry. We'll run the sessions for two hours, more or less. If we need to go overtime, we'll get some sandwiches or take a short break." She wanted to get on with the real work today, but she desperately needed air. With a trembling hand, she dabbed drops of perspiration from her brow and glanced at her watch. "Speaking of which, why don't we take a short break for coffee and return here in fifteen?" She stood up, pushing her chair back with her knees. "Excuse me," she muttered as she rushed out the door to the ladies room.

This can't be happening! It felt like a bad dream. How many times had she naively imagined— no *fantasized* about— Simon Sharpe suddenly reappearing in her life? It was the principal scene that had replayed over and over in her obsessive mind. She wanted him so badly. Oh, not anymore, but during the worst years of her depression. She was always, in her mind, overcome with joy and hope.

Now look at me! Under fluorescent lighting, her image in the bathroom mirror wasn't flattering. Her face was green and mottled, her hair hung in lank, ratty strands pasted to her damp brow and cheeks. Her eyes... she could hardly stand the darkness she saw there. Seeing Simon again— she was coming apart, experiencing some kind of relapse— a freak anxiety attack. She still felt weak, sweaty and chilled. Actually physically sick, despite having already emptied the contents of her stomach. This was no dream. And instead of thrills what she felt was sheer terror.

Her cell phone vibrated in her bag on the vanity. Pulling it out, she confirmed that it was Jay again. Suddenly he seemed comforting. "Hello, Jay." Her voice was weak and watery.

"Hi, Beautiful. Have you been avoiding my calls?"

"You know I can't talk when I'm working."

"You haven't been answering my calls in the evenings either," he said.

"I've been... really busy."

"I need to see you. I miss you. How about dinner Saturday?" That's because she was avoiding him. She suffered a twinge of conscience.

"Um... I don't know." She tutted. " I can't decide right now." And wasn't that an understatement. How could she think about Jay when her mind was full of Simon?

"Come on sweetheart. You can't torture me like this. I've got a surprise for you." He laughed, warming and confusing her. He was awfully charming.

She rubbed the dampness at the back of her neck, fluffing her hair. "Maybe. I'll let you know later."

He remained silent for a moment, the line quiet.

"How about now?" Kate heard the smile in his voice.

"Ja-ay."

"Please."

Her laugh was feeble and she looked at herself in the mirror again, mopping her brow with a wadded tissue. "I don't know." *Quit waffling.*

"I didn't get your answer about that dinner."

"I don't think so. I need a little me time right now."

"Please, Katie."

She sighed. Was this what everyone went through when faced with a lifelong commitment? "We'll get together soon, I promise."

"Whatever's going on with you I know I can fix it. I have ways." His warm sexy, laughter filled her head. "I'll make you laugh and you'll feel better. We'll have a good time like we always do."

An image of Simon flashed in her agitated mind, and she pushed it away.

"Maybe I'm not in the mood to laugh right now."

"All the more reason for us to spend time together." He laughed. "Saturday?"

It was comforting to hear his voice. But now he wanted forever, and she had to decide whether that was something she could do.

Could she face the question? "No. I don't know. Maybe." Her
voice shook. What she really needed was to talk to Alexa.
"Are you okay? You don't sound well."
"I'm feeling a bit nauseated. Might be coming down with
something. Call me tonight?"
"Sure. Okay. Later." He paused. "Love you, angel."
Yes. Coming down with something. Something like a nervous
freaking breakdown! But she could pass it off as a stomach virus.
That's it. She'd wrap up today's session early. She needed time to
think about her reaction to Simon, and come up with a strategy.
She had to get control of herself. She had to deal with Jay's immi-
nent proposal. Her clients needed her. And she needed them.

two

After the movie, she was even more subdued than she had been during dinner at Flying Wedge Pizza. The evening air was mild and fresh, and they strolled to a Starbuck's nearby.

"Well. That was okay, I guess. But I would have rather seen *the action flick*." Jay shuffled along beside her, hands shoved deep in the pockets of his overcoat.

She didn't respond. He was cute, but dense sometimes. It was comforting to be with him, but her mind was elsewhere.

"I hear Harrison Ford is excellent. I bet you would have liked it better."

She walked on in silence. Such a boy. She wished she knew what to do about him. It was times like these she found it hard to imagine spending the rest of her life with Jay. They just weren't on the same page.

He slung an arm over her shoulders and squeezed. "Are you sure you're feeling okay, honey?" Jay asked, eyes quizzical, concern in his voice. "You're so quiet."

She put on an agreeable face. "I'm fine." She forced a smile. "I liked the movie, didn't you?"

He shrugged. "I guess. For a chick flick."

"I think they're called rom-coms."

"Huh?"

"Never mind. You didn't get anything out of it?"

He pulled a long face, casting his eyes upward. "Um." His eyes circled, searching. "Gay guys are more style conscious?" He shook his head at her deadpan expression. "They make better girlfriends than girls?" He was trying to make her laugh. She gave him a weak smile.

Kate sighed. She did like that he was lighthearted and funny, but it'd be nice to have a serious discussion with him, for once. "Didn't it make you wonder, even a teensy bit, how you know when you should spend the rest of your life with someone?" He flashed her a sly grin, and she blinked hard. She didn't mean to lead him on, she really didn't. But the closer he got to popping the question, the more she agonized about what was the right thing to do.

"Didn't it make you think about the fact that we waste so much time worrying about..." She waved a hand about, "... about superficial things, like how a person looks, or whether they're from a certain type of family, or their job?

Jay sniffed and adjusted his coat with a shrug. "That stuff's pretty important. That's what it was about?"

Kate stared at him critically. Perhaps that wasn't a fair question. She knew he did care about those things, more than she did. Maybe she was obsessing. "Didn't Julia Roberts' character raise any questions for you?"

He sulked. "I thought it was a comedy."

Kate was relieved to spend a relaxed Saturday evening with Jay, even though she'd been avoiding him, and was preoccupied. She'd been resisting his company in direct proportion to his obvious hints about his approaching proposal. But after her traumatic and distressing week, it was a comfort to fall back into their routine even though she was more conscious than ever of his shortcomings. It's not that she found fault with Jay, only that he left her wanting more.

An image of Simon flashed in her mind, and she pushed it away. Her memories of what they shared fifteen years ago had no bearing on her relationship with Jay. Yet she felt a sense of loss.

Jay brought their drinks and they squeezed onto a couple of chairs against the wall in the crowded café, their backs and elbows pressed against their neighbors, the general buzz of conversation loud enough to force them close together to be heard. She noticed a couple of female heads turn to openly admire Jay, and him return a cocky grin, eating it up.

"Jay?" She felt a frisson of irritation.

He took her hand. "I know what you're hinting at. Be patient. I wasn't going to —" he glanced around the crowded, steamy cafe. "What the hell." Jay leaned closer, dropping his voice. "Kate. You know what I'm going to say. Marry me, Angel."

"Ah, Jay, don't. I need—" She dropped her head into her hand. "How do you know who you're supposed to spend the rest of your life with?" She peered at Jay earnestly, trying to get through to him.

He grinned and laughed out loud. "Me, of course." He ruffled her hair. "Isn't it obvious?"

She wanted to scream. "Seriously, Jay." She frowned at him. "What if you make a mistake?"

He sobered. "Damn it, Kate." He set down his coffee mug with a too-loud thunk and turned to face her. "I know exactly what I want. What we have is good. You mean what if *you* make a mistake?"

"I'm sorry. I have to be sure." She gazed down into her teacup, and twirled it round and round restlessly. "And I'm not."

Jay thrust his face nearer to hers, his voice rising. "I never know what's going on in your head. You're always pulling away. Why don't you tell me what you're so afraid of?"

"Shhhh." She glanced up and could see him fulminating, his umber eyes glassy under furrowed dark brows. She was aware that other people were looking at them, picking up on their tension. A wave of guilt overcame her, thickening her throat. She dipped her head. Whatever her problems were, he didn't deserve this.

She took a deep breath, closed her eyes and pushed the hair back from her forehead. "Let me try to explain."

Jay didn't reply.

She reached out and gently lifted his large hand from his knee, her stomach knotting. She could share something. Open up a bit. "Let me tell you about this guy I went out with."

"What guy?" Jay's expression darkened, his jaw jutting.

Jeez-us. It's a good thing he didn't know about Simon. She squeezed his hand and clarified. "He was my *high*school boyfriend." She felt Jay relax a bit. "I was so in love." Kate gazed wistfully over his shoulder, shaking her head. "At the time I thought he was the one I would spend the rest of my life with."

At Jay's puzzled expression, she quickly concluded her story. "He dumped me quite unceremoniously in the middle of first-year university." The story sounded stupid now. Irrelevant. How could anyone ever understand what she'd been through. "He broke my heart."

Jay's response was a blend of compassion and righteousness.

"Poor baby. You think I would drop you like that?" He wrapped his strong arm around her and pulled her close, kissing her hair. "I'm no eighteen-year-old puppy. I want you forever, Kate. I mean it."

She remained limp and unresponsive in his embrace, remembering the utter dejection and lost self-esteem that she'd felt until Simon came along to distract her. "No, no. Don't take it the wrong way." Her voice was pleading. "I know that was only a teen romance. But I was wrong once. And I could be wrong again. So could you." She sat upright and met his eyes with fervor. "We should be certain."

She'd been wrong more than once. Maybe that's all she'd had with Simon, too. A trivial childish romance. It was a lot easier to file away their history when she thought of it that way. Wasn't it? But it felt like so much more, and she couldn't let it go.

"I need a little more time to think this through." Now that Jay had asked the question, she had to make up her mind.

Jay heaved a sigh. "Okay. Okay." His voice was tight, determined. "I can't force you, can I? I'll give you the time you need. But know that I am certain. And I'm not going away."

Despite her doubts about the depth of their connection, he was a good man and he truly loved her. It wouldn't be a bad thing. She should just say yes. She probably would. If only she could trust her own heart.

After several desperate phone messages, Kate had finally connected with her best friend on Sunday night for dinner at their favorite cheap Italian restaurant on the Drive. They sat huddled over a candle at a small red-gingham covered table in the corner of the dimly lit room. All Alexa wanted to talk about was Jay and his proposal, while Kate kept coming back to Simon and her reaction to him.

"I know how much Simon meant to you," Alexa said, pressing her hand over Kate's on the stained paper tablecloth. "But, Katie. That was years ago. Why are you freaking out now? Especially now that Jay has popped the question. Why does it matter anymore?"

"This is not just any guy, Alex. You know. Nobody ever—"

Kate's stomach knotted into a hard fist, and her throat closed up, choking off her words. It's Simon. Kate lifted her large glass of red wine with a trembling hand and took another big gulp, filling her nose with the sharp, dark cherry aroma.

She had already drunk too *much* with dinner, hoping to take the edge off her creeping anxiety, but it had only made her foggy and confused. She needed Alexa's help to sort through the turmoil in her head. They'd been friends forever. Alexa had stood by Kate through the tough years of depression and counseling, and watched her put herself back together. Now Kate needed to figure out how to respond to Jay, and how to move forward with some kind of strategy to work this case, even with Simon there, like a shadow from the past, week after week, messing with her head. But Alexa didn't know the whole story. Filled with a vague dread, Kate looked up.

Alexa's cropped dark hair swung as she shook her head in confusion, her dark brows furrowed. "I know you had it bad for him, and I understand what it's like to get dumped by a guy you think is hot, especially when you're nineteen. It's happened to all of us. But... so what? What's so special about Simon that you're still hung up on him after all these years? Why can't you move on?"

Kate studied the pattern of pasta sauce splats and red wine arcs printed on the paper tablecloth. She ran her fingertip across yet another drip that slid slowly down the side of the bowl, and put her finger in her mouth to lick it off. Why? That was the question. She knew Alex didn't have the whole picture. Would it help if she did? She swallowed the lump of fear that formed in her throat.

"I can't seem to get past it. Being in the room with him, being able to see his face, his hands, hear his voice, look in his eyes, if I dare. It rattles me completely." Kate looked at her trembling hands, clenching them into fists. "I haven't had these anxiety attacks for years. Not since I went through my training."

"He's just a man."

"Not for me. That's why I'm questioning my relationship with Jay. Simon was everything I ever wanted. Beautiful, smart, sensitive, strong. He wasn't one of those brutish, macho guys. And we had such a deep connection. If I wasn't so messed up back then, I would have held onto him forever."

"Well, if it's so bad, then don't do it. Drop the case. You've got plenty of others, you don't need the hassle."

If only it were that easy, but she had to work through this. She needed to face her demons and purge herself of the anxiety and self-doubt. "But I do. It's so complicated. I've got a few other cases open right now, but none of them are couples counseling *and* potential reconciliation. This one is."

"So?" Alexa shrugged, sloppily refilling their wine glasses. Drips splashed onto the table, splattering into a galaxy of purple starbursts.

"It's this award the society is giving me in January. It's huge. My professional success and reputation are built on my reconciliation methodology. Not only is this my fiftieth case, it's an excellent case study to present at the awards dinner. It's what they're expecting. I need it."

Alexa screwed up her face. "Can't you pull an old one out of your files?"

Kate tutted. "It's not the same. My ideas have evolved over the years. Going into this one knowing I'll be sharing my notes with my colleagues gives me the chance to record things..." she circled a hand. "Insights that occur to me as I'm working, specific moments when I use certain strategies and why. My own emotional responses to the dialogue. I've never written most of that down before. I usually just... do it."

"I see. But under the circumstances..."

Kate scrubbed her fingers through her hair. "It's more than that. I like this couple. There are multiple obstacles to reconciliation. Red-hot emotions. Interfering parents. Confrontational lawyers. It's volatile. I'm afraid another mediator won't be as invested in reconciliation as I am, and my gut tells me I can get them through all that. I've already won their trust."

"Then what about telling him he can't stay. Get another lawyer to come instead."

Kate nodded. "I tried that. But my client is already bonded with him, and I don't think the other guy is available. I can't impose because of my own issues." Kate ignored the truth tugging at her consciousness like a stubborn ghost. She wanted Simon there. She was as fascinated by him as she had ever been. It haunted her. That was part of the problem. Perhaps that was all of the problem.

Alexa remained silent for a while, staring into her wine, avoiding Kate's eyes.

Kate's stomach clenched. "What? Spit it out."

"You're rationalizing. It sounds to me like you don't want to get out of this. You're secretly thrilled to have crossed paths with Simon and you want more."

"Alex!" Her heart rate tripled, hammering against her ribcage. It was as though Alexa had read her mind. But it couldn't be true. She was miserable. Pushed and pulled. Sick with anxiety. "He's married!"

Her eyebrows peeked up above her dark-framed glasses. "Is he?"

"Well, divorced, I think."

Alexa tilted her head down. Her dark eyelashes lifted slowly, and her smoke-and-moss eyes peered intently into Kate's over her frames, narrowing, wordlessly challenging her.

"Okay. Yes! You know me too well." Kate swallowed. "But I didn't know it was true until this moment." She pushed her face into her hands, moaning. "Oh, my God. What's wrong with me?"

"Damned if I know. Especially with the delicious Jay waiting in the wings. What could you possibly gain by tangling with Simon again?"

"Nothing, nothing at all. I'm torturing myself. But—"

"But?"

"Well—"

"Well—?"

"There's more. And I can't avoid it."

Alexa's mouth quirked into a wry smile. "You gonna share that with me?"

Kate screwed up her face, diligently studying the Jackson Pollock emerging on the tablecloth. Tight bands of fear wrapped her chest, squeezing her heart until it fluttered like a dying bird, crushing the air from her lungs. Her head flushed hot as a furnace. Her voice, when it emerged, was a strangled whisper. "It means... it means I'll have to tell you a dark secret."

Alexa's tone twisted with sarcasm. "Something I don't already know about you. Seriously? That exists?"

A gust of embarrassed laughter escaped from Kate, merging into a mangled groan. "Yeah." She bit down on her thumbnail. "I'm so afraid you'll be angry with me Al."

Alexa was suddenly wide awake and leaning in. "Kate? What the fuck is it?"

Kate glanced around them. The restaurant crowd was thinning. Not many customers were left, and none were within earshot. She took a few shaky Pranayama breaths to calm herself. "So. Remember back in third year. When I got more and more crazy obsessed with him?"

Alexa nodded slowly, pinching her eyes together.

"Remember that party?"

"Simon's birthday party. Where you dragged me even though we didn't know anyone?"

"Yeah. That's the one."

"The one where I had to sleep in a chair half the night, and then walk about ten kilometers home as the sun came up because you slept with him and then desperately had to sneak out?"

Kate's heart fell to the pit of her stomach like a rock. "Yeah. That one." Trust Alexa to remember the humiliating details.

Alexa pursed her lips. "I always did wonder about that. You never mentioned him again."

"Nope."

"Oh, fuck. Did he do something nasty? I'll kill the bastard."

"No! No." Kate's breath came fast and shallow, her vision narrowing and getting spotty. "Not like that. It was unpleasant, that's all. See... I pretty much threw myself at him that night. He wasn't very friendly, but in the end we did go to his.... We hardly spoke. I can't remember... then we finally... you know..." she nodded, and Alexa nodded back in understanding.

"He was... angry, I guess? Kind of cold and mean. He didn't hurt me." She shook her head, not wanting Alex to misconstrue. Her voice dropped to a whisper. "Not physically. But it was clear he didn't like me, didn't really want me there. I cried the whole time, wishing for something I couldn't have."

"That's sick."

Kate drew a deep shuddering breath, paused, and let it out. "I still don't understand why he didn't ignore me or kick me out. Just being a dumb guy, I guess—a lay is a lay. Anyway, it was confusing and humiliating. I was devastated."

"So that must be pretty uncomfortable for both of you."

Kate nodded, shrugged, feeling as though the room had shrunk and Alexa and she sat huddled together in a small dark box without air. Her skin felt raw and tight, as though she'd been peeled alive. "I have no idea what he's thinking." She focused on Alex's eyes, worrying her cheek, and hung on, knowing she could trust her friend with anything, and she'd be okay. She'd be okay. "There's more."

Alex exhaled and sat back, breaking eye contact.

"Don't leave me, Alex." Kate reached out and grabbed Alexa's hand. Alexa leaned in and placed her other hand on top of Kate's, squeezing. "I'm still here, honey. You can tell me."

"Something else happened to me that night. I remembered something."

"What do you mean?"

"I didn't understand it at the time. It crept up gradually. But something about that ugly night with Simon triggered delayed recall. I started getting flashes. Fragments of something."

Alexa nodded, and Kate could see the question in her eyes, awareness dawning.

"A memory of getting... raped... on a high school trip, that I had essentially...forgotten... for years."

Alexa sat stunned, her mouth open. "Is that even possible? I read–"

"I know. I thought so too. There's all kinds of controversy and misinformation out there about the subject. But I know what I experienced."

Alexa's face crumpled in sympathy. "Oh, baby. Why didn't you ever tell me?" Her eyes flooded with tears, triggering Kate's own, which burned paths down her cheeks. A sob ripped from her chest, as though the wall of tension holding her together had suddenly ruptured like a balloon, and she pulled a hand back to smother it, pressing her palm against wet, trembling lips. For several moments, she couldn't speak, could only feel waves of pain and shame surge through her body. Alexa waited, drawing a thumb back and forth over the back of Kate's other hand, soothing. Finally, the quaking eased, and she could draw a full breath.

Her jaw was too cramped to allow speech, lines of tension forking down her neck and shoulders. "I didn't understand for another three years. But that moment triggered the recovery of my memories, and then depression followed. As you know, there was counseling after that, lots of it."

Alexa nodded, her green eyes intense on Kate's face. "I know but, you really didn't know until then?"

"There is plenty of evidence to support the idea that some people experience dissociative avoidance strategies, a kind of selective amnesia, to reduce trauma-related distress."

"Now you're talking psycho-babble at me."

"Trust me, I researched it to death. I needed to understand this. And while I was studying psychology and mediation, I found out a lot. The actual learning and therapy helped me both understand and recover from the experience."

"Did you?"

Kate nodded. "I had a lot of baggage to work through. Insecurity, self-loathing, shame, anger. In fact I thought I was fully recovered... until I saw Simon again. Then something snapped. I began to experience some of the stress and anxiety I felt back then."

"And... he triggers those memories for you?"

"He did. Therapy helped me to understand why I was so obsessed with Simon in the first place. And then when he... well, I learned about a thing called transference. His angry rejection somehow echoed the rape itself, and released a flood of memories. Or maybe I was just ready to deal with it. So then they were all tangled up together."

"So despite being a jerk that night, Simon isn't to blame for your emotional reaction, is he? He dredges up all the painful memories. But obviously there are unresolved issues."

"Yeah. Apparently. I thought I was past it. But I hadn't seen him since then. How could I know?" Kate felt small. As though her bones had shrunk, and her flesh and skin had collapsed down onto her smaller frame. Her arms were heavy and weak, and there was no longer any room for her to draw a breath, or space for her heart to beat.

"Wow. I think I understand a lot of things now, in this new light. Your entire relationship history has been tainted by this."

"With Simon?"

"With everyone," Alexa clarified. "No wonder you can't commit to Jay."

Kate reflected on her relationships with men over the past decade or so, including the confusing and stagnating two-year relationship she was in with Jay, and agreed with Alexa's point. It was definitely holding her back. She would never have a future if she didn't deal with her past.

Alexa sat up taller, meeting Kate's eye. "Seems to me, it's even more clear that you have to quit this nonsense."

"What?"

Alexa leaned forward on her elbows, intent. "You can't keep

on with this case, Katie. You have to get out of there before you get hurt again."

"No. No, I see now that I have to work through it. To get past this." She had to purge herself of the confusion, anxiety and self-doubt that had hung on all these years.

"You're delusional! It's not rational to dig around in this stuff."

Kate felt a surge of resentment toward her best friend. And disappointment. "I'm being extremely rational. I thought you would understand." She loved Alex, but she was no psychologist, nor was she a relationship expert. In fact her own aversion to commitment led her into any number of dysfunctional relationships.

"I do. You're not thinking clearly."

Kate shook her head. No. She had to follow her gut. "I am. I have to do this."

Tuesday arrived grey and gloomy. Temperatures had remained steady, hovering just above freezing, and the damp air hung thick and oppressive. Kate stepped off the bus onto a bleak street-scape and stopped for a morning coffee and bagel, before walking to Sharon's office. Fingers of cold damp penetrated her overcoat, making her shiver, almost as much as the prospect of facing Simon again.

She was apprehensive about meeting Eli and D'arcy and their lawyers again after her peculiar behavior last Friday morning. Her intention had been to resume the mediated discussion after coffee break, but the anxiety attack had come on so precipitously, she just couldn't pull herself together and had to get the hell out of there.

Afterwards, while discretely questioning Sharon on the phone, she learned first that Simon was married to a beautiful and talented lawyer, a close friend of Sharon's, and then that he was in fact separated, which only added to her confusion. Not that his marital status was relevant. She was quite certain he loathed her, and she was prepared to keep a polite distance in order to do her work. Her muddled thoughts and feelings fueled her concern over the proper course of action regarding ethical conduct.

Nonetheless, today Kate was feeling much better about the

new case. Unburdening her cares to Alexa and gaining a new perspective gave her the confidence that she could manage the case and do her job even with Simon in the room. Kate had made one more call on Monday morning, concerned about the impact this problem might have on her upcoming award and presentation. She didn't want to take any chances with her reputation. Her old mentor and teacher at the Justice Institute, Rose MacIlhaney, was just the person to advise her on the ethical question that was bothering her. She conveniently left out the detail of her failure to disclose the details. She was relieved to hear Rose's verdict.

"It's a very grey area, Kate," she had said. "You no longer have a relationship with the man, and haven't seen each other for a very long time. It's not likely to affect your judgment regarding the couple.

"But Rose. This is *the* guy I told you about."

"I understand, Kate. It's up to you to decide if your performance is negatively affected in any way by his presence, based on your past together and your own feelings for him. You know what you're doing. Only you can answer that."

Kate had decided that, despite Alexa's skepticism, she had to face whatever painful memories Simon kindled and purge them forever. She was determined that, once she got used to the idea, she'd be herself again. And so she looked forward to hearing what D'arcy and Eli had to say today. Though it was unsettling to face Simon again, she needed to be strong and focus on her clients.

Kate arrived first and rearranged the seating from the previous week. The dreary view from the window was too depressing so she closed the blinds, fiddled with the light switches to brighten the room, and after a moment's hesitation, dragged a potted palm to a new location. *Better.* She would place D'arcy and Eli side by side opposite her, facing the trio of framed landscapes– abstract, vibrant, Mediterranean, hopeful. This seating arrangement was designed to keep everyone comfortable and to avoid confrontation. They were to feel like teammates rather than opponents.

When Sharon entered, she sat at the end. Kate studied her warily from a distance. A deathly pale and ghostly mortician in stark black and white, she was stoic today, saying little. Good. Maybe she would behave herself on this case after all. It's just a shame the table is so darn big.

Or not, she thought after everyone had been seated, and Simon took his place beside her. He wasn't so rumpled today, she noted. His navy blue blazer set off a crisp white shirt, and an interesting tan, white, and red graphic Escher tie. She'd always liked him in white. He was even more handsome, if possible. Searing heat flashed down the side of her body, escalating her pulse, but she told herself it was just nerves.

"Before we go any further, I feel it's necessary to disclose... something I failed to on Friday. I feel it's my professional obligation to tell you that Mr. Sharpe and I were more than mere... acquaintances in college." She raised her eyes to Simon's warily, noting that his widened slightly at her words. "In fact we... we knew each other rather well." She swallowed, waiting for her clients' reactions.

Eli sat up. "No kidding? That's cool."

D'arcee's face spread in a long, slow smile, and Kate imagined what inferences she was busy making. "What a strange coincidence, Kate. Isn't it?"

Kate frowned, casting her eyes across the faces of her clients, her heart fluttering wildly. A sharp vertical line formed between Sharon's pale brows, but she said nothing, her eyes darting toward Simon for verification.

Simon nodded, his face impassive. Then a ghost of a smile flickered across his bow-shaped lips. "Indeed. We did."

That's it? That's all he was going to say? Thank God! He neither made a big deal out of it nor contradicted her. Kate drew a breath and returned her attention to her clients. It was their reaction that mattered most. She swallowed, her throat hard. "If that concerns you... I mean if you are bothered by that... now is the time to say so. I will gladly refer you to another mediator–" *Please say no.*

"Don't be ridiculous, Kate," D'arcy said. "You've come to us highly recommended. I don't think my Mother would–"

"Oh, if D'arcee's *mother* recommended you, Kate, then there's no question. No one else will do."

Kate peered at Eli, puzzled by the note of sarcasm in his drawling voice. "Are you sure?"

Eli's face softened, and his smile grew warm and genuine. "Really. No one cares what happened in college. Stop worrying about it. It's all good." He glanced at Simon. "Right? You're cool with it, huh?"

Kate glanced sideways and caught Simon's nod, his brief enigmatic smile. "Of course. That was many years ago."

She steadied her rapid breathing with a hand on her windpipe, wishing her pulse would settle down, and took comfort from her Celtic knot pendant. She nodded and nodded again, wetting her dry lips. "Alright then. Let's continue. I'd like to discuss the nature of your dialogue at the moment. You were very quiet last week, and I hope you are both comfortable talking to each other right now, and talking about your relationship over the past while. Did you each have time to prepare as I asked you to?"

Eli clutched a page scrawled with spiderwebs, and nodded. He looked a little anxious, but eager, she thought. He wore the same leather jacket as last week. He always managed to look careless, a little dangerous, like a sexy college student.

Oh, geez. Don't think about sexy college students, Kate!

D'arcy, on the other hand, was somber and sullen. She was dressed as stylishly as before, with a chunky, tweed jacket over a loose, untucked blue blouse, and a dark pencil skirt with high boots. But her posture was slumped. A study in contradictions, that one.

Kate addressed Eli. "Why don't you go first? No one will interrupt until you're finished, at which time I may prompt you." She turned to D'arcy. "Then, you'll have a turn."

D'arcy made no reply, her eyes darting up and down furtively, like one of those high-strung monkeys at the zoo, always looking guilty, or scheming.

Eli's voice was low, soft, reluctant. "Um. Well, things were getting kinda rough at home. I was busy with shows and openings last winter. I thought D'arcee'd be really happy for me, y'know? After all the struggles. But she starts nagging, eh? 'You're never home anymore...You're drinking too much...I don't want all those strangers in the house at all hours...Who was *she?*'" Eli complained in a simpering falsetto, punctuating his words with a jabbing forefinger in the air. D'arcy perked up at that, tutting and rolling her eyes toward the ceiling in outrage. Kate held up a staying hand and sent a soothing glance in her direction.

Eli continued. "Always something. I was getting pretty sick of it. After more than a few battles, I split. I tried going back a couple times, to make up, but it just got worse. I've been staying with friends, or at my studio, since July."

Three months separated. Kate leaned forward onto her elbows and nodded to encourage him to continue, making sure to lock eyes with him, to let him know he had her undivided attention, and making a mental note to record how she read and used non-verbal behaviors in session. She sensed Simon, beside her, echoing her gesture by leaning forward, his hands steepled in front of his firm lips, a thoughtful gesture she recognized as signature.

"So. She didn't like the changes." He straightened his spine, shaking his head. "I'm an artist, right? There's no guarantee you're ever gonna make a buck. You do it because... well ya just gotta. It's a passion." His attractive face looked as earnest as a child's. "So when you get a big break, damn! What are the odds, eh? Ya gotta go with it." He flashed a bright smile. D'arcy sat back and crossed her arms suddenly, tossing both her head and her eyes away from Eli, as though he'd slapped her.

Eli squirmed, and darted a glance at D'arcy beside him before continuing. "You gotta understand. A lot of what's been happening is completely outta my control."

Kate nodded again, her eyebrows raised in question.

"There's a big machine out there. The 'Art World', ya know? One day you're alone in your studio, the next, you're part of it. Geoffrey, my new agent, told me, we're gonna do *this,* ya gotta be *there.*" Eli's hands flipped open on one side, then the other, to illustrate his story. "So, suddenly there are all these people in my life." Eli's face opened as if to share his incredulity that this might have occurred. His enthusiasm was infectious.

"When Geoffrey sets up an opening, a showing, something... I have to be there. It's expected. I had to go on a couple trips. And I met some people... artists, gallery owners, some collectors, ya know? So I have some new friends, and they're great people, sophisticated, exciting. Suddenly I belong somewhere and I'm respected." Eli pulled his shoulders back. "And there are groupies. Who knew? Everybody loves me all of a sudden." He shrugged, his eyes wide. Though these changes might have taken him by surprise, it was no secret he was enjoying the attention and praise.

Simon cleared his throat, and Kate shot a worried glance in his direction, but barely registered his expression, she was so intent on Eli's story.

D'arcy and Sharon both leaned in, as though they couldn't wait to hear the next part. They both shot looks at him that would kill, and he squirmed under their scrutiny, hiding his furtive dark eyes under a furrowed brow. Sharon had hinted to Kate that there might have been an affair or two.

"Oh, yeah. They think they've got somethin' on me, but she's got it all wrong." Eli leaned back, darting a desperate glance across at Simon, as though calling for a lifeline. "Like I can help it when they're throwing themselves at me night and day." Eli's threw his arms wide, the look of a persecuted saint upon his features. Kate glanced up quickly to assess the women's reactions, and was not surprised to find they both had arch, suspicious expressions on their faces. D'arcee's anger appeared to be simmering to the surface, but Sharon was as smug as a fat house cat with telltale feathers clinging to her lips.

"You slept with them, Eli, or at least one of them. Don't try to deny it." D'arcee's voice was grim. She looked utterly deflated. Kate realized this was, understandably, perhaps the worst thing Eli could possibly have done.

"Objection," Simon murmured, and Kate turned, momentarily meeting his eyes, sharing a second of understanding. She swallowed and turned back to Eli.

"Slept," he guffawed. "Exactly. The thing is, I didn't do anything. Nothing! They're just always there fawning and hanging all over me. What am I gonna do, push them away? I can't say I don't like the attention. But that, well... " He floundered, " ... you, you saw it before I did. You know I was asleep. I didn't even know they were there."

"Do I look like a fool?" D'arcee's cupie-doll lips curled in contempt.

Kate gently raised a hand to restrain D'arcy. "Can I ask for a few more details, please Eli? Since I didn't see anything, I'm having trouble following the story."

Simon looked up from his file notes and gently touched her sleeve, sending a shiver of awareness through her. "Perhaps I can explain, Kate. Eli refers to the time in late July when D'arcy returned home one night to find Eli asleep in their bed with two... er... scantily clad young ladies. Apparently there were a few people over, and he had had a few too many drinks that evening and passed out. He says the... ladies... must have joined him after he was unconscious, that nothing untoward happened.

You can see that it was a somewhat compromising situation in which to be discovered." Simon's expression was determinedly stoic. He shifted in his seat, and his knee brushed against hers under the table, making her flinch. Kate blinked, uncomfortably aware of a spark of laughter in his eyes, meant only for her.

"Compromising indeed," offered Sharon, one pale eyebrow raised. D'arcy steamed like a kettle about to boil over, the colour on her cheeks high, her eyes bright.

"Doesn't mean I cheated on my wife, though, does it? Circumstantial evidence." Eli's fist clenched around his fountain pen, turning to Simon. "Am I right? And effing convenient. I know what this is all about, you can't fool me." His voice was clipped, becoming more agitated. "All this bitching is just to shift attention away from the real issues." He pointed a finger at D'arcy. "She resents my success. It was all right when I was helpless and dependent… made her feel superior. Now I'm successful, she's not interested anymore. She can't control me anymore. I'm no use to her."

Kate sat up, alert. Hold on. "No use?"

"Yah. No friggin' use. You were only interested in keeping me around while I was a thorn in Daddy's side. Aaand Mummy's. I still don't know who hates me more. Now you're all looking for a convenient way to get rid of me."

"*I* hate you more! Leave my family out of it. This has nothing to do with them," D'arcy burst in. She seemed unable to contain the outrage that had been building while Eli regaled them with his version of the facts. Kate knew she had to slow them down, but there were some very interesting insights emerging.

"Hate is a strong word," she murmured.

"This has everything to do with them! Our marriage is one big ol' political campaign for you, isn't it? Well, I'm tired of being manipulated."

D'arcee's face became animated, her eyes bulging, her mouth quivering. Kate held up one finger at her, with a stern, warning glare, as a last subtle attempt at restraining her, but D'arcy persevered. "What's really eating you is the whole idea that you've been supported all these years. Your manly ego's bruised, that's what. Now you've got a little money you… you're… "

"Like a kid in a candy store?" offered Sharon.

"Okay, okay! Hold it right there, D'arcy," Kate barked, shooting an incredulous glance at Sharon. "Calm down, both of you.

Nobody. Speak." She held out both hands in a braking gesture and paused for effect, studying the loss of composure and sudden change of direction. She concentrated on making notes for a few minutes while they sat seething in silence. Was Eli diverting attention, as he accused D'arcy of doing? Or did he honestly believe D'arcy was trying to use him to hurt her parents? She glanced at Simon, who sat stoically silent with steepled fingers, his eyes sharp and wondered if he was as good a judge of character and motivation as she was, and what he thought of all this.

"Now, D'arcy, I understand it's difficult to listen to Eli's feelings, but it is still his turn to tell his story, and your turn to *listen*. You promised. Your turn is coming. Okay?"

D'arcy looked chagrinned. She was breathing quickly through flared nostrils, but contained any further urge to speak, her eyes burning a hole into the print on the wall over Kate's shoulder.

"Eli." Kate looked steadily at him for a long moment, until he was able to look calmly back at her. "Perhaps you could address yourself to me. D'arcy finds it difficult not to respond when you address her directly. That time will come."

He nodded.

"I'm getting the picture. Can you go back to where things started to go wrong? Can you talk about how you were affected by your sudden success and how D'arcee's reaction made you feel?"

Eli sat silently thinking for a moment longer, his fountain pen scratching thoughtful lines on his sketchpad. Then he spoke calmly, his eyes on D'arcy, though addressing Kate. "Like I said before — discarded. For years we were fighting for the same things. We had a good marriage. No—a *great* marriage. It was more than a partnership. We had romance, excitement, dreams to fight for. When we finally achieved something, I felt... abandoned." Kate's gut clenched in sympathy. She knew what abandonment felt like. He shrugged his shoulder. "Like she didn't care anymore about all those things. Suddenly she sounded like a harping housewife, worried about the furniture, bills and getting a good night's sleep. I didn't recognize her. I felt... alone."

"That's good, Eli, thank you," Kate said. "Very good." She waited for more, but he seemed spent, for the moment. She was curious to know more about his relationship with D'arcee's parents, but it was a good time to pass the baton. The mood was right. She would dig that out another time. She nodded. "D'arcy? Your turn."

three

Kate felt more confident as the hour progressed. She'd found her stride, and was becoming immersed in her clients' story. That's all she needed to do. She was naturally good at this. That's what she had to remember as her attention kept getting drawn by the enigmatic man beside her. It was taking all her willpower to ignore him and the effect he was having on her. That, she would have to ponder later, when she was alone. She nodded at D'arcy.

D'arcy spoke, her eyes on her hands. "I've always been Eli's biggest supporter, not just financially, though there was that, but I mean, his admirer, too. I believed in him, in his work. I knew one day the rest of the world would discover what I already knew… " D'arcy paused, drawing a deep breath, and shot a glance at Eli. Her face creased into a sad little frown as she did so, her full lips pursing into a moue.

"I was always there for him. He can be very moody, and if things aren't going well with his painting, he gets… well, weird. His behavior has always been erratic. I accept that." D'arcy paused, glancing at Eli as though he might combust if she revealed family secrets. A tight grimace pulled at his face. "But no matter what was going on, high or low, fast or slow, he always included me. We were always in it together. Until… now.

"I'm the one that found Geoffrey for him. Actually, it was Mother, if you must know." She shot Eli a resentful glare. Kate watched for Eli's reaction, which was a sour, brooding look. "She referred him to us. What a change! He loved and understood Eli's art. He really took Eli's career seriously. And then, overnight, it was like I didn't exist anymore. Suddenly he didn't need me and he didn't have the time of day for me, either." D'arcy shook her head emphatically.

"It felt like..." Kate prompted.

"When you had all those parties... it felt like my needs weren't being considered. Our home was suddenly a flop house for all kinds of strangers."

"Hah," grunted Eli, lifting his chin, sneering. "You liked artists well enough before, when you could be the great *patrona*."

Kate studied Eli carefully. A little chip on his shoulder.

"Eli. Please. You'll have another chance." Kate reminded him, gently but firmly. With one eye she noticed that Simon had turned in his chair, studying her over his fingertips, eyes narrow. Her heart jumped.

Eli gave himself a shake and turned his whole body away from D'arcy, tossing his hair back. He picked up his fountain pen and sketched on the notepad in front of him, as though he were alone. Kate watched Eli's long graceful fingers work with assurance. In just a few seconds, his finesse with a pen became evident. Against her better judgment, she glanced at Simon's hands, reminding herself of his long, elegant, sensitive fingers, and what they were capable of. She tore her eyes away.

Kate jotted notes, listening, waiting.

"He thinks *he* feels discarded." D'arcy's lip quivered, but she got herself under control and stared intently at her hands. "I felt... I felt as though he couldn't care less about me anymore. I had plenty of time to sit at home alone and think about it, too. He was always out, or traveling. He had new friends. It's like he's drunk on his success. In love with it, you know? You'd think all those years of hard work and patience and frustration never happened."

D'arcy's eyes glazed, unfocussed. Kate waited, not speaking, just watching D'arcy, giving her time.

"Eli was suddenly a big shot. That's what I resented. It was crass. It seemed false, to me. I didn't know him anymore." D'arcy seemed to cringe, remembering. "Suddenly he was this huge spender, buying things, giving gifts, and throwing money around.

"One day, he came home with a ridiculous, extravagant yellow sports car. What was that?" D'arcy said incredulously, her hands spread wide. "That's not even you!" She enumerated his purchases one by one on her precisely manicured fingers. "New clothes. Electronics. Jewelry. Fancy restaurants. I mean, what is he trying to prove? We've always had enough, but we've lived within our means."

"*Ad infinitum* -- I have a spread sheet showing spending for the year to date. It's very enlightening–" offered Sharon, holding out a sheet of lined paper. D'arcy ignored her, as did everyone else except Eli, who cast a hostile glower her way, sneering. "–if you're interested."

Kate squinted at her. "Thank you. Sharon." Simon rubbed his hands over his face, and Kate was shocked to see the corner of his mouth turned up in a sly grin. For a moment, she lost the thread of D'arcy's narrative, she was so distracted by Simon's suppressed mirth.

"...eating into our savings. My trust income is more or less fixed, you know. It's not a bottomless pit. I was concerned. I *am* concerned. I didn't know if or when it would stop." D'arcy shook her head. "I can't live like that."

Kate leaned in, concentrating hard on her clients' words, willing her nerve endings to ignore the man beside her, whose intellect and warmth intimidated and intrigued her by turns.

Eli's mouth twisted. "You could have said something. How do I know you're getting so uptight about a few indulgences?"

"I did say something. You seem to think *that* was the problem." D'arcy retorted.

"I meant *talk*, not nag until I can't stand it anymore. And then call your mother and complain about me. I feel hen-pecked."

"How can I talk to you, Eli, when you never listen, you never sit still? You're never home."

Eli's hand flew up to the back of his neck, rubbing, then he patted his pockets, fingering the outline of his cigarette pack. "That's a load of crap. The harping came first. You drove me out."

"Okay, let's–" Kate tried, but they rode over her.

"You're just a little boy, Eli. It's not harping, it's communicating. That's what married people do."

"I said I would change..."

As the bickering continued, Kate felt Simon tense beside her.

"I tried to come home, D'arcy. But I just couldn't... I couldn't be there anymore."

"Not with me, anyway," D'arcy shot back, dripping sarcasm, her arched eyebrows elevated.

Eli shot to his feet, disgusted, turning away from the table. "Not fair. I told you what happened. Why don't you trust me?"

"What you *think* happened," she spat.

"It's the truth." Eli's face was flushed with colour, and his dark eyes glinted.

"Okay. That's enough for now." Kate cut in. "I think, D'arcy, we've gone off on a tangent here. But that's okay. You've begun an exchange. That's very good. You're really talking, and that's wonderful." She stood up, so Eli didn't seem so conspicuous in the midst of his outburst. "We've been at this quite a while. Let's take a breather. I took the liberty of ordering beverages and snacks this morning, so we can resume our work sooner."

Kate had listened to the spontaneous exchange without interrupting, though she knew D'arcy had more to say. They were listening to each other, though not carefully enough. She believed they were beginning to hear some of what the other had to say through a mountain of mistrust and resentment. It was a start.

But, they were both heating up; the exchange was taking on the character of a domestic quarrel. They needed some guidance, and she needed a more active role to keep her thoughts from dwelling on Simon's distracting presence.

Kate tried to ignore Simon's eyes on her as she left the room, returning a moment later with Siobhan on her heels, pushing the tea trolley. Siobhan parked it by the window, smiling shyly at Simon and colouring prettily. Kate thanked her and she quietly left. Even though he was nearly twice her age, Siobhan obviously found him attractive—Kate stole a surreptitious peek—he really did look handsome today. He'd been a lovely, lanky teenager, but now he was a large, graceful and powerful man, like a tawny mountain lion. She sighed. Kate remembered feeling weak-kneed over him, and congratulated herself that she had made it halfway through the session this morning without letting his presence rattle her concentration—much. She really was in control of herself, after all. It was deeply gratifying, and she intended to keep it that way. She stood taller and pushed her shoulders back, filling her lungs with a deep *Pranayama* breath, only to shrink back when her movement drew Simon's gaze, scanning up and down her torso, bringing a self-conscious hand up to tuck back her hair. *Blast!*

Everyone seemed more than a little relieved to have an excuse to break, and stood up and stretched, no one making eye contact.

"I've ordered good strong coffee, and also a selection of

teas. I hope you find what you like," she said to no one in particular. She hung back as Eli and Sharon dived at the coffee pot first, pouring themselves cupfuls with obvious relish. Eli helped himself to the muffins, Danishes and scones. D'arcy waited until they were seated, then moved in nonchalantly and flipped through the tea bags, finally selecting, Kate was interested to note, a fruity herbal one. No tobacco, no caffeine. It seemed to go against character. Finally Simon looked at her, inclined his head and gestured for her to help herself.

"Go ahead," she said stiffly, taking a jerky step closer. What was wrong with her? Every cell in her body was drawn to him, like some weird petrie dish experiment, scattered and agitated.

He, too, looked through the tea bags, and selected a green tea. "I hope it's up to your standards," she said, feeling strangely shy and awkward, tracing the impossible pattern on his tie with her eyes. Her voice sounded tight and shrill to her ears.

A smile tugged at the corners of Simon's lips. "I'm actually quite easy to please. And I don't always drink green tea. It's a habit that comes from eating Asian food so often," he replied, his voice hushed.

She chose Earl Grey and stood there, steeping the bag, absorbing the heady aroma of bergamot. Her feet felt cemented to the carpet. She glanced over her shoulder. Eli was staring out the window, drinking in solitude, already tapping an unlit cigarette in anticipation of stepping outdoors. Sharon sat with D'arcy, their heads close together, speaking softly. D'arcy wolfed her muffin like she hadn't eaten in a week.

"Really? What's your favorite?" she asked, meeting his eye briefly, though why she was engaging in small talk with Simon Sharpe she couldn't fathom. About food, no less.

"Hmm. That's a tough question. I like so many," replied Simon after a few moments consideration. "I'd have to say Japanese. And Thai, definitely Thai. But I like them all. Malaysian, Indonesian, Korean, Schezuan… " He tapered off.

"Do you count Indian food as Asian?" she asked, pondering this passion of his.

"Oh, sort of. Though it's a category unto itself," he said.

She laughed softly, agreeing. "It's one of my favourites. I like to cook with all those aromatic spices."

"I'm surprised you find the time," he deadpanned, eyebrows raised. Kate recoiled under his implied criticism. What did she do to deserve that? Her mind shied from the obvious answer. "I prefer to cook Thai. But then, there are so many good restaurants in Vancouver, why kill yourself trying to learn how to make them all?"

He cooked? He cooked Thai food? He smiled, and she felt her face flush warmly, and darted a glance around the room, looking for an escape, or at least a witty comeback. Eli had left the room, and D'arcy moved in their direction.

"I just have to have another muffin," she said. She blushed suddenly bright pink and turned to the trolley. Kate moved aside for her.

"How can you resist when Kate's tempted us with so many delights," Simon turned his relaxed charm on D'arcy at the trolley, perusing the platter of baking, selecting a Danish glistening with sugar glaze, and sharing a conspiratorial wink with D'arcy as he took a gigantic bite, glazing his lips with sugar.

Simon caught Kate's eye, his eyes twinkling with humor as he licked his lips and chewed. She smiled and shrugged at his easy manners, though she felt a ripple of self-conscious anxiety flutter through her intestines. How odd — that they'd come to this already, she thought — this familiar non-verbal communication, as though they'd known each other for years. Oh! Except they had! She felt a tight clenching in her gut. Her hands jerked suddenly, slopping scalding tea over her wrist. "Oh, darn." She dropped her eyes to his tie, then tore them away, reaching for the serviette he held out, and mopping the spill from her stinging skin. The warmth she felt in her face crept through her body like a fever. She couldn't talk to him; and pretending she was cool stirred up too many emotions.

She was grateful for the diversion. "I... uh... excuse me." Kate tried to smile and slunk away. *What a buffoon I am! I've regressed to an awkward teenager. How humiliating.* She exchanged a few words with Sharon, then sat down and made notes until Eli returned in a cloud of cigarette fumes carried on cool air. When they'd all sat down, and she felt calmer, she began again.

"I really want you two to carry on with your exchange. But before you do, I think it would be helpful for everyone if I summarized a few of my observations." She shot a fleeting glance at Simon as her eyes scanned the room, an unfamiliar unease gnawing at her confidence. "Sound good?" Eli smiled halfheartedly. D'arcy polished off her second muffin and dabbed crumbs from her cupie-doll mouth.

Kate paused. The more concise she could be with her summary, the more effective it would be, but her thoughts were scattered and undisciplined. The discussion would congeal around whichever key points she decided to make. She could pave the way for accord. She chose her words carefully as she read from her notes.

Kate smiled. She really loved what she did. Communication was such a funny thing — like a large, unruly, potentially dangerous beast that had to be repeatedly stroked and soothed before it behaved the way you wanted it to. She was able to guide them where she wanted them to go because she was a skilled listener. They didn't always comply, but it was gratifying when they saw things her way.

She continued. "Also, despite efforts to reconcile, the difficulty seems to be a mutual lack of trust." Kate let that suggestion sink in for a moment before elaborating. "Eli, you feel that D'arcy finds fault rather than sharing her feelings with you. Is that so? " Eli scowled thoughtfully, his pen moving again, pouring his emotional turmoil onto the page in jagged black lines. "D'arcy, you feel that Eli also has found other sources of emotional support. Correct?" D'arcy looked stricken.

"Very concise," interjected Simon, his eyes flat. What was that supposed to mean? She didn't like his tone, and glared at him, forcing herself to continue. What happened to the charmer at the tea trolley?

"Would you also agree that you've been unable to resolve your differences so far mainly because of difficulty communicating? And this lack of communication has become perceived as a lack of caring?" Kate paused, referring to her notes, dropping the volume of her voice to just above a whisper. "But that is not necessarily so, is it? I believe I can clearly hear you both saying that you feel hurt and abandoned. Is that right?" She looked at them both, and found that they were both embarrassed. Unable to look at each other, squirming, their eyes shifting. Eli's focus on his sketching intensified. D'arcy's restless hands reached for her handbag and settled on a piece of gum.

"It's a very easy psychological trap to fall into—to assume that the other person isn't listening, and therefore doesn't care anymore, or values different things than we do. The more we're hurting, the more assumptions we lock onto about the other person's point of view. This is perfectly normal. It doesn't make either of you the villain here." Simon cleared his throat and Kate shot him another questioning glance, realizing she didn't have a clue what was in his mind. What? Was he criticizing her? She shut her mind to thoughts of Simon and persevered.

Kate paused to smile reassuringly at D'arcy and Eli, willing them to look at her. "So would you agree that you haven't really given yourselves a chance to resolve your differences yet? You don't yet know for certain that they are irreconcilable." This time, they looked up—thoughtful, questioning—and met each other's eyes, wavering, uncertain. Kate smiled. *Now we're getting somewhere. I can see what they want.*

Sharon, predictably, bristled at this suggestion. Her somber expression, together with the starkly black suit and white shirt that further bleached her pale complexion and severe hair, lent her the disposition of an anemic undertaker. Kate almost smiled at the image, until she caught her attempt to draw Simon in. Lord, how she wished she could be alone with her clients to work her mediation magic without distraction!

"And I have one more point. It's this: that before you are able to work through your differences, all of your issues and all the necessary information must be on the table. No secrets. Does that make sense to you?" Eli's pen suddenly flipped out of his hand onto the table with a rattle.

"Sorry," he muttered, retrieving it.

"Indeed," came Simon's editorial. Was that supposed to be a comment about Eli, D'arcy, or was he referring to their own dirty secrets? Why couldn't he just keep quiet? She clenched her teeth in frustration. Was it her own paranoia that made it seem like he was criticizing her every move? She felt raw and exposed.

Eli looked confused and a little suspicious, as though she were fishing for a confession, and he glanced nervously at Simon. The regular rhythm of D'arcy's gum chewing slowed. Kate noticed Simon staring at D'arcy with a narrowed, pensive eyes.

"Now," Kate said, "Let's practice listening. And I'm looking for affirmations not accusations. D'arcy would you like to open the exchange?"

D'arcy hesitated for a long moment, her gum-chewing continuing in slow motion. "We-ell. My biggest concern has to be Eli's lack of responsibility. I know he's always been spontaneous and carefree, and I've always liked that about him, but there's a point at which a person has to accept his share of responsibilities. Has to be an adult." D'arcy paused, and looked at Kate, her eyebrows raised.

"That's great, D'arcy. You can address Eli directly now. He's listening." She inclined her head at Eli.

"Eli's… " D'arcy turned to him awkwardly, her eyes faltering, her voice dropping in tenor, " …you've… always let me take care of things, and I've done that, but I won't always be able to," she raised both hands in a silent plea, "to pay the bills, fix the cars, clean the house, cook meals. Look after you." Why was D'arcy so afraid? Perhaps she's ill?

Kate turned her eyes from the exchange between D'arcy and Eli to scan the room, and jolted to notice Simon's gaze resting pensively on her! Again his attention pulled her mind from her clients to wonder about him, and who had been taking care of him these past fifteen years, and why he carried with him an aura of sadness. She tried to pull her focus back.

"I never asked you to look after me," Eli's voice held a note of defiance. "You're not my mother."

"Exactly. I'm not your mother," she agreed, a little too earnestly. Their timbre of their discussion escalated, while D'arcy complained about doing all the work while Eli played. Tempers flared. They needed her.

Eli's agitation was reflected in a rapid tapping of his pen.

D'arcy's face crumpled. "I'm too busy taking care of you to do my own thing. What if I got sick? What if we run out of money? The way you're spending money… it's crazy." D'arcee's eyes searched Eli's, desperate for acknowledgement.

A flicker of questioning concern in his eyes was replaced by indignation. "I've got my own money now. I don't need yours and I don't need permission to spend it. I'm not affecting you." Kate bit down on her lips, silently urging him to lower his defenses. She willed him with her whole being to be courageous.

"It *does* affect me." D'arcy cast her eyes around the room, unfocussed and glistening, while she expressed her concerns about their future security. "We're married."

"You're always so uptight; it's no big deal," said Eli.

Oh Eli! You totally dropped the ball, baby. Kate pressed her lips together and gave him a disappointed shake of her head. He dropped his eyes and stared gloomily at his sketchpad, clearly aware he was being childish.

D'arcy seemed to know she'd scored a point. Her speech slowed, becoming more enunciated, tears shimmering in her round, hazel eyes. "When are you going to grow up?"

Simon cleared his throat, and glancing over, Kate saw him scowling, his jaw set. She flinched when he turned his hard gaze in her direction. He bugged his eyes at her, his hands twitching, as though he wanted to wring her neck, demanding something from her. Her heart thudded. What?

Breathless, Kate cut in, "Okay, D'arcy. I suspect Eli's feeling a bit defensive at the moment." *Not the only one!* She turned to face him. "Eli. Can you tell me, tell D'arcy, what you hear her saying. What is *she* worried about?" She felt Simon's tension slacken beside her, and the tight band around her own ribs eased with it, as though her nerve endings were tethered to his. What was this?

Eli sat, sulking, reluctant to play by Kate's rules or be drawn out. She met his eye, stern but sympathetic and encouraging. His voice was just above a mumble. All he managed to express were irrational fears of oppression and loss of artistic freedom.

"Are you saying what you hear D'arcy saying, or what you're afraid of?" Kate asked, looking steadily at him. From the corner of her eye, Kate noticed Simon lower his hands and lean forward.

Eli stared hard at her for a long moment. "Okay. Maybe I'm overreacting. I dunno. For years, she never asked me to be anything that wasn't me." Eli was subdued, speaking softly. "I was good enough for her before. Why the change now?"

Kate paraphrased Eli's concerns. She could certainly relate to fears of lost identity and integrity.

"That's ridiculous." D'arcy replied, then hesitated and softened her voice. "All I'm saying is: chip in, that's all. I'm looking for Eli to contribute, not just with the money he's earned, but by caring, by showing an interest in the things we have invested in together, our future, our dreams," D'arcy hesitated, " … in me, you know?"

"Eli?" Kate prompted. "What do you hear now?"

"Yeah. I hear. I hear," he said, looking down, his lip pressed into a thin line. His fountain pen rested on the page, ink bleeding slowly outward in a growing ragged blot.

"Do you want to think about that for a while?"

Eli nodded. He wasn't making eye contact with anyone now. He wasn't sketching either, but staring sightlessly at the Rorschach splotch on his notepad.

Kate stole a glance at her watch. She reckoned that both her clients had had about enough for one day. Furthermore, she had quite a lot of information to digest and record in her notes. Not just their words — though those were interesting enough — but all the non-verbal signals and signs that they were emanating. She'd wrap up the meeting, and then by next Tuesday, she'd have a fresh approach mapped out.

"I think we should stop there for today. It's a good start, though you're both falling into your old habits. I think you know that. You've both shared a lot of information and feelings and we all need time to digest and consider. Sharon, you've been very quiet. Do you have any questions or comments before we wrap up for this morning?"

Sharon was ill-disguising her critical thoughts of the disloyal and irresponsible Eli. "No, thank you. I think I've heard enough for today." She scratched a few brief notes in her notebook and closed it with a slap.

"Simon? Any questions?" Kate didn't look up from her notes while she spoke, though she peeked at him through her dropped lashes.

"Hmm. Many. But, I, too, have had enough for one day," he said, his mouth curving up mysteriously to one side, as though his secret thoughts were quite amusing, and might involve her. He abruptly turned away, "How about a *post mortem* over sushi, Eli?" The two of them said their good-byes and left immediately, followed shortly afterwards by D'arcy and Sharon, who stood and talked softly in the corridor for a few moments.

Kate quietly made notes while she waited for everyone to leave. It was a good start. The first step was always to deal with emotions, and both Eli and D'arcy had been fairly expressive and open, and, she felt honest. There was a lot of hurting and mistrust, and if they could get that out in the open, the material issues might just go away. She'd talk about the agreement next time.

She felt she'd begun to uncover D'arcy and Eli's needs, concerns, hopes and fears. It occurred to her to question her own while she was about it. Things were going more or less as she expected with D'arcy and Eli, and altogether outside of her expectations regarding Simon. She was doing all right, wasn't she? Instead of feeling calmer in his presence, however, she was becoming increasingly agitated, distracted and confused. She felt a strange intimacy with him, with his body. It was as though fifteen years hadn't passed, and they were still connected somehow.

"Ah, there you are." A stiff British accent that she didn't recognize.

"Excuse me? Who's calling please?" said Kate upon answering her phone the following day.

"Helen Duchamp. I left several messages."

All this morning? Aah. "I'm sorry, I just got in. We haven't met. You're ... D'arcy's mother then?"

"Yes, dear." The condescension was dripping off of her voice like icicles. "Of course."

Oh, of course. "And what can I do for you, Mrs. Duchamp?"

"What can you do for me?" The woman's voice was as brittle and cold as ice crystals. "The least I would have expected is a courtesy call to discuss my objectives for these sessions that I'm paying for before they get too far along."

Aha. It was like that, was it? Kate slowed her breathing. "I take it D'arcy doesn't know you're calling."

"Don't be ridiculous!" Mrs. Duchamp's laugh was shrill. "This is strictly confidential. Just between you and I."

"Excuse *me*, Mrs. Duchamp. Let me clarify for you how mediation works." She paused, gritting her teeth. "Firstly, my clients are *both* D'arcy and Eli, and I will invoice them for my fees. How they are financing the payments is none of my concern. Secondly, *my* objective for the sessions, as it should be, is to mediate discussions between my clients, and, if possible, facilitate a reconciliation."

"Yes, yes. But you and I know how these things really work."

"Do we?" Kate knew she couldn't be rude to this woman. Mustn't hang up on her, but she was sorely tempted.

"This marriage is a farce and it's high time it ended. This man can only hurt my daughter more. He'll ruin her life if it goes on much longer. She needs someone more suited to her own station in life, who can support her."

"Mrs. Duchamp, please— "

"My daughter is a dreamer, Miss O'Day. She seems incapable of seeing what she's gotten into. He's gotten what he wanted from our family, and it's time for him to move along. I'm relying upon you to use these sessions to shine a hard light on that man. She *must* see him for the user that he is. Surely you understand, I have only my daughter's best interests at heart."

If she called Eli *that man* one more time Kate was going to scream. "Mrs. Duchamp," Kate tried again to interrupt the tirade. "I too have your daughter's best interests in mind... "

"Then you do see things my way," Mrs. Duchamp interrupted with syrupy condescension.

"No. No I don't. I appreciate your sharing your concerns with me. But my job... my professional and ethical obligation is to be objective and non-judgmental. That's how mediation works. It's up to them to decide what will make them happy. Furthermore, client confidentiality prohibits me from discussing the case with you, Mrs. Duchamp."

"*I* know what's best for my little girl, Miss O'Day. I only consented to these irregular sessions because he was obstructing divorce proceedings, and she was getting so upset. They were making it difficult for the lawyers and costing me a fortune. This is intended to speed things up."

Kate had had enough. "Mrs. Duchamp. Surely you've noticed that your daughter is a grown woman. I trust that she can decide for herself what is best for her. Now if you'll excuse me, I have work to do." She hung up, wondering if that little chat would have any fallout.

four

❦

The day broke clear, warm and sunny, offering a sudden reprieve from two weeks of dull and mostly rainy weather. It worked like a tonic. Everyone Kate passed beamed beatifically in gratitude, and she was not immune to its effects. The city shone radiantly in its brittle light, the shadows all-the-sharper for their equinoctal angles. Blue and green glass curtain walls reflected rays of sunlight; creamy stone and soft grey concrete towers gleamed, scrubbed immaculate by the rain.

She approached the nine-thirty session full of optimism. Over the intervening week, her impressions became clearer each time she reviewed her notes. She knew beyond a shadow of a doubt that she could help Eli and D'arcy reconcile. All the pieces were there. As long as Eli hadn't broken trust by sleeping with that woman, or any other, everything would be fine. And her instinct told her that he hadn't. No, she thought she understood him pretty well, though her goal was to get to know him even better.

Eli wasn't uncaring at all, simply uninitiated. All he really sought was respect, and he couldn't yet tell the difference between the fawning attention of the fashionable, and the real McCoy. That's why she'd gone in search of his paintings on the weekend. She knew a thing or two about art.

The paintings she'd located at the Redmond-Lightstone Gallery had been a revelation. Far more refined than the artist appeared. The 'dark side of the human soul' was a phrase that came to mind. One canvas spoke to her so powerfully that it drew tears, right there in the gallery.

It was simple to see why he had a fan club. It would be easy to fall in love with a man who could paint like that. Combined with his saturnine, sexy good looks and joie-de-vivre, he was dangerous indeed. Or maybe he was the innocent, the one at risk. His adolescent personality was at odds with the sophistication of his paintings. He could be easily misunderstood, and possibly manipulated. A complex man.

When she arrived, she opened the blinds, and sat with her back to them, so her clients could enjoy the spectacular view, and benefit from all those uplifting rays of sunlight. This would be the last meeting in this space, she determined. She was glad when Eli was the first to arrive, and he was followed moments later by Sharon. She was back in pseudo-military form, with a belted taupe pant-suit that Kate thought made her look even more petite and drab. She sat with her hands folded on her notebook like the teacher's pet in the front row of class, lips pressed primly together.

Eli's greeting was warm and he exuded energy like the sun itself. His smile was disarming, Kate thought, as she admired his smooth handsome face. He carried a motorcycle helmet, which he tossed on the table with a pair of dark sunglasses. His personal sense of cool urban style no doubt encouraged his fan club. His agent might even have exploited this deliberately.

Kate decided she would risk annoying Sharon and bond anyway. "I dropped into the Redmond-Lightstone Gallery this weekend, Eli," she said. His eyes popped open. "I have to tell you that I was simply astounded by your work."

"Thank you," he said simply, beaming at her compliment. "Which was your favourite?" he deadpanned, a mysterious twinkle in his dark eyes.

Had to be a trick question. "Mmm. I'd have to say... 'Magdalene of the East Side'. The light... and her expression. She exudes a kind of acceptance or something—a fecund receptivity." She nodded thoughtfully, and gave him a knowing look.

He glowed under her praise.

"I'm sure I didn't understand half the allegorical bits." She shrugged. "It really got to me, though."

His smile broadened to a grin. She'd passed the test, apparently.

"What is it like, then?" enquired Sharon, unwilling to be left out.

Kate shared a look with Eli, then said, as lightly as possible, so as not to alienate, "You'd really have to see it yourself, Sharon.

It's impossible to do Eli's work justice with a simple description. The canvasses are huge and complex. They are masterpieces, truly. It's no wonder he's being collected."

"You exaggerate, Kate," Eli said, "but I'm flattered."

Simon entered the room just then. "Greetings to you all this glorious morn," he said upon entering, encompassing them all with a broad smile. Kate caught her breath. In deference to the warmer weather, he wore a simple blue oxford cloth shirt with a preppy striped tie that had been loosened already. The look was fabulously sexy on his tall frame. Sunlight flooding in the window caught his golden hair, and the blue of his eyes glowed as brightly as his shirt. It was hard not to stare.

Then he caught her eye and she faltered, returning quickly to her notes while her every pore strained to take in more of him.

"We are blessed indeed by this Indian Summer."

Everyone murmured words of agreement. How did he manage to speak that way and yet not come across like a dork? Kate wondered, mesmerized. He was hypnotic.

"We were just discussing Eli's paintings, Simon," Sharon said ingratiatingly. "Have you seen them?" Kate caught Eli's eye and they exchanged a small smile. Sharon was plainly looking for an ally in her ignorance, but was disappointed.

"Yes. Yes, actually," replied Simon. "I'm quite a fan already."

Sharon looked peeved. Kate, however, was impressed at his confident assessment, and noted Eli's open pleasure at the restrained compliment.

D'arcy's entrance interrupted anything further Simon might have said. D'arcy removed sunglasses to reveal dark circles punctuating red-rimmed eyes in a puffy face. Her dark hair hung limp as linguini, as did the loose dull grey turtleneck sweater she wore. She embodied the antithesis of the bright day. Kate wondered again if she was unwell. She noted an echo of her concern reflected in Eli's face.

"Good morning," said D'arcy simply, and sat down next to Eli, squinting at the bright sunlight out the window, and twirling her sunglasses in her trim fingers as though tempted to don them again.

"Shall I draw the blinds, D'arcy?" asked Kate.

The room erupted with murmurs of protest. D'arcy answered, "No, no. It's fine. Enjoy the sun while it lasts."

"Okay, then." Kate began, and with very little preamble, walked them quickly through a recap of the last week's discussion, summarized and highlighted to reveal underlying truths, conveniently erasing most of the more obnoxious and confrontational attacks.

The expressions on their faces said it all. It was amazing how people crumpled or unfurled like marionette's puppets depending upon whether they were misunderstood or validated. Confident in her initial assessment that D'arcy and Eli really did want to reconcile, she decided to pull another of her signature exercises out and give it a try. This one always had interesting results, and would add color to her presentation as well.

"Today, we're going to take a slightly unconventional tack. Instead of rehashing the things that have gone awry this year, we're going to focus on memories and dreams. First I want you each to talk about the past, how you met and got to know each other… and then the future, what you each would like, in an ideal world, to see your lives look like in, say, five or ten years." Kate paused and looked at Eli and D'arcy in turn.

She stole a glance at Sharon, who was remarkably quiet, her head bent. She focused all her attention on paring her pencil, and shaking the shavings into a small plastic box brought, evidently, for that purpose. Kate's quirky methods were like a bitter pill to her, judging by the pinched and sour expression on her round face.

Eli reminisced about meeting D'arcy and the dreams they once shared. Kate glanced in Simon's direction, noted him gazing thoughtfully at her, and as quickly away, before she could catch his eye. Listening to D'arcy and Eli recount the early days of their romance, her mind involuntarily probed back to when she'd met Simon. Although they were young and socially awkward at nineteen, there was that same instant connection at the dorm beer night. Something that drew them together, making the rest of the crowd fade away. Something that felt inevitable. For her, it wasn't only his leonine beauty, gangly as he was, but something compelling in his blue eyes. A deep intelligence and seriousness, like he could really see her. With effort, she forced her attention back to her clients.

"...sometimes you just connect with someone, and it's mystical. Time stands still, like you've known each other forever... " Eli stole a glance at D'arcy and paused a moment, then glanced away again. "We couldn't imagine *not* being together." Eli stopped and glanced around, dazed.

Yes! Kate had felt the same way once. She thought Simon had, too. But it hadn't worked out that way at all. She pulled her lips between her teeth and tucked a stray strand of hair behind her ear, keeping her eyes averted from Simon's, lest he catch a glimpse of the pain and regret that still haunted her.

"Thank you, Eli," said Kate. She looked at D'arcy. "Would you like to have a turn?"

D'arcee's eyes were wide and glassy, and her throat tightened and released, but she gained control of herself, and spoke of their meeting in a quiet, meek, faraway voice, as though she'd been transported back in time, too. After a while, she paused and clearly wasn't going to speak again.

Kate watched as Eli and D'arcy's gaze met, recognition sparking.

Time for a break. Kate suggested everyone go outside for some sunshine, and meet back in half an hour. Sharon excused herself to make phone calls in her office. Eli and D'arcy drifted out together, and Kate noticed Eli gently tug her hand and smile shyly in invitation as they moved toward the reception area.

Simon and Kate were left alone. He stood up and stretched, turning to the window. She sat quietly making notes in her book, head bent, but he didn't leave.

five

With a mumbled, "Excuse me," Kate escaped to the ladies room with barely a glance in Simon's direction. She had to put some space between them and get control of her thoughts. She locked herself in a toilet stall and sat down, trying to calm herself, head in hands. The morning had gone incredibly well, but as time passed, she was unable to rid herself of flashes of memory—things she hadn't thought of for many, many years—about the night she met Simon.

She could remember her response when he first banged on the door of her dorm room at three in the morning after they'd spent the night dancing and talking over warm beer, and said another awkward goodnight on the sidewalk. Horror. "Kat-eee. C'n I come in? I wanna talk s'more." His tousled hair. His glassy, inebriated eyes and pouting, sexy lips. She refused to be harassed by some drunk, no matter how cute he was. But he was a gentleman, and he'd won her over. By that time, the other girls had figured out there was something going on, and she could hear a chorus of hushed giggles from down the hall. To them it undoubtedly seemed very romantic, though perhaps a trifle sleazy, too. But they were only nineteen. What did they know?

She'd been in a funk for weeks after her Ben's Dear John letter arrived. There was nothing negotiable about Ben's letter. She was only his high school sweetheart and now it was over. He had moved on. To her dismay, he obviously didn't feel the way she had. She had thought this was it. Ben, apparently, had not. At that point in her life, she'd been too frail emotionally to deal with the loss. He'd been her familiar anchor in a disintegrating world after the attack.

In any case, Alexa and the other girls had barely managed to urge her out into the social milieu again, and now there was this gorgeous new guy literally throwing himself at her door, begging to be admitted to her heart. Talk about a rebound romance. She wasn't certain what to make of that. Initially she'd let him in because he was so pitifully cute, and seemed harmless. He knocked, he begged and pleaded, he whimpered, and she gave in.

"Pleash. Kate." His voice was slurred. Why did boys have to drink themselves into a stupor? "I jush wanna talk w'you." When she first met Simon, that's exactly what they did. In public, in daylight, he was shy to the point of being awkward. But she knew there was more to him because of the way the other guys admired him and flocked around him. He radiated intelligence and charm, and there was that something special in his eyes. He tried to stiffen his spine with a few drinks, and invariably showed up at odd hours of the night in quite a state. And made her laugh.

She knew she shouldn't have liked it, but she also knew it was only that he was so shy. He was deep, gentle and funny without his inhibitions. He'd flop down on her bunk, and she'd make him a cup of tea to sober him up. They would stare at each other for a while and then they would talk and talk, probing, questioning each other's ideas and dreams, until finally, exhausted, he'd pass out on her bed, his damp golden locks spread across her pillow, his lax, smooth face as innocent as a baby's. If her roommate hadn't been out of town on weekends, she'd have spent those hours in a chair. Well, undoubtedly she wouldn't have let him in at all. But she'd lie down on Sheryl's bunk, and doze until he stirred and fumbled out early in the morning, embarrassed and apologetic, and no doubt nursing a wicked hangover. She thought he was adorable.

The whirlwind of attention had yanked her out of her funk over Ben, perhaps more quickly than it ought. She really liked Simon, and soon looked forward to his visits. It was perhaps the fourth or fifth visit, she recalled, that he wasn't quite so drunk, and that their long, philosophical, intimate discussion led to other things, more intimate. They were both surprised by the intensity.

Afterwards, it was different. They never dated, per se. They didn't need to, both captives of the university life. They sought each other out on campus, at the pub, at dances. They spent a lot of time together over the following three months, making love again and again, unable to quench their mutual desire. By the time the term ended in May, she thought she was in love again, though no words to that effect were ever spoken. It was implied through looks, gestures, poetry and passion.

Kate hadn't thought about these things in so long. The details that came back to her were incredible. She emerged from the stall, still feeling disoriented in time and space. She patted a damp paper towel against her face and neck, trying to regain some composure. Her eyes were drawn to the silver knot pendant she always wore, and she swallowed, drawing strength from its message. How would she continue to face Simon when such memories were flooding back? Instead of keeping a cool distance between them, she felt herself drawn toward him as though her helpless years of obsession had never ended. She wanted to wrap herself around him and love him all over again. She couldn't let that happen.

Exiting the ladies room, she let out a pitiful high-pitched shriek as Simon materialized, as though from the fog of her memory, springing away from the wall by the elevator like a big cat. He was obviously waiting for her.

"Come for a cup of tea?" He grinned, and placed his fingertips lightly on her elbow. She felt her resolve melt.

He led the way to a small, folksy café down the block.

Quelling the warning voice in her head, she pulled out her sunglasses and donned them, tossing her head back and smiling benignly at the sun. Warmth uncurled inside her.

Simon squinted at the glare reflecting from the glass and chrome trim of the parked cars they passed. She was elated to discover the café had small tables outside under the street trees where they could sit, and Simon offered to bring her tea.

"Earl Grey this morning?" he asked.

"Mmm. No. Ceylon today, please," she replied.

"Certainly. Anything to eat?"

"I am a bit peckish. How about a scone?" He bowed slightly and turned in to the café. He returned shortly with just what she'd ordered and even brought her homemade strawberry jam.

"Delightful!" she exclaimed. "If I'd known there was such a nice café here, I wouldn't have made plans to move the sessions to a new location next week."

"A new location? Why?"

She sobered. "It's important that the space is conducive to the relationships, and the positive outcomes we want." He nodded, listening, his eyes intent on her face. "I really dislike Sharon's board room. They'll make better progress in a more informal and intimate setting. It's one of the things I do a little differently."

Simon looked intrigued. "There's more to it than I imagined." He took a sip of tea. "I've been really impressed with your techniques. Today, for example. It seemed gimmicky, but then you really moved them along. I could see what you were doing." He paused. "I'm still impressed."

She smiled, chewed a bit of her scone, swallowed and said, "It's all about timing. I manage the exchange very carefully, and build on each step when they are receptive."

"Are you sure they're ready to reconcile? Surely it's not that simple."

Kate nodded. "There are still issues to be resolved. But desire and intent are there, so my gut tells me we can do it."

He squinted up at the canopy of umber, bronze, russet and green overhead, outlined against the intense blue of the sky. "You're not the way I thought."

Her brows knit as she puzzled over that. "What?"

"I mean, when I first saw you, you seemed stiff and distant. I thought perhaps arrogant. I assumed you were like... this other mediator I knew, kind of hard and cold."

"Whoa. So you wrote off my entire profession on a case study of one?"

He scrambled to explain, lifting his palms to face her. "Don't take me wrong. I'm not trying to ruffle your feathers. And I'm not trashing all mediators. It's just a certain type I have unfortunate experience with. I'm wary, that's all."

She continued to look at him through narrowed eyes. His reticence seemed to be of a different kind than Sharon's skepticism. A few awkward moments of silence passed. She gave him a tentative smile. "I had good reason to be cool. I was taken completely off guard when you came in. I didn't have time to think."

Simon hesitated. "I was surprised, too. I'd had no idea you'd be there." He laughed softly.

She was astonished. They'd silently, politely transitioned into acknowledging their past.

"Strange coincidence, wasn't it?" She paused, her eyes darting to meet his before glancing away. "I'm still worried about whether we should have disclosed more. I didn't think it would be a problem or I would." She flushed, and stared at her plate, her hand fluttering.

"It was so long ago." He waved it away with an air of indifference, and she was grateful. She was making too big a deal out of it.

"How is it that I've never seen you before, if you work in the city?"

He nodded. "That's relatively recent. I both lived and worked in Richmond until last year, and had little opportunity to come downtown. Then, when I changed firms, I couldn't make the commute across the bridge work anymore, with daycare and all that."

Daycare equaled kids. Separated with kids. She nodded while the questions swirled in her brain. She would not ask.

He continued. "I was still living in the condo we'd bought years ago, but we were outgrowing it anyway. So I found a comfy old bungalow in Kits. It's nice to be back in the city."

"I see. And I've always lived here, in the centre." She shrugged.

"So tell me," he continued, "I'm curious. Whatever happened to Urban Planning?"

He remembered her major? "A lot. I got involved in crisis counseling, and had a talent for it, as it turned out. It was gratifying. I wanted to help people. One thing led to another. I changed." She shrugged, and he seemed to accept her explanation at face value. At least they'd established some ground rules for their conversations: easy, inconsequential, nonchalante.

He assessed her quietly, sipping his tea. "I believe you have." He grinned and wolfed down the rest of his sticky Danish, licking his fingers.

"I see you still have a sweet tooth," she observed. Simon froze, finger between his lips, and his ears grew red.

"Mmhmm." He chewed slowly.

She studied him for a moment, smiling shyly. "Are you frustrated with being sidelined?" She closed her eyes and smoothed her eyebrow with the fingers of one hand, shaking her head slowly. "In the mediation process, I mean?" She watched his mouth as he licked his lips, and he lifted a napkin to wipe them, hiding a smile, though it showed in his crinkled blue eyes.

He pulled his face into repose. "Not at all. I'm interested in your methods. And I'm also curious to see the outcome. Eli and I have talked. I know he wants to reconcile. He knows he needs to compromise to make this work, but it's hard for him."

"It's not all his fault, of course. It's complex," countered Kate. "D'arcy has some issues she needs to face. Today's reminiscence brought them forward."

"She has issues, alright. Control issues. And trust issues. But something else bothers me about her. I think there's more. I mean I hardly know her, but her behavior is ... well, just weird. Edgy."

"You know, with instincts like that, you might make a decent mediator yourself," Kate said, slipping her sunglasses on. "We'd better get back." It was going to be increasingly difficult to keep her cool and continue to pretend that the past they shared was inconsequential.

As Kate and Simon approached Sharon's office building, a warm, fuzzy feeling enveloped her, despite her nerves around Simon. She was enjoying being around him so much, she felt a fizz of energy tingling all through her. Her step felt as light as air, even while she cautioned herself to be sensible. She was jolted back to earth to see D'arcy marching indignantly toward the door, trailing hair, coat, purse, and Eli three yards behind her. He was calling out to her, waving his arms wildly, apparently angry, but she wasn't waiting to hear him out, striding onward with her chin jutting. He ran to catch her, grabbing her arm to spin her around, and Kate could see the fury on their faces.

"Uh, oh," said Simon.

"What's happened?" Kate cried in despair, hurrying to catch up with them at the elevator. They were hissing and spitting at each other like alley cats. She stepped between them, wrapping an arm around each. "Take a deep breath, you two. Let's take it upstairs." Their silent ascent was somber, Eli and D'arcy silently fuming, Kate catching Simon's perplexed and sympathetic look, until they reached the relative privacy of the boardroom.

"That's it. I've had enough of this charade," D'arcy said, sweeping inside and flinging her tight fists down to her sides just inside the door.

Sharon, awaiting their return, shot up with an expression of shock and concern. "What happened? What's he done now?" she asked D'arcy.

"I'm getting out of here," D'arcy said, twisting around like a caged animal, tears welling in her eyes. "This is *such* a waste of time." She turned on Eli, "How could you be so hypocritical? How can you be so—"

"You're hysterical!" Eli fought back. "You're so—"

"—dishonest?" she spat. "You think you can fool me with your romantic—"

"I told you, you can't trust him," Sharon said stiffly. Kate gave her a sharp look and turned back to Eli and D'arcy. Simon quietly closed the boardroom door and leaned against it. They stood in a huddle.

Eli ignored Sharon, jabbing his pointed finger in D'arcy's face. "—determined to find evidence to support your suspicions, you can't even see what's —" Kate watched, tense, trying to decipher their overlapping words. She caught Simon's eye again, watching him listen, observe and absorb all that was going on around them, glad to have at least one sane person in the room.

"—stories. I'll never trust you again!" D'arcy cried, tears glistening.

"That's it, isn't it? You never did trust me. What have I ever done to make you feel—?" Eli pleaded.

"What can you expect from such an irresponsible philanderer—?" Sharon said.

"Shut up, will you?" Eli screamed in Sharon's face, spittle flying.

Kate had had enough. "Stop right there! All of you." She turned away. "Sit down, please. Everyone." She moved to her seat and stood, tapping the table with her fingertips, waiting for everyone to take their places, and sank into her chair with her spine straight as a pike. She let them wait while she turned her cool gaze at each of them, and sent a particularly reproachful glare at Sharon. When her eyes met Simon's she was aware of a bright intensity there—was it approval? admiration? His lips tightened ever so slightly in a small smile meant only for her that made her feel an inch taller and sent a tingling warmth through her middle. She couldn't explain why, but it was suddenly important to her that he respect and admire her for her work.

When it was quiet, she made notes, gathering her thoughts.

She was loath to ask them what had incited the dispute, but…
it had to be done. "Okay. Everyone take another deep breath.
We're going to discuss this like adults, calm and rational."

Sharon sniffed and raised her chin. "You needn't address us
like school children, Kate. Clearly something's happened to upset D'arcy, and if she feels justified in… "

"Excuse me, Sharon." Kate cut in, her voice a whisper of
steel. "You're behaving like school children. If you don't mind:
Were you there? Did you see or hear what happened?"

"Well, no, but… "

"Well then. I would also like to remind you of your commitment to support the mediation process. Please refrain from
accusations and name-calling in future. It's unprofessional. And
unhelpful." Kate's voice was as hard and sharp as a nail, though
she felt enormous frustration.

Sharon's mouth hung open. Kate closed her eyes for a brief
moment, gritting her teeth, and drew a deep breath. When she
opened them, she could see Sharon's face pinched in fury, her
shoulders drawn up. Later, shrew.

"Now. D'arcy. In as few words as possible, describe what
could have possibly happened during a half hour coffee break to
cause such an outburst."

D'arcy sniffled, indignant and distraught. "We went for a
coffee down the street. We sat down at a table and were talking.
Everything was fine." Her voice rose in pitch and cracked. "Then
this bimbo with her navel-ring hanging out of jeans down to
here," she sliced herself across the midriff, " —bounced into the
shop and squealed— 'Eli, oh, Eli baby, what a surprise,' —and
threw herself at him. He jumped out of his chair and grabbed
her in a huge hug, and then he kissed her and pawed her, right in
front of me! I was stunned. I couldn't imagine who this little tart
was, but he didn't even introduce me. I was like, like—" she stuttered, searching for the word, "—like wallpaper or something.
He completely ignored me while he made a date with her, for
Chrissake!"

Kate made notes, glancing at her watch. "Okay, thank you
D'arcy. Stop there. Eli? Your version please." With deliberate
calm, Kate refused to judge the truth based only on D'arcy's in-
terpretation of it.

Eli didn't hesitate to launch to his own defense, bursting
with righteous indignation. "This is just what happened last

time." He looked pointedly at Kate. "She sees what she expects to see and jumps to conclusions."

"Just describe and explain events, Eli, please," said Kate in a soft monotone. She noted Simon squinting at Eli, as curious to hear his explanation as she was.

"The 'bimbo' in question is Cara, my agent Jeffrey's seventeen-year-old daughter!" He sat grim-faced, his dark brows joined in an angry line across his eyes, which glinted as black and unfathomable as coal. "We're friends. She's been out of town and was happy to see me. I did *not* kiss her. She kissed *me*. I did hug her. Why wouldn't I? I was happy to see her, too. She's been in Italy since May." His lip curled in disgust. "And the 'date' D'arcy refers to is a reception at Jeffrey's gallery on Thursday evening that she ought to know about. We're celebrating the sale of two large canvases to a collector in London. All my *friends* will be there."

"Okay, stop there." Kate paused again, letting the facts sink slowly into everyone's brain. After a few moments, she spoke. "D'arcy, how did this make you feel?"

"I felt… " her expression was graphic: her mouth warped into a frown, her brow creased, eyes pained, chin quivering. "I felt humiliated. I felt rejected… and betrayed. He didn't tell me who she was, or even acknowledge me to her. How is that supposed to make me feel?"

Kate nodded and gave her a small, reassuring smile. "And you? What emotions are you feeling, Eli?"

"That's easy. Anger. And resentment." Eli was still fuming, nostrils flared, his body tense as a sprung bow.

Kate talked them both through the event, showing them how it looked from the other's point of view, and trying to frame their respective behavior in terms of their good qualities, instead of allowing their fears and biases to color the experience.

"Eli, this sounds like consideration and good manners. Do you typically introduce D'arcy when you meet friends that she doesn't know?"

"I'm not a complete idiot, you know! I didn't get a chance." He was getting worked up, his voice escalating as he rose from his chair in agitation. "You people talk to me like you think I'm an idiot." He wiped saliva from his mouth with the back of his hand, and Kate met his eye and silently sent him soothing energy.

Sharon perked up, leaning back in her chair and glaring at Eli. "If he's going to get violent, I'm afraid we can't continue until he learns to behave."

Kate shot Sharon a staying glance. "Hold on, Eli. Stay with me." She reached out an open hand. "I'm trying to explore past patterns of behavior, to see how this fits in. D'arcy, has Eli always been openly affectionate with friends, with you? Is he demonstrative, I mean?"

"What are you getting at?" Eli interrupted.

D'arcy's face relaxed, her eyes sliding sideways, "I suppose, yes. His Mom is like that too, all hugs and kisses."

"What's that supposed to mean?" Eli demanded.

Simon's eyes widened with alarm, and he lay a calming hand on Eli's arm. "Take it easy buddy." Kate released a breath, feeling grateful for his presence.

Eli was undeterred, his voice jeering, pugnacious and petulant. "This makes perfect sense. It's been there all along." Eli turned on D'arcy, belligerent now, leaning over her, jabbing his finger. "You never respected me. You're just as prejudiced as your precious Mother and Daddy. You don't trust me to behave nicey-nicey because I'm such a cad; not raised properly and all that. Should have thought of that before you married me, eh?"

Whoa, touched a nerve there. Why was he overreacting like this?

"Don't misunderstand me, Eli," Kate cautioned. "I'm trying to—"

He turned to Kate. "I can hear it in your voice, too. Judgment." Foam gathered at the corners of his lips, which were working in a sneer. "You've all declared me guilty without a shred of evidence. You already think you know what I am. But you're wrong." He turned to D'arcy. "You know me, cher. You know what I'm like. I wouldn't do that!"

Abruptly, Simon rose and touched Kate's shoulder, sending a current of warming energy down her arm and across her ribs, steadying her racing pulse. His face had shuttered, become grave. His shaggy brows bristled, shadowing his steely eyes and his voice was dangerously calm, taut and quiet, like the whisper of steel on whetstone. He took hold of Eli's arm with a firm grip, ushering him toward the door. "Please excuse us, ladies. We'll be back in just a moment."

Kate was grateful the kerfuffle was over, but she felt an unexpected surge of resentment toward Simon for taking control. It wasn't like she hadn't dealt with unruly or distraught clients before. It was her job, after all, what she was trained to do. Does he think I can't handle it? She scowled. But she knew Eli respected and admired Simon and would listen to him, and tried to damp down her irritation.

While they waited, she took the opportunity to work with D'arcy. It was, actually— she was loath to admit to herself— a good time for a spontaneous breakout session. With Eli out of the way, the atmosphere calmed and Kate was able to get D'arcy to see how Eli's tendency to be expressive, openly affectionate and careless of etiquette, though he wasn't intentionally insensitive, fed her fears that he was flirting and having affairs. She admitted that one of the things she loved about him was his ability to completely lose himself in the moment, the person, the idea. When his fancy was caught, his passion was immediate and engrossing, and he was completely unselfconscious in his devotion to it.

"That can be a dangerous tendency, if you ask me," offered Sharon. "Everyone needs to exercise control over their emotions."

"Sometimes that's true, Sharon. But if everyone did all the time, there would be no artists, no musicians, no lovers in the world," Kate said, meeting D'arcy's eye with a knowing smile.

D'arcy admitted that in the past she had felt jealous of the way he became absorbed in conversations with people, to the exclusion of her or anyone else in the room. But she understood it and accepted it. "Lately, though, I've had a harder time with it." She admitted it was her own needs that perhaps had changed.

Ever vigilant, Sharon chose the opportunity to raise the alleged infidelity again, asking how she could trust him after catching him in such a compromising situation. "What kind of man would do that? It isn't right."

"Well, D'arcy? How are you feeling about that now?" asked Kate. "Do you still believe Eli slept with one of those women?"

D'arcy was pensive, her voice wistful when she spoke. "I don't know, Kate. Maybe I–"

"But you were certain," exclaimed Sharon. "That's what drove you to file for divorce, wasn't it?"

"Oh, I don't know, Sharon ... the evidence was damning, yes, I admit, but pretty circumstantial. I really wouldn't put it past Eli to pass out at his own party," D'arcy lowered her face into her hands and ground at her temples with her carmine-tipped fingers. She looked dog-tired.

"I'm telling you, a word to the wise is enough," Sharon shook her head, tight-lipped.

"Meaning... ?"

"Meaning... he's already shown you his colors. If he didn't sleep with those girls, how long until he's tempted again?" Sharon's hands sliced down onto the table like small square guillotines, unforgiving. D'arcee's eyes widened in distress, and she inserted her little finger between her teeth, nibbling.

Kate grimaced and, resisting the urge to roll her eyes, said, "Sharon, I'm sorry, but I have to ask you point blank. What exactly is your objective here?" She opened her hands, remembering the phone-call from Darcy's mother. "Have you been retained to ensure D'arcy and Eli are divorced despite their wishes?" It was difficult to keep the sarcasm out of her tone; Sharon's motives were so obvious. "You're doing a great job of helping them along, if that's the case."

Sharon huffed, her nostrils flaring like a small dragon, but there was no opportunity to further the topic, as the door opened. Simon and Eli returned, Eli shuffling. Simon glanced at him significantly, eyebrow cocked.

"Er." Eli angled toward his chair, gripping its back. "I... uh... I'm sorry. I kinda lost my cool, there." Kate met his eye cautiously, not smiling. "M'sorry Kate. I didn't mean what I said, honest. I just get worked up into a lather." Eli dared a peek at D'arcy, who offered him a shy, tentative smile of acceptance.

Kate reluctantly acknowledged that Simon had done a very effective job of turning Eli around. "Good. Alright then. Please sit down and we'll resume." They did sit, and Kate tried not to scowl at Simon. He answered with a bemused expression, filled with unaffected warmth, empathy and confidence, and a little shrug. Somehow it annoyed her even more.

"Right. I'm sorry we lost the momentum we gained earlier this morning, but, perhaps we learned something valuable in the process," Kate opened her hands, palm up. "D'arcy, why don't you tell Eli what you discovered this morning?"

Tentatively, D'arcy admitted she had been too willing to leap to the wrong conclusions lately about his behavior, especially toward other women. She wanted to give him the benefit of the doubt, to trust him. "I guess I need reassurance, instead of resentment."

Eli glanced at Simon. Simon sat forward, his hands clasped together against his chin, as though he sheltered the most precious, tiny treasure trapped between them, his blue eyes bright with expectation, like a summer sky. Kate could almost hear him cheering Eli on. Eli squared his shoulders. "I know, D'arcy." He swallowed, his prominent Adam's apple sliding up and down his tanned neck. "I think... no, I'm pretty sure a lot of... of my flying off the handle is just my old insecurities."

"I think I know that," said D'arcy. She laid a hand lightly over his on the table.

"I mean, it's not even you. I'm still pretty blown away by what's happening. Maybe I'm afraid it won't last. That I'll be found out, knocked down a peg, y'know?" Eli's eyebrows tilted like brackets in his creased brow, and the earnest, anxious expression in his dark chocolate eyes melted Kate's heart.

Gosh, she wanted so much for these two to work it out. It was so obvious to her that they loved each other very much. Kate stood straighter, pulling in a deep breath, filling her lungs. I'm good at this. I really am able to help them. We're making progress.

"Oh, I should know that about you." D'arcy's smoky hazel eyes were glazed with unshed tears. "But I also know, I've been pretty hard on you, babe. I can see how my demands are responsible for pushing you away." She offered a quavering smile.

"Brilliant. I'm so excited. We're getting to the heart of the matter, here, you two. I think it's plain to see what we need to work on is trust. Are you with me?" She queried them with her eyes, searching for consensus. She recapped her observations. Closing her folder, Kate sat up straight and rummaged in her bag for a moment, giving her clients a moment to gather themselves together.

"Okay. We're done for today. Do you think you're prepared to begin next week with a plan of action? I think we're ready to move on to talking about the future." When they both tore their eyes away from each other and looked up at her, blinking their confusion, she answered their implicit question. Sharon was scowling again. Simon, in contrast, leaned back with his face open and amused. She wondered, not for the first time, what he found so damn humorous about the whole process. At least now she understood how skeptical he was about her work. "In mediation, we collectively draft an agreement that lays out each party's wants and commits to actions in the future. It's an important step on the road to reconciliation." Her smile of reassurance was met with blank stares. "I'm assuming that's what you want out of this?"

"Don't you think moving to an agreement without more discussion would be a bit hasty, considering the morning?" asked Simon, his eyes skeptical.

"I agree. It seems a rather tenuous leap of faith," said Sharon. *Stay calm.* They didn't understand her methods. "Not at all. Trust me, I've been through this a hundred times." Or fifty, anyway. "This is all part of how this process should unfold," she said. "I'll explain in detail next week, but suffice it to say, I want to send you away with very specific goals. It won't be so easy to slip back into troubled waters if you have an action plan made up of wants, needs, and a commitment to changes in behavior that you can then go home and apply. The work's not over yet." She laughed softly at their bewilderment. "Last thing," she stood up, and passed around cards. "Next week, we'll try out a new meeting space. Here's the address. It's a bit unconventional, but I think we'll be more comfortable there. I hope that's not too inconvenient for you Sharon." She smiled tightly, but there was venom in her heart. She'd be only too pleased if Sharon couldn't attend.

Now the conflict was diffused, the atmosphere was lighthearted as everyone stood to leave. Eli offered to take D'arcy for a ride on his bike around Stanley Park in the sunshine. When she hesitated, he picked up his helmet and said, "I've got a spare. C'm'on, cher." He pulled on her arm, a most alluring smile in his sparkling, dark eyes. How could D'arcy resist? He plucked a cigarette out of the pack in his pocket and tucked it between his lips, grinning. D'arcy smiled back, shook her head, and yanked the cigarette out again, tossing it aside.

"Hey!" he complained.

Before they left the boardroom, Kate pulled D'arcy to one side, and said under her breath, "Get some sleep this week, hey?" giving her arm an affectionate squeeze. Simon, Sharon and Kate stood and watched as Eli and D'arcy left, and there were smirks of approval as they saw Eli twine his fingers between D'arcy's. "Hmmph. I never would have guessed it," said Sharon. "Well, good day you two. Until next week, then," and she followed them out. At the last minute, she turned back. "Oh, Simon. Will we see you on Saturday night, then?"

"Erm. I... probably, yes."

"Good. Good. I'll see you there."

Kate felt a twinge of annoyance. What could Simon and Sharon could be doing *together* on the weekend. They seemed an unlikely pairing. But then she recalled that Sharon was a friend of Simon's wife. Undoubtedly, they moved in the same social circle. It was nothing to her, in any case. His private life was none of her business. Certainly she wasn't envious. Not a bit.

As usual, Kate sat down again to make her case notes after everyone else left. Simon caught her eye on his way out. She couldn't help herself. "By the way, Simon. Although I'm certain your actions were well-intentioned, in future I'd appreciate if you'd check with me if you want a break-out session with your client instead of dashing from the room. I'm quite accustomed to dealing with my clients outbursts, you know."

He stared silently, his face passive. If he was angry she couldn't tell. "Alright." After a moment, he nodded slowly and left, leaving her with the memory of his perplexed expression.

six

Dazzling afternoon sun blinded Kate as she stepped out onto the street and, squinting, stopped to fish her sunglasses out of her bag. Remembering her tea with Simon, she smiled to herself and thought how pleasant it would be to sit outside again. This was likely the last bit of sunshine she would see before next spring. She would treat herself to a nice restaurant lunch and take her mind off of both her temperamental clients and their interfering, exasperating barristers. *I know just the spot.*

Two blocks over, she approached Luigi's, but was dismayed to find a cluster of people in the doorway with similar intentions. She'd have a long wait for a table. She paused on the sidewalk, glancing at her watch and surveying the crowd. A flash of movement caught her eye, and glancing over, she was amazed to see Simon sitting alone at a small table outside, waving a menu in the air. She strolled over, her stomach tightening, feeling awkward after their parting words.

"Hey, this isn't an Asian restaurant. What are you doing here?" She forced a laugh.

He smirked, a knowing light shining in his blue eyes. "Were you trying to avoid me by choosing Italian?" He twirled a glass of red wine, the only ornament on the plastic covered red and white checked tablecloth.

She feared her hot face exposed her distress. "Don't be ridiculous. I've been here before, the food's excellent."

"Join me," he invited. "You'll have quite a wait otherwise. It seems I got here just in time."

What? She hesitated, biting her lip. "Sure." She shrugged, stepping around the barrier. "You're not expecting anyone?"

"Only you," he smiled, as she pulled out a chair and perched across from him. "Here," he handed the menu to her, "I've already decided."

"Oh, I think I know what I'll order already, unless there are specials to tempt me," she replied, flipping open the menu to glance at the fresh sheet. "Hmm. I'll stick with the pesto."

"Good choice. You know he grows his own organic basil..." A young waiter sidled through the crowded patio smiling at them.

"Buon giorno, signore. You have company." He took their orders, Simon ordering the pesto too. The young man grinned at Simon. *"Signorina,"* he bowed his head slightly and met her eye with a mischievous grin.

"That looks awfully good," said Kate, eyeing Simon's wine, "I think I'll have one, too," she told the waiter before he turned away. "I don't know where they find young Italians to wait tables here in Vancouver, but it sure helps the ambiance."

Simon chuckled. "Octavio was born here, over near the Drive, though his parents and grandparents immigrated. I think he gets better tips with the accent."

She laughed. Waiting for the food, they reviewed the morning. "Sorry if I didn't follow protocol," he said, his sincerity unmistakable. "I just reacted when I saw Eli losing it. I didn't want him to say something he couldn't take back. I was trying to help."

Kate dropped her eyes, acknowledging his apology. "What did you say to him, anyway?"

Simon's mouth twisted to the side, and his eyes dropped. "Er. Guy stuff. Confidential."

Whatever it was, he seemed to have a way with Eli and she said so, her resentment evaporating in response to his bashful smile.

"I'm a lot more comfortable one-on-one with my clients than in the public arena of a courtroom," Simon explained. "Too introverted, I guess."

"That reminds, me," Kate sipped her wine, "Is that what happened to criminal law? You used to be so fervent about that. I figured by now you'd be..." she hesitated. Perhaps this was not a diplomatic line of questioning. "I don't know... " She waved a hand in the air, tossing the question away, and reached for a piece of bread instead.

He laughed. "It's okay. Some days I wonder what happened to my dreams, too." He pulled apart some bread and nibbled at it thoughtfully. "It's complicated I guess. I did work in criminal law for a while, until I passed the bar and then a bit longer." He hesitated, and added softly. "I was still with Rachel then, before Maddie was born. We were both very driven."

She glanced up quickly. "Sharon mentioned. You're divorced?" She knew it was none of her business, but some part of her couldn't help digging for details.

"No, not yet. Separated two years. My wife's a lawyer, too, and a very good one. She didn't slow down when our daughter was born, so I had to." He shrugged and offered a skewed smile to Kate, and she saw that it was full of sadness. "I made the shift to business law first. But I really didn't fit in, anyway. Sometimes… " he looked up at the canopy of trees that cast filigreed shadows across the table, ruffling in the gentle breeze, " …sometimes things just don't turn out the way you expect them to."

Kate nodded. *You can say that again.* But she didn't want to interrupt his wistful rambling. She urged him to continue with her eyes alone, sipping her wine.

Simon sighed. "Then I found corporate law just too tedious to bear. I don't really have a mind for business, so I shifted into divorce and personal services a couple years ago. It may not have the panache or the upside potential, but it's easier, that's certain, with more regular hours. But that's not the only reason I made the changes. Just being around all those ruthless, greedy people made me feel sick. Someone was always trying to take advantage of someone else. I couldn't bury myself in that world day after day. *Not…* " he added, "…that I don't see ruthlessness and greed in divorce law." He laughed. "It wasn't the thrill I expected it to be in my idealistic youth," he threw a lopsided grin at her, making light of it.

"So, do you see much of your daughter?" Kate asked.

Simon tossed his head back and exploded with laughter. "Every day." In response to her puzzled expression, he chortled, reaching out to pat the back of her hand. Rather than feeling reassurance, his touch sent a frisson of excitement though her. He sobered and said, "When Rachel and I separated two years ago, Maddie stayed with me. Though we haven't moved forward on the divorce settlement much," he added, almost as an afterthought. "I want full custody of Madison. Rachel never had time for her in the first place, so she isn't involved much these days. But she's holding out for shared custody anyway, just to aggravate me. I think."

It took Kate a moment to process what he was saying. As the realization dawned, she opened her mouth, hesitated and then said, "Are you telling me your daughter lives with you full time?"

"I am. Rachel travels a lot. She just plain works more than I do. It makes sense. That's why I bought the house." He smiled and shrugged. "I always did most of the parenting anyhow. Maddie's my little girl, so I couldn't have parted with her, even part time." He studied his glass, twirling it around and around.

Kate's heart swelled with compassion. She could hardly imagine Simon as a father, let alone a single parent. What a disconcerting notion to try to integrate into her image of him. She really had no idea who he was, but she liked this new Simon too much, far too much for her own good.

"You must be very close," Kate said. "I mean, don't the courts usually… " she stopped, and looked askance, embarrassed. "Never mind. I'm sorry."

"No, no. It's okay." Simon raised his brows, his eyes guarded. "It is much less common, definitely. Though it's not unheard of. I basically raised her. And Rachel would offer no opposition to Maddie living full time with me… at least so she says, most days. When she's feeling cooperative." His laugh was taught and brittle, and he pressed his lips into a thin resolute line. "That's why we're still married. I see a lot of kids go home with their mothers, even when they shouldn't. I'm not ready to test the courts archaic views. I don't want Maddie to lose her mother, but I'm determined that she not lose her father."

What a heart-wrenching dilemma. What kind of mother *wouldn't* want custody of her little girl? Kate wondered if that was the main reason he wasn't divorced, or whether he still harbored hopes of reconciliation with Rachel. She was curious about Simon's wife, and the impact this must have had on his career, but couldn't pry any further. "So. Now that you're a divorce lawyer, are you enjoying it? Have you worked with a mediator before?"

Simon tensed, his eyes unfocussed. Several moments passed. "Simon?"

"What? I'm sorry, you asked about… divorce law?"

She smiled and nodded, studying him through narrowed eyes, hiding her mouth behind a delicate dabbing of her napkin. "Um. Do I like it? Well. Yes and no. I'm very good at it, perhaps because I'm in the middle of it myself. I seem to have a talent for moving the really volatile cases forward. I think it's because I avoid being inflammatory, unlike many attorneys." He paused. "I encourage my clients to separate the emotional battles from the legal ones."

Just then, the waiter brought their pasta, and it was a few minutes before they could resume. Kate tucked into her lunch and let him continue.

"You eat like you really mean it," he laughed.

She looked up, surprised. "It's pasta," she said in her defense.

He lifted his wine and took a sip. "I guess I can't bear to see people ripping each other apart. People aren't all that happy to destroy each other once the court case begins. Everyone suffers, especially the kids. They all walk away damaged."

"I would have a hard time with that too," she sympathized, her eyes cast down as she rearranged her napkin. She felt a strong affinity with his views, and liked that he was comfortable talking about the things that mattered to her.

"I guess I'm old-fashioned, or sentimental, or— "

"Idealistic?" she suggested, meeting his eyes.

He grunted. Understanding sparked between them. "Mmm. Perhaps that's it. I like to see families whole."

Kate nodded again. "And mediation? Have you had any experience with it?"

His face crumpled, his cheeks flushing, and she wondered if he would finally confess that he thought it was a bunch of baloney, like Sharon did. "Clients of mine have gone to mediation, mostly over child custody issues, but I haven't been involved." He hesitated. "The only time I've experienced mediation, I was the... client." He dipped his chin and grimaced.

"O-oh?"

He cleared his throat and took a sip of wine. "We... Rachel and I tried... about a year... it wasn't very...He let out an exasperated sigh, grimacing, and still she just looked at him. "Um. I... uh... I walked out. The... it seemed to me the mediator was quite... not objective. I found the process very frustrating." He stabbed his fork into his linguini, avoiding her gaze.

"Oh. I see." She'd had clients abandon sessions before. But she would have pegged him as calmer, more rational than that. He looked up. "You doubt me?"

She was perplexed. She knew it wasn't impossible that some mediators took sides, despite their training. It was a shame, and gave them all a bad name. "I'm sorry." She placed a forkful of pesto into her mouth and chewed. "It shouldn't be that way."

After another moment he said, "Have you been very successful helping clients reconcile?"

"Pretty successful. You can't help everyone." She hesitated. "Are you... still hoping to reconcile with Rachel?"

"No." Simon's eyes flashed. "I'm not sure I was then, either. I just felt I had to give it a try. Rachel never wanted to stay with us. But I guess I had a hard time letting go of Maddie's mother."

"Some people really shouldn't be together." Kate concentrated on her food. "But though I work on other kinds of cases... no even when I do, I always try to bring families together again. Even if couples end up going through with divorce, they tend to do it more amicably. But my philosophy is therapeutic, and I've built my reputation on my success in reconciliation." Kate pondered the case study she planned to present at the awards ceremony in January. It was going well, so far, and she no longer worried about Simon making her work more difficult. In fact, it felt like he was on her side.

"That's right. There are other... philosophies then?"

"Oh, yes. But of course there are mediators working in a wide array of settings — corporate, union, government... " she trailed off. "They have different objectives. The relationship is usually an important factor, though, if not paramount."

"Do you do only divorce mediation?"

"No. Family mediation, and some community work. You'd be surprised at the things people fight about. Child custody, of course. Family businesses. Abuse. Property. Wills and estates. That's a popular one." She laughed.

"That would interest me," Simon leaned forward, earnest. "It's an extension of what I'm doing now, with a different aim - more positive."

"Perhaps you should think of shifting into mediation. Many mediators are lawyers, you know.

Simon made a wry face. "That *would* be ironic."

They talked about the business of mediation for a while longer. "You mentioned you got into mediation through crisis counseling. How did that happen, if I'm not prying?" Simon ate his lunch, waiting for her answer.

Her chest tightened, and she dipped her chin, swallowing. "Well. You are. But... it's okay." Kate hesitated. She could share without making the connection with him, with them. "I discovered crisis counseling the hard way. It really made a big difference in my life when I was at a low point. Afterwards, I volunteered. After a few months, I realized that, not only did it make me feel wonderful to help others that way, but, I had a real talent for it."

Simon frowned but said nothing.

"I took a few courses, here and there, and then I discovered the program at the Justice Institute. My background's not in Psychology, per se, or law, but I supplemented. All in all, I studied for a few years before qualifying. It was quick. To be a Clinical Psychologist, I would have had to go back to school for another six or seven years, get a doctorate... I really didn't have the patience for that. This way, I was able to get working right away." Kate held one hand open, palm up. "Not that I'm a counselor, of course," she added.

"So it's more a kind of specialty on top of other training. That's why lawyers do it, I suppose, and shrinks."

She nodded.

"And it's more goal oriented, I imagine, than family or marriage counseling, which can just go on and on and then peter out."

"Exactly. I think you'd make a great mediator. You have empathy," she her eyes to his, felt her face heat, and a small smile pulling at her lips. "You keep your cool around difficult people. That's challenging for some." She raised her index finger, her enthusiasm brimming over, "And, you're a keen student of human behavior. I've seen the way you observe. Study. Analyze. Those are just the qualities you need." In that moment, Kate felt as though they were alone, and that his attention was as focussed on her as hers was on him.

He tilted his head to study her face. "You've almost got me convinced. You obviously love what you do."

"I do. It's a great feeling to find what you're meant to do in life. It's very empowering and energizing. I love going to work every day." It was true. She loved her work.

"I'm not sure I've got your... I don't know. Commitment, I guess." He sipped his wine. "So how about you. I gather you're not married?"

"No. Never been. I've been seeing someone for a couple of years."

"Serious?"

She lifted one shoulder. "My life is mostly about my work."

His eyes narrowed, but he said nothing.

Their conversation swung to lighter topics, food, books and travel. Kate listened with curiosity to Simon tell of his travels in Japan, Hong Kong and Thailand, and his discovery of various new culinary and cultural experiences along the way. Suddenly, despite her apprehensions of being with him, she couldn't get enough. She leaned in on her elbows.

"Each new trip I plan, I try to visit a country or region I haven't seen before. At the moment I'm thinking I might be ready for some trekking in the Himalayas. I'm not sure. It's hard not to go back to the places I've really enjoyed. It's tempting just to lie in a hammock in Phuket. These days it's a toss-up between the food and culture and experiencing the spiritual meccas."

"Does Madison stay with your wife when you go?" Kate asked, wondering what exactly he did at a spiritual mecca.

A sharp bark of laughter escaped his lips. "Oh. No. Not for the two or three weeks I need. I'm very fortunate in that; my parents and my brother help out a lot."

"So, you're interested in Eastern philosophies as well?" Her head was spinning with his myriad interests and activities. It was difficult for her to reconcile this sensitive complex spiritual man with the brilliant, career driven party guy she once knew. She was intrigued.

"Yes, more and more so as I get older. When I'm not traveling, I read a great deal. The classics, poetry and philosophy. I know it sounds, well, eccentric. Maybe a bit flaky. But... "

She shook her head, about to protest, but he continued.

"You're very polite." He laughed softly, with the self-deprecating, bashful grin and shy, dropped eyelids that she had always found so endearing. "Usually when I warm to my subject, people squirm. I'm afraid my interests have become a bit esoteric over the years."

"Well, I remember you being quite the aficionado of rock music, professional sports and, um, beer," she laughed, and he joined her with a rollicking guffaw, tossing his head back. She was touched by his easy grace, the unselfconscious way he held his body. It was very appealing.

"Everyone changes, not that I've given up those pursuits entirely," he said, shaking his head and pressing his forehead into his interlocked hands. "I guess I've never stopped looking for answers. I certainly didn't find them in the lyrics of rock songs, though they might have seemed relevant when I was nineteen. If anything, they only raised more questions." He looked up at her, humor sparkling in the cerulean depths of his eyes. "What about you? Have you traveled much?"

Kate bobbed her head ambiguously. "Not quite as much as you, but I've been to Europe a couple of times. And Alex and I have been to the Yucatan. I seem to be more drawn to European history, and art, when I travel. I never get enough of the Great Masters."

"Alex... is he–?" His brows drew together in a question.

She hesitated. "Alexa Jenner? You might remember her."

Kate shrugged, feeling momentarily awkward at the prod to their memories. Perhaps he wouldn't. She wasn't sure how much he paid attention to back then. He sure didn't seem to miss much now, though.

"Yes. I do remember. Short little brunette? She was in your dorm," he nodded, his eyes faltered and slid sideways. "I went to Greece and Italy once, years ago. But I'd end up sitting on a rock contemplating ruined civilizations, thinking about life, rather than touring museums and stuff."

He paused.

"What are your thoughts on Eli's work?" he enquired, his expression giving nothing away of his own opinions.

She remembered his comments in the boardroom. "You seemed to think it had merit, as I recall. Were you being polite?"

"Aah. But I asked you first." His mouth lifted to one side, teasing, with a sexy flash of white teeth.

She smiled back. "You missed my comments that day. I had just finished telling Eli that I liked his work very much. And I was not just being polite. I think he's amazing. Really talented and very, very smart."

"Mmhmm. Me too, though I meant to have another look." He grinned. "If you ever get the chance to travel in Asia, you might be surprised by the art and architecture there. When I was in Japan—" he was interrupted by the trilling of his cell phone, and stopped to dig it out of his pocket. "Excuse me. Sorry. Hello?"

Kate sat quietly sipping her wine, watching Simon. He was so well-rounded and thoughtful, and all of this on top of being a full time single father to his daughter. How did he manage it? The waiter took the opportunity to whisk away their empty plates, smiling warmly at her. "Cappuccino, Signorina? Espresso?" he asked quietly, and she held up a hand to indicate they needed a minute. He nodded and drifted away again. Simon's countenance changed quickly from curious to concerned as he listened on the phone.

"She was fine this morning. When did this start?" He listened. "Did she eat anything?" Another pause. "Okay. Yes. I'll be there right away. Give me twenty minutes or so. Right. Thanks." He clicked off, and rose from his chair.

"Trouble?" asked Kate, sensing, her bright mood dampened, that their lunch was over.

"Yes. I'm afraid so. That was Maddie's day care. She seems to have come down with something after lunch. She's barfing and running a fever. I've got to go get her. I'm sorry." He pinched the bridge of his nose, frowning, though he had shut down, mentally having left already. He pulled his mouth into a tight attempt to smile, and bent to pick up his briefcase.

She felt the light, fizzy sense of happiness they'd shared over lunch drain away, and her heart seemed to sink into the pit of her stomach. She felt the powerful pull of her attraction, and something more. A desire to comfort him. She sensed that, despite help from his family, he was very much alone. "It's okay. She needs you. And we're done here anyway. It's been a great lunch. Thank you so much for... everything. It was fun."

"I'm glad you found me." Simon said, taking the time to meet her eyes, and she believed him, though it was obvious he was distracted and worried. His face flickered with alarm, and he sucked in a breath. "The bill!" He rummaged for his wallet.

"I've got it. Don't even think about it." She placed a hand lightly on his arm to stop him. "Really. I hope Madison's alright. I'm sure she is... Just go."

He shook his head, reaching to curl a hand over her shoulder, his thumb squeezing gently, gliding over the edge of her collarbone. That small gesture felt like a momentous embrace, stopping her breath. "Thank you. Thanks a lot. I'll see you next week."

And he was gone, leaving Kate to sit and ponder the astonishing amount of information he had shared about himself, feeling as if her shoulder was on fire, throbbing with his heat, and the memory of his touch. She couldn't recall meeting anyone like him, perhaps ever. Not even himself at nineteen. There always was that dreamy side to him, even then, she thought. Strangest of all was trying to fathom how he'd traveled along that road, how he'd gotten from there to here, with everything else going on in his life. The waiter returned, his jaw hanging, apparently confused to find the charming tête-à-tête ended so abruptly. Kate ordered a cup of green tea, determined to sit awhile longer and contemplate the astonishing reappearance of Simon Sharpe in her life.

Kate was glad to have a night out, and an excuse to wear the new violet chiffon gown she'd bought recently. The Children's Hospital Fundraiser ball was the perfect venue, and she looked forward to catching up with the old work colleagues who had invited her to join them.

She pressed through the dense crowd, eager to get her first glass of wine. Too many bodies, most of them taller than her, pressed close, a pungent mix of colognes, alcoholic breath and, even at this early hour, perspiration assaulting her senses. On the other hand, it was nice to see people dressed up, especially the men in their tuxedos. A tall, broad-shouldered specimen up ahead caught her eye. The warm light of the crystal chandeliers overhead sparkled in his golden waves. She felt suddenly breathless, the skin on the back of her neck tingling. He looked almost like—he turned his head— hey, it actually was Simon.

Her pulse fluttering wildly, she lifted her voice to hail him. "Hey neighbor. I would have expected you to be home with a book on Confucius or the I Ching tonight, not rubbing elbows with the glitterati in your tux."

Simon whirled around at the familiar voice, his eyes searching the dense crowd.

"Here," she said, with a little wave. "Excuse me," she elbowed her way between two men and approached him. He stared at her, his jaw slack, but still hadn't spoken. "You look rather Bond this evening. Or you might if you didn't have such a vacuous expression on your face," she teased.

Then he spoke, his voice throaty and deep. *"Your two great eyes will slay me suddenly/Their beauty shakes me who was once serene/Straight through my heart... the wound is quick and keen."*

"Hmm?" Her grin vanished, and she stared, uncomprehending. What did he say?

"Chaucer," he murmured. He swallowed. "Sorry. I'm not hitting on you. I just mean to say, you look... amazing."

Her pulse kicked into higher gear. "Oh." She looked at his tie, feeling her face heat. "Thank you."

"Can I get you a drink?"

"I was on my way," she said, gripping her beaded evening bag. "I was thinking about a glass of white wine."

"How about Champagne?" he suggested. When she nodded, he elbowed up to the bar, looping his arm behind her, steering her closer, laying his fingertips lightly against the bare skin of her back to keep her beside him. She stiffened slightly, shivering, and drew her shoulders up, goose-bumps rising on her flesh. He ordered two glasses, then raised them high to turn toward her.

"Shouldn't you be drinking a martini? You know, shaken... "

"That's not me," he laughed, shaking his head, handing her a glass. She took a sip, and wrinkled her nose as the bubbles tickled it. His mouth lifted into a crooked smile.

"There you go again laughing at your own private joke." She clicked her tongue with feigned annoyance, secretly thrilled at his nearness, and his attention on her again. "And I was seeing you as this... sort of ... bearded mystic on a hilltop."

"Hah! That may be closer to the truth. I've been known to forget to shave, or forgo a haircut, but my daughter keeps me in line. She likes her guys clean shaven."

"A woman after my own heart," replied Kate, their eyes briefly meeting before she glanced away.

"How is she, by the way? Last I saw you she was ill."

"Much better, thanks. It was a short-lived stomach virus, I guess. She was back at pre-school yesterday, good as new."

Just then, the MC announced that dinner would be served shortly.

"They bounce back quickly, don't they?"

"Where are you seated for dinner?" he ventured, and

reached for her elbow, which tingled again at his touch. "Are you here with someone?"

She flinched, picturing Jay, who loathed formal fundraisers, refusing to accompany her tonight, and replied, a little breathless, glancing across the room, "Oh, table twelve, over there. A bunch I sort of know from my volunteer work at the hospital. Social workers and psychiatric nurses, mostly." She spoke too quickly.

"I should have known you'd be involved with the patients somehow," he said.

"It's nothing. The hospital social worker calls me up from time to time when there's a little problem with the families," she shrugged, her sheer shawl slipped, baring one shoulder. Simon stared, and she pulled up her shawl self-consciously.

"Uh. Well if your boyfriend's not here with you, would you care to join me? There's room at my table," he hurried to explain, "and a group of very dull old lawyers whose evening your company would distinguish, not to mention my own."

A little wave of guilt washed over her. Could she abandon the colleagues who invited her? She knew they'd understand and cheer her on. "Maybe for a while?"

At her hesitation, he added, "I won't bite."

"I... ah... I suppose. Sure." She tilted her head. "I'll just let them know. What table?"

"Thirty-one. Just there." He pointed, standing close to her so she could share his line of sight, and she inhaled deeply the fresh, crisp masculine scent of his hair and skin, a hint of his citrusy cologne, vaguely familiar, making her head spin. "I'll be waiting." He strolled slowly away from her toward the table, and stood by his chair watching her across the room.

She felt awkward explaining Simon to her friends, especially since a couple of them had met Jay. "He's just an old friend," she said, shaking her head, trying to convince herself as much as them. Several of them turned to check him out, and then gave her approving mischievous glances and nods. "I'll catch you later." She bent to retrieve her auction ticket. Blushing, she gave a little wave to her colleagues, and turned back in his direction.

The older lawyers at his table were bold and lewd. As Simon introduced her to the partners from the firm where he'd articled years ago, they stood, bowing and fawning over her like schoolboys. But she was more than used to holding her own among professional men, even younger and more aggressive ones. And their interest was more avuncular, in truth, than real. One old guy had a face like a shriveled apple doll.

As dinner was served, Simon watched her silently. Her efforts at conversation felt forced, and she squirmed under his gaze. *What is he doing?* They ate in shy silence, she attempting small talk, and he staring and smiling, with heat in his eyes.

As the dinner plates were being cleared, and the live auction was wrapping up, he leaned toward her and whispered, "If I leave you alone with these old lechers for a minute, will you manage?" She simply laughed, and cocked an eyebrow. He sauntered away slowly.

Between bids and banter, the older men at her table eventually turned their attentions away. It allowed her a chance to return to her table of friends and chat awhile, though she had to rebuff their questions about the mystery man. "We're working together on a case, that's all." Simon's temporary absence also gave her a little space to contemplate the strange evening, especially now that her was not staring at her so relentlessly.

She still was stunned to have found him here. But more than that, his demeanor left her in a coil. He was behaving like a besotted lover, staring at her and (gasp) reciting poetry, inviting her to join him for dinner. But then, he just sat there, aloof, observing her with that infuriating half-smile on his handsome face and a question in his hooded eyes, barely saying two words together. She imagined his busy brain brooding, questioning who she was, how she'd changed, just as she was. She'd felt obliged to fill the silence with empty chatter, which made her feel vapid and awkward. His attentions both warmed and worried her. *Is he still shy? Is he toying with me? What on earth is he thinking about?* Her mind bounced to Jay again. *Why am I even thinking these thoughts?*

Discretely, she kept one restless eye on his progress across the room. He strode with a polished and confident air, and struck a dashing figure in his black tuxedo, with his height, broad shoulders and slender hips. He moved with elfin grace, the candlelight glinting off his golden hair. She had assumed he went to the men's room, but he stopped abruptly and exchanged words with a stunning beauty in an elegant navy blue sheath. Her gleaming chestnut hair streamed down her back like a racehorse's mane, and she had a sleek, sinewy model's physique to match.

They made a striking couple. Standing close together—she was almost as tall as Simon—their degree of intimacy was obvious from the nearness of their faces and their steady eye contact. Kate's forte was reading non-verbal behavior and it was clear they knew each other well. Simon stood rigidly with his back to her, arms at his sides, his hands clenched in fists, but the woman's expression was sultry and seductive, and Kate couldn't help wondering who she was, and what claim she had on Simon's attention.

But, Kate caught herself, *what claim do I have on it?* She was being ridiculous, just because of some innocent flirtation and a little superficial flattery. It was dangerous to entertain such thoughts. She fell instantly to imagining Simon as he was all those years ago– when he was hers. Though then he was not so polished and worldly, he was both romantic and passionate. Why did he make her feel such strong emotions, when in truth she hardly knew him? She'd become enthralled by him again, so easily. It was too easy to imagine herself the object of his desire, too.

It frightened her to allow the thoughts playtime, and she quelled them with ruthless reminders of how he'd rejected her, and how she'd fallen to pieces. A shiver skittered over her bare skin, and she tugged at the edges of her thin shawl. She couldn't trust herself to judge her true feelings, even though it felt wonderful to imagine that kind of infatuation and desire overtaking her. Surely he was only playing, and meant nothing by his flirtation. The room tilted as dizziness invaded her head, her stomach squeezed and surged. She sat upright, stiffening, and closed her eyes, trying to breath through it. It was best to put a stop to this before it went any further. She would turn away both eyes and heart from his encounters with other women. It was none of her business.

When she saw him returning to their table, she excused herself and made her way back. But when he arrived, he was altered, and she found she no longer had to withstand his heated regard. She tried not to care; though he spoke no more or less than before, he was tense, fidgety, more reserved, and looked not at her but at his utensils. He made desultory conversation with the man to his right, ignoring her for long periods, as dessert was laid before them, and coffee and tea served. What happened to him? Abruptly, she felt cold and unwelcome. *I should say good-night and rejoin my friends.*

Kate's appetite for sweets was gone, and although she told herself she didn't mind, she couldn't help feeling dejected. She felt heat in her head building. She missed his eyes on her, though they made her tremulous and queasy, as if she were an amateur on stage, her lines forgotten. After another empty exchange with the lawyer to her left ended, she could no longer pretend she hadn't notice Simon's mood.

"You've gone quiet," she observed.

There was a long pause as he sipped and set down his tea-cup. "I often am." Now he was curt. Not the charming roman-tic from an hour earlier. He seemed to regret his harsh words, and relenting, said, "I bumped into Sharon on my way back." He pressed his three middle fingers to his creased brow, rubbing with an abstracted air.

"Oh? She's here too?" The conversation felt forced, with long awkward pauses, and she was certain he would rather be anywhere than sitting here with her. He must be embarrassed that Sharon would see them together. "I can't picture her at an event like this."

"She's actually quite civic-minded. She got me the ticket, insisted I come," he replied, glancing at her chin. His jaw was working, dimpling as he clenched his teeth, thin-lipped.

Kate remembered their exchange on Tuesday. "You seem up-set. Did she say something?"

His eyes closed slowly and opened again, flicking skyward. "Almost everything she says annoys me. It appears she's figured out that we…" he flicked a finger back and forth between them to indicate which 'we' he meant, "…were much more than ac-quaintances back in university. I hope she doesn't make trouble. I wouldn't put it past her."

"Ooh. Oh! I worried that we should have disclosed more. Now what?" Kate pondered aloud, nibbling the inside of her cheek. This could get sticky, especially if Sharon decided to press the issue publicly. "I mean… not that anything–"

"Now? Nothing. We'll be certain to give them nothing fur-ther to talk about." There was a cold distance in the tarn blue of his eyes, a flatness she hadn't encountered for a long, long time. It made her shudder to remember that other side of him.

He could be ruthless when enraged; as hard and cold as a steel blade. The message was clear enough, though.

Nothing for *whom* to talk about? Her stomach clenched. "I wonder how she figured it out?" Kate mused, poking indifferently at her mousse. She didn't want those glacial eyes aimed at her anymore.

He sneered. "Some women make it their business to poke into other people's concerns and use whatever they find out against them. Sharon's a pretty typical professional, clawing and scratching her way to the top, stepping on people as she goes." Simon's jaw was set like granite, and his eyes did not meet hers while he delivered his verdict.

She could hardly believe her ears. Where did that come from? Kate felt a hard jolt of rage slam through her, and gripped her fork with white knuckled fingers, pointing it at him. "Professional *woman*, I suppose you mean? I can't believe you would make such a blatantly sexist and petty comment. You sound like a misogynist, when I know you're not. Maybe it's you who has issues about competition in the workplace, not Sharon."

He tongued his cheek and shot a wary glance at her hostile fork, his nostrils flaring, and replied, "There's truth in what I said and you know it. It wasn't my intention to offend you."

"Too late, I'm afraid." She glared at him for a long moment, assessing, while her buzzing nerves made her tremble so hard she could hardly draw breath. Her chest ached with tension. Inside she was in turmoil. Perhaps he wasn't the enlightened male she took him for, or that he pretended to be. Maybe it was all an act, to get rid of her, so he could return to the company of that goddess in the blue dress. Or maybe she'd only imagined his charm and insight, dredged up from the years of fantasies she'd conjured. She turned her head from side to side, gnawing her upper lip. Either way, she'd had enough. Infuriating man. "I think I'll head over and visit with my friends from the hospital. Excuse me." She stood up. "Good night."

seven

Alexa scowled. "I'm worried about you Kate."

"I'm okay. Really. It's just so weird. I don't know what to think."

"You should have stayed away from him. It's probably a careless act he's been perfecting for years to impress and snare women." Alexa concluded, stabbing a broccoli floret with venom.

"Well, it's more in keeping with his hot and cold behavior back... then," Kate reassured herself. She crunched thoughtfully on a mouthful of salad. Thankfully Alexa was here to share her tumult of conflicted feelings after her disturbing encounter with Simon last night.

"He hasn't changed, after all. He's just more polished. Maybe he's not even conscious of flicking his charm on and off like a switch." Last night's abrupt about-face was probably meant to dismiss her, or let her know he was only playing with her, since he was obviously flirting with that gorgeous redhead as well. "He seemed really embarrassed that Sharon found out about us. I know I am." Kate felt a painful knot twist in her stomach, and suppressed a belch. She pushed aside a bright red tomato wedge, examining the remains of her salad. "Are you sure this feta is okay?"

"Well, I wouldn't give him the benefit of the doubt," Alexa said. "Men like that know exactly what they're doing. I've known a few. I wouldn't trust him, or take his flirting seriously." She stood to clear away their plates and tossed them on the pile of unwashed dishes in her kitchen sink. Turning, she pointed at Kate. "Which would be fine, if you weren't so vulnerable. Why wasn't Jay with you, anyway?"

"Wouldn't come." Kate shook her head. "I wish I weren't so gullible."

"It's only because it's *him*, you know. If you had a thicker skin, and just wanted to play and move on, I wouldn't worry so much about you. It's this naive obsession with happily ever after that gets you in trouble."

Alexa set two cups of steaming coffee in front of her and sat down again.

"Maybe." It was a relief to finally peg him and move on with a clear head and a calm heart. But she didn't feel calm. "Still, there was no reason for him to become so nasty last night. We have to work together, after all, and it seems less than politic to offend me." Something didn't fit.

"It would be easier for you to work if he weren't there at all. You need to forget about guys and focus on your career." Their eyes met, Alexa's criticism implicit. "So why wouldn't Jay go with you?"

Kate rolled her gaze to the ceiling. "Because I couldn't give him an answer, and he's miffed with me."

"And why is that?"

Kate shrugged. She took a sip of coffee and cringed at the bitter taste. "Don't know. Not ready, I guess."

"Why aren't you ready? You were expecting him to propose. You told me so. Why can't you decide?"

Kate slumped in her chair. "I'm not sure it's the right thing. It feels like settling."

"Well, you said that, too. But it's what you want. Stability. Security. A family."

"But… something's missing. I just don't have strong enough feelings about Jay."

"As opposed to Simon."

Kate looked up.

Alexa had correctly deduced that Kate was flattered and disconcerted by Simon's attention last night, and was worried that it would go to her head. Kate had not let on how deeply disturbed she was, neither by the flirtation, nor by his sudden indifference.

"He does shake me up."

She told herself it didn't matter, but his words had hurt her. Again.

We'll be certain to give them nothing further to talk about.

Well, what did she expect? Just because she still went weak in the knees at the sight of him, didn't mean he was eager to jump back into a relationship with her. It ripped her apart, exposing raw wounds she had thought long healed, and undermined her confidence as nothing had in years. The feeling of betrayal was too familiar. She didn't know herself, she was so confused; desire, anxiety, anger and insecurity mixing in a toxic brew despite her rationalizations.

Alexa said nothing, just sat drinking her coffee and gazing thoughtfully at Kate.

"I know it's irrational! And it's probably unfair to Jay. I feel horrible. It's not his fault. But shouldn't I have strong feelings for the man I'm going to spend the rest of my life with?"

A walk on the beach was just the thing to sooth Kate and help her think. Last night's drizzle had left everything glistening with wet, but the sky had cleared, and she looked forward to some time outdoors in the fresh washed air. She cut diagonally across the waterfront park toward Kits beach. As she walked, the spring returned to her step. Maybe she would even continue on to Granville Island so she could pick up some groceries from the farmers' market and take a water taxi home.

Autumn in Vancouver was never what it was out east where cold dry weather provided spectacular colour. But still, there were moments, and being by the water on a cool, sunny day was a treat she wouldn't have traded for anything. Though the leaves on the maples and elms in the park were a subdued mix of russet, green-gold and brown, and the trampled wet grass was slick with rotten fuscous leaves, the afternoon sun glinted off the water in English Bay and the indigo North Shore mountains rose above the water. Everything shimmered, the blue and green vivid and alive. She had a great life, she concluded, her spirits lifting. She had her health, work she loved, a beautiful home, good friends and supportive family. What more could anyone want out of life? If she chose it, she could even have marriage and a family. She could still have it all.

Jay had sent over some roses this morning with a sweet note: *I'm sorry. That was the most unromantic proposal in history. I take it back. I can do better. I felt you slipping away and I panicked. I love you.* Was that really a retraction? Was he having second thoughts? Even though she didn't feel what she knew she ought for him right now, he was very sweet. It's only that he'd moved too fast. Maybe in time, love would grow.

On the other hand, part of her wondered if her extreme reaction to Simon wasn't just her head telling her she needed to take a break from Jay.

She wouldn't let this episode with Simon get to her. His appearance had triggered something in her, some echo of the trouble she'd once suffered, and her old anxieties and obsessions had raised their ugly little heads. She was hyper-sensitive, where Simon was concerned. She just had to sort out her feelings and everything would be back to normal. What she'd perceived as flattery and flirtation were just his natural charm, and likely he meant nothing by it.

Just as well, given their professional relationship and Sharon's unwelcome scrutiny. It was a relief to know that there were no further barriers to a successful resolution to the case. It was too important to her to mess it up with second-guessing and neurotic romantic fantasies.

She drew in a deep lungful of clean, cool, moist air and, face tilted to the sun, continued on her way past the nearly empty playground. She might have walked right by but for the delighted squeal of a tiny girl on the monkey bars piercing the tranquil atmosphere.

"Daddy! Look at me, Daddy!"

Kate looked just in time to see Simon smile and wave at the child and reply, "I'm watching, honey. I see you."

Oh God! She halted in her tracks, frozen to the spot, her stomach dropping like a stone. *How could this keep happening?* She hadn't seen him in fifteen years and suddenly she was tripping over him everywhere she went. Had he been there all along, on the fringes of her world, and she'd never noticed? Was it one of those three-degrees-of-separation kind of things?

Kate looked left and right, swallowing the wedge of dread that thrust its way into her throat. She was in plain sight of them if he should turn around, no place to hide in the open field. Uncertain what to do, she stood at the edge of the playground gawking at them for a few moments. If she carried on her route, he was sure to see her. But she could hardly snub him, despite his rudeness the night before. Yet, she found herself unable to step forward and call out a greeting.

Rooted there, unseen, on the periphery of his life, an unwelcome spectator, she felt a wave of nausea overtake her. She was sweating, trembling, and felt strangely faint. Images of achingly similar incidents in long ago times and different places flashed in her mind, and she felt a powerful urge to run despite the consequences.

The little girl stopped, perched atop the structure, and stared at her.

"Hi," she called out, waving. Kate was trapped, holding her breath. Simon slowly turned toward her, curious, unsuspecting.

She looked at him, answering his daughter and greeting him in one self-conscious gesture; flicking a hand, she croaked, "Hi." His face was a cinematic parade of emotions projected plainly one after the other — shock, pleasure, embarrassment, chagrin, and confusion.

"Kate?" His voice was surprised though subdued. She approached tentatively. "I won't bite, you know," he said, one corner of his mouth quirking upward.

"Really," she deadpanned, suppressing a smile; his discomfiture was so obvious and good-humored. Or was it? She pumped her fists uncertainly. *Why am I so incapable of objectivity around him?* She stopped beside him, her hands thrust into her pockets, and gazed at the girl who was struggling to get down the ladder, curious about the stranger who had intruded. She had a tousled mop of light cocoa curls, and was wearing little green quilted coat.

"Daddy, help me down," she called out. Simon strode over and lifted her down as though weightless, carrying her back to where Kate stood.

"Madison, this is Kate. Kate, meet my daughter Maddie." He beamed at Madison with pride and affection.

"It's nice to meet you, Madison," said Kate, her heart squeezing at he sight of the beautiful little girl.

"Hi." Madison said, studying Kate intently, her light green eyes framed by long brown lashes and her round little cheeks apple red. She frowned. "Are you Daddy's girlfriend?"

Kate's mouth fell open. "Uh. No, honey. We… we work together."

"Oh." Maddie squirmed and kicked until Simon set her down again, clearly uninterested in work colleagues, and ran off. "Watch me climb," she demanded.

Simon stood shoulder to shoulder with Kate watching Madison struggle up the rope ladder. "I owe you an apology."

No, don't say that! I just got you figured out. "Not me," she said, trying to keep her cool.

His soft laugh held a cynical note. "Perhaps I do owe all professional women an apology. But it's you I offended last night, so I'm apologizing to you. I tend to generalize when I'm upset."

"Yes, rather." Kate shuffled her boots over the damp bark mulch, releasing its musty cedar scent.

He was silent a moment, then he turned toward her. "I feel rotten about spoiling the evening like that. We were having a nice time. I really would like to explain, if you'll let me."

She could not avoid turning toward him and meeting his eyes, though with trepidation. They were translucent and sincere, and her heart melted with her resolve. "I can hardly deny you that." Her eyes slid away, afraid of the persistent tug of attraction that snaked through her.

"Where are you headed? Can you come have a cup of tea with us? We stopped here on our way home, and we've been here a while; Maddie needs to eat."

"Um. Okay." She smiled and shook her head, torn. *Oh, crap.* She fingered her pendant nervously. *Is this a test?*

"C'mon, Maddie. Let's go get a snack," he called out, and Maddie came running immediately, a fact that Kate noted with some amazement. Weren't preschoolers supposed to be whiny and defiant?

They walked back the way she had come, over to a strip of cafes and shops on Cornwall Street. On the way, he explained that he'd just picked up Madison from her mother's in Richmond where she'd been all weekend and that his house was not far away. Close enough to Alexa's apartment that Kate wondered they hadn't run into each other before today. He led them to a small coffee shop on the corner with a banged up bright orange door and a hand-painted wooden sign that announced they'd arrived at Aster's Cafe. "It's kind of an old hippy hangout, but they make great home-made muffins, and they have toys," he said, lifting his brows significantly. They sat by the window in a wide beam of sunshine that slanted across the mosaic-tiled tabletops, setting shards of red, yellow and cobalt blue ceramic glaze afire. Settling Maddie on a chair, he went up to the counter to order and returned shortly with tea, muffins and a pink plastic cup of milk.

"I want juice," Maddie pouted.

"I know. But it's time for milk," he replied serenely, smiling at Kate. Maddie protested no further, but drank her milk and ate the half muffin Simon distractedly set on a napkin in front of her. She was oblivious to the mustache of milk and crumbs that clung to her sweet cheeks, and her sulking lasted only a couple of minutes. Kate, on the other hand, was mesmerized by Simon in the role of father and could hardly concentrate. Soon, Maddie was twisting around on her chair and watching a large golden retriever tied up on the sidewalk.

"I was more upset than I let on last night for a couple of reasons," Simon said. Kate looked up, questioning. He continued. "Before I met Sharon, I saw my wife."

Aha! So that's who she was. "I noticed you stop to talk with someone," she offered in a neutral tone, glancing at Maddie and the dog. "Your wife is very beautiful."

"Hm. Yes, people think so. She's anorexic. But more to the point, she shouldn't have been there." Simon glanced at Maddie. "If you're finished your milk Maddie you can go to the play area." She spun around in her chair and gulped her remaining milk, wiping her face on her sleeve and leaping down in one blurred movement. Simon shook his head.

"She's very good," Kate smiled, drinking her hot tea appreciatively, watching Maddie sit down in the play corner and dig with determination into a pile of grubby dolls and cars with missing body parts.

"Yes. She is. Usually." He added, pursing his lips. "I'm surprised she doesn't act out more. She has to deal with a lot of disappointment. She's supposed to spend every second weekend with Rachel, but Rachel quite often cancels for some reason or another. She travels… It's very frustrating for both of us, as you can imagine. Maddie doesn't understand."

"Ah. I see. So this was Rachel's weekend and—"

"She left her with a sitter —a stranger– after she'd been ill last week. I was furious." He spoke through clenched teeth, his face darkening with his words, and Kate believed him. Clearly he only wanted what was best for his daughter.

"I can certainly understand why that would ruin your mood," said Kate with sympathy. She appreciated what he had to contend with. Not only did Maddie rarely see her mother, but poor Simon had no time to himself.

"That's not all. I'm afraid she made some comment about you, and I was already so riled up, I told her we were old... lovers, just to annoy her." He winced. "I'm the guilty party." Kate's face must have shown her dismay, because Simon nodded and looked down, continuing. "After Sharon's snide comments, I knew how big a mistake it was. I should have realized she would run straight to Rachel to blab. It was foolish, and I'm truly sorry." He looked up at her, his eyes pleading. "Afterwards, I was as angry at myself as I was at the two of them."

She hesitated. It was very difficult not to be swayed. She sighed. "Well. You're forgiven. I wonder what will come of it."

Simon admitted he was relieved to have a chance to apologize before their meeting Tuesday.

"I am too," replied Kate, "I think." She paused. "I'm having difficulty taking your measure." He gazed at her, his sandy brows pinched together. The wide swath of sunlight from the window had arced across the table as the afternoon wore on, and now painted a brighter trapezoid of azure like a frame on the cobalt wall behind them. Along the way it highlighted his windswept hair, picking out pale strands among the burnished gold and illuminating the course texture of his sheepskin collar.

"I'm not so mysterious. You know me better than you think." She glanced nervously at him. "Tell me about you instead. What happened to you after graduation? What made you change fields?"

She toyed with her teacup, twirling it round and round in her fingers. She studied Simon through the curtain of her tangled bangs.

"I guess it was the counseling experience that did it," she said finally. "First I was on the receiving end, after a bad spell in my... twenties," she paused, meeting his eyes briefly, "and it was so significant that I later volunteered at Speakeasy; you remember that student peer counseling service the Alma Mater Society ran?"

He nodded.

"After that, I worked for a short while at a rape crisis center."

His eyebrows went up like flags, but he said nothing.

She hurried on. "Like I said before, I seemed to be good at it. Though I had intended to go back to grad school to study Urban Planning, my heart wasn't in it. I simply changed my mind." She shrugged and smiled. "It seems I was meant to help people more directly."

"So you *did* go back to school?" he asked.

"Yes and no. I took a few of courses, just to see if I was on the right track, in Ethics and Psychology at UBC. That's where I first ran into Sharon, actually." She made a face that pretty much summed up their experience of Sharon. "Then I discovered the Mediation Program at the Justice Institute, and there really weren't any prerequisites. It was quick. In about two years I was ready to go to work."

"Well. I think you did the right thing." He smiled. "I can't picture you behind a desk at City Hall. I think you're very effective as a mediator, from what I've seen so far. Your genuine empathy shows; it literally glows on your face," he added, "and I think people sense it, and open up to you." A hot flush rose to his ear tips, turning them fuscia.

"Yourself included?" she smirked. "Or are you so sincere with everyone you meet?"

"Uh. I don't know how to answer that, so I won't even try," he laughed. He hid his embarrassment by turning to see how Maddie was doing in the play area. She was engrossed in some imaginary game, providing barely audible voice-over for her broken dolls' unfolding drama. "What about when you're not mediating. What entertains you?"

She suppressed another knowing smile, and clicked her tongue thoughtfully. "I do yoga, most days," she said, tilting her head and staring at the ceiling. "And I draw and paint a little." She gave him a significant look. "But don't ever ask to see them. And, let's see…I read a lot. I like to read."

"What do you like to read?" he wondered, leaning forward on his elbow peering into her eyes.

"Nothing so arcane as yourself. I read novels, biographies. I like people, remember. I'm hooked on dysfunctional relationships. People's dramas." She laughed at her self-deprecating humour, and he laughed with her.

"And you like Indian food," he prompted. She nodded and he asked, "Have you ever been there?"

"No. No." Shaking her head, she added, "Alexa and I always talk about going, but work keeps us both so busy. She's an Architect, did you know?"

"No. I didn't." He paused thoughtfully, and his lips quirked. "I imagine she does well in that environment."

"You mean, in a traditionally male profession?" enquired Kate with an arch smile. "Yes. You should see her in a hard hat. She kicks some butt." That prompted a full grin from him, and Kate found herself mimicking him. She sobered. "She's also a really talented designer."

"That is interesting. It always amazes me what people turn out to be good at." They continued along this vein for some time, talking about various people they knew and their latent talents, laughing. Then, Maddie appeared at his elbow, tugging.

"Daddy. I have to pee," she offered in a stage whisper that had the other café patrons smiling. He moved to stand up.

"Excuse me. We'll be just a moment," he said.

"I'd better push off, anyway," said Kate. "It's getting late, and I was planning to shop on my way home."

"Can we give you a lift?" he offered. "I was hoping to talk about Sharon, maybe figure out some strategy before Tuesday."

"Oh." She took a deep breath. "Why don't we wait and see what she does. I think our best bet might be to be honest but play it down. We don't want to jeopardize the case. It really was such a long time ago, we might have forgotten altogether, you know." She blushed, avoiding his gaze. "The details aren't important to anyone, right?"

"Ri-ight," he answered skeptically. "Although, there's no crime in reminiscing a bit," he added, "or in getting to know each other again, for that matter."

She forced a smile to cover the thrill and terror his words inspired.

"Daddy!" Madison urged.

"Okay. Well. See you Tuesday, then," Kate said, and stood up, reaching for her canvas backpack.

Maddie dragged Simon toward the narrow corridor at the back of the café, and he disappeared with an apologetic glance over his shoulder.

eight

❧

Kate had just returned from an emergency trip to the corner store for fresh coffee cream when the buzzer rang, sounding not unlike the gears grinding in the transmission of a very large truck and jarring her, as it always did. She plucked at her sweater nervously and went to the phone to answer it.

"Kate. It's me D'arcy, and Simon's here, too."

She glanced around her loft once more to make sure she hadn't forgotten to put away any personal stuff. Everything looked tidy, the cool grey light flooding in through industrial sized windows. *Okay. I'm ready.* "Come on up," she said and pressed the buttons.

A few minutes later, Kate flung open the door, welcoming them in with a smile, and an invitation to make themselves comfortable, hurrying back to the kitchen in pursuit of a whistling kettle.

Without meaning to, she overheard snippets of their conversation as they removed their coats and looked around her loft.

"Is this her home or her office?" said Simon.

"Hard to tell. It's pretty slick. Look at the view! You can see Science World though that gap. And the marina."

She peaked around the doorjamb to see Simon tossing the same sheepskin coat he wore on Sunday over a chair, and lean close, squinting at the art on the long brick wall.

"What's this?" asked D'arcy. Kate ducked back into the kitchen and checked on her muffins.

"Looks like an old cable spool," said Simon. Kate missed the mumbled discussion that followed, smiling at their reaction to her coffee table. Alexa hated it, but she'd never regretted saving that old piece of junk, and people always commented.

"I can't believe this place," D'arcy gasped. "It 's really gorgeous." Kate heard D'arcy's heels click in her direction. "Kate?" she called.

"In here," Kate called from the archway, noting Simon wandering around, touching things in a curious manner. A vase here, a book there. She watched him move through a strong beam of sunlight, the air filled with suspended motes of dust, and he seemed like a character in a scene from some old movie. He moved toward the side window, and she turned away.

"Is this your home?" D'arcy asked, leaning in the doorway as Kate arranged mugs and plates on a tray.

"Shh. It is, but I keep my personal stuff tucked out of sight, and my living space kind of neutral. It's homey but not too... too, you know?"

The buzzer sounded again, and Kate carried the tray of dishes, resting it on the edge of her oak barley twist table, shoving a stack of books aside, and supported it with one hip to grab the phone.

"Hello," she sang into it. "Oh, Sharon. Hi. Come on up, fifth floor, yellow door." She put the phone down and picked up the tray, heading for the sofa. "Right on time. Hi, Simon. Have a seat if you like, we'll be right out. I've got D'arcy watching the oven. My muffins are about to beep." She flashed him a shy smile.

"Muffins?" he said.

She blushed. "It's nothing." She set the tray down and waved a hand vaguely in the air.

"This place is incredible," he said quietly, shaking his head. "You live here?"

She folded her arms across her chest, looking at the floor, scuffing a foot on the concrete. "It's Alexa's design. I was lucky to buy this place early. All the new so-called lofts are so small. Carved up into little rabbit warrens," she said. Her heart was beating a staccato rhythm, and her breathing was far too rapid. "But I couldn't afford an office and an apartment, so..." She stopped abruptly, feeling her face flush with heat, and shrugged. "I'll just get the coffee." She spun and strode off again. There was a knock and she opened the door as she passed by. "Come in, Sharon."

Sharon entered the space and looked around. "Ah. Simon," she said, finally, noticing him, and strode in his direction. Kate watched Sharon pull open her brief case and set up shop like a merchant laying out her wares in a street bazaar stall, and Simon, not surprisingly, continued his jaunt, heading in the direction of her desk. Reference books and magazines were piled high, even though she always carefully locked away client paperwork and case notes. She groaned, wondering what he was thinking, and returned to the kitchen. What was worse, having Simon snooping around her work space, or having him sit while Sharon gave him the third degree?

A few minutes later, when she came out, she stifled a laugh. He was talking to Oscar in a sing-song voice.

"Hullo," he said to him. In response, Oscar uncoiled his long thin torso, stretching his gangly legs, claws fully unsheathed, through the spindles of the chair back, and gave him a lazy green stare. Simon recoiled, disgusted. "Who beat you up, buddy? You are positively the ugliest cat I have ever seen," he said.

Kate smiled and snuck up behind him. "That's Oscar." Simon jumped. "He's had a hard life," she laughed softly.

"I'll say," replied Simon, his ears turning pink.

Kate stooped to pick up the lump of bone and fur, curling him up on her arm and scratching his skinny neck. He turned his face toward her chest and buried it there, a loud sawing noise immediately emitting from his belly, and kneaded at her like a lump of dough.

"He obviously knows which side his bread is buttered on."

"I found him in a dumpster, half dead, some years ago and took him to the shelter. But then I just couldn't leave him there, with his mangy fur and chewed ears. No one else would have him. He's very happy to have a home here now," she said, cooing at him, "Aren't you old boy?" and pulling his ugly mug out of her oxter to look him in the eye. "He's very affectionate, if you like cats, but he does stink, I'll warn you. He can't help it. He has more than a few chronic health problems." She reached forward with the cat hanging like a limp rag mop from her hands, and Simon had no choice but to take him, blinking.

He curled up his nose. "I do like cats. We have one, actually. Lucy. She's diabetic."

What was this, a pissing match to see who was more compassionate towards pathetic animals? She smiled wanly and walked away, leaving them to get acquainted.

"Ow! Fffk." She heard Simon utter a quiet oath as she walked away. "Alright. I've got it, don't touch your undercarriage," he muttered, as Oscar dashed away, and she laughed to herself.

D'arcy carried in the tray of steaming muffins, and Kate followed with a teapot in her hand. "Are we still missing Eli?" she asked no one in particular. "What time is it?"

Simon flipped his wrist over to glance at his watch. "It's 9:45," he reported. He followed Kate, sucking his finger, and sat down.

Sharon was at last off the phone, and commented to Kate that her loft was lovely, then complained about Eli. "What's going on? We can't wait all day."

"I'll give him a call. Maybe he's lost or something," offered Simon. He dialed and waited. "No answer," he reported. Just then, Kate's phone rang, and she excused herself. Sure enough, it was Eli and she buzzed him in. He wore his usual brown leather jacket and jeans, motorcycle helmet in hand.

"Hiya Kate. Sorry for being late. I got turned around." He looked around openmouthed. "Awesome place. Wow, could I live and paint here. The light!"

"Help yourself to coffee or tea, everyone, and grab a muffin while they're hot. Let's get started."

"You baked muffins," Sharon deadpanned, as the others reached for plates and mugs. Sharon gave Simon a strange look, and he merely raised his eyebrows haughtily in response, settling in next to Sharon with a muffin balanced on his knee, the corners of his mouth quirked.

Kate sat in an armchair at the open end of the sectional sofa, waiting for everyone else to sit down. She smiled warmly at Eli and D'arcy, who were sitting next to each other, and at Sharon. Kate would like nothing better than to give Sharon a piece of her mind for always finding something to criticize, but she had to admit that at the moment Sharon held the ace and they had to tread carefully. She was waiting for Sharon's revelation, but it never came. Maybe she was waiting for them to confess to some sordid affair.

Ignoring the feeling of dread that encroached, Kate recapped key points from the previous session, highlighting Eli and D'arcy's strengths, and also summarizing their concerns, distilling all their words and actions into a tidy package that everyone could easily digest. Though she had introduced the notion at the beginning of their sessions, she spent a half hour explaining the purpose of a reconciliation agreement that would include an action plan made up of wants, needs, and a commitment to changes in behavior, as well as a statement of common goals. Many people found it a strange idea, until she explained that its creation was the entire point of it. D'arcy and Eli were listening intently, Eli lightly holding D'arcy's hand in his lap, less restless than usual.

After a while, Kate handed them both forms and asked them to fill in the blanks as a basis for a draft agreement, after which she would outline a document for them to review. While they scratched away, Sharon peering over at Darcy, Simon excused himself, standing up and setting his plate down on the table. "Erm. Where's the... ?"

"Oh. Around the corner from the kitchen." She pointed at the screen divider. "Just behind there, on the left."

Kate watched Sharon fidget, unable to keep her eyes from following Simon's progress across the room. Kate was just as tense waiting for him to return. He was taking an awfully long time in the bathroom. After several more minutes, Sharon finally stood and excused herself as well, and Kate wished she could chase after her and prevent her from confronting Simon about what she'd learned. She tucked a strand of hair behind her ear, and wiped her sweaty palms along her pant legs, wishing there was something she could do, hoping Simon could keep his cool under pressure.

When neither of them returned, Kate worried they were embroiled in an argument. The best she could do was wrap up the session and get everyone out of there as soon as possible. After much mumbled discussion, it was approaching noon as Eli and D'arcy completed their forms, so she stood up and said her farewells as she led them in the direction of the door. It had been a productive and peaceful session - at least on the surface.

At last Simon and Sharon emerged from the gallery, side by side. Kate turned to face them, holding her breath, trying to read Simon's face. "There you are." She tried to smile, but her face felt tight. Simon offered her a subtle smile of reassurance, but she picked up on his tension. She tried to put on a cheerful manner. "We've got the ingredients for a reconciliation agreement hammered out here, which I'm going to draft. D'arcy and Eli have some homework, but I'm hoping we can pull it together next week."

"Well. Congratulations," offered Simon, "I look forward to going over that with you Eli."

Eli smiled. "You'd better, Simon. Just to make sure I haven't promised to give up painting, or eating and drinking." Fingering his cigarette pack, he laughed and glanced at D'arcy.

"Eli!" she gave him an affectionate elbow in the ribs and pouted coyly, and he wrapped an arm around her, planting a loud kiss on her lips. She blushed and looked down, but let her body relax against his as he continued to hold her. Eli glanced at Simon, and his smile tugged to one side, self-conscious.

"Well, we'd better head out. 'Til next week then, everyone," said Eli, turning for the door. "Lunch, cheri?" he said against D'arcy's hair, his tone flirtatious.

"I'll call you," Simon said.

"I'll buy you lunch too, Simon. Next time," Eli smiled again, placing a cigarette between his lips and heading out the door.

"I'm afraid I have a lunch meeting, or I would offer to take the two of you out," Sharon said, narrowing her eyes, and peering from Simon to Kate and back. "We could continue our little chat, Simon." Kate shuddered as Sharon's eagle eyes turned toward her. "But there is one thing I'd like to talk privately with you about, Kate. Can I call you?" She almost purred, but Kate was sure she was dealing with a very large predatory cat.

"Sure, Sharon. I'm free tomorrow morning, any time it's convenient," Kate replied, a touch of a waver in her voice. She crossed her arms, reaching for her pendant, reminding herself there was a reason for this too.

Sharon shot Simon a warning glare as she turned for the door, her briefcase gripped in her tight little fist. "Can I walk you out, Simon?"

Simon hesitated. "There's some information I have to get from— uh, Kate before I leave. You go on ahead." She scowled and moved to the door. "You were going to show me that Mediation program syllabus, remember?" he added to Kate, showing his teeth, a hopeful expression on his face.

They both breathed an audible sigh of relief as the door clicked behind Sharon, listening to her heels tick tock toward the elevator, then turned toward each other with exhaled laughter.

She covered her mouth with a hand, shaking her head. "I'm so relieved she didn't say anything publicly," said Kate, pressing her fingers against her brow, "but I think she's going to let me have it tomorrow." She knew perfectly well what Sharon wanted to talk to her about. "I think today went very well. Why can't she simply let it go?" she implored, clenching both fists in frustration. "Obviously there's no conflict of interest. There's nothing going on. And we're nearly done with the case."

"She seems determined to think otherwise. Everything *I* do seems suspect, anyway. I feel like she's policing me."

"Oh." said Kate, suddenly flustered, her brows knitting. "You'd better not linger."

"She's gone already. We're not doing anything wrong here," Simon rationalized.

"Yes, I know," was Kate's only comment, but she was worried nonetheless. "What did she say to you, exactly?" she asked, as she walked back over to the coffee table and piled cups and saucers onto a tray. Simon followed her and helped pick up dishes.

"Let me," he said, taking the laden tray from her. "I can't figure out her motives." He stood watching her punch throw cushions and toss them onto the sofa. She followed him toward the kitchen while he talked. "On the one hand, we weren't completely honest about our history. Then she saw us sitting together at the..." He carried the tray through the kitchen archway and looked around.

"Put it there," Kate said, pointing. "But she knew perfectly well that we didn't even know we would meet there. She got your ticket herself, for goodness sake."

"I know. I can see why she has some suspicions, but I think the real issue is that I was a bit of an ass with Rachel." He set the tray down and looked at her, chagrinned, his lanky frame leaning on the counter, shoulders hunched. "In any case, she's not emphasizing the conflict issue with me. She was always Rachel's friend; we were never close. Now she seems to have this notion that I'm in need of her protection and charity. She's offering meals and company, as though I were some kind of hopeless recluse. It's weird."

"Ha ha. I'll just bet," Kate said, opening the dishwasher.

"What's that supposed to mean?" Simon helped her to pile mugs into the tray.

"I mean... " she hesitated, standing up. *What the hell?* "I mean, you're... uh... quite eligible now. What makes you think she's offering charity? Maybe she wants something from you." She looked at him pointedly. Simon looked up, his eyes wide.

"Aah. Hardly. I've known her for years. She's not interested in me that way."

"I wouldn't be so sure. Maybe she's been waiting for an opening. You're a nice... man, good looking, professional, why not?"

He stared at her closely. "Thanks, but... Well besides Rachel, I come with baggage," he said, his face somber. "And she doesn't strike me as the mothering type any more than Rachel is."

"Are you calling Madison baggage?" She meant to be teasing, but he seemed intent on taking her seriously.

He turned to place a plate in the lower tray. "You know what I mean. I adore her, of course. She's my baby. But having a young kid puts a damper on your lifestyle."

"I think the only baggage you've got is in your head. Madison is an asset. She's a beautiful, sweet little girl. What woman *wouldn't* want a ready-made family that includes her?"

He was standing with his back to her. "Including you?"

Kate's heart pounded in her chest. What did he mean by that? Probably nothing, she decided in an instant. *Get a grip, Kate! Play it down.* "Uh. Sure. I want a family someday. But the point is, Sharon's a normal healthy woman, intelligent, attractive even though she comes across like a tank. And she does know you. I wouldn't rule out that possibility. Are you interested in her?"

The sound that emitted from him was more gurgle than giggle. "No." He said with clear emphasis, and paused. "Anyway, I don't know. Her tactics seem a bit aggressive for seduction." He shuddered, his mouth twisting. "She scares me, actually." He was absentmindedly picking crumbs from the muffin tin that lay on the counter and nibbling them.

"I'll bet," Kate laughed too. "She does lack a certain something."

"Ye-ah. Like warm blood."

Laughing, she piled her muffin tin and a few odd utensils into the kitchen sink, and wiped the crumbs from the counter, wondering, for the first time, how long he was planning to hang around. "Are you hungry?"

Simon shrugged, scowling slightly, as though he hadn't thought of it yet. Then, on cue, his stomach growled loudly. Colour rushed up to his face and neck. "Apparently," he apologized. "Why don't we nip out for something? I'll buy you a sandwich."

"I've got a pot of homemade soup, if you're interested," she offered, lifting her brows in question. It would do no harm to offer him lunch, she rationalized. His face lit up.

He raised an unconvincing hand. "I wouldn't want to impose, or make you feel... you know... "

She sighed. "Like you said, no one's watching. And it's only soup. It's easier to eat at home in this neighbourhood. There are a few lunch places, but they're mediocre and I get pretty bored with them." She opened the fridge and hauled out a big pot, setting it on the range and lighting it.

He stood watching her. "Do you enjoy cooking?" he asked after a moment. *Is he just making idle conversation or am I being interviewed?*

"I like it well enough. A person has to eat, after all. And you can't eat in restaurants every day." She pulled out a wooden stir spoon and opened the lid.

"You seem so... domestic," he commented. "You remind me of my mother."

She looked at him askance. "Thanks a lot! That's not so bad, is it?" She grimaced, backpeddling. "Being domestic, I mean. I couldn't say about your mother." She turned to the sink, feeling a hot and cold tingling tickle her spine and the back of her neck. *What an idiot!*

He blinked at her, as though really considering the question. She squirmed under his penetrating blue gaze. He drew a breath and said, "No. I'm sorry. I meant it as a compliment. It's different than what I'm used to, that's all."

"You don't cook, yourself, then?"

"I do, actually, quite a bit. I have to obviously, with Maddie. But Rachel didn't. Not ever. Not even an egg." He laughed softly, his scorn reflected in his expression.

Kate could well imagine that. She couldn't picture that statuesque, elegant woman in the kitchen with an apron. "So you assumed kitchen duties in the family, then?" She stirred the soup slowly.

"Mmm. I guess. I was always competent as a bachelor. You know, burgers and spaghetti, that sort of thing. But once Maddie came along, I pretty much had to take care of everything domestic. That was the deal." He seemed to ponder a moment, leaning back on the counter with his arms folded across his chest. "The nanny helped, for a few years. But since Rachel left, I guess I've spent more time at home. And honestly, I wouldn't see friends if I didn't have dinner parties. So I've been learning, experimenting. I think I'm a pretty decent cook now."

"You don't go out much? Get a sitter sometimes?" Kate prodded, curious how curtailed his life seemed to be.

He sighed, his face tight. "Maddie's family life is already so dysfunctional, I don't like to leave her with strangers. She stays with my folks sometimes, and with my brother, when he's between girlfriends," he laughed. "But I haven't found someone yet that she's really comfortable with. The nanny's only been gone a few months, so we're still adjusting. That smells really good."

She stirred the soup once more, bending forward to sniff the fragrant steam emerging from the pot. She scooped out a spoonful and blew on it briefly, turning to him and offering him a taste. "Does it need salt, do you think?"

His eyes widened with pleasure and surprise when he tried a small spoonful. "No. Wow, is that ever good. What is it?"

"Oh, I don't know. Leftover garlic roasted chicken, corn, potato and whatever chowder. I just threw it together." She opened a cupboard beside his head and pulled out two bowls, setting them on the counter and fishing a ladle from a drawer to fill them. "There are some bread buns in there," she gestured at another cupboard with the ladle, "Do you mind?" He didn't seem fazed by her invitation to help. How refreshing, she thought, to find a man who really was comfortable in the kitchen. Jay, in particular, seemed to take it for granted that she'd feed him and serve him. It had always irked her, foreshadowing other problems down the road. Then she stopped herself. She wasn't dating Simon, for goodness sake! Why was she comparing him to Jay, who was practically her fiancé? Almost. Sort of.

Why did that thought depress her?

After Kate piled the lunch things on the tray, she said, "If you can carry that, I'll clear a space on the table"

He dug in with gusto once they sat. "This is really delicious soup," he said. "And you didn't use a recipe?"

"No. Soup is a kind of intuitive thing. I have a rough framework." She took another spoonful and considered it, shrugging. "So what did you mean by Sharon wanting to protect you'?"

He frowned, thinking. He broke a bun open, hesitating. "She seems to think you're a bit... uh... perhaps mercenary or something. I'm not sure. I'm reading between the lines." He smiled across the table at her, his eyes laughing. "You're not mercenary, are you?"

She didn't know what to say, shaking her head in disbelief. Why would Sharon imply that about her? What had she ever done to her? But then, perhaps her theory was correct. Sharon might be simply fending off perceived competition. She smiled. "Hardly. I hope she doesn't make my life too miserable while she moves in for the kill."

His eyes widened in mock fear. "Help me, Kate."

"Are you kidding? I'm keeping well clear of both of you. I know what's good for me." She was joking with him, but hoped he got the hidden message. She wasn't about to compromise her career over a careless flirtation, or allow her attraction to him or her confused memories interfere with her calm, clear professional management of this case, or her orderly life for that matter. "You're on your own, buddy." She laughed. "More?"

He nodded eagerly and she took his bowl back to the kitchen to refill it and put the kettle on for tea. When she returned, she tried to steer the conversation away from their joint problem with Sharon. She'd find out soon enough what Sharon had planned. They were silent for a few moments while he ate his seconds. She was surprised how easy it was to be with him, all things considered. Even though there remained a gnawing tension in her gut, almost like stage fright, she couldn't prevent herself from simply enjoying his warm, intelligent company. She leaned back, supporting her chin on one fist.

"Tell me more about Rachel. What went wrong?"

He looked up, his face shutting in a frown and she instantly regretted overstepping her bounds. *Damn it, Kate! Always playing the mediator, never just a friend.* A bowl of soup didn't grant her access to his deepest secrets.

"I'm sorry. I shouldn't have… "

"No." He wiped his mouth with a napkin, shaking his head. "It's okay." He thought for a moment longer, pulling on his chin, mirroring her pose. She noticed his scratched finger for the first time, and cursed her psychotic cat.

He began to tell his story.

The brilliant legal mind, sexy body and intense, vibrant ambition that so excited him in grad school turned out to be his undoing. He fell head over heels in love with Rachel, convinced her to marry him right out of school, and then…

"I was so naïve. I don't know what I expected." There was no honeymoon. Just work, work, and more work. And when Rachel did play, she played hard. Like she was running from something, though it took him a few years to find out what it was. He felt that she never made the kind of commitment to their marriage that he had. She was aloof and emotionally alienating. There was always more time for her male colleagues than for him. He scowled, remembering. Kate had the impression that Rachel did more than just work with her colleagues.

He related how beautiful she had been. At least he'd thought so. "My ideal woman," he said with scorn in his voice. But over the years, her vanity and shallowness grew. The diets, the implants, the dyed hair, the over-plucked brows, the collagen injections. All the expensive designer clothes and jewelry. She was perfect, he'd thought, and became, step by inexorable step, grotesque. "I only gradually came to understand how hopelessly insecure she is."

"But she truly is a beautiful, elegant woman."

"I guess, on the surface. I came to see her true nature, which was in fact monstrous. I couldn't get close to her. She looked like a runway model, but she felt like a mannequin." Kate felt so sorry for him, his face was tightly lined, and his gaze turned inward.

"Rachel resented Maddie's existence the moment she got pregnant, which was an accident, of course. I had to literally beg her to keep the baby. She was horrified at the idea of being a mother. She... got worse." He hesitated. "You see... Rachel's family was... how can I say it." He groped at the air for words, a deep sadness reflected in his eyes. "Her father was very powerful and distant, and emotionally abusive, toward her mom anyway. And her mother took refuge in her imagined illnesses, her valium and sleeping pills. She wasn't there for Rachel either. Rachel grew up watching her cower and shrivel and grow fat. Rachel's spent her life grasping at both the kind of power and freedom she imagined her father and her older brothers enjoyed, and at the same time trying to be beautiful and glamorous enough to deserve the love she so desperately needed. She's never satisfied. Having Maddie seemed to push her over the edge. Her on-and-off anorexia developed into bulimia, her obsessions and fears grew, she pushed us away. She's been hiding behind that façade for so long now, I don't know if she'll ever find her way out." Simon's eyes were distant, glassy. "I kept hoping... "

Kate listened in silent horror. No wonder he was so dev-astated by their separation, and so frustrated by her neglect of Maddie. She felt tears burning at her eyelids and at the back of her throat. "Has she been in therapy?" Surely with therapy Rachel could have been saved, along with their family, if only something had been done earlier.

"This is not a woman to admit to weakness." Simon's smile was wry and deeply sad. "She handed Maddie over to my care the day she was born. I was thrilled to be a father." She was back at work in a week, leaving him to work out the logistics of par-enting and childcare. Kate could hardly bear to look in his eyes; they were liquid pools of pain and disappointment. He ended up taking the six-month parental leave his firm allowed, and then setting up a nanny at home.

"That was four years ago."

"I'm sorry. It must have been very hard for you."

"Not hard, in the sense that—it was a relatively normal life—just disappointing that I had to do it alone. The Rachel I thought I married just didn't exist. I had dreamt of things being very different." His voice faded. She wondered there was any fight left in him.

Kate took advantage of the lull in conversation to fetch the tea, and, remembering his sweet tooth, grabbed a bag of store-bought oatmeal cookies out of the cupboard. He dug into the cookies the way other people ate potato chips, by the handful, dipping them into his tea and continuing his story. Currently, Rachel was supposed to take Maddie every two weeks for the weekend. They were lucky if she came through once a month. That was why he'd lost his cool on Saturday night. Poor Maddie. Maybe she was young enough it wouldn't matter much in the long run. Kate doubted that. Madison needed a mother, a real mother; every child did, no matter how wonderful her father was. Four. Five. Six, she counted the cookies he ate.

"And you never met anyone else?" Seven. Eight.

Simon shrugged. "It's only been two years. There hasn't been time for dating. Besides, I'm still too angry and too... ex-hausted." Simon ground his knuckles into his eye sockets, and she could see it was true. "And Maddie comes first. Always." His face was set in determination.

He reached for another two cookies. "Okay, that's nine already." He froze with his hand in the bag, looking up with a guilty expression.

"You're counting?"

Kate grinned at him, happy to distract him from his tragic tale. "I'm teasing, go ahead. But how do you stay slim if you eat sugar and carbs like that?" She figured he'd had enough serious reflection.

"I run, mainly. And a few odd sports when I get a chance, hockey, basketball, whatever." He shrugged. "And I suppose I come by it naturally." He bit into number ten with a grin.

"I'm sorry about your finger, by the way," she said, indicating his bandage. "Oscar can be moody."

He laughed. "My own fault. Don't worry about it."

Not long after, he apologized for spending the whole afternoon eating up her food and her time. "What is it about you? You make me want to tell you all my secrets?" he'd said, touching her chin with a fingertip, and left, extracting a promise that she'd keep him informed about Sharon's maneuvers.

How had the day progressed in such a fashion? She'd begun the day determined to put more distance between them. Instead, he'd spent hours in her personal space, poured out his heart to her, and she'd come to feel more warmth and compassion toward him than ever. Each time they shared a meal, she reflected, she got deeper into trouble. Well, it was one thing to become friends. She'd just have to work harder to keep herself apart, both physically and emotionally.

nine

Kate arrived at the community center to meet Alexa for their regular squash game, every Wednesday at four-thirty. It was hard to get away some days, but Kate managed. They had made it a priority years ago, when their busy schedules had caused them to drift apart, trying to kill two birds with one stone, stay fit and keep in touch. It was one of Kate's favourite times. And over time she'd become quite a formidable squash player.

After checking in, she went to the locker room to change into her gear, watching for Alexa. She was often late, squashing their late afternoon squash appointment in between meetings and more meetings. Architecture didn't seem to allow her to work a regular schedule. Alexa was a loyal friend, but unreliable.

While she dressed, Kate thought about how long she and Alex had been friends, since meeting in an Art History class when they were eighteen, and discovering they lived in the same dorm. Simon had reminded her of her youthful interest in Urban Planning, and she wondered if she would have ended up a consultant like Alexa, at her clients' beck and call, living from deadline to deadline. Well, she shrugged, it was a moot point now.

Instead, she had found her calling in mediation. She was happy. And she was helping people in a way that was more direct and immediate than work as a planner would have been, and that, she'd learned, was important to her. All that bureaucracy would probably have driven her crazy, anyway. She locked up her things and made her way through the weight room to the squash courts. All the more reason not to risk screwing up her big opportunity for recognition, and blowing this important case study, by being weak and naive about Simon. She couldn't afford to be off her game right now.

Sharon's high-handed phone call this morning had infuriated her, but she knew there was some truth in her accusations. Though there was ostensibly nothing unseemly going on between herself and Simon, except getting reacquainted, there was a disturbing undertone, and she wasn't sure what it meant. He made her nervous. She seemed to become so sentimental and flustered in his presence, and really had no idea whether it was being near him now, or remembering their time together then, that caused this reaction. She was angry with herself for such lack of control, but even more, for not knowing herself better. She'd worked so hard in counseling and training to learn to separate her objective mind from her emotions, this state of confusion felt like a major setback.

Having tossed her racquet, towel and water bottle inside the court, she was pacing around in the hallway, glancing at the large wall clock every few minutes. It was already ten minutes into their court time; something must have held up Alexa. The muffled sounds of squeaking shoes and shouts echoed from adjacent courts. She paced back and forth and fidgeted, frustrated to be missing her workout. She needed to let off steam.

"You look fit to be tied," said a familiar tenor from behind her. She jumped and spun.

"Huh?" Speak of the devil. "You again!" Simon, of all people, was standing in the hall in gym gear, glistening with sweat, his dark blond hair clinging in damp tendrils to his neck and forehead.

"This is getting kind of woo-woo, huh?" he laughed. He had his arms folded across his chest, a squash racket tucked under his arm, and was soaked with perspiration down the front of his shirt. He had a bemused grin on his handsome face that made her insides lurch and her pulse flutter wildly. Or was it the long, lean muscles of his bare arms and legs?

"I'm here *every* week," she said, shaking her head in disbelief. "Are you stalking me?" Oh, God. How could she say that?

"I'm not. Just subbing for a friend today." Rivulets of sweat trickled down the sides of his face and he grabbed the towel from around his neck and mopped himself, messing up his hair even more. "Did your partner stand you up?" he asked languidly, looking her up and down, taking in her attire and apparent possession of the empty court beside them.

She was taken aback by the relaxed physicality of him. He

was so tall and thin that a suit concealed his lanky strength. Looking at him now, she was reminded of the sinewy muscu- lature of him. His long limbs were lean but strong, like a long distance runner's. Liquid heat unfurled in her core, making her nipples contract, and arrowing downward. She crossed her arms over her chest, succeeding only in drawing his attention there. "Um. It looks like... maybe." She couldn't think of anything else to say, she was so unnerved by his half-dressed, sweaty pres- ence. "Uh, Alexa's often late," she added awkwardly.

"Well, I just finished my game," he drawled, "but I'd be happy to help you warm up while you wait." He glanced at the empty court again.

"Oh. I don't know... " She was getting warmer by the min- ute. Did she want to play squash against him?

"If she shows up, fine. If not, we can play a game. I'm wiped, but... " he shrugged.

Kate shrugged too. She couldn't think of a gracious way to decline his offer. It seemed kindly meant, and she didn't want to offend him. "Thank you," she said. *Why can't I get away from him?*

"I'll just get a drink of water and be right back," he said, and turned down the hall and strode away on those long, lean legs. She watched his butt for a moment, transfixed, then gave herself a mental shake and entered the court. She picked up her racket and bounced the ball in the air a few times before flicking it against the wall.

At last her phone dinged, and she read Alexa's text: *Sorry, sorry! I'll explain later.*

When he returned a few minutes later, he had toweled off and changed into a fresh snow white t-shirt. He looked even sex- ier, if that was possible. He stood close enough that she could smell the heady mix of fresh laundered cotton warmed by his body, mingled with the masculine musk of his sweat and a hint of soap.

"No Alexa yet?" he asked.

"Not coming. I guess she got sidetracked with work," re- plied Kate, restless now. "Let's get started." They decide to launch right into a game. At first, they were courteous and vol- leyed agreeably *bing, bonk, bing, bonk.* She thought he was more tired than he admitted. *Or does he think I'm such an amateur he can take me on in his exhausted state? I need a challenge.* Neither of them had missed a single shot, so Kate decided to lever up the speed and aggressiveness of her play, to see what he would do. He matched her shot for shot without apparent effort. Finally she scored a point, then he did, and so on. He smiled serenely while he played, saying nothing. *He thinks he's toying with me. What nerve!* The intensity built minute by minute until Kate was playing more the way she was accustomed to; they were very evenly matched. She was getting hot. In more ways than one. Even the skin on her knees and shins prickled with sweat.

"I'm not sure why I put a clean shirt on," he laughed when they stopped for a drink of water between sets. His t-shirt was soaked under his arms, and down the center of his back and chest already. She pulled her t-shirt off over her head and tossed it on the floor. Underneath she wore a stretchy yoga tank top, a bit revealing, but she couldn't bear the heat. It was her serve. He seemed distracted, and watched her shot whizz by. She turned around with her eyebrows raised and a smirk on her face.

"Was that too fast for you? Or did you just stand there because you're determined to be a gentleman and lose? That won't be necessary, you know. You'll lose anyway. Gracefully or otherwise." She laughed, grabbed the ball and turned away before he could reply. "Here's your second chance. Don't screw it up."

The ball smacked the front wall and headed in his direction with ferocious speed and precision. He lunged at the side wall snapping his wrist, but just couldn't get near enough.

"No fair," he whined. "You took your shirt off. That's fighting dirty." He smiled sheepishly when she looked at him, her eyes large and astonished.

"Oh, really. We're using lame excuses now, are we?"

"Well… I am getting a bit worn out; I've been at this an hour and a half already," he said.

"You must be getting old. That didn't used to be a problem, as I recall," she teased, then immediately smacked a hand over her mouth, her face suddenly burning hot. At his raised eyebrows, she mumbled, "Oh. My. God. Did I actually say that out loud?" *How could I do such a stupid thing?*

He looked amused at her reference to their past intimacy. She had fastidiously avoided any specific mention of their romance, not just in front of others, but even when they chanced to be alone. Now this.

His mouth curled up and he stepped toward her shaking his head. "It's okay. Sooner or later one of us had to mention it. Maybe its time we talked about it, got it out in the open."

Her stomach twisted as he stepped closer, panic rising. She rubbed her arms, feeling even more heat flood through her. "I was really hoping we wouldn't, actually," she tried, unsuccessfully, to smile, and her eyes danced across his gleaming shoulders.

"Well, why not?" he asked, suddenly serious. "I've been following your lead, but I really don't understand why we're playing games. Who are we fooling, anyway?"

"I would rather pretend it never happened, actually," she said, aware that her breathing and her heart-rate were escalating. She looked back and forth at the floor, avoiding his eyes, wishing she could be anywhere but here, having this conversation with Simon. They stood where they were, facing each other in the squash court, a few feet apart.

"Don't say that. Those are some of my fondest memories," he laughed, trying to lighten the mood. His eyes shone as he spoke, and his eyes dropped to her mouth, lower, and up again to meet her eyes.

"Ooh. You can't be serious," she hissed. *How could he...What did he think...?*

"I certainly am. I mean, really. I thought you enjoyed our time together too. Maybe I was wrong."

"I can't believe we're having this conversation." Her face tingled with heat, and she rubbed her brow with her hand, head down, still clutching her squash racquet with white knuckles.

He strode toward her and stopped, a foot away, gently placing his fingertips on her bare shoulder, warm and slick with perspiration. She flinched and stiffened at the jolt of electricity that made her skin tingle. "Hey. You're really having a hard time with this, aren't you?" He lifted her chin with one finger and tried to meet her eyes, but she kept them averted, trying to hide the tears that welled and burned.

She turned her head to the side, rubbing at her chin where he'd touched her.

He suddenly dipped his head and kissed her tense lips, quickly and firmly, sending a shock of heat through her, confusing her further. He pressed his mouth harder onto hers with a small moan.

Stop! No! She pushed away, sucked in her breath and stood immobilized, staring at him as though she'd seen a ghost, her heart thrumming. *Did I do this? Did I encourage him?* She checked herself. She'd learned not to blame herself for everything that went wrong in her life. But she couldn't very well pretend any longer that this chemistry between them wasn't real, or that he wasn't interested in her.

He backed away with a wan smile, his eyes searching hers. "Let's go to the cafeteria and sit down. It would be good to talk a bit," he suggested. "I think we're done with squash for today."

She nodded stiffly, avoiding eye contact, and they gathered their things and left the court. Numbly, she followed him to a small cafe to one side of the reception desk, and they sat at a table near the window overlooking the street.

The sky was clear intense blue and vivid, and a brisk wind jostled and shivered the still clinging brown shriveled leaves on the sidewalk trees, like Lilliputian flags. A steady stream of people came and went, people in suits and overcoats, mothers with strollers and kids in tow, some dressed for sport and others in street clothes, hunched against the wind, their clothing flapping violently.

For several minutes, they sat in silence staring out the window. Kate searched for some understanding of her extreme agitation. It wasn't what she'd expected. She felt him turn to gaze steadily at her, searching, then he spoke in a subdued voice.

"Look, I know it didn't end well. I'm not sure I understand exactly what happened back then."

She squinted at him accusingly, skeptically, but he continued. Could she blame him for being clueless about busting her heart?

"But it was such a long time ago and we were just kids. Can't we just chalk it up to experience and move on? We're adults now." He stretched his hand toward her. "We've been getting to know each other... liking each other, haven't we? Can't we just keep doing that and relax?" He reached across suddenly and picked up her hand, which lay limply on the table between them, stroking it lightly with his thumb.

She yanked her hand away. *How dare you?* Her reaction was immediate and violent. She glared at him, frowning furiously. "Don't think for one minute that because you kissed me, I'm suddenly ripe for picking. I'm no easy target. The past doesn't give you... I'm not interested in starting... starting... something!"

"Whoa." He drew back, lifting both hands, palm out. "I thought... I know you're seeing someone, but it seemed to me we were heading here. Take it easy. I thought you... I just wanted to make the point that we don't have to sweat the past. Just forget about it. Let's start over."

She drew herself up, nostrils flaring. *What arrogance! How could he be so glib, so heartless?* "Well maybe your faulty memory is to blame," she said icily. "I happen to remember every detail of our so-called relationship. Including the ending. And to me, it was rather a big deal. Thank you for the reminder. I now clearly recall how callous and unfeeling you can be."

He opened his mouth to speak, shook his head, and shut it again.

She gnawed on her lip and glared at him from under her brows, her vision darkening and narrowing, then shot to her feet and spun on her heel, grabbed her racquet and stalked out the door without another word, desperate to put as much distance between herself and Simon as possible. *What a fool! How could I put myself in such a position again? Have I learned nothing?!*

She strode away in her court shoes, her arms and legs bare in the cold October sunshine. A gust of wind raised gooseflesh and she shivered. She marched angrily for several minutes and then sat down with a huff on a retaining wall, breathing heavily, furiously gnashing her teeth. *Ooooh.* Why was her life suddenly in such turmoil? *Shanti-mukti-shanti-mukti,* she forced her breathing to slow down, and her vision returned to normal. She sat, observing dry brown leaves lifted from the plaza on eddies of wind, spiraling upward, tossing erratically in the moving air, falling down elsewhere, only to be yanked away again by the next squall. She felt a particular empathy with them, passive victims to their fate.

Why did Simon have the power to work her up into such a passion? If it wasn't nerves, it was lust or anger, or obsession. Never in two years with Jay had she felt such a tumult of emotion. Maybe that was what held her back from making a commitment. On the other hand, hadn't she been avoiding exactly this sense of lost self-control for years? Reflexively, she fingered her eternal knot pendant, wondering if all this chaos was designed to teach her a lesson.

It occurred to her she would have to return to get her clothes and car keys from the locker room. She'd be sure to wait until Simon was long gone.

"Kathryn O'Day." She grabbed the phone, her mind still on her case notes, thinking it was Jay about Halloween. She was regretting agreeing to go to the party, but she'd promised.

"Um. Kate? It's Simon." An empty, electronic silence reverberated on the line. "Listen. Don't hang up."

"I don't hang up on people." Her heart pounded. Why was he calling? She'd moved through the past two days like a robot, determinedly unthinking.

"No... just storm off. You were very upset. I don't like to leave things hanging that way. You seem skittish," he broached carefully.

"I'm not a cat." There were several more minutes of silence. Now she sounded peevish and immature. She released a heavy sigh. "You were out of line, but I overreacted. That's all. I'm sorry. Let's forget about it."

"I don't want to forget about it. I want to resolve it. We both have memories of what happened. I imagine we had very different experiences and... well, I'd like to understand yours, talk it through." His voice was exceptionally calm, and he spoke slowly, as though he was dealing with a psychopath or a child.

Eurghh! "What if I don't want to?"

"Please, Kate. I won't force you to say what you don't feel comfortable saying. But I'd like to have a chance. I just think it's a good idea to... to... clear the air. We still have to work together. I think it will help diffuse the tension. Please."

She made him wait a few moments. He had a point. How could they resume their sessions like this? She let out another long sigh. "Alright. When?"

"Before the next session. But I've got to take Maddie out Trick-or-Treating tonight. How about tomorrow evening? Maddie's with Rachel this weekend." He paused. "Can I take you to my favourite Indian restaurant?"

She clicked her tongue. Damn. He knew she liked Indian food. "Just talking, then. That's all."

"And eating. Don't forget eating." There was a hint of laughter in his voice. "I can pick you up—"

"Nope. I'll meet you. Where is it?" This was not a date. She wouldn't make it easy for him. She picked up a pen, tapping impatiently on a pad of paper.

He sighed. "Alright. It's Balki Tandoori, on Victoria Drive. Seven o'clock?"

"Right. I'll be there."

ten

A loud rapping at her door a while later brought Kate's heart to her throat.

Had Simon decided to push his luck and show up at her place today? But no. That was ridiculous. He would never do that. Even her eccentric neighbour Lena called first, though she was just across the hall. There's only one person who would show up without warning.

She walked to the door and peeked out. Yup. It was Jay, with his arms full of a big soft bundle and a stupid grin on his handsome face. She sighed and shook her head, opening the door and pulling it wide.

"Jay."

"Hey, baby." He barged past her, right up to the sofa and dumped his load down. The plastic bags let out a shushing sigh and a puff of damp and mothball scented cold air. "Wait till you see what I've got."

She closed the door and followed him, trying to suppress the feeling of irritation at his sudden intrusion. She hadn't been very nice to him lately. She had to try harder.

He turned and swooped down on her, capturing her face between his cold hands and planting a long, hungry, possessive kiss on her mouth. "Mmmm. God, I've missed you. Haven't seen nearly enough of you lately. What've you been doing?"

She shrugged. "Work, mostly. I'm quite involved in this new case. Making notes for my award speech in January. I really like the couple, and we've moved on to a draft reconciliation agreement already, so it's going well."

He planted another quick kiss on her lips. "That's because you're so brilliant." He shucked off his coat and tossed it on the sofa. "Go out at all?"

Her ribs tightened with waves of guilt as she recalled her encounters with Simon at the ball, their long talk the next day, their shared lunches, and their impromptu squash game. Not to mention dinner tomorrow. She swallowed. She'd seen more of Simon lately than of Jay. "Saw Alex a couple times."

Jay wrestled with the zippers on two bulky garment bags. "What's all this?"

He grinned at her over his shoulder. "Our costumes! I just picked them up."

She cringed. "Er. You know I hate dressing up."

He pulled something frilly out and held it up to her, then crushed the costume between their bodies and kissed her again while grinding his hips into hers. "Don't say that. I so want to see you in this." He stepped back.

She looked down and immediately recognized a stereotypical English maid costume, Playboy-bunny style, and groaned. "No way! I'm not wearing this!"

He put on a coy, puppy dog expression. "Please. You'll be so hot in this. I'll be wanting you all night, and you can torture me." His hand scooped around her hip and pulled her against him again, demonstrating that he needed neither torturing nor skimpy costumes to get him worked up. "The anticipation'll be so sweet," he growled.

Anticipation of what? Her insides clenched involuntarily, her body remembering his enthusiastic lovemaking. It had been a couple of weeks. He was virile and athletic, and they'd always had a good time in bed. But the thought of sleeping with him tonight worried her. It felt... wrong.

She put the maid's outfit down. "It's just not me, Jay. Do we have to go to this party? I'm really not in the mood."

He raised a devilish brow. "I know what you mean. We could get dressed up and make our own party here. Starting right now."

It was only four in the afternoon. "No way. I still have work to do."

"Just kidding. Anyway, we've got to go to Miles's party. We're in the middle of negotiating a big contract. This could cinch it for me. I'll get outta your hair for a couple of hours. But you have to try it on for me first."

She pulled a face. "What's yours?"

He made yet another mischievous face. "That's why I brought mine over here. You have to help me with the make-up."

"What kind of make up?"

He shrugged. "Blood and stuff."

She closed her eyes. He was like a twelve year old. Why couldn't he dress like some obscure eighteenth century philosopher? A Roman senator or Fitzwilliam Darcy. Something dignified. Why was it always a zombie or something? "What are you supposed to be?"

"Chop-Top Sawyer!" He twisted his head to the side and leered at her in a very creepy way. It reminded her of Igor, but she was sure it was even worse than that.

She was afraid to ask. "Who?"

"From Texas Chainsaw Massacre Two. You seriously don't know?"

"You have to ask?"

He laughed. "Ah, well. It's okay. I've got photos." He rummaged in his bags. "You should see these ugly brown teeth I found. And a bald cap with stringy hair."

"And this is supposed to be sexy?"

His face fell, confused. "No. Did you want me to be sexy?"

"You always want *me* to be something sexy." And tacky. And skanky.

"Yeah. Well?"

"Well? It goes both ways, you know. Axe murderers aren't exactly sexy."

"Chainsaw... But this is way more fun."

Kate drew in a large breath and sighed heavily, wondering if he was planning on wielding an actual chainsaw to the party. There was no getting him to see it from her perspective.

He pushed the maid suit at her. "Go try it on. Be a good sport. Please?"

He wouldn't back down. Gritting her teeth, she grabbed the bundle and marched to her bedroom to oblige him. She tore off her yoga pants and sweatshirt and wiggled into the ridiculously skimpy little dress that barely covered her crotch, tying the miniature white apron over it. She glared at herself in her dresser mirror. Her boobs were practically hanging out the low cut top. It was even skankier that she anticipated, and she looked stupid and cheap. Jay probably expected heels as well. She'd be cold and uncomfortable all night, fighting off the groping paws of every guy at the party, including the smarmy Miles whom she loathed. Not a chance in hell was she wearing this in public.

"What's taking so long?" Jay hollered from the other room.

"Just a minute!"

She flopped down on her bed to think. How was she going to get out of this one? With Jay, it was always one thing or another. They never seemed to want the same things, enjoy the same things. It was always a battle. He was like a big kid, a little wild, wanting to play, but his idea of play invariably made her uncomfortable. And he was obtuse when she tried to explain the things she liked. She'd always smile and put up with it because he was so good-natured and fun-loving. Now she was coming to realize how this ongoing struggle was part of the problem. They were so very different.

He was a party animal, always wanting to go to bars and parties, drinking and dancing with groups of friends, or more often pseudo-friends who were more work colleagues or potential clients of his. He drank too much and behaved coarsely. But whenever she wanted him to accompany her to a social function of her choice, like a play or the charity ball, he cried off, pleading death by boredom.

They didn't enjoy the same food or music or movies. The same with vacations. She loved to travel to different cultures to explore and experience new things. He would only go to Florida, Hawaii or Mexico to drink and lie by the pool. Or more likely drink while lying by the pool, and party and dance with other drunken strangers. In two years they'd been on exactly two trips together, one of her choosing and one of his. They'd both been miserable.

Then there were moments when their time together was lovely and romantic, when they'd somehow hit a happy medium, and their mutual attraction peaked. He was funny and charming. Attentive and admiring. Generous with dinners and gifts and always available. Sex was always lively and hot with Jay. But there again, it was always on his terms. Her moods and preferences seldom registered with him.

She began to wonder why his immaturity and narcissism, because that's how she saw it now, never felt like a deal breaker before. She supposed it was because nothing better had come along. And because he wanted her. And it felt good to be desired.

She gnawed her lip and questioned whether she'd really fully dealt with her self-esteem issues during therapy. If she was completely honest, she was afraid she'd never find someone to spend her life with that was a perfect companion and complement to her. It was reasonable to have to compromise, wasn't it?

Or was it?

"Katie!"

She hauled herself up. She had had to make a decision about Jay. Her chin dropped as she gazed blindly at the floor for long minutes. She hated to disappoint him when he had nothing but the best intentions. But now was as good a time as ever to face the truth. Better than modeling the stupid maid costume, or going to the boring party later. Better than having to endure sex with a drunken Chop-Top whoever after the party. Better than continuing on with the lies.

Kate had to tell Jay the truth. She couldn't marry him.

She quickly changed back into her own clothing and gathered up the frilly costume, along with her resolve, to deal with Jay's disappointment and inevitable hurt.

"Coming!" She forced herself to go back to the living room where Jay waited.

"Hey, why aren't you–?"

"We need to talk, Jay."

His dark brows bunched.

She turned away from his challenging stare, then forced herself to look back at him with foreboding. He seemed frozen, the pieces of his costume hanging in his limp hands. His dark hair was damp, a stray lock lay ruffled across his forehead. It made him seem oddly innocent, like a young boy.

"Jay, I—"

"What's going on?" He didn't seem to be in a mood for listening, but she knew what she had to do.

"I've had a lot on my mind."

Recognition lit his dark eyes. "Don't do this, Katie. I've told you, I can wait."

"I know…"

His voice was terse. "I don't think you'll find another man who would wait while being kept at arm's length. This isn't the way I imagined this going, Kate. We've been serious for two years. I thought… I feel as though… " He shot a wary glance at her, and cast his eyes down, reflecting his agitation. "This isn't just about you. I feel betrayed."

Kate winced. Her chest tightened, guilt swamping her, mixed with the apprehension of finally ending it.

His mouth moved, his eyes searching her face. Perhaps he knew the answer before he spoke. His voice came out tight and quiet. "Will you marry me or won't you? Why won't you answer me?"

Kate gnawed her lips, swallowing the searing sensation in her throat, and raised fearful eyes to his. "No. Of course, you're right. I can't." As she spoke, her face crumpled and she lost her composure, tears burning her eyes. How could she explain that he had too much style and not enough depth? That their values just didn't align? How could she tell him that without hurting his feelings even more? She clenched a fist and held it to her heart, feeling like a terrible person. "I'm sorry, Jay. You're a wonderful man. But you are not the right man for me. I know you're frustrated and hurt." Her voice wobbled and broke "You have every right to be."

Through her tears, she could see his eyes fill, too. His nostrils flared and he clenched his jaw in his effort to control himself. His head shook minutely from side to side, a hard white line outlining his lips. Eventually he spoke. "I just don't believe it. I thought..." His brow furrowed, and she could see his pain metamorphose into anger.

"Just tell me why, damn it. What could you possibly want that I can't give you?"

She shook her head. "Nothing at all. You're a good person. Kind, generous and fun. You're very attractive. You are everything any woman could want. You've been good to me, and I'm very fond of you. But..." Her eyes fell away, her lips trembling.

"But?"

"I don't feel what I ought for you. I don't love you... enough."

Jay glared at her in silence, a muscle in his jaw twitching. Then his brown eyes lost their focus, turning inward and his jaw went slack. "But I love you, Kate. I really do."

She could only nod, and nod again. "I believe you, Jay. You'll find someone else to love, I know you will. But I don't feel that we're right for each other." She spoke through the tears that slid down her face.

Kate's splayed hand lay on the open pages of the novel resting in her lap, her heart heavy. Her eyes stared unfocussed at the blackened bus window and the lively layered multi-hued reflections of the other riders bundled in their winter coats, scarves and hats. Overheated bodies made the atmosphere humid, stale and stifling, but she was glad to be among a group of strangers on the bus, alone with her thoughts, all the same. She felt relief to have finally responded to Jay. And guilt to feel that relief, and over the crushing pain she saw on his face when she'd broken it off with him last night. That hadn't stopped him from showing up at her place again this afternoon, heart in hand.

His usual bravado had been replaced by a plaintive manner, tinged with desperation. Outright refusing his marriage proposal had made an impression on him this time. He understood she was dealing with some tough issues, that it wasn't only fear of commitment. It was more complicated than that.

His eyes were glassy when he said, "Please don't say never, Kate. I love you. Let me take you to dinner tonight and we'll talk it over. I know I rushed things. I can be patient. I promise."

"That's not a good idea, Jay. Besides, I actually have a dinner date tonight. I'm just on my way to the bus."

His face had fallen. "A date? With Alexa? To rake me over the coals?"

"No. An old college friend. No one you know." There was no sense upsetting him unnecessarily. It wasn't like tonight was a real date anyway.

"I forgot to mention, I got the roses Monday. Thank you."

His eyes pinched at the corners even as he smiled hopefully. "I'll give you a lift. My car's around the corner."

"No. Thank you. I'll be fine. I have a book with me. I need some solitude before I get there." She had turned away, paused and turned back. A fresh wave of guilt swamped her as she suddenly remembered the good times they'd shared over the past two years. Jay was good and kind, a smart, hard-working guy, and fun to be with, at least some of the time.

Kate didn't know if there was such a thing as a soul mate, but it wasn't Jay's fault he wasn't hers, or that he didn't meet some imaginary standard she had imprinted on her heart. Placing a hand on his broad chest, she'd met his dark worried eyes and said, "You're very sweet. I'm so sorry." She pressed her lips together and shook her head slightly, could say no more. Then she shrugged and walked away, forcing the image of Simon from her mind.

The bus lurched to a stop and a man in a puffy slick blue down parka fell heavily onto the seat beside her with an "Oomph!" releasing a noxious cloud of onions and stale cigarettes, and she turned her face away. She erased a lens in the breath-fogged glass and peered out at the black night, trying to make out her location. There was no moon to see by tonight, only the intermittent pools of greenish streetlight providing a patchwork to navigate by, illuminating the occasional strand of damp toilet tissue strewn across a lawn or hedge, remnants of last nights revelry. Another few blocks and she'd ring the bell.

Maybe she should've told Jay she just needed space to see other people. But she was afraid his possessiveness and jealousy would work against her, and he'd apply even more pressure. She didn't really want to see anyone, anyway. She'd agreed to have dinner with Simon only to talk. Whatever Simon was thinking, she was determined to keep it platonic, merely trying to get their relationship back on a peaceful, friendly plane before work next week forced them into each other's company. He really seemed to need some kind of reckoning after their quarrel. Perhaps he felt guilty.

Her stomach clenchd again with a fresh wave of regret over letting Jay go. It was possible her was the last good thing left between her and a long and lonely life as a single woman. Or not that exactly, but that she didn't have the time or energy to go back out there, or to work on building another new relationship. She shouldn't worry about it, really. She was self-sufficient and independent. She didn't need to marry. It's only that she didn't want to be alone.

But, the truth was, she still dreamt of all those things, traditional and contradictory though they might be, despite her years of stubborn rebellion against her mother's and society's expectations. She did want children, after all. To admit it felt like a betrayal of all that she'd fought for, all that was dear to her, but it was still true. She was manifestly one of a generation of women caught between two conflicting value systems, two very different dreams that sometimes seemed virtually incompatible.

She rang the bell and stood up, trying to ignore a small voice in her head that warned: *Your stubborn independence is just a mask to hide your fear of rejection.*

Well, she'd taken care of that by rejecting every decent man she'd ever dated.

Tucking her unread book into her satchel, she alit from the half empty bus into a gust of cold northern wind that slapped her hair across her face and tossed her scarf. Pulling her coat collar tighter to her chin, she bent her head for the short hike to Victoria Drive, the dark night sky enveloping her in a cloak of solitude.

Filled with trepidation, Kate pulled open the door of the small Indian restaurant, warm air drawing her in from the harsh autumn night, tiny brass chimes heralding her arrival. She lifted a gloved hand to push away the stray strands of hair caught in her mouth and lashes. She ardently wished she could have found a way to avoid this showdown. The pit of her stomach felt as hard and heavy as granite. Why couldn't she simply have said no? She didn't have any trouble setting boundaries at work. Her chest felt hollow, and each breath she drew was too thin and hard, as if her ribs were bruised.

No matter how determined she was to put distance between herself and Simon, she seemed compelled to become more and more entangled with him. And here they were, breaking bread again. No matter how uncomfortable she was dealing with her past, she still found Simon irresistible. Everything that Jay wasn't, Simon was, and it drew her in. He was so determined to examine old wounds that there was no way to avoid it, even though the very thought of it made her feel physically ill.

He had no idea he was opening Pandora's box.

Ching ching ching. She caught her breath. It was like entering another world. The long narrow space was dimly lit, yet crouched within the darkness was a sense of something exotic and alive, like a crocodile asleep beneath still waters. The first thing that hit her was a wall of rich, complex aromas: turmeric, cumin, fenugreek, cinnamon and curry, a hint of anise as she passed the small dish of *sonf* on the reception podium. Soft sitar music wove its way into her consciousness, though it was so subtle she had to strain to hear it. In the darkness, small oil lanterns flickered on the tables that glowed in the lamplight with an array of colourful *sari* silks trapped under glass: saffron, indigo, and magenta. The contrast to the colours and textures of her everyday world had a narcotic effect.

The atmosphere was hypnotic. Kate could not tell if Simon sat somewhere in the shadows watching her bewildered arrival.

A handsome middle-aged man with a black shoe-brush mustache, and touches of white at his temples approached her. He wore an ecru Nehru-collared tunic and dark trousers, his white teeth flashing in his café-au-lait face, welcoming. "Good evening, good evening. You would like a table?"

"I'm meeting someone," she said.

"Aah. Yes. Simon?" Dark brows poised above his black sparkling eyes.

She nodded tentatively, frowning.

His smile broadened. "Simon is not yet arrived. Please. This way. I have our very best table ready for you."

The man led her to what looked to her to be a perfectly typical table near the far wall away from the cold blind windows overlooking the deserted street. Despite the gauzy curtains that screened the lower part of these windows, they had a forlorn aspect to them and she was glad. Her table was special only in that the tapestry that hung over it was larger than the others. Its tablecloth was deep indigo blue embroidered with tiny metallic gold stars and moons and she thought perhaps it was sari silk as she fingered the edge. It was very beautiful. Perhaps these celestial bodies would guide her along this mystifying stage of her journey.

She perched on her chair, shuddering as the chill left her body, and peeled off her coat, gloves and scarf, glancing around. Small painted and embroidered tapestries hung from dark wooden poles along the side walls, mythic Hindu narratives sketched in blue, green, black, pink and silver, tiny embedded mirrors shimmering and foil tassels trembling in the faintly moving air. Palanquins bearing princes; various gods and goddesses; mentally she ticked them off, all the usual suspects.

Twisting her head, she peered at the large tapestry beside her. Illustrations from the Kama Sutra floated above her. She pondered them, the proud yogic posture of the maidens, their naked breasts jutting in invitation, long ropes of shining black hair, the strong masculine profiles of their young lovers, their entwined limbs and large, evocative, khol-dark eyes. She felt a visceral response in her abdomen and picked up the menu to peruse and take her mind off the suspended sensuality of the images around her, wondering if their choice of artwork had cost them their family-friendly rating.

The waiter was on his way back when the door opened again with a tinkle of tiny brass chimes, ushering in a gust of cold wind that ruffled the tablecloths and tapestries momentarily, settling as quickly as the door closed. They both looked up to see Simon's tall form huddled in the entryway. The waiter bustled over.

"Simon. How very good to see you, my friend," he said in a resonant voice, reaching out both hands. There were a few other patrons, but he did not seem concerned about disturbing their meals.

"Lali, how have you been?" Simon greeted him, gripping, brown leather gloves to brown skin. Then, to Kate's astonishment, they released each other and hugged briefly, slapping each other's backs and laughing.

"Excellent. Excellent." Lali discretely took the brown-bagged bottle that Simon clutched in his gloved fist and, gesturing toward Kate, swept it away, chanting something in Hindi toward the rear of the restaurant.

A woman's voice rang out from the back of the restaurant, a quiet musical contralto, it stretched nonetheless, "Simon, darling, how are you?"

"Hey, Sarita," Simon replied, waving to the unseen voice. He turned his attention to Kate, one corner of his mouth lifting as he neared. "Good evening. Sorry I'm late. I'm having some trouble... uh, reaching Rachel."

She said nothing in return, simply raising her eyebrows. She wasn't going to surrender that easily, though it gave her an irrational pleasure to see him standing before her, shaking off his sheepskin coat and sinking down. Her chest swelled and she was suffused with warmth, like a shot of good brandy going down.

He pulled his cell phone out of his pocket, glanced at the screen, and set it carefully beside him. Apologizing, he explained he'd been waiting for Rachel to call him back for two days, and it was important. He seemed tense.

"Everything okay?"

"Yeah, sure. Coordination issues." He leaned forward, releasing a current of cool air and masculine aromas, fresh and crisp. "Have you been waiting long?"

"Just arrived," she said. "You seem to be a familiar here."

Laughing, he said, "Sarita's younger brother Rajit was in law school with me. We came here many times in search of a hot meal and escape from the madness. It was like a second home, and Sarita and Lali feel almost like family."

"They're very warm and welcoming."

He nodded and smiled, looking up as Lali returned with an opened bottle of white wine in an ice bucket.

"What do you know, Simon, I found this highly unusual bottle of wine in the cellar. I thought you might like to sample it." He filled their small glasses to the brim and set it down on the table, arranging a linen towel around its long green neck. He stood beaming at them, until Kate pondered his purpose. She lifted her glass and tasted the wine, waiting for something to happen.

Simon cleared his throat. "Kate, Lali would like me to introduce you. Lali, meet Kate O'Day, a work colleague." He said the latter with emphasis.

Lali turned and gave a little bow. "A pleasure to meet you Kate O'Day," he said, and backed away. "I hope very much you enjoy your meal with us." He turned and disappeared.

She lifted her glass. "So what's the deal? You brought this."

"You noticed. I've complained for years about Lali's wine list, but he claims there is little demand for wine and his clients are happy with the cheap schlock he stocks. So we've worked out a little arrangement." He smirked and raised his glass. "To something palatable."

She clinked glasses with him and took another sip. "It's very good."

"It's a favourite of mine, from Alsace-Lorraine, a Sylvaner varietal. I find it goes better with Indian food. The spiciness of a Gewürztraminer competes with curry, somehow. It's better with Asian food." He sipped and glanced around. "So what do you think?"

"It's a charming place. I like it, though of course I have to reserve judgment until I taste dinner." She inclined her head.

"No worries there. You won't be disappointed. Sarita is a fabulous cook, and she has good help back there on weekends."

She wanted to comment on the tapestries, but felt the oppressive presence of the one above their heads, and thought better of mentioning them.

But it was not to be. "Isn't the decor great? They redecorated last spring. I love the new colours in here. Makes me feel like I'm a million miles away," said Simon dreamily, echoing her own response, "or in another time, long ago. That's my favourite—there—the blue ones." He pointed.

"That's Rama, one of Vishnu's incarnations, and his wife, Sita. They're considered the ideal man and... " She stopped herself, blushing and catching her lip in her teeth. " ...woman." *Why can't I keep my mouth shut?* He raised his brows in astonishment.

"And you know this because... "

"I took a history of Eastern Art years ago, and I've continued studying Hindu mythology. I told you I wanted to go someday, didn't I?"

"Okay. Now you have to tell me the rest." He nodded, smiling in expectation, gesturing at the walls with a sweep of his hand.

She clicked her tongue and sighed, narrowing her eyes. It was so easy to fall under the spell of his charm. "Very well. The other side of Rama and Sita, the very sparkly one, that's Indra, god of the firmament, with her one thousand eyes."

"A female god who sees all?"

"Oh, I don't think gender means much to the Hindus. Then," she pointed, "in the middle is Brahma, of course, the creator, with his four heads."

He squinted and nodded. "Handy."

"You mean heady." She quirked her lips. "Beside him is Shiva doing his rapturous dance. He's the god of death and rebirth, sort of." She swung her head around. "Oh, and there, the fat one with the elephant head and several arms, that's Ganesha. And see his rat there, at his feet? That's his helper. Businesses like him. He removes obstacles." She laughed softly.

"Fascinating. What about that one?" He pointed to a small one on the end wall.

She twisted around in her chair, and through the corner of her eye, caught him checking his cell phone again, his jaw tight, his brow furrowed. "Mmm. Looks like Krishna. See, he's got the lotus, the conch shell and a mace. And that small woman beside him is his lover and devotee, Radha. *She* is a mere mortal." *Please don't look up,* she begged silently. She held her breath as she watched him scan the room, and finally crane his neck up, his mouth opening.

"And these folks?"

She took a deep breath. "They're not gods either." She hesitated, regarding his attentive expression through narrowed eyes. "It looks like an illustration from the Kama Sutra, to me. Probably the four embraces."

She watched as his head whipped around, wincing, but no words emitting from his open mouth. Then he seemed to regain his composure and turned and studied it again, chewing his lip.

"I imagine that's why Lali thinks this is his best table, reserved for friends," she added wryly, tongue in cheek.

"I'm sorry. I really didn't know." She could see from his hangdog expression that he was telling the truth, though the irony of it obviously hadn't escaped him either. He was biting back a smile, two spots of color flaring on his ears. He glanced up at it again. "It's quite beautiful. A flash of grin escaped and changed the subject. "Shall we order?"

Whew. Moving on. She nodded enthusiastically. She was eager to sample the cooking.

"Do you have any favourites? Or is that a stupid question?" he asked.

Kate laughed and opened her menu, scanning it, though she expected she would find mostly familiar dishes. "I'm fond of *bhartha*. Do you like eggplant?"

"Sure. They do a great lamb korma here," he suggested.

She made a face. "I avoid red meat as a rule. But go ahead."

"No. That's okay. How about the fish korma, then?"

She nodded in agreement. They discussed a few other options. With his nose buried in the menu, Simon said, "And I always leave room for... "

"Butter chicken?"

He looked up, grinning. "How'd you know?"

"Who doesn't like butter chicken?" She shrugged.

They ordered their food, which they agreed was more than enough, but that one could hardly complain about taking a little leftover curry home. With their freshly refilled wine glasses, Simon lifted his and offered a toast. "To... good food, and good... friends." She toasted, silently, and sipped her wine. She supposed he was on the verge of broaching the subject of their past, and waited, the tension building both inside her, and crackling between them. Tucking a strand of hair behind an ear, she examined her fingernails carefully, her breath shallow.

Instead, he launched into a funny story about his travels in Thailand. He'd made friends with some interesting young people who had taken him home, and he'd spent nearly a week shadowing their mother, learning to cook at her elbow. "They all thought I was positively odd. While they went dancing, I was fighting through throngs at the market and chopping vegetables."

She laughed. "You're remarkable."

He waited until their dishes were set before them, the rich aromas of the wonderful food wafting up to fill their nostrils. He served her before filling his own plate and stood poised with his fork held up. "*Bon appetit.*"

It was excellent food and Kate sampled the various dishes, along with the trio of homemade chutney's Lali brought in one of those quintessentially Indian serving dishes, with three tiny silver pots on a tripod and three tiny spoons. "Try the tamarind," she suggested.

With the first wave of their hunger satisfied, they took seconds and ate more slowly, sipping the wine, which, she noted, was an excellent complement to the food, with it's fruity aroma and mineral base note. She'd have to remember that.

They talked of many things. He was worldly, philosophical, well traveled, adventurous, unpretentious, spiritual, very well read. Kate thought they could really enjoy each other's company, if only it wasn't so complicated for her. The contrast to Jay was jarring. Simon frankly fascinated her. He was open to new experiences, and life-long learning, and the wisdom of others, even children. He spoke dotingly about Madison, how amazing she is, how awed he is by her every day. Kate discovered that he still read, watched TV and listened to music simultaneously. She laughed at the memory. He had quite the intellect, but didn't take himself too seriously.

At a lull in the conversation, he checked his phone once more. Then he took an audible breath. "Look, Kate. I don't want to poison this." He waited, searching her face. She stared warily into his lucid blue eyes, the food in her stomach suddenly oppressively heavy. "Regardless of Sharon's threats, I'm really... really enjoying getting to know you again. I don't want to ruin it, but... we can't dance around it. It almost feels like we're not the same people we were all those years ago. And maybe we're not.

We were only nineteen, Kate. And we saw something in each other then that's still there, now. But we weren't really adults yet, were we?"

He made a valid point, but... "We weren't children either."

"Which is not to say our experiences weren't real." He shook his head. "What I mean to say is, I think the me you knew then was pretty raw. I had a lot to learn. I look back on that time of my life, and— I have regrets. Don't we all?"

No kidding! She puffed air through her cheeks, suddenly on edge. She couldn't believe she was sitting across from Simon Sharpe after all these years, actually talking about one of the most traumatic events in her young life. The feeling was unreal, as though she were in a dreamscape, or twisted nightmare. Lali appeared from the shadows and silently swept away their dirty dishes, sensitive to the fact that they were engrossed in private conversation. She nodded for Simon to continue. As long as he was talking, she didn't have to.

He stared into his wine glass, sluicing it around. "After we went home for the summer that year, I kind of assumed we'd moved on. That was pretty much my *modus operandi* back then. It was careless. I guess I was cowardly when it came to feelings, but I was too young to consider anything beyond..." He shrugged. "Fun. Anything deeper just wasn't on my radar yet. I had a plan."

"I suppose you were quite freaked out when I called then," she said, cool and curious. She distinctly remembered pining for him all summer long, wondering why he hadn't called or written, her heart breaking a little more each day. Foolishly, she assumed they would pick up in September where they left off in May.

"I was a typical guy, I guess. I wasn't looking for anything long-term. Maybe we had something that was worth pursuing. I don't know. We probably did. But I wasn't ready for that sort of thing."

I was! I was in love with you! I thought you felt the same way. Instead she said, "I guess young girls are more romantic, more idealistic perhaps." *If you only knew how in love with you I was!* How enraptured, how disgustingly dependent. Part of her wished he could understand what he'd meant to her, but the other part shied away from revealing how damaged she was. Her love was a sickness. Maybe she could get through this with her pride intact. If only it didn't make her heart ache so, remembering.

"I'm not so sure about that," he shook his head, closing his eyes. "I had a pretty fixed idea of the ideal woman I was searching for back then. I probably broke a few hearts as I sifted through the options. It's not that I... found fault... exactly." he said, evidently embarrassed by this admission. "It's only that I was... looking for something specific."

"Rachel?" she suggested, raising a brow.

He barked with laughter. "That's the ultimate irony, isn't it? I guess I got exactly what I deserved." His eyes darted to his phone, his expression exasperated.

"What were you were looking for?"

He studied her face for a long moment, his brows low, and she felt peculiarly exposed under his scrutiny, as though he were measuring her against that obsolete standard. "I think, in my naïveté, I thought the perfect woman wouldn't really depend on me, the way my parents' generation did. She would be self-sufficient and autonomous, having her own life." His eyebrows came up, chagrinned, as if to say– *I got more than I bargained for.* "That way, I could have my cake and eat it too. It was something to do with self-determination... freedom. I was terrified of having to sacrifice or share or really commit myself, I don't know. Just a selfish, immature cad, I suppose. Like you said last week."

She bit her lip, remembering. "I'm sorry I blew up at you like that. I don't know what I was thinking."

"It's okay. It got *me* thinking. Which is a good thing." He sucked air in through his teeth and ran his hands through his hair. "This is an appropriate time in my life to revisit some of those earlier ideas. I think I've come full circle." He paused, and reached across for her hand, stopping himself, and tentatively touching the tips of his fingers to hers. It was like an electric current, the heat traveling up her arm, and through her body, alarming her. "I'm truly sorry, Kate, if I hurt you. And I assume I did. It matters little now how I justify it."

Her heart thawed at his words. His apology was sincere, but she sensed, as well, some residual bitterness at his broken dreams, and along with that, a profound sense of loneliness. "You must have wanted to run in the opposite direction whenever you saw me coming, that next fall." Ugh! Why couldn't she leave well enough alone?

"No." His eyes drifted up to the ceiling while he hitched his shoulders. "I was stupid enough to believe that everyone shared my world view. I really had no idea you were hoping for more. But I still enjoyed seeing you… in a way." His laugh held a skeptical note.

"I felt like a cast-off," she dared. His honesty gave her courage. "I really thought that… what we had was… something unique," she ventured, glancing up at the tapestry. "To you I must have seemed like a clinging vine, choking you. I was naïve too, obviously." She drew out the last word, feeling foolish that her life had fallen apart over something so seemingly innocent.

He gripped her hand now, his face pained. "I'm so sorry. I never meant to cause so much pain. I can't understand why you didn't avoid *me,* given what I did. We seemed to bump into each other an awful lot, over the next couple years."

She cringed, recalling how much time and energy she'd expended keeping tabs on him, lurking, hoping he would appear. He was her sun and moon and stars. Along with the images came the feelings, long suppressed. Kate's stomach tightened as she felt the anxiety coming on. Churning gut, cold sweat, shaking. Her vision narrowed, darkened and blurred. There was a buzzing in her ears. She wanted to run, and run far and fast.

He noticed. "Kate? Are you alright? You look like you're going to faint."

She thought it was a distinct possibility. She gripped his hands with white fingers.

"I'm sorry. I'm so embarrassed. You must have thought I was… was… stalking you or something." Her head was spinning, dizzy.

He screwed up his face. "Nooo. But, I guess I did get kind of worried. You seemed so forlorn, after a while, and kind of…" he paused.

"Pathetic?" she offered. She squeezed her eyes closed, echoes of shame and sadness for her screwed up self filling her mind, pressing down on her, and she felt beads of perspiration bloom on her forehead.

"Maybe—needy?—is a better word. I didn't really know what you wanted from me. By then, I'd met Rachel and I didn't know what to do when you were around. I couldn't ask you out. But I thought that party would be safe. A gesture…" He shrugged and squirmed in his seat. "Maybe you would see me with Rachel and take the hint." Memories of that night hung like a specter over them, persistent, toxic and destructive. She wished she could purge it from their shared memory.

"Is *that* why you invited me?" Kate stared in disbelief.

"Problem is, *she* never showed up that night," he nodded, chagrinned, "and *you* did. Things were never meant to end up that way." He pressed her hands, reassuring.

Fragmented images of their cold, fraught, violent coupling flashed in her mind, stirring a nauseous, squeezing reaction in her gut. He'd seemed so frustrated and... what? Furious? Why? She felt numb, detached as he explained his own thoughts and feelings that night. It never occurred to her to wonder what *he* had been going through.

"I was angry at Rachel for not showing on my birthday. And hurt, deeply hurt. I'd fallen hard for her, but she was hot and cold. I think I took that anger and hurt out on you, for being there instead of her. There you were, your eyes... staring at me." His eyes glazed over. Finally, he was remembering. "I'm ashamed that I was such a mindless brute, not really caring about you at all, or why you wanted to be there with me," he whispered. His face reflected something of the pain she felt. "I don't know why. I couldn't stand the... the *look* in your eyes anymore. I guess I wanted to drive you away..." His voice tapered off. "Sex... should never be like that– so cold. I'm sorry."

Her eyes welled with tears. She shook her head. Her voice was barely audible, quavering. "You didn't hurt me, Simon, except..." she pressed her shaking hand to her breast, "...except here. I was ill... vulnerable, depressed. I didn't know what I was doing. It wasn't really about you; I only... thought it was. I'm so sorry." Her lips quivered and she squeezed her eyes shut, releasing hot tears that fell onto her hands.

"You're sorry." He looked as if he was on the verge of tears himself, his jaw tight and working. He stood up abruptly. "Look. Let's get out of here. We can go to my place. I make a pretty mean cup of *chai*," he said with forced brightness. "Did you drive?"

She shook her head jerkily. "No, I took the bus." Her words were wooden, and she swiped at her helpless tears with an angry hand, turning her face to the wall.

"Good." He turned and went to take care of the bill while she sat in stony silence, her eyes following him. Simon was drawn into a friendly debate with Lali, who kept pushing his credit card away and laughing. Finally, Simon acquiesced.

"Good night, Lali." Simon shook his head and returned to the table, surreptitiously checking his phone again. "Let's go."

Kate wrinkled up her nose. "You seem preoccupied with this situation. Maybe I'll just head home."

He frowned, lifted her coat up and held it while she slipped it on, then pulled his own on. "No, please. I want to spend time with you. It's just, I'd like to be at home in case Rachel drops off Maddie." He cleared his throat.

Out the door, the cold wind whipped their clothing. He wrapped one arm about her shoulders and held on tight, leading her half a block away to where his car was parked.

They drove in silence, regrouping, remembering, pulling themselves together.

His jingling cell phone jarred her nerves. He jumped and seized it quickly. "'lo?" He stole a glance at Kate. She stared out the window, expressionless, giving him space.

He voice was steely hard. "Yesss. Damn it, you can't do that Rachel! Where the hell have you been?"

She bit her lip and rubbed her hands on her pant legs, picking up on his tension.

He listened a moment. "You should have talked to me first. I felt like an idiot when the school called looking for her. What kind of parents— " He peered again at Kate, who glanced at him now in concern, her brows knit, and he grimaced.

His face registered disbelief. "When are you bringing her home?" He paused, listening. "We'll talk later."

He hung up his phone and seethed for several minutes, his knuckles white on the steering wheel, before stealing another look at Kate.

She eyed him nervously. "Everything... alright?"

He nodded weakly, closing his eyes in a slow blink. "It is now. She picked up Maddie from preschool Wednesday afternoon without telling me her plans." He shook his head, concentrating on the dark road. "She's never done that before. If anything, she usually brings Maddie back early."

"I'm sorry. All this time... you must have been worried sick."

He nodded silently, his jaw clenched tight. "Maybe I'm being paranoid, but lately... I don't know. I'm worried that she's suddenly taken more of an interest in Maddie. I think she's doing it as a power trip, to mess with my head about custody, but... it sends a confusing message to Maddie, too.

The poor man. Kate reached out a hand and gently squeezed his arm. Now she understood how Rachel's erratic behavior posed a threat.

eleven

Once at his house, he settled her on the sofa and quickly built a fire in the fireplace, then slipped into the kitchen to toss the leftovers in the fridge and make a pot of chai. The air filled with the soft sounds of blues guitar. A few minutes later he carried the tray of tea into the living room and set it down in front of her. The fire crackled nicely, warming the room. He looked self-conscious, fidgeting. "Look, I'm sorry about that."

She smiled, waving away his concerns. "You have a nice house," she said, to put him at ease.

He poured two mugs of tea, the warm spicy cinnamon and cardamom aromas filling the air.

"Thank you," she said, taking the mug he handed to her.

He plopped himself down next to her on the sofa and picked up his tea. "Thanks. It's a good house. Pretty traditional though. Not like your place. I still can't get over that loft. It really suits you."

"It's me, but it's also Alexa. I had to put up with a lot of nagging before she gave up and let me throw my mix of antiques and moderns and weird art together. It was my compromise. If it were up to her, it would be as sleek and cold as a Bauhaus showroom." She took a sip.

"Were any of those paintings on the wall yours?"

She looked at him and away. "Ah. No. Mine's more therapy than art for public viewing."

They sat in comfortable silence for a few minutes, drinking their tea.

"I was wondering about your muffins."

"Wha–? "You want the recipe?" She took a warming sip of her *chai,* meeting his eye playfully over the rim of her mug.

"Yes, actually. But that's not the point. You said baking was easier than shopping, but… I have the impression it was more strategic than that." He studied her reaction.

A slow smile spread across her face. He was smarter than your average bear. "You got me. It's well worth my trouble to bake muffins just to fill the space with the scent of cinnamon, apples, vanilla and such. It does wonders for reconciliation."

He shook his head. "And here I was, thinking how charmingly domestic you were, and you're experimenting in human engineering."

"It works." She shuddered with silent laughter.

He leaned toward her, laying his arm along the sofa back behind her shoulders and gave her a heated look, fluttering his eyebrows suggestively, and wobbling his head. "Is it that you are liking your chai, lady?" he asked in a deep, seductive voice with a fairly decent imitation of Lali's accent.

She sat upright, mock indignation on her face, and a laugh building deep in her belly. "You've used my own devious methods against me!" They laughed together, and she relaxed into his arm and smiled up at him, exhaling. How could she be afraid of him? She'd never known a gentler, kinder man. "Very therapeutic."

Their eyes met and held, and she felt her breath shorten and her heart accelerate. She inhaled his warm, clean, masculine smell, blended with exotic spices from India. The heat of his arm at her neck and his spicy breath on her face mingled, and her mind filled with the embroidered images of Indian maids and men in tangled embraces. The mix was intoxicating.

Earnest, he searched her face for clues. "I know I shouldn't do this, because of your guy…" He swallowed. "But if I kiss you again, will you shout at me and storm out into the night?" Her nostrils flared, an arrow of heat slicing through to her core. She was still afraid, but tingling with anticipation, too.

"No," she whispered. "Um. That's… over."

His eyes darkened to steel, gold stars reflecting the crackling fire. He closed the short distance between them and touched his lips gently to her mouth. It was electrifying. At first she didn't move, but then she responded, returning the press of his kiss. He pulled back slightly, dipping his head. "I was unkind to you Kate. I was cruel. You didn't deserve to be treated that way." He stroked her face gently, lifting her chin up so he could gaze into her eyes.

Dark memories flashed in her mind, jumbled together, slashing and tearing at her peace. Irrational. Stop. Just forget. "Simon, I— " She trembled again.

"Don't fear me, Kate," he whispered against her lips, "I won't hurt you again. Let me show you." He kissed her eyes, her nose, her cheeks and ears. He laced his fingers in her hair and drew it away from her neck, planting kisses there.

A soft moan sounded deep in her throat and she dropped her head back into his cupped hand, allowing him closer and he devoured her softness.

"I want you, Kate. You have no idea how much I've wanted you since I first saw you again." He kissed her again and this time she surrendered to his plundering tongue, allowing hers to dance and parry, and lost herself in the soft wet interior of his mouth. They tumbled back onto the cushions of the sofa and it seemed as though the years slipped away and they were as intimate and hungry for each other as they had been in their optimistic and innocent youth.

As his hands roamed over the contours of her body, she was amazed that the chemistry they had known sixteen years ago was undiminished. They may be different people now, mature, shaped by their separate lives, but their bodies, ah, their bodies remembered. They were made for each other.

He deftly unbuttoned her blouse and slipped a hand inside, stroking his nails lightly over the silken rise of her breast.

She gasped. "Simon, please… " She arched upward, meeting his straining desire and he bent to kiss, and then lick, her collarbone, the hollow of her throat, and the softly rising mounds of her breasts.

After that, she had no memory, only impressions of frenzied tearing of clothes and tumbling among cushions onto the rug by the hearth, where they abandoned themselves to their mutual passion. She could only wonder what intriguing, metaphorical names the Kama Sutra had for the way their bodies meshed, like two parts of a whole, limbs entwined, blood throbbing and pulsing, joined. In due course, they found sleep tangled like sesame and rice in their discarded clothing, drenched in perspiration, spent, the fire burning low and warming their slick skin.

Some time in the middle of the night, there was a screech and a thump on top of them, followed by a crash, awakening them with a start, her heart thundering. "Wha– ?" Kate bolted upright, disoriented. "Where?"

Simon laughed. "It's only Lucy, my cat. She hasn't been fed her supper tonight." He dragged himself up and to the kitchen to feed her, returning to find Kate shivering amongst the pond of discarded clothing and strewn cushions, staring dazedly at the last glowing coals in the hearth. "Let's go upstairs and get comfortable. I'm too old for this." He reached for her hand and pulled up her lax form and she followed him up the stairs, admiring the green-gold highlights the streetlight picked out along his lean limbs and the smooth rise of his muscular shoulders and bare buttocks. He led the way to his bedroom, where, softened by sleep, they made love again, slowly, hypnotically, and deliciously, and fell asleep again, her head nestled against his shoulder.

What do you want from me? Simon's voice emerged as a growl from between tightly clenched teeth. *What do you want from me?* His face bore down on her, inflamed with rage, his eyes cold and hard as ice, lips pulled back in a sneer. His words cut her like a knife, and Kate felt a sharp searing pain rip through her, welling up from her deep dark hidden center. Hot tears erupted and squeezed out from behind her closed lids onto her cheeks, and an anguished sob wracked her body.

The force of it wrenched her upright, and sitting in the bed, shaking, her throat tight with the pressure of unshed tears, she surfaced, panic-stricken, from the nightmare that had returned after many years dormant. It left her in a cold sweat, shaking, dizzy and nauseous. Grey pre-dawn light filled the dim room like a gauze shroud.

Beside her, Simon mumbled and rolled over, his arm reaching for her, and sliding off her rigid side, back down, slack onto the rumpled sheets. He didn't wake. She must have dreamt of sobbing aloud. His face was serene in slumber, his short blond waves pushed this way and that, his lips slack and sensual. He was such a beautiful man.

Waves of heat reverberated through her body, remembering their night of passion. *How could I do that?* This was Simon Sharpe. *How could I resist?* This was Simon, after all. Her Simon.

Kate sat quietly, wiping her wet eyes, measuring her breathing as she was taught to do, soothing herself, listening to his even breathing, a comfort. After some minutes, her tears abated and she was able to reflect calmly on the dream. It used to come more often, and during her training and therapy, more and more often, with more detail as she revisited her trauma.

It was only with Rose's help, and careful recounting of the details of the dream that they were, together, able to understand that Kate had transferred suppressed memories of her high school rape to the painful, stupid encounter with Simon years later. The convoluted twists and turns of the human mind baffled her still.

Sleeping with Simon, making love to him again after all these years, must have triggered those memories again. Thorough analysis and careful reconstruction of the two, completely separate and unrelated events had allowed Kate to pulls the strands apart and come to an understanding. With Rose's help, she was able to see how her pain and humiliation at Simon's rejection and his baffling anger and harshness when they were supposed to be making love—but no, that was her fantasy. That night, that was only a fuck. A desperate one for her, in her deluded attempt to win Simon back. For him it was— well, now she understood a little better, a bitter and resentful one. A tortured one. A tortured fuck.

Well if that wasn't a good enough clue as to why the encounter had allowed deeply suppressed memories to surface of that rape in her last year of high school, then nothing was. A mirthless, silent laugh shook her. At least she could see the irony in it now.

Rose said that it was common enough, for memories of a traumatic event to be completely suppressed for years, sometimes forever. It was the brain's way of protecting itself from what it couldn't understand, couldn't handle. She supposed that was true. For all her smarts and ambition as a young woman, she had been remarkably naive, sheltered and immune to the harsh realities of the world. Who knew that a high school graduation trip to Greece could provide such a rude awakening for a small town girl. Too rude, apparently. She'd shut it away. Until Simon, unwittingly, had unlocked the door.

Goosebumps rose up on her bare arms and back, and she shivered. She lay back and pulled the covers over her naked body, laying apart from him. She turned onto her side and stared at his sleeping face in the shadows of his room, remembering that night, re-examining it in a new light.

Kate had been beyond thrilled at the invitation to the party at his house—actually at his house—she was intoxicated and dizzy with anticipation. It was his twenty-first birthday. Alexa had reluctantly agreed to go with her, a comfort and a safety net. Other than crossing paths on campus, she hadn't seen him socially in almost two years, though she knew his every move. *This* was momentous.

Once there, she searched the house for him, prowling like a hungry lioness. She was fixated on Simon, her longing eating her alive, utterly obsessed.

Already slightly disoriented with drink, she could see him sitting in a chair, staring back at her, the hunted, his body pulsing nearer, farther, nearer, farther, the cinematographic effect of some psychotic director's vision, as though she focused the scope on her weapon, zeroing in on her prey. Everything but him was lost to view, to focus, to comprehension. Him, only him. She studied his features as they became magnified, exaggerated, distorted by her thrall. Was he as perfect and beautiful as she believed? He was brooding and dark and seemed mesmerized by her staring. They exchanged no civilities. They'd both had plenty to drink. He stood up portentously, not breaking eye contact, and she followed him—sensuality and seduction lost, into his bedroom. Why was she here? She didn't know the answer now. Maybe she was already on the verge of a breakdown, and her encounter with Simon was just an unfortunate coincidence.

She remembered, much later, that she and Alex had walked a long, long way home, in the wee hours of the morning, the sky fading from black to violet to blue, even as her ego disintegrated into a heap of fine grey ash. Her life, after that night, was an enormous gaping hole. A deep depression set in, and that was the start of her slippery slide down the road of a mental breakdown.

She shivered again, inching closer to him for warmth. Sleepily, he rolled on his side and wrapped his arm around her, drawing her closer, pulling her into the heat of his embrace. She nestled there, feeling safe, for the moment. Part of her wanted to confide in him and share her experience. Perhaps it would help him understand, and perhaps even forgive, her erratic, bizarre behavior with regard to him and their relationship, both back then, and now.

Eventually, with help, she'd come to understand that her whole relationship with Simon was doomed. She'd used him as a crutch at a vulnerable time, as an escape from what happened in Europe. That spring, her self-esteem was at an all time low. Simon appeared as her knight in shining armour. How could she ever see him in any other light? He was just a man– a very young one. It wasn't fair to him. And it wasn't a real relationship either. It could never be.

But those were her darkest days. Did she really want him to know that about her? She'd never told anyone, except Rose and now, Alexa. Certainly not Jay, or any other lover. Easier, in fact, far better, to walk away now. She might be healthy now, but somehow, when it came to Simon, she felt so fragile. She could never allow herself to be that vulnerable again. Every moment she spent with him brought those memories closer and made them more visceral, less abstract. They would always be a part of her, she realized. How could she ever trust her own attraction to him? Her motives would be forever muddled in her mind. She would be better off a long way from him, and he would be better off without her, she thought as she finally drifted back to sleep.

The second time she awoke, for the moment forgetting the dream, it was because something was brushing softly against her thigh, tickling. Calm now, she opened her eyes slowly, taking in the clean, bright square room. She tried to understand where she was. Soft brown walls, bright white ceiling and trim, sheer luminous curtains in the large, traditional window to her side, billowing gently in the warm air rising from the heat register. In the center of the ceiling, an elegant, old-fashioned Depression glass and bronze light fixture hung, partially obscuring a white plaster medallion. Simon's bedroom, she realized, the night before flooding back in awesome detail. It– Simon's cat?– tickled her again and she reached down to touch it. Instead, she found her hand suddenly in a warm firm grip.

"Don't touch that unless you're prepared for the consequences." Simon's hoarse, sleepy voice, warm against the top of her head, contained laughter.

Oh!

"I thought you were still asleep." He released her hand and she felt the weight of his arm across her as he pulled her, rolling her body toward him, his hand gliding down her bare back to her butt cheek beneath the sheet, and pulling her tighter. His morning erection, not a cat after all, was now trapped between them, pressing insistently against her abdomen. A coil of sizzling heat unfurled in her center.

Tipping her head back, she gazed into his eyes, which shone a bright, translucent pool blue in the morning sunlight from the window behind her.

"Good morning, Kate." He smiled sleepily and kissed her. Her body took off without her permission, her insides liquefying and boiling, her heart accelerating, without regard for her earlier resolution. Last night's passion reverberated in her veins, and throbbed between her legs.

"Aren't you worn out?" She smiled.

"Not at all. I'm just getting started. You?" His face questioning.

"Noooo. Not—" He stole her breath with an urgent kiss and her heart leapt to her throat, drumming its demands.

He pulled back, his blue eyes sparkling with mischief. "Tell me about the tapestry. The four embraces."

She scrunched her eyes tight and huffing out a tiny laugh, smiling. "Er, okay. Let's see, at the top, there was 'the twining vine'. Beside it, 'climbing the tree'."

He screwed up his face and rolled his eyes to the ceiling as if trying to remember the images over the table last night. "Right. I remember." He gave his head a little shake, and bent to trail tender kisses down her neck, and along the top of her breasts.

She shivered, and an arrow of heat shot down between her legs, pulsing at the memory of their ardor in the night. "In the bottom left corner, was 'sesame and rice', I think, but I've never been able to figure out if they mean plants or food." She recalled the two recumbent bodies, their arms and legs tangled.

"Now we're coming to my favourite," he said. "It seems the most romantic. With the woman curled in the man's lap, their arms enfolded so tightly." Simon met her eyes, naked and clear.

"The last one represents 'milk and water'. It's the embrace of a man and woman very much in love. " Kate recalled the figures' aquiline noses and foreheads touching intimately, eyes locked, and her heart squeezed with longing. She cleared her throat, looking away.

"So you've taken a course on the Kama Sutra, too?" he teased, caressing her ribs with a feather light touch.

"Nooo. Just a little light reading." She smiled, and could feel the heat rising into her cheeks, competing with the flush that radiated outward from his fingertips as he traced a delicate line down her thigh. "Haven't you? You're the Eastern mystic."

"I never considered the Kama Sutra mystical," he murmured, his lips against the skin in the hollow between her ribs.

"O-oh. It's a very philosophical document. It states that even an ignorant man can gain respect if he knows the sixty-four ways."

"I see. I'll have to look into it. Obviously my studies are incomplete." He pushed himself up above her, his shoulders and chest flexing as he nipped at her upper lip, licking and kissing, his need as demanding and impatient upon awakening as the morning sun straining on the horizon. Dropping to his elbows, his mouth moved down her neck and throat to lick and nibble her breasts, and in seconds she was moaning with pleasure and arching in anticipation as he slid slowly inside her. Every cell of her skin where they touched ignited. Her body was awake and alive and aching for his in a way she hadn't known for years and years. What was it about him that unraveled her? He was refreshed, and his stamina renewed. They made love languorously, luxuriously, savouring each delightful sensation their bodies created in each other, and came together in a long, slow breathless crest of satisfaction, his blue eyes dark and intense on hers.

Afterward, they remained joined, legs tangled, their breath mingled, panting, grinning foolishly until their hearts slowed and they became drowsy again. "Now we are sesame and rice," he mumbled, his eyes closed. They lay motionless in the beam of sunshine that stretched across the creased white sheets. He caressed her skin slowly, sleepily, exploring each curve and crevasse, sliding down and then up, teasing her nipples. His interest quickened, and amazingly she could feel him swell again inside her as he moved his lean hips and long thighs back and forth. Kate was amazed that Simon seemed ready again so soon. How many minutes had they lain here? Ten maybe. He seemed tireless.

"How old are you, kid?" she asked, teasing.

"Um. Ah… thirty… mm… something. I can't seem to do the math at the moment." He chuckled. "I think thirty-five. Yes, that's it. Is it important all of a sudden?" He buried his face against her neck and nuzzled, kissing her earlobe and began to move with a slow, sensuous, liquid thrusting in and out, gradually quickening his pace and intensity.

"When you used to do this," she murmured, "I thought it was just youthful exuberance and virility." Amazingly, she felt herself responding to his slow seductive movements, though she was quite certain she couldn't move a finger.

He laughed softly into her neck. "Well, I can't speak for others. But it's nothing to do with age." He raised his tousled blond head and looked deeply into her eyes, holding her there in a blanket of warmth and intense yearning. "It's you, Kate. I can't get enough. I can't satisfy my hunger for you." He did not look away, with each deliberate thrust taking them both gradually up and up and up and over, like hawks on an updraft, hovering, drifting, descending, watching her, making certain she stayed with him beat for beat, holding her in his eyes.

No one, no one else had ever made her feel this way.

How could she resist the powerful pull of this beautiful, beautiful man, when he was all and everything she had ever wanted? And now, he wanted her too. Or he thought he did. No. No, she had to be strong. She felt the heat of tears building in her throat. This had to be good-bye. Her heart squeezed painfully and tears flooded her eyes, blurring his face. His eyes too glistened with unshed tears. How could something that felt so right be so very, very wrong?

Afterwards, lying truly spent, Simon toyed with a lock of her hair, saying nothing for the longest time. "Kate?"

"Mmm?"

"I could get very comfortable with this," he whispered.

She waited, unable to say anything. Her breath was held hostage by such powerful feelings, she thought she might be swallowed whole and carried away, like Jonas in the whale.

"I didn't think I would ever feel these feelings again, with anyone. You make me want to take risks, and live again. I feel safe with you, Kate."

Kate felt panic rising, washing over her in a wave of heat and chills, setting her trembling from the inside out. She too felt something akin to love welling inside her. But it didn't make her feel safe. She was too afraid of it to name it. She knew she wanted him; she couldn't help that. But she wasn't naïve anymore. True love, the kind that lasted, if it existed at all, must be a far heavier, more sensible thing, not this wild, fluttering flight of fancy that lifted her and threatened to shatter her into pieces, this desperate consuming need. It was too intense and out of control for her. These feelings couldn't be trusted. She didn't know what this was, but her pulse raced and she felt the urgent need to flee.

"Oh, Simon. Don't go there, please." She pulled away from him and the spell was broken.

"Don't run away," he pleaded softly. "I'm not asking for anything. I'm only giv—"

She jerked upright, feeling lightheaded and dizzy. "I'd better go." She looked around frantically, feeling a sudden need to be alone, to meditate until she was calm and could gather her scattered thoughts. "Where are my clothes?"

"What are you doing? Don't do this." He sat up and touched her lightly on the shoulder. "I'm trying to tell you something."

Kate stiffened, shrinking from his touch. "I know what you're trying to say, Simon." She shot him a hard look over her shoulder and turned away. "I don't know if you're glib, or hopelessly romantic. I don't know who you are." She buried her face in her hands, grinding the heels into her eye sockets to suppress the flood of hysterical tears that threatened to erupt. What had she done? She'd been so caught up in Simon, she hadn't even thought of Jay. How could she do this so soon after breaking up with Jay? "I do know who I am not. I am not the girl who loved you fifteen years ago. I am not who you think you want to be with. Neither am I the clinging vine you ran away from." Her voice rose and cracked.

Simon bristled and stood up, pulling on his robe, and stalked around to her side of the bed, facing her. When he spoke, his voice came out harsh. "Give me some credit for knowing my own heart, Kate. I'm not talking about the past. We're not kids anymore." He huffed out an exasperated sigh, knelt by her at the side of the bed and looked up, earnest. "I'm talking about you and me right now, right here." He took her hand and placed it against his chest. "Feel this. This is real."

No. Please, God, give me strength. This intensity of feeling is what she'd felt before. And that was a lie. It was her undoing. "You can't know me. You are just as prone to falling in love with some abstract notion now as you ever were. It's love you're in love with. You're fooling yourself. Believe me, I know what I'm talking about. I'm not the answer to your dreams or the solution to your family problems. Get real. Grow up. What you're looking for doesn't exist. And if it does, I'm *certainly* not it!"

Kate didn't know if she was talking to Simon, or to that part of herself that wanted to let go and be head-over-heels in love with him again.

Simon's face twisted, his mouth puckered as though he'd eaten a bitter pill. "You're wrong. It's you who can't see the truth. Or don't want to, because you're afraid of something. I'm not a young fool. If there's one thing I've learned the hard way, it's that real relationships are a two-way street. Nobody's perfect, Kate. But we all need someone."

Kate closed her eyes. She mustn't give in to his arguments, however tempting, however much she wished for a simple, romantic outcome to this debacle. She couldn't lose herself in him again.

Kate could not meet his eye, steeling herself, forcing her will to dominate her heart. She crossed her arms over her bare breasts, one hand over the pendant at her throat, and turned to face him, her eyes averted, her jaw jutting. "Look. This was a mistake. A big mistake. With all the baggage of our past, your fragile family situation, and the added complications of dealing with conflict of interest claims, we should have known better than to let this happen. "This situation is impossible. This just can't happen."

He seemed to deflate, and she knew she'd trumped him. For the moment. "It is happening, Kate. You can't stop it. Why don't you trust me? Trust yourself? What is it with you?"

She stood up abruptly and yanked the sheet off the bed, wrapping herself in it and looking away. She held up a hand to silence him and push away his reaching hand, and left the room determined to find her clothes.

twelve

She saw the hurt in his eyes as she left, and felt her own aching sense of loss and disorientation. The room was suddenly airless. She could hardly draw breath. What a fool she was to put herself in this vulnerable situation. She raced down the stairs, almost tripping on the sheet she dragged along, and grabbed her strewn clothing from the living room sofa and floor, searching for her bag. The chaotic scene of their passionate lovemaking the previous night filled her with panic. *What have I done? What have I started here?* Had she no sense? No self control at all? She found a guest bathroom downstairs and quickly washed her face, running wet hands through her tangled hair, shaking it out, putting herself back together as best she could, painfully reminded of her dream and her furtive dawn departure fourteen years ago.

When she emerged from the bathroom, she found him standing in the hall in faded low-rise jeans, bare-chested and barefooted, his arms crossed. She could not bear the look of pain and scorn on his handsome features. "Want some tea?" he offered, his voice flat, and he waited, tight-lipped.

It was too tempting to go to him, to touch him. He looked so vulnerable in that moment she could almost forget that it was she who was in danger. She willed her heart to cease its pounding in her chest. She shook her head quickly. "I have to go."

"Don't leave like this," he pleaded.

She stopped and drew in a ragged breath. "Please understand me, Simon. I don't want to hurt you. I genuinely like you. But this whole thing has become a confusing mess. We've rushed into something without considering the consequences for who knows what tangled reasons. Our lives are too complicated. I'm not what you need. And you certainly aren't what I need. We can't go back." She held up both hands, palm out. "We're playing with fire here. You may be willing to take risks with your career, and your family, but I'm not."

"You sound just like me sixteen years ago." His voice was filled with disdain. "Are you afraid of intimacy? Is that it? Or is commitment the problem? What's *your* excuse?

She clicked her tongue and rolled her eyes, then met his with a steely glare. She ignored the voice in her head that acknowledged how close he'd come to the truth. "You can take it any way you like. It's irrelevant. I'm leaving and I don't want to pursue this." She sliced the air with her hand.

Stealing a glance at him, she was alarmed by his grim face and set jaw. His sandy brows were drawn across his eyes, which were ice cold and flat, as was his voice when he spoke. "I really thought I understood you. You're saying one thing but your actions tell me something else. Who are you lying to Kate, me or yourself?"

The scorn in Simon's voice rose as his lip curled derisively. "Perhaps my first impression of you was closer to the truth, after all. Are you just another cold-hearted woman who only cares about her career?" His jaw jutted forward.

"Don't be…" She stopped herself.

Was he trying to start a brawl? She ground her teeth as her body quivered with tension. Anger grabbed her gut in its fist and crushed it to pulp. She had a sudden urge to smack that insolent face. She shot him a venomous glare and turned toward the door, flinging it open with such force it crashed against the wall. She needed the violence to stay the tears that threatened to erupt—again. She was crying all the time lately. He followed her out onto the covered wooden porch, saying nothing. What was there left to say?

"Who's playing with whose feelings here? Why *are* you still married anyway? Have you asked yourself that question?" They were both panting and bristling when she spun away and almost crashed into a young man leaping up the steps. She gasped in surprise.

"Will!" It was Simon who spoke first, under his breath, shocked.

"Si-mon." The man stood to one side, his eyes darting from Simon's half-dressed state to Kate and back again. "Good morning?" he said, a note of concern in his voice.

Simon shot him a silencing look. "Kate. I don't think you've met my younger brother Will. Will, Kate." His voice was clipped and he said no more. Kate imagined how the scene must appear and she glanced awkwardly at Simon and Will in turn. Though Simon got the edge in height and good looks, there was a distinct family resemblance.

Simon looked meaningfully at Will past her shoulder. "Anything wrong?" he said with a tight smile.

"No-oo." Will glanced uncomfortably at Kate. "Need to pick up my hockey gear. Got an early game today." Will smiled feebly at Kate, but his eyes were searching and curious.

Simon cleared his throat. "Right. Uh. The gear's in the garage. I'll get it out for you." He turned and strode to the side of the house. Kate tried to swallow her anger and pretend a calm she didn't feel, but she was shaking.

She and Will stood in awkward silence for a few minutes. Kate sighed. Was there no way out of this ridiculous situation? She glanced away, scanning the street. Could she just walk off down the street in search of a bus stop?

Will's narrowed eyes scanned her up and down, lingering on her wet hair. "You spent the night?"

Kate lifted her chin. "I don't see how that's any of your concern, actually," she snapped.

"I look out for my brother. Is that so extraordinary?"

She shrugged and turned her head away.

"You both seem strangely testy for new lovers, if you ask me."

"I didn't. What do you know about it?"

"I know more than a thing or two about Simon's love life. He doesn't have one. The truth is, I'm shocked to find you here at all." He squinted at her, as though by sheer dint of concentration, he could glean the facts.

"Perhaps you don't know everything about him." Why was she engaging in a contest with this man? She didn't know him. She would likely never see him again. He could think what he liked for all she cared. She glared at him, tempted to walk away without saying goodbye to Simon, but it felt wrong.

Will shook his head knowingly. "Simon doesn't sleep around. He always puts Maddie's needs ahead of his own." His head tilted to one side. "But it seems you've broken the pattern, whoever you are, Kate." He said her name meaningfully and cocked one eyebrow in a strange echo of Simon's familiar gesture, considering her. "He's a lonely and vulnerable dreamer. I just hope he doesn't get hurt... again." It sounded more like a threat than a wish.

She bristled. "I assure you that I have no designs on your brother, who can take care of himself and is fully responsible for his own vulnerable heart, as we all are. We're old friends from university." Will lifted his eyebrows clearly astonished at this detail. She crossed her arms, plucking at her pendant, and tapped her foot. "Look, can you just tell him that I–"

Just then, Simon appeared clutching a hockey stick, a large duffel bag slung over his shoulder. A ripple of physical awareness shook her at the sight of his bare chest, his lean hips, and she pushed it away. He dropped the bag on the edge of the driveway and sauntered up, handing the stick to Will, and taking in their expressions. "I see you've been getting acquainted. Weren't you supposed to pick up Maddie?"

Will frowned. His head shook slightly, his eyes questioning.

"Rachel said she'd called you. Have you checked your messages?" Simon asked.

"Yeah. I never heard from her. Whassup?"

Simon chewed his lip thoughtfully, his eyebrows drawn. "I don't know. She's been acting weird this week. She's had Maddie since Wednesday."

Disbelief registered on Will's face. "Wow. That is weird."

"Well, sorry to interrupt your musings, gentlemen, but I really have to push off, so I'll say good-bye... until Tuesday, then," she said brightly, forcing a smile, hoping to escape before any more threats were made or questions asked.

"Wait. I'll give you a lift," Simon offered. Though his manner was still stiff, he seemed despondent now.

"No, thanks. I'll walk to the... bus." She pulled her jacket closer to her neck, glancing up. The sky was dense and grey, the air cold and damp.

"It's going to rain any minute. I'll take you home." Simon insisted testily.

No! She shook her head, her throat tightening. Kate couldn't trust herself to be alone with him just now; her feelings were so conflicted and confused. She'd surely cry and say things she'd regret. She wanted to throw herself into his arms and beg forgiveness. She mustn't even allow such thoughts.

"Hey, I'm leaving anyway. Can I drop you somewhere?" Will

looked at Kate. The look said he didn't care one way or another, but she sensed he was digging for more dirt.

She chewed her lip, considered her options: Simon's resentful eyes, the dark sky looming overhead, Will's lecturing. She could better handle the brother. "Thanks. I'd appreciate it." She and Simon exchanged one long hard look before she got into Will's rusty Dodge pick-up and slammed the door. She stopped herself from glancing out the window at Simon, and her chest squeezed with a terrible sense of loss.

Despite Kate's fears that Will would renew his probing questions on the way to the bus stop, he said nothing at all, and Kate sat silently, ramrod straight, staring out the window, wondering about this protective little brother and his cautionary words. The sooner she got far away from both of them, the better.

When they finally stopped, he half-turned to her. "I'm sorry for walking in on your lover's spat. I know it's none of my business." He stuck out a placating hand. "But you have to understand that my brother hasn't dated since the split with Rachel. Not once." Will squeezed his eyes shut briefly and shook his head, his jaw dimpling with tension. "I hate it. I worshiped him, before she brought him down. He might have been anything." He paused, and shot a glance her way.

She gaped mutely, shocked. *Is he serious?*

"I don't know what you're fighting about, but it doesn't look like the result of a one-night stand. There's something more going on here. I also know that you wouldn't even be in Simon's house, or in his life, if you weren't someone very important to him." He paused, and scowled at her, his teeth worrying his cheek.

She said nothing, but returned his stare.

"I just hope, whatever the problem is, that you work it out. For *his* sake. I don't think he'd survive another heartbreak."

God save me! thought Kate as she got out of the truck. *This isn't difficult enough. I need guilt on top of everything else.* It was enough to make her wonder if Simon was the victim and she the villain in the scene. How would the protective brother feel if he knew that Simon wanted a relationship, and Kate had shot him down. She knew she was doing a bad thing, and she was hurting him, but she was doing it for the right reason. Kate just couldn't take the risk.

thirteen

Her gauzy window screens veiled a flat silver sky, only partially mediating the imposing effect of the frigid, wintery morning. Kate shivered. She'd tried to compensate for the cold weather with fresh coffee and spice tea, and warm muffins, wistfully remembering her conversation with Simon.

He was the last to arrive, clearly by intention, and Kate was so tense she didn't know how she'd get through the session. *Focus! Discipline!* Today they had to review the preliminary draft agreement and then they were on the home stretch. This case could finally end, and the turmoil it had brought to her life could end with it. Hopefully.

Sharon opened the door for him, and he strolled over to the seating area and quietly took his place on one of the low upholstered black cubes that closed the gap in the sectional, his long legs folding like a grasshopper's, his knees meeting his elbows. He looked uncomfortable.

D'arcy carefully chewed a muffin with an intensity of focus that typified her peculiar, boundless appetite. It struck Kate that D'arcy seemed always to be eating lately, and the results were becoming evident. Her round face, instead of chiseled and glamourous, looked just plain plump. She supposed it was stress.

Kate got right down to business. When she read aloud the draft, with a few suggested modifications, Sharon pitched in. "I believe the draft is still too vague on the issue of economics. No matter how well-intentioned D'arcy and Eli are going into this, money matters are always a source of conflict and things could easily get derailed again over them, given their unusual financial history."

Kate conceded Sharon's point, confessing that she had downplayed financial issues. "I agree with you, Sharon. Money will always be a sensitive topic between D'arcy and Eli, given their beginnings. Though it can never be prescriptive. The future is always an unknown." She offered a sample clause. "How do you feel about that?" she asked, turning to Eli and D'arcy, who sat in their usual spot side-by-side on the long sofa, their thighs touching like two electrodes, an invisible but tangible current of hope passing between them.

"That sounds reasonable," D'arcy replied, scanning the papers she held. Eli fidgeted, drumming his long fingers on his knee and fingering the rectangular outline of the cigarette pack in his pocket with a longing caress.

Suggestions and ideas for a framework of financial responsibilities were critiqued and discussed, until they had added a couple of clauses that satisfied everyone.

Kate tried not to look at Simon at all, but when she, against her will and better judgment, found herself glancing in his direction, he was almost always staring at her, creases etched between his brows, his hand rubbing his mouth or jaw pensively. He hardly spoke.

"Simon. You're very quiet. Any comments?" Sharon asked, apparently noticing the same. Startled, he looked up, scanning the group, and his eyes caught Kate's for the first time. She looked away quickly, as did he.

He sat up straighter. "Not on money matters. I'm in agreement with the changes you've proposed there." He paused. "I did want to suggest, however, that we go over the section on family. I think there are some loose—"

Kate cleared her throat, irritated. "Okay. That's fine. I'd like to tidy up the next two sections before we move on." She glanced up, but her eyes rose only to his chin, her lips pressed tightly together.

"Whatever," he muttered.

She returned to her draft, and a moment later was startled by his, "Oh, Kate?"

She looked up sharply, this time directly into his eyes. "Yes?" He sent her a silent angry message. *Are you still there?* Her eyes fluttered, unable to hold his gaze. She was culpable.

He blinked slowly and looked away, point made. "Never mind. It can wait." Kate's brows knit and she blinked once, twice and looked down with a glower. What kind of game was he playing? *He's trying to piss me off, behaving like a spurned lover.* Even though that's exactly what he is, a little voice nagged.

After an uncomfortable pause, Kate lifted her chin and resumed. "The next section I'd like to review involves responsibilities in the domestic sphere. Here, in paragraph thirty-two, I think we've made a start, but it's much too brief and... well, abstract, quite frankly."

"But I can't cook," complained Eli. "Not at all," he whined.

"Neither could I when I left home," D'arcy rebutted. Eli made a face.

Simon jumped in to help D'arcy and Kate persuade Eli that sharing in the family cooking was not only his responsibility, but a great opportunity to be creative.

D'arcy leaned in and planted a big kiss on his cheek. "It'll be fun. I promise." They all shared a laugh. "Of course that means doing dishes, too."

Eli looked like he might cry, though he was hamming it up now. "Couldn't we just hire help?" He pulled out his cigarette pack with practiced ease and tapped it nervously.

Everyone frowned at him. "Eli!" they cried in unison.

"Maybe eventually. You two are hardly destitute." Kate said. "But it's about getting yourselves established first. Working out your roles. Remember all those discussions we had about extravagant purchases and gifts. No one is saying that those things are wrong, or that your generous spirit is a bad thing. It's about balancing that impulse with responsibility, to D'arcy and to your future."

Simon and Eli exchanged a meaningful look, and Eli nodded and took a deep breath, placing an unlit cigarette between his sensual lips. He leaned back and draped an arm around D'arcy's shoulders and she shot a smile at him.

"It's really about outlining options and using some objective standards. So, let's try this wording... " suggested Kate, and she read from her notes, while the others made marks on their draft agreements.

Simon excused himself quietly and sauntered across the loft while they finished the next two sections. A part of Kate's mind went with him, missing him even though they could hardly look at each other, never mind talk.

Some minutes later, Simon returned and stood behind the sofa, shifting his weight from foot to foot. Awareness slowly dawned that an unpleasant odor had wafted into the room. *Oh God, Oscar*. She stood up.

"Simon?"

"Uh... Kate. I... er... I think perhaps you might want to..." He gestured helplessly. He looked beseechingly at Kate, his eyebrows tilted in pitiful brackets, all anger forgotten for the moment as she caught his eye.

Just at that moment, before she could speak, the culprit himself made a dramatic entrance. Oscar dashed across the room as though pursued by the devil, up onto the hall table, leaving a vase of flowers tottering.

"Oscar!" Kate jumped up. "You naughty boy." She quickly bent to pick him up. "Please excuse us a moment." Blushing, she hurried toward the bathroom with the guilty cat. "Bad kitty," she whispered as Eli guffawed and Sharon clucked.

"I'll just..." Simon cleared his throat and followed her to a chorus of muffled laughter.

"Oh, Oscar, are you feeling unwell, kitty?" She set him down in her bedroom and closed the door, then opened the connecting door between her guest bathroom and private en suite where she kept Oscar's litter box, efficiently eliminating the problem— Oscar had missed his litter box by six inches. She flushed the offending matter away, spritzed the rooms with deodorizer, flicked on the fan, and was disinfecting the floor when she realized Simon was leaning in the door frame watching her.

"I smelled it, but I didn't see where... you know..." He was choking, trying not to laugh. It was too bizarre to believe.

"Don't be silly, it's nothing you could deal with. I'm so embarrassed. I try hard to keep my personal... stuff separate from my workspace, but– Sometimes his illnesses get a bit messy." She stood up and gave her hands a thorough scrubbing in her own sink, while he stood awkwardly behind her with is hands thrust like incriminating evidence into his pockets, peering through to her bedroom.

At last she looked up and caught his eye in the mirror. Their serious expressions gave way to smirks, then grins, and finally crumpled into guffaws of laughter that brought tears to their eyes.

She dried her hands and turned to face him, still laughing, and his smile suddenly fell. "Kate," he whispered.

Her heart leapt to her throat, thrashing like a trapped bird. Discerning his intention, she sobered. "Don't."

He grasped her shoulders and pulled her towards him earnestly. "We have to talk. We can't leave things as they are."

"There is nothing to discuss." She tried to pull away.

"Kate." He searched her eyes. She shook her head silently, dropping her eyes. He bent his head quickly and brushed his lips to hers, but she turned her head, and caught her breath. "Don't run from me." He caught her chin with his fingertips and moved to kiss her again, but she turned her body away.

"Simon," she hissed. "For God's sake. Have some sense." She slipped out of the bathroom, shutting the connecting door, and strode away from him. Her pulse hammered, and she was sure her flushed face would give her away. How could she go on if he insisted on behaving this way?

Kate returned to the group, covering her discomfort with strained, excited laughter and apologized for Oscar's poor hygiene and bad timing and offered fresh coffee in a breathless, agitated voice that sounded slightly hysterical even to her own ears. Simon rejoined them and sat down sullenly without another word.

Sharon squinted at him suspiciously and he flashed her an insincere grin, and Kate felt as though she were teetering on the edge of a precipice. Any fool could see there was something wrong now. And Sharon was no fool.

"Alright. Where were we?" Kate resumed in a shrill, synthetic tone.

"We were just finishing up the section on consultation and joint decision making. I drafted something while you were gone. Have a look." Sharon handed a page to Kate, who looked it over. Sharon was being terribly helpful now, as though she couldn't wait for these sessions to end.

Kate nodded stiffly, made a small amendment and handed it over to D'arcy and Eli. "This might work. What do you think?" Eli held the paper while they read and then passed it to Simon, who scanned it quickly.

As much as she would like to, she couldn't forget that Simon had asked to make a point earlier. "Simon. You had something you wanted to add to the section on family?"

"Yes." He flipped a page. "Yes, here are my notes. I thought the draft was a little one-sided. I know the concern has been about interference. But, really there should be room for family in every couple's life. D'arcee's parents are already across the country."

Kate noticed Eli stiffen. "But some families truly do harm with their meddling," Kate said pointedly, remembering Mrs. Duchamp's officious phone call, meeting Simon's gaze steadily and then retreating again.

"Undoubtedly. But it's my belief that most families interfere because they care." He lifted his chin. "Perhaps the problem could be solved, or at least alleviated, not by excluding family involvement, but by spending enough time together to ensure there is a strong foundation to the relationship, and a better appreciation for each other's character."

"You haven't met my in-laws, Simon," said Eli with a sharp look, his jaw jutting. "They never gave me a half a chance. Even before they met me, they'd written me off as some kind of deadbeat loser. I've hardly seen them since we got married, and they're barely civil when I answer the phone."

"Have you gone to Montreal for a visit since you've been together?" enquired Kate. She didn't want to agree with Simon, but he made a valid point.

"Of course," said D'arcy. "Right away, when we decided to get married. It didn't go well." Her voice trailed off.

Eli snorted bitterly. "That's an understatement."

"We ended up getting married here, without them." D'arcy added.

"And you haven't seen them since?" Simon asked.

"I haven't spent time with them, no, and with good reason," Eli replied, scowling. "They despise me."

"Eli! That's not true. I know you have a hard time believing it, but Mother and Papa do like you. They just worry a lot. They are very protective of me, so the whole thing was a shock for them," D'arcy explained.

"It's been six years, cherie," said Eli, leaning back and crossing his arms.

Simon jumped in. "That's my point, right there." He jabbed his forefinger into the air. "You got off to a rough start six years ago, and you've never recovered from it. Instead of tolerating this partial estrangement, which can hardly be easy for D'arcy and isn't practical if you have kids and they become grandparents, why not assume that you need to start over." He drew a long breath, and spread he hands in supplication. "I mean make a point of spending time together and getting to know each other?" Simon folded his hands together and looked around expectantly. "Bond a little."

"I go back regularly, but they won't speak to each other," D'arcy said quietly. "Every year they invite us to visit. Both of us. In fact there is a standing invitation for Christmas." D'arcy sat forward, earnest. "Why don't we go this year?"

"No way!" Eli raised his hands in protest. "After the things they said to me?"

"What things?" asked Simon.

Wait a minute? Who's running this show? Kate glared at Simon, her nostrils flaring in annoyance. "Stay calm, please, Eli. Maybe you could tell us what happened six years ago that got you off to such a bad start."

He stiffened, dropping his eyes. "There's nothing to tell. They never liked me."

"Eli. They do. You have to give them a chance, too," D'arcy said.

Eli shot to his feet and took a few steps away from the group. Kate's heart raced wildly. *What's going on?* Kate shot Simon a look. *Do something!* Sharon was staring at Eli as though he might explode, and Kate thought she might be right. Simon stood up too, and moved toward Eli, speaking softly. "Sit down. Tell us more."

Eli's dark eyes were tormented. He stood with clenched fists. "No. Just drop it. I won't go groveling to those people."

Kate approached them, conciliatory, her voice calm and gentle. "Please sit down. Perhaps we came at this from the wrong angle. I think I understand what Simon is getting at, but it doesn't have to be threatening for you. Let's just talk it out a bit." She lay a gentle hand on Eli's arm, trying to coax him back to his seat. D'arcy's face was grim. Eli yanked his arm free and strode a few feet away, turning his back.

D'arcy stood up and followed him. "Babe, why don't we call them right now. You don't have to go back there. Maybe we could invite them here for Christmas. We can show them our place, take them on a tour of your studio and the gallery. It would be a real eye opener for them. And then you'd see too. They aren't against you." D'arcy's voice rose and fell in a soothing lullaby, while Eli's shoulders drew up, even more tense.

Oh, this was bad. Really, really bad. Tension in the room was building. Kate could feel Eli moving closer to catastrophe. She stepped toward Simon and leaned close, hissing, "Why did you bring this up? We were so close."

Simon whirled on her, nothing like his usual serene self. "You call this close? You've got to be... It was just glossed over. I saw it right away. This is a major stumbling block..." He lowered his voice. "They have to work through it."

"You didn't have to rile them up," she said indignantly. She clenched her fists, frowning. Damn it, she was frazzled. She wasn't behaving like a mediator at all.

"I didn't rile them. It's already there. You can't hide from old wounds. You have to face them," he looked searchingly into her eyes, and she could see that he was speaking to her, about her, as well as Eli and D'arcy.

"Why are you doing this?" Kate was seething, and the words escaped in a moan through her gritted teeth. They were only a few inches apart, and their conversation did not go unnoticed by the others, she knew that.

"I'm an honest man. And I expect honesty from everyone else." He met her eye steadily. "There are too many secrets and lies in this room." He drew a deep breath, and dropped his shoulders, exhaling.

Kate noticed Sharon glaring at them. She knew he was right. Not only was there something weird going on with D'arcy that she hadn't been able to figure out, but Eli held onto some deeply rooted issues with his in-laws that were always going to stand in the way of their relationship if they were never resolved. But Simon should have spoken to her privately. As if he'd had a chance. She sighed, stroking her furrowed brow with her fingertips.

Sharon's face suddenly appeared between them like a darting cobra, her smile rigid and hostile. "Don't think for one second I don't know what's going on here," she spat. "And you thought I would make trouble for you. It looks like you've brought it on yourself, this time." She moved off toward D'arcy, who was still pleading with Eli.

"Eli, please reconsider. If we invited them... Better yet, if you invited them for Christmas, it would mean so much. You have no idea how that would turn things around," D'arcy begged, her voice a desolate whine.

"That'll be the day, D'arcy." Eli was suddenly cool and calm, in a dangerous way that unnerved Kate, her senses prickling.

"Eli, please." D'arcy wailed, moving close to him, her hand on his arm.

"Abso-fuckin'-lutely not! They would have to come crawling on hands and knees in abject apology before I would even consider it." His smile was sardonic, and he tilted his head as he gazed at D'arcy, his ebony eyes glinting.

D'arcy flinched, backing away. "We have to work this out. You know we do."

"You do, chere. You have to decide who you trust. Me or them. If you choose me, I'll be there for you. But if you want Mother and Papa in your life, you can count me out.!"

"Eli. No ultimatums. Please, be reasonable." Kate tried to interject, but she knew it was too late.

"No. It's not an ultimatum." He was disconcertingly calm, his voice flat. "I just realized that I'm so fucking tired of being a pawn in someone else's game. I've got my own life to live. I don't need this." Eli grabbed his jacket from the back of a dining room chair and strolled to the door, as though he hadn't just tossed his marriage away without a care. He opened it and left, not bothering to close it behind him.

"No-ooo." D'arcy sobbed helplessly. She turned her back on the others, and rummaged in her bag for a tissue, weeping into it, her shoulders shaking.

Kate moved closer, and rubbed her back. "Calm yourself, D'arcy. You know how volatile he can be. Don't give up. We'll work this out yet."

"Hah." Sharon cracked. "I'm not so sure. I knew this would never work. Madame Duchamp was right all along. This is what she predicted."

"What?" Darcy whirled around, her face streaked with mascara.

"When your mother retained me, she said it would be Eli who walked out in the end. She said he was a stubborn little boy who had to have his own way."

"I know Mother doesn't approve of him, but she would never cheer for us to break up. She knows I love Eli." The flow of tears resumed as her face crumpled pitifully.

"She knows you'll be better off without him," scolded Sharon.

Kate embraced D'arcy and rubbed her back again, trying to sooth. She turned on Sharon bitterly. "I suspected you had a vested interest all along, Sharon. More than just skepticism about mediation. Tell me the truth. Were you hired to make sure it didn't work out? Is that it?" Kate jutted her chin at Sharon, her voice rising in anger.

"You'd like that wouldn't you," Sharon's voice was filled with rancor. "That would make it so easy for you. Then you wouldn't have to admit to failure. But no, I'm afraid it's not true. Skeptical or not, I'm here in good faith. The Duchamps really do want whatever makes their little girl happy, however foolish it seems to them. No, I'm afraid you'll have to face up to the limitation of your idealistic methods. That's the point isn't it? You've been more invested in a reconciliation for your own reasons than because it's right for your clients." Sharon narrowed her eyes. "I know about your little award, you know. I believe your romantic entanglement has thrown you off your game, and compromised your professional integrity." She threw her head back defiantly, her small feral teeth showing between narrow unsmiling lips, and Kate's heart went cold. "You can expect me to file a complaint, by the way."

"Sharon. Don't, please," Simon entreated sharply.

Ignoring him, Sharon, too, picked up her coat, and threw a withering glance at Simon. "Let me know when you want the divorce proceedings to recommence, dear," she said in a cool voice to D'arcy, and walked calmly out the open door.

D'arcy's erupted into fresh tears and Kate held her for some time until she was calmer. "It's not over. Don't worry. Everyone's emotional today. Let's give ourselves some time to calm down and think a bit. I'll call you in a couple of days. We'll go over it all and we'll make a plan." She held D'arcy's face in her palms and nodded with an encouraging smile, though her resolve was faint. Just what would that plan be? Things couldn't be much worse.

D'arcy's head came up, her brows knit, and she looked so young and vulnerable. "What was Sharon talking about? What complaint?"

Kate closed her eyes, resigned. It was time to face her problems head on. "Sit down a minute, D'arcy." She led D'arcy back to the sofa and sat across from her, leaning forward, elbows on knees. "I should have talked to you about this long ago." Simon lingered, standing with his arms crossed watching them, chewing the inside of his cheek. She sighed. "What Sharon is referring to... is the fact that Simon and I... were more than acquaintances in college. Much more." Darcy's eyes widened. "Technically, we should have divulged that fact the moment he walked into the boardroom that first day." She squirmed in her seat. "But, it was such a long time ago and we hadn't stayed in touch. I... don't know why, but I just let it go. And Simon too." She peered into D'arcy's face. "That was wrong."

"Go on..."

"Well that's it. We've become reacquainted, obviously. Then Sharon found out that we knew... that we had ahh... a relationship back in college and she's been making a fuss ever since."

"A—are you together again?" asked D'arcy, her eyes wide.

Kate's breath froze in her chest. "No!"

"Yes." Simon spoke simultaneously. Kate shot him a hard glare.

D'arcy's looked from one to the other, the light dawning in her eyes. "Oh. I see."

Kate drew a deep breath. "It's complicated, D'arcy. Because of the past. But I promise, as long as I'm representing you, my focus is exclusively on you and Eli and your needs. You can trust me to be completely impartial, and to advise and represent you both. Our..." She waved a hand between Simon and herself "... relationship can have no bearing on your case, no matter what Sharon might imply. She's just trying to make trouble." She smiled reassuringly.

"She's succeeding, isn't she?" D'arcy said.

Kate pressed her lips together. "That remains to be seen. She knows I'm to be presented with a career award in the new year. So she thinks she's got me by the tail. Anyway, it shouldn't concern you, so don't worry about it. I'll take care of it." Kate glanced over at Simon, who stood, tight lipped, his arms folded over his chest. A ripple of nerves fluttered through her, from her knees to her throat.

Simon walked D'arcy to the door and, closing it behind her when she left, turned to face Kate, a look of apprehension in his eyes, his jaw set, the corner of his mouth twitching.

In that moment, Simon seemed to be the cause of all her problems. Her frayed emotions snapped their bindings. "What the hell do you think you're doing? We almost had this case resolved."

Simon shrugged and moved towards her. "There was no opportunity to speak to you about my concerns about Eli or

D'arcy. Maybe you would have handled it differently. But under the circumstances... " He lifted both hands, palms open, and shrugged. "It had to come out. I could see it festering."

Anger rose up inside her, her voice stuck in her tight throat, threatening to break. A rock hard tension gathered in her chest and stomach. "You can bet I would have handled it differently. What makes you an expert mediator, all of a sudden? You're the one that fanned that fire. It wouldn't have been an issue."

"Bullshit. Don't tell me you didn't see it. That you're satisfied with such a superficial analysis," Simon's voice rose in indignation, and his face darkened. "It would have blown up in their faces. They would have been back in divorce court in months. Be honest. You're better than that. You can't have sent them off in the belief that everything was fine."

"We were on the verge of a resolution. Why are you trying to sabotage this case? It's important to me. My reputation is at stake here." Kate was trembling now, her anger ebbing away as she shifted her focus to her clients instead of her own emotional turmoil.

"That's ridiculous. I'm trying to help." Simon's hands flew up, pleading as he turned away.

"How can a big face off between Eli and D'arcy's family help them? Eli has no deeper problem with the in-laws than class difference. It's his insecurities. Trying to force them together will only be painful for everyone."

"I didn't say it would be easy," Simon quietly agreed.

"Eli's temper is so capricious." Kate thought that Simon might be right. "He was strange today."

"Yeah. Dangerously cool. It gave me a very uneasy feeling."

"Has he told you something you're not at liberty to say?"

"No. I wish he had." Simon raised a loose fist to his chin and nodded with these words. "I should call him and see what I can find out."

She bristled again. "No." She didn't want him so closely involved in her work. "I mean, don't get his back up. I want to be able to talk to him, too. Maybe even meet one-on-one. We have a good rapport. He might confide in me," said Kate. "You don't have to worry about it."

"*You* need to work on D'arcy," said Simon.

Oh. The tendons in her neck tightened. Now he was telling her what to do.

"I'm more convinced than ever that she's withholding something. She seems stressed. She's gained weight. She's so... emotional all of a sudden," he added pensively.

What an asinine, sexist comment. Kate's frustration was building. "Why wouldn't she be stressed? Look what she's going through. Women are emotional. So are men. So what?"

"Don't get so defensive." He stepped back slightly, his brows coming up in alarm. "I mean, she's changed so much in the past month; she's like a different woman. I thought I got a pretty good reading when I first met her. But now, she's less confident. And I feel like she's hiding something. It's the other thing that needs to surface before they can reconcile. I'm convinced of it."

Kate found it difficult to meet his eyes. She gazed broodingly out the window at the ceaseless rain. She felt cold suddenly, and shivered. "I don't know. I think she's just feeling vulnerable," she mumbled. "And why wouldn't she be? She's finding it difficult to trust you given your past behavior."

Simon started. He was silent, and studied her for a moment. "You mean—Eli?—His past behavior?"

"That's what I said." She glanced at him, feeling restless and irritable, and shifted her weight. Isn't it?

"Right." He stood silently for a moment, considering her. "I think Eli's come a long way, actually. I believe he's really committed to the changes. But now it's D'arcy's turn to come clean. She has to be honest with herself and with him. But there's something more... " he paused.

"Why are you picking on D'arcy?" Kate crossed her arms.

He shook his head, plainly perplexed. "I'm not picking on her. It's very subtle. I think because of the power imbalance, she's accustomed to..." He scowled in thought. "In order for him to take responsibility, she has to give him some room. She has to trust him, and rely on him. She has to let go of her control. Soften up a little."

She stiffened. "Why are you so hard on independent women? I get the impression you would like them all to be soft little maidens, all innocence and dependence."

Simon's mouth fell open in astonishment, his eyes widening. "Where is this coming from? I'm talking about D'arcy."

"Are you?" Kate shook her head, looking at him. "It's almost like you're afraid of strong women. You've transferred all your own fears about powerful women to D'arcy. And maybe to me, too. Is that why you have to undermine my efforts to mediate?"

He stared at her for a long moment, his lips pursed thoughtfully. "It's the opposite. I thought I married a strong woman. But I've learned what real strength looks like, that's all. And it's not hard. It's about having the courage to be open and vulnerable." Simon stepped closer and dipped his head to peer deeply into her eyes, "And I'm not trying to interfere with your role here. I'm truly trying to help you to help them. I care about these two. But they won't make a go of it with skeletons in their closets."

"I don't believe you," she cried, turning away, her arms akimbo.

"God, you can be stubborn, woman. You're in denial. Maybe Sharon's right. You've missed some critical problems, here. I don't think you're thinking clearly." His voice dropped to a whisper. "I know I'm not." He took another step toward her and reached out one hand, running his fingertips lightly across her shoulder.

His touch seared her and unleashed all the emotions she'd been holding in so tightly for three days. "Don't touch me!" She whirled, pulling away from his hand.

"You can't go on pretending nothing is happening. That you're not affected by it." He stood quietly beside her.

Why did he have to be so calm? So mature? She felt as though she was being boxed into a corner. A sudden, desperate thought surfaced.

"Oh, I think I understand. You want this case to end so you can pursue your own selfish interests. You don't care about Eli and D'arcy at all, do you? You just want to end this case to get it out of your way. That's it, isn't it?"

He grunted cynically. "Look who's talking." He shook his head, grimacing. "You know that's not fair. I did it because it's *right*. If I wanted the case to hurry up and end, all I had to do was keep my mouth shut. As you said, we were wrapping up. You could have sent them away happy and washed your hands of them. But I do care what happens to them. I can't pretend not to see what I plainly see. That would have been dishonest and irresponsible."

She knew he was right. Knowing that he did see it and she had missed it is what upset her the most. She tucked her loose hair behind her ears. Her emotional turmoil over her relationship with Simon had truly dulled her insight. Sharon had every right to report her to the Mediators' Society. She had allowed private feelings to interfere with her objectivity and effectiveness at work.

Suddenly, she was overwhelmed with the foreboding that all her years of hard work making herself into a respected, competent mediator had come undone. Her breath felt short and her chest too tight. Her throat constricted as she felt burning behind her eyes. *Why is this happening? What have I done to deserve all this chaos and disruption?* Simon's face blurred behind a curtain of tears, and a small whimper escaped.

Then his arms came around her and she could hold back no longer, letting her tears and her fears and disappointments spill over unchecked. She could feel his soft hands stroking her back and hair and hear his muffled voice crooning soothing words against her ear. "Shhhh. It's okay. It's going to be okay."

Some minutes later, she raised her head, spent, and sniffling, accepted the handkerchief he held out for her. She turned aside, wiping her eyes and blowing her nose and then, pocketing the sodden hanky, stood uncertainly, her eyes downcast.

"Better?" he asked. He bent his head and gently pressed his lips against her forehead for a few exquisite moments, and gently stroked her hair once more.

She nodded, and a hiccup escaped her throat. She was surprised how much better she felt, for just having been held by him, despite the fact that nothing had changed. It shouldn't be that way. But it was. Oh, how she longed to lose herself in his arms, and forget everything.

"You don't really believe what you told D'arcy, do you? That everything will be okay?" he asked.

She looked up at him. His expression was pensive, his eyes searching. "No. I don't. I don't know." Maybe it wouldn't be as dire as Sharon implied, but something would happen. Kate gripped her knot pendant, gnawing her cheek. Maybe she deserved to be reprimanded.

His mouth twitched into a half-hearted, asymmetrical smile, and fell again. "I do, actually."

"How can you? You've just admitted that neither of us has been thinking clearly lately. I plainly am not able to concentrate, and am not in tune with my clients as I should be, however much I disagree with what you did today."

"Everyone has a private life. But people are expected to deal with it and carry on doing their jobs. This is no different, Kate."

He shrugged. "We may be involved with each other, but it poses no conflict with our roles as agents for D'arcy and Eli." He paused. "As long as we can be honest about it."

"You really believe that?" It was a comforting thought. The problem was Kate wasn't sure she bought it.

"I do. Can I make you some fresh tea?"

She nodded gratefully. That was the trouble with Simon, she thought. Just when she ought to be tossing him out on his ear, she really cherished having him around. She had come to rely on him as a trusted friend. And right now, she really needed a friend. *How the devil am I going to deal with this?*

He carried two mugs of steaming tea back to the living room, and they sat down on the sofa, facing the rain-streaked window. She settled back, tucking her legs under her, and held her tea cupped between two hands, letting the steam rise up to warm her face before braving a sip of the soothing hot liquid. A comfortable silence stretched on, during which Kate was viscerally aware of his presence.

Finally, he spoke. "I have to admit, I've underestimated Sharon's trouble-making capacity. I should have made an effort to short-circuit this before now."

"So. You finally see my point?" she asked, with a wan smile.

He turned to face her. Too near, she could feel the heat of his body, and it did wild, frenzied things to her blood. He drew a breath and gazed at her. "I do. Yes. And I'm willing to… give it a rest until this case is resolved. I don't know how I'll stand it. But let me be perfectly clear. You're not through with me. When this is over, I'll be knocking on your door, and wanting to pick up the pieces." His clear blue eyes pierced hers intently as he delivered these words. There was no misunderstanding them.

Her heart leapt into her throat, unbidden. Kate couldn't be sure if she was ecstatic or terrified by this admission. She needed time to sort out her own feelings. It was just as well then, that Simon was willing to give her some space.

It wasn't easy to ignore his rangy body draped across her sofa, the warm musky, masculine smell of him, the creases in his smooth blue cotton shirt and the waving tendrils of golden hair against his collar and over his elfin ears, casually sipping tea with her as though he belonged here. But at least he wasn't devouring her with his eyes. His presence was comforting, but also disconcerting and distracting. *I can get through this without falling apart. I can stay calm and in control.*

She dared to look into his eyes. All she saw there was naked honesty and kindness. Nothing threatening. But she was frightened all the same. "I won't promise anything, Simon. It might be for the best if we just leave things where they are. I don't know. We'll see."

He didn't reply at once, but gazed at her, his sky blue eyes shining with emotion, and at the same time shadowed with questions and doubts. She could see the muscles in his jaw clenching, his nostrils flaring, and his soft, sensual mouth twitching involuntarily as his thoughts swirled. She could hear him breathing against the backdrop of steadily drumming rain on the windowpanes. Finally, he dropped his eyes and nodded once, without a word. When he looked up a moment later, he had put away his raw emotions and his need, and pasted a determinedly cheerful expression on his face, though she still sensed his tension in the flare of his nostrils and set of his jaw.

She offered him a conciliatory smile. No matter what happened, she didn't want to fight with him.

He polished off his tea. "I'd better get going. I have a client coming in this afternoon." He stood up and then hesitated, expectant. He seemed to be as aware as she was that everything was left hanging, uncertain. Was this good-bye, then, for the time being?

She stood and walked with him toward the door. "I'll keep you posted."

Turning at the door, Simon nodded and lifted a hand, reaching toward her cheek, but stopping short. Kate's eyes widened, and she pulled back slightly. If he touched her now, there was no telling what she might do. He dropped his hand with a sigh of resignation.

When he was gone, she stood for a long while by the door, thinking. One thing for certain, Simon's return had turned her entire life upside down, and he wasn't going to let her bury her feelings anymore. Her fingers traced the outline of her eternity knot pendant, as she did when she was stressed, or had difficult questions to ponder. She wore it for a reason. To remind her of the interconnectedness of all phenomena. In other words, to remind her that none of these events were happening in isolation, and that perhaps there was a reason for it all.

If she was serious about her job, her life's work, and truly wanted to help people with their relationships, and maybe help herself, too, then she had two things she knew she had to do. Kate vowed to uncover both Eli and D'arcee's secrets, whatever they might be. And she promised herself that she would have an honest visit with her past. It was time to clean the skeletons out of her own closet.

fourteen

The November rains continued unabated, painting an unbroken haze of grey days without boundaries. After a few days had passed, and Kate had heard from no one on the case, she tried reaching D'arcy. Even though Kate had no explicit strategy as yet, D'arcy undoubtedly needed reassurance. Maybe she could make a lunch date and try to inspire her confidence. If Simon was correct, and she was harbouring a secret, the timing might be just right to bring it out. But there was no answer, and after repeated tries, she decided to switch tacks and try Eli.

Eli remained elusive. She kept getting his voice mail, and when he failed to return her messages, she wondered if there was a remote chance they'd gone away together somewhere. When she finally got through to him early Sunday morning, correctly assuming that she'd catch him in bed, he informed her that he'd been working. That's all. Working. He sounded distracted and aloof. He hadn't spoken to D'arcy and had no idea where she was or if she was alright. It seemed he'd made no effort to contact her in almost a week. He did a good job pretending that he didn't care about his marriage and she had the distinct impression he hung up and crawled right back into bed.

When Kate had caught up on her other work, done her filing, shopping, and even cleaned her fridge, she could no longer avoid calling Sharon. She sat drinking tea while she folded laundry and absent-mindedly watched the Remembrance Day ceremonies on TV. To a backdrop of plaintive bagpipes, she watched dignitaries place battered wreaths against the steps of the war memorial, and her heart squeezed for those poor frail old men huddled bravely against the cold wind and drizzle, their thinning numbers tenaciously holding onto memories of the most horrific, traumatic experiences from their lost youth. Was that really a good thing? It seemed an inevitable part of the human condition, to hold on to pain, to make it a part of your life. Contemplating the meaning of courage, she slowly pressed the mute button and picked up the phone at last, dialing Sharon's cell number, in the off chance she was not at her office.

"Ah. There you are. I was wondering when I'd hear from you," Sharon said.

"I rather thought that I'd be hearing from you," Kate rebutted.

"What can I do for you?"

"I've tried unsuccessfully to reach D'arcy. And Eli doesn't seem to know where she is. Perhaps you've heard something?"

"She's been in Montreal for the past week. Visiting her parents. She's due back on the twentieth." Sharon sounded smug. Kate felt her dander rising. Why wouldn't Sharon know? D'arcy was her client. The rebuff felt like a coded message. Had Kate's confession about Simon alienated D'arcy? Or had Sharon poisoned her against Kate?

"Oh. I see," she replied. "I wanted to meet with her. I guess it will have to wait." What else could she say? She certainly wasn't going to bring up the conflict of interest issue.

"I'll call you when I've spoken with her. If she's interested in meeting with you. I'll let you know."

"Yeah. Thanks." You bitch! Kate ground her teeth until a sharp pain shot through her temples. If she's interested? She didn't need Sharon's approval to meet with D'arcy. She's my client too. Who do you think you are? "I'd appreciate that."

Sharon said nothing for a few uncomfortable moments. Her voice, when she spoke, was a soft growl of contentment. She was really enjoying torturing Kate, like a cat toying with a mouse. "I haven't dropped the professional conduct claim, in case you're wondering. I've looked into the process with the Mediator Roster Society. I'm actually getting the paperwork organized as we speak. You can assume I'll be filing it shortly." Kate felt her stomach drop to the ground. She was actually going to go through with it.

Kate donned a cool, indifferent voice like a cape of courage, which barely hid her rage and trepidation. "Do what you have to do, Sharon."

Sharon cleared her throat. "I guess you and Simon are enjoying getting cozy while the case is on hold."

A tense, relentless silence stretched between them. "Simon and I have not seen each other; nor are we *seeing each other,* Sharon. Your threats don't intimidate me. There is no foundation to your claim."

"Hmmm. We'll see what your executive think about that," Sharon answered haughtily. "Obviously you're willing to gamble your accolades on a not-so-sure thing"

Kate was so agitated after hanging up the phone she found herself standing with her fists clenched, staring into the muted television screen and fuming about Sharon's threats. Looking down at last, she saw she'd crushed the clean handkerchief Simon had handed her last week during her bout of tears. She'd have to iron it now.

With some sense of perspective, Kate called up Alexa to confirm their spa appointment the next afternoon. Kate had not had a chance to talk to her yet about recent events. Meanwhile, she needed a walk to clear her head.

The bracing November air slapped her face and tossed her hair as she made her way from Yaletown down to the boardwalk on the north side of False Creek. She decided to walk toward Science World and admire the boats in the marina en route. Though it was a holiday, the cold wind and gusts of wetness that shuddered down from the sky kept the crowds thin. A blast of cold air and a sudden shower of fat icy raindrops made her stop and tug the hood of her anorak closer, hunching her shoulders. She turned to the white steel railing for a moment, her back to the weather. Metal rigging and stays on the sailboats tied up at the dock swayed and rattled loudly against their steel masts, drowning the sound of the wind momentarily.

From the corner of her eye, she thought she saw a familiar dark-clad figure approaching on the boardwalk behind her, but when she turned to look, nothing was there but a retreating cyclist wobbling slightly against the wind, and some people in bright jackets strolling in the far distance. She continued her walk, pondering Sharon's troublesome interference. She could make Kate's life incredibly difficult if she pursued this course of action. But perhaps she was only bluffing. It was bad enough the case had gone so badly off the rails, and now this. She was distressed to think how the society executive would see what she had done, or failed to do. It was, potentially, a huge embarrassment, especially because she was in the limelight right now. A professional reprimand, because surely that's the worst they would do to her, would cast a pall over her award and presentation at the AGM. Especially since notices of reprimands and disciplinary measures were circulated to the membership. But could she wish her relationship with Simon away, simply because it was inconvenient or difficult for her? *Do I really want to?*

Relationship. She wasn't even sure that's what it was. So much emotional baggage, and for what? No matter what eventually happened with Simon, the feelings he had aroused in her made it clear, she needed more. She could never be satisfied with less. Staying with Jay would have been a terrible mistake. Both of them would live to regret it.

She had to resolve these questions once and for all. She had to be strong, and fight both her fear of being alone, and her fear of intimacy.

"Mmm." Alexa's eyes were closed behind her severe angular frames. "This is just what I needed."

Wrapped in fluffy white terrycloth robes, they were perched side by side on high faux-leather reclining chairs overlooking a tropical oasis with palm trees and a softly bubbling waterfall, their feet immersed in identical tubs of hot soapy water. A ceramic dish of dried fruit and nuts sat between them.

"Me too. Much better than squash," Kate murmured, wiggling her toes in the hot water, inhaling the soothing scent of essential oils– something tropical and sweetly floral. She felt herself relaxing into the sound of the burbling fountain. Sighing, she said, "We should go to Maui again someday soon."

"I'm sorry about the past two weeks. Work's been so intense. Two project deadlines, three proposals. And Krystof wanted my help hiring a couple new interns, so there were interviews, etc."

"Mmm." Kate secretly fumed whenever Alexa mentioned her boss. She tried to keep too much judgment out of her tone of voice, not wishing to ruin the mood. "And how is Krystof?" She reached for a slice of mango and nibbled it's sweet chewy flesh.

Alexa sighed. "You know. He's back with his wife… again."

"I guess I don't have to ask if you're still sleeping with him."

"Not right now." Alexa shifted in her chair and flexed her wet feet in the tub. "Only when he's separated from his wife."

Kate ground her teeth together. They'd had this debate a million times. "Has it occurred to you that you shouldn't do it at all, as long as he's still married to her?" She suffered a twist of guilt, realizing that she'd somehow fallen into a parallel situation with Simon.

Alexa exhaled and peered over her frames. "Not every married couple is meant to be together. You're somewhat biased in that department. I know you'd like to but you can't fix every failed marriage."

Two young aestheticians entered the room and settled down opposite each of their clients, pulling out towels and toolkits. Cheerful greeting were exchanged, pink and claret red polish colours selected, and they set to work. Alexa let out a long slow breath.

"How about you? What's new?" Alexa grabbed a fistful of nuts and fruit, popping them into her open mouth.

Tension swirled through Kate's muscles, and she felt light-headed. She didn't reply, even though she knew Alexa eventually would squeeze every detail out of her.

Alexa sat up, pulling down her dark glasses and glaring at Kate over their tops. "You're scaring me. Prolonged silence from you can only mean one thing. C'mon. Spill the beans."

"I don't know where to begin," Kate said, a hot tingling pressing at her eyes.

"At the beginning of course."

The two young women bent their heads over their clients' toes, working diligently.

Kate filled Alexa in on her squash game with Simon and its disturbing fallout. "He asked me out for dinner. Just to talk… you know… about the past."

"Uh-huh." Alexa's eyes sparkled.

Kate was feeling sheepish. She knew Alexa was way ahead of her, and just needed the details, but it was uncomfortable to have to relate the facts, now that so much had happened. It made it more real somehow. "We went for Indian food. And there was a huge tapestry from the Kama Sutra right over our table." Kate gave her a pained expression. Alexa laughed heartily at Kate's description of the murals, and Simon's obvious discomfort upon finding them sitting under such sensual images. "It was all downhill from there."

"Downhill? Don't you mean smooth sailing?"

Kate squirmed and kept her gaze fixed on the trickling waterfall across from them. The aesthetician poked and pruned and scrubbed at her feet, distracting her.

"So then he took you home."

"Not so fast," Kate said. "First I had to have another whopper of an anxiety attack. Then of course he had to take me home." Kate wished her story stopped there.

"Aaaand...?" Alexa prompted while the aestheticians held their breath.

Kate glanced at them, lowering her voice. "Well, I don't know what I was thinking but..." Kate felt a shiver of remembered sensual pleasure. "Oh, Alex. It's so complicated. You can't imagine how hard this is for me."

"I can imagine, yes." She didn't skip a beat. "But did you sleep with him?"

"Shhhh."

A small intake of breath emanated from one of the girls, prompting a severe glance from her companion as she reached for her clippers.

"What's going on exactly? What did he say? What did he do? What did *you* do?" Alexa leaned in expectantly. "How did it compare to Jay? He's pretty hot."

She groaned. Thinking of Jay just made her feel worse. Despicable, discomposed.

The aesthetician shifted Kate's feet, wrapping them in soft blue towels. Kate shared her fears about becoming intimate with Simon again, and how she'd really wanted to avoid it, but something else had happened, so much beyond her control.

"No comparison. It was an amazing evening —night— I guess I should say. Like a reunion with a lost part of myself. I forgot everything. We fit together so beautifully. And he seemed to feel the same way."

"That sounds like a good thing." Alexa caught the aestheticians gaping open mouthed, but her narrowed eyes sent them quickly back to work, painting perfect red crescents of polish in expert strokes.

"But in the morning— " Kate winced, remembering the painful collision of his tender feelings and her naked terror. "In the morning, it was so— he started to say *something*..."

"No way." Alexa stopped, a handful of dried apricots and almonds half-way to her open mouth, smoky green eyes piercing Kate over her dark-framed spectacles.

"Well, I may have jumped to conclusions, but in that moment I was suddenly so afraid, I knew we couldn't go on. I was feeling quite overwhelmed. There's just no knowing what I might have said. And I knew, I just knew, that I couldn't trust my feelings."

"I suppose you're falling in love with him again, aren't you?" Alexa's face was twisted into the familiar wry smile she wore whenever the subject of love came up, as though she were referring to fairies or alien abductions.

"But how do I know that? How do I know it's love, and not just some sick dependency? Or a fear of being alone? Maybe my perfect mate hasn't even shown up yet. Why is this so hard for me?"

"What about Jay?" Alexa sobered. "Did you give him an answer yet?"

Kate gave her a sad smile and shook her head. "On Halloween. I finally told him I just didn't have the right feelings for him. That I never would. Do you honestly think I could have been with Simon if I hadn't broken off with Jay?"

"I guess not. Not you." Alexa shook her head sadly. "What a waste. But you do have feelings for Simon."

"Yes. I don't know. I mean, how do I know it's *real* and not imaginary? I mean, he's still married, and has a daughter. How can I trust this thing? I don't know what's worse, blithely carrying on and then getting dumped because I've imagined some grand love affair, and having to crawl out of the ashes again, or waking up in a few years and thinking, 'Who the hell is this guy? I don't even know him!'"

Alexa frowned, understanding Kate's fear. "You've got trust issues, you know that. But Simon is the one man you seem to feel strongly about. From what you've told me, what's not to love? Just because you fell in love with him before, and are falling again, doesn't mean it's *not* real. Maybe he *is* the one. Maybe that's exactly what it feels like." She made a wry face. "Hey. What do I know about love? I'm not even convinced it exists."

Kate reached across and squeezed her hand.

"How does he compare to Jay, or Grant, for example? Grant was great, too, and that fizzled." Grant was Kate's previous boyfriend, almost three years ago, a darkly handsome architect that Alex had introduced her to, who had finally stormed out in frustration at Kate's lack of commitment, or, she had to admit to herself, attention. She had been content to sail along in a static state of semi-attachment, relieved that there were at least no difficulties to overcome. So she had thought. She had felt safe. There hadn't really been anything wrong with Grant, either. Not quite tall enough, perhaps... It was all kind of lukewarm, that's all, just like Jay, and she hadn't missed him when he was gone.

Kate sighed deeply in reply. "I agree with you. When I'm calm, and I'm with him, I love everything about Simon. But I'm a nervous wreck lately. These attacks— I've been getting paranoid. I-I think Simon has triggered memories. I've been having dreams. I know I've made the right decision with Jay, but I've passed up an opportunity to be with a really good man –handsome, successful, fun, and I know he really loved me– because of something that's wrong with *me*. What if I broke up with him for the wrong reasons? What if my past has ruined me forever, Alex? Am I so damaged I can't make a relationship work with anyone?"

Alexa thought about that for a long time. It was so quiet it was clear the aestheticians had stopped breathing altogether.

Then Alex met Kate's eye with a steady gaze. "I don't have the answers, Kate, but you might be onto something. Let me throw this idea at you. What if it isn't about the guy, and whether he's the right one for you? What if your focus on the perfect partnership is a way to avoid commitment? Because if you made a commitment to someone, you'd have to open up completely, and give more of yourself than you're comfortable giving."

Kate scowled. Simon's voice suddenly echoed in her head. The morning she'd stormed out of his bedroom, he'd said, *Nobody's perfect, Kate. But we all need someone.*

Do we?

After their pedicure, Kate finished her story in the locker room, with the news of Sharon's aggressive stance on professional conduct, and a general idea of her tough day with her clients.

"That's good. It can't hurt the conduct claim if nothing happens for a while. It will probably blow over. It'll become clearer with more time to think." Trust Alex to see the upside of even the long delay.

"It looks like time away from Simon is exactly what I'm going to get, whether I need it or not. It's another week until the wife returns, and who knows if I'll be able to get the husband back to the table." She bent to slip on flip-flops. Thinking uncomfortably of how long her obsession with Simon had gone on with no encouragement at all, she said with a wry smile, "Time isn't always the best test, you know."

Alexa buttoned her shirt and studied Kate intently for a few moments. "You know, I wouldn't worry, honey. You may be feeling confused, but there's a little fantasy in every love story. What's important is, is it mutual? Is there mutual liking and respect? Enough to make it last? Honestly, I don't know anyone that agonizes over relationships the way you do. I think you're over-thinking the whole thing. That's your problem– too much therapy. You've done the work. You're not deluded, just phobic. But falling in love again doesn't mean you're going to have another nervous breakdown. That doesn't even make sense." She stood up. "You have to learn to trust yourself. I suppose, any real meaningful relationship is going to require the kind of intimacy that means putting yourself out there, getting vulnerable. You've got to believe that you'll survive no matter what happens. Believe in yourself, that you're worth it." Opening her black leather handbag, she pulled out her wallet and dropped a ten-dollar bill on the credenza.

It sounded like Alexa wasn't sure if Kate could trust herself either, understandably, since she'd dragged her through her every emotional trial of the past sixteen years.

"So you're an expert on intimacy all of a sudden," Kate said, smirking at her friend.

"Yeah, well…" Alexa opened her arms for a hug. "I know it's different this time, honey. You seem really wound up. You've been through a lot. Maybe you need some more time. Take it slow."

Kate wrapped her arms around Alexa and gave her a big bear hug and an air kiss.

"I've gotta run. Believe it or not, I've got some drawings to review before I can go to bed."

"You work way too hard." Kate watched her friend rush out into the wet night, wondering if Alexa was right. In any case, it made her feel much better to have her say so. Funny, she'd been half expecting Alex to tell her to forget about Simon. She was always the one who was hardest on men, especially the ones Kate had dated over the years. No one was ever good enough for her friend Kate. It hadn't stopped Alex from dating the longest string of losers Kate had ever met, including Krystof. But then, Alex could always take care of herself. *The question now is, can I?*

fifteen

Kate spent most of the next day meeting with her other clients away from her loft, which was an exhausting affair because of the endless rain, and the challenge of driving, parking and getting around without getting soaked. Vancouver was a dreadfully dreary place in November, and it could be very discouraging. It was a relief to finally return home in the late afternoon. Her chat with Alexa had been oddly energizing, and despite the long tiring day, Kate had gathered her courage and decided to take the bull by the horns—that bull being Sharon, of course. She hung up her drenched overcoat, left her umbrella open to dry, and quickly made a cup of tea before she lost her nerve.

Picking up the phone, she called Sharon's office and asked to speak to her directly. "Hello Sharon. How are you?" she greeted her matter-of-factly when she came on the line.

"How can I help you?" Sharon's voice held its usual icy inflection. Always polite and anything but friendly.

"I don't want to beat around the bush. I'd like to deal as honestly and directly with this concern of yours as possible, put it to bed so we can get on with our work."

"Interesting choice of words," replied Sharon cattily.

Good grief, would she not let up? "It's not my way to play power games. I want to speak frankly with you about Simon."

"Go on. I'm listening." Sharon sounded intrigued.

"I'm not denying that we knew each other back in university. I'm not even trying to tell you we didn't have a very close relationship. But we're talking about sixteen years ago, when we were very young students, and relationships then could be quite superficial. It's more of an embarrassment than anything, to find ourselves working together now. You can imagine how we felt that day he walked in the board room."

"Mmm. Perhaps."

"The point is, it was a mistake not to disclose the depth of our relationship to the group, I admit that, but in the moment we were taken by surprise. Afterwards, it seemed petty to bring it up, so we let it slide. That was an error in protocol, but not one that was motivated by a concern for our performance. There is no conflict of interest here, Sharon." As she spoke the words, Kate believed them wholeheartedly. Under the surface, however, there still lingered the fear that while her judgment was not impaired, her concentration was.

"Your explanation for the distant past is all well and good, Kate, but you can't deny that there is a new relationship growing, whether on the foundations of the old one or not is immaterial. You can't deny that you're interested in Simon... romantically, I mean, of course."

"Simon is an interesting man, as you well know. I won't deny that we've become reacquainted, but how is that different from any two people who work together? It has nothing to do with our prior relationship, in any case." *Not the way you think.* "You've known Simon better than I do, and for longer. If I didn't know better, I could easily assume that you were interested in romance with Simon. He's a very eligible man, after all."

It was a very veiled counter-threat. It was a dangerous move, Kate knew, but if she could just get Sharon down off her high horse long enough to agree to give her some breathing space, she might get through this case.

"Nice try." Sharon didn't sound particularly amused. Perhaps Kate had touched a nerve. Who could tell with this ice-maiden? "I'll admit one thing. Simon is a friend, and he's been through quite the ordeal with his marriage and separation. Anyone who cares about him would try to protect him from further pain. This isn't the first time I've felt the need to intervene when some ambitious woman has pursued him."

Really?! Simon would undoubtedly be interested to discover that Sharon had been functioning for some time as his unofficial chaperone. But why? "That's not my business. *I'm* not pursuing Simon. In fact I'm trying very hard to avoid any entanglements." *And it isn't always easy!* "But I've always been devoted to my clients, and you know me to be highly ethical in my practice. We may not always agree on methodology, but I know my business, and I also know that I'm good at what I do. In fact I may be D'arcy and Eli's only hope of reconciliation. Everyone else seems quite willing to let them self-destruct, though it's plain to me they want to work it out."

"I'll concede that point. Though I'm still not convinced it's in my client's best interest," Sharon said.

"I believe it is. They both have growing up to do. Eli is as capable of being as devoted, responsible a husband as any man. I'm convinced of it." Kate took a breath. She knew she couldn't trust Sharon, but she somehow felt much better for having had a frank discussion. "Anyway, I really am looking forward to meeting with D'arcy next week when she returns. I'm sure Eli will be ready to resume by then."

"I understand... her mother is traveling back to Vancouver with her," Sharon offered.

Interesting. "I see." She paused. "Well, perhaps I can meet with the two of them. Maybe we'll make some progress."

Sharon's response was to laugh, a cynical cackle that made Kate shudder. "Good luck with that."

Perhaps she ought to get a little more information from Eli before venturing forward with that plan. Suddenly she couldn't wait to get rid of Sharon and call Eli. She hated to broach the subject again, but she had to know what her situation at the Society would be. "So, will you drop the conflict claim?"

"Too late, I'm afraid. I faxed over the Breach of Society Standards complaint form and letter this morning. It's done."

It felt as if a great weight pressed down on Kate's heart. Sharon's voice didn't carry a hint of regret. *Damn it!* "I see." What was there left for her to say? It was unstoppable now. She would be forced to make a formal response, and deal with the consequences. So much for keeping the whole thing private. She forced her words though her tight throat when she replied. "Good-bye, then. I'll see you next week." This was the last thing she needed, and it put a sour note on her special award. She'd be too humiliated to accept it, never mind stand at the podium and crow about her methodology. She couldn't think about it right now. She'd do her job, and deal with it as necessary, but still she felt hot tears of frustration sting her eyes as she hung up the phone.

Then she forced herself to dial Eli, despite her shaking hand, and as quickly hung up again. No. This was too important to put herself at the mercy of his evasive maneuvers. Too much depended on getting Eli and D'arcy back to the table. Too much was at stake. If this case fell apart, in the midst of an unprofessional conduct claim, she would look even more foolish.

And even more important than her reputation was her responsibility to her clients. What if she had missed something critical, as Simon suggested, misdirected them, abused their trust, because she was absorbed in her own problems? She'd never forgive herself.

She grabbed her coat and flew out the door. It was four o'clock Friday afternoon. How long did she have before Eli decided it was time to quit work for the day and join his friends for a drink? She fled down to his studio at the docks.

A skeptical porcelain moon stared down at Kate through a shadowed veil of secrecy and shame, tracing her slow progress through "the stroll" on Powell Street. She cruised through the Downtown East Side past the old Rogers' sugar refinery on the harbour side of the railroad tracks, trying to locate the warehouse where she knew Eli's studio was located, but her knowledge of the area was sketchy. She prayed he would still be there, if she could find him.

She slowed, searching in the dying light for the entry gate in the chain link fence that ran parallel to the road. Kate felt the pull of dark eyes upon her like daggers, and was compelled to return the haunted stares of the prostitutes lingering on every street corner, huddled under umbrellas, their gaunt shadowed faces and bare legs portents to their past and future. She shivered and her mission suddenly felt ominous and foolhardy. Mediators don't make house calls. *What do I think I'm doing?*

But Kate knew she had to go on. Her reputation, her very career could rest on getting Eli and Darcy back to the table. It was a matter of personal integrity now.

It got harder to see as daylight ebbed, though the rain had let up a little. She slipped her car slowly into a narrow laneway between two identical long corrugated metal dockyard buildings, her sense of doom mounting, and was about to surrender when she noticed a sign that indicated the building address. A little further along she spotted a garage door with a big green 14E painted on it. That's it!

Stepping out of the car into the deepening shadows of the dockyard, her anxiety increased, and she glanced over her shoulder more than once. Tentatively she knocked on the metal door adjacent to the large number. No sound but the softly lapping waves on the concrete dockside. She tried the knob and, finding it open, crept warily inside.

"Eli," she called out tremulously. *I must be mad, coming here alone at this hour.* "Eli, are you here?"

The corridor was dimly lit by a single bare bulb hanging a few yards along. Pungent odors of oil paint and turpentine, tobacco, dust and decaying sea life assaulted her nostrils. She squinted at piles of debris, a haphazard stack of wood framing, rolls of canvas, cardboard boxes, bits of wire cable, empty paint cans and crumpled rags. A fire waiting to happen. "Eli?" She ought to leave. This was insane.

Picking her way through the junk, she reminded herself why she had come... how important this was, both for her clients and her career. She made her way to the end, where the space suddenly opened up into a cavernous warehouse with a dusty concrete floor. She stepped in, turning around to scan the space with wide, darting eyes. The last cool glow of daylight on this dull, drizzling day was fading fast. She could make out only vague shapes in the dusky light. Her heart sank. Even though he couldn't possibly be far, he didn't appear to be here.

Turning to leave, her breath caught in her throat as the large round factory lights that swung on long cords from the ceiling suddenly blinked and gradually, eerily awoke, first with a dull orange glow, then a soft yellow flicker and finally bright sulphurous greenish-white light. "Is someone here?" she said in a small voice. "Eli?"

There was no reply, and blinking in the brightness, she stepped quickly toward the doorway, her tense shoulders pulled up to her ears, her arms crossed. *I have to get out of here.*

A disembodied voice came from behind her. "If you're planning to steal one of my paintings, you should have brought a panel van. I don't have anything that will fit into that little coupe."

"Aaaahhh!" she half gasped, half yelped, a hand flying to her throat. Her body went rigid.

Eli chuckled. "Over here." She turned towards his voice, and found there was a small doorway in the wall concealed between the stacked paintings. He leaned lazily on the jamb, holding a beer and cigarette in one hand, a thread of smoke curling up around his ears.

She let out a deep sigh, shuddering. "Thank God." She held a hand against the heart pounding against her ribcage. "How did you know it was me?"

He laughed again. "I have security cameras mounted outside and in. I watched you approach and unlocked the door for you." He shifted his weight. "Can I offer you a drink?" He held his beer bottle aloft, grinning. His normally smooth, handsome face was almost masked by a heavy weeks' worth of black facial hair. A length of rag held back his curling dark locks, grimy with dust, tendrils of which hung forward over his face. He wore a paint-smeared plaid work shirt and tattered and splattered jeans.

Security cameras? She gazed around. "Well, you are full of surprises," Kate replied, smiling and shaking her head. "Come in," he turned and disappeared through the doorway, past a tiny yellow kitchen, where she could see her car flickering in grainy black and white on an old laptop resting on the counter, along with stacks of unwashed dishes and greasy take-out boxes, paper cups, empty beer bottles and Coke cans. She followed Eli into another smallish room cluttered with more of the same, along with ashtrays and mugs teaming with cigarette butts and murky moldy liquid. A rumpled blue sleeping bag lay on the ugliest threadbare brown sofa Kate had ever seen. What sparse furniture there was seemed to have been salvaged from a back lane dumpster in East Van in the late sixties.

"This is quite the place," she observed, looking around. "Have you been... *living* here?" It certainly looked like he hadn't left in a while.

"Yeah. Well. Sort of." He shrugged, chagrinned. "How 'bout that drink?"

She waved a hand in protest. "Oh, no thanks. I shouldn't even be here, never mind drink. Good God, if Sharon found out... " She thought of asking for a Coke, but was uncertain whether he owned a clean glass.

He lifted his index finger, his face opening in thoughtful delight. "I have just the thing." He jogged into his kitchen, and she heard cupboard doors banging and a thud on the countertop. A moment later he returned with a Styrofoam cup that he proudly handed to her. "I remembered I had a bottle of twelve-year old single malt someone gave me long ago. It's even older now." At her expression he added, "Go on. I won't tell if you don't. Let's assume you're off duty, hey?" He pushed the cup into her hand.

She accepted the cup, peering over the rim at the half-inch of golden liquid. If it wasn't perfectly clean, at least the scotch might sterilize it, she thought. "Thanks." Upon closer inspection, both the cup and the scotch looked fine, though the juxtaposition seemed incongruous to say the least. She sat where he gestured, and he dropped himself onto the sofa beside her, grinning. "What are you smiling at?" she asked.

"Oh. It's just nice to have company. Someone who speaks English and doesn't smell like diesel or fish. I haven't seen anyone for several days."

She laughed. "Oh. Well. If I'd known you'd be so happy to see me, I would have come much sooner." Kate braved a small sip of the scotch, and discovered that it was wonderfully smooth. Her nose tingled with the earthy aroma as the tawny liquid burned a path down her throat. It bolstered her courage. She settled back on the sofa, no longer concerned with the filth, and took a larger swig, smiling and feeling the warmth take hold in her belly. "So *have* you been living here?"

"Not exactly. I go home to shower and get food and beer." She raised her eyebrows at him and his surroundings, prompting the further, " … just not lately."

She laughed again. "So what have you been working on?"

"Mmm. A new series I've been thinking about. Sketches. Cartoons. The last one grabbed hold of me, so I got out the oils and haven't stopped."

She was more than curious. "Is it a secret?"

He tilted his head. "Yes and no. *You* can see it. Come on." He jumped up from the sofa and led the way back into the studio. She followed eagerly to the giant easel, thinking that he was a different man in his own environment, relaxed, energized and powerful, and waited as he climbed a step ladder and pulled back a huge, paint splattered canvas tarp from one edge. She stepped back, trying to take in what she saw.

The stretched canvas was very large, perhaps eight feet wide, and more, maybe ten feet high. Most of it was quite bare, with large thin washes of beige and grey veiling but not covering his bold, charcoal lines. Two figures, their arms tangled as they clutched at each other, stood almost back-to-back. They were gaunt, underfed, their musculature explicitly drawn in dark lines. Even without the benefit of light, shadow and colour, Eli had been able to capture their striving, their effort, with posture and gesture alone. Kate stood transfixed.

Finally she could speak. "It's like a Matisse, with gravitas, angst, and anorexia. Are they fighting or dancing?"

He chortled. "Both, I guess."

"My God, Eli. You really know what you're doing."

"Hm. No, actually. That's what I'm trying to figure out," his voice was wistful, and he had clearly taken her meaning the wrong way. He shrugged and turned away.

She studied him for a long time. "Let's go sit down," she suggested. He followed her back to the lounge, stopping to pick up the bottle of malt from the counter, and refilled her cup. Somehow she'd managed to drain it.

He fetched himself another beer and sat down again next to her, tucked a cigarette between his lips and flicked on his lighter.

"How are you feeling? Still angry?" she asked.

"Aah. No. I'm long past anger," he inhaled, his voice quiet, the tip of his cigarette glowing red.

She thought for a moment, looking into her cup. He sounded desolate. "D'arcy went to Montreal."

He frowned. "That doesn't surprise me." He took a long swig of his beer.

"She's coming back Thursday— with her mother." She studied his face carefully. Whatever he thought of that, he didn't show it, but she thought she detected some tension around his dark eyes. "There's something else I've been wanting to talk to you about... "

Eli leaned forward, resting his elbows on his knees, his beer bottle dangling in between. "Mmm?"

"Sharon has decided to file a professional conduct complaint against me, and maybe Simon, I don't know." She shot a nervous glance at him.

He sneered. "What's that shrew got up her ass?"

"I should have said something right away," Kate said. "Simon and I were quite romantically involved years ago, and Sharon found out. She's claiming we've renewed our relationship."

"I should hope so." He sat upright, smiling broadly. "He's had plenty of time to make his move. How slow could the man go?"

"What?"

"Simon told me when we first met, about your history. I figured you'd be into a steamy affair by now," he smirked and waggled his eyebrows.

"We're not allowed to do that. We're working together. We can't be in… in… in*volved* with each other."

"Why not? How can it affect us?"

"Well, that's the question. I can't see how it could bias our thinking about you two, though it has been distracting. But technically, Sharon has a case, if only because we *weren't* truthful at first."

"Well. You can call me as a witness. I'm all for it. You two *ought* to be together." He drank again.

"Ought to be?"

"Oh, yeah. You're cut from the same cloth, you two." His stomach growled viciously, and he clutched it making a face.

What a strange thing to say. "Well. It's not that simple." She swept a hand through the air. "But anyway, we have to deal with Sharon and her protocol now. I wanted you to know. How 'bout I take you out for a real meal?"

He grimaced, gesturing across his state of dress. "I'm hardly presentable. I could get a pizza." She smiled and nodded. Maybe she could get him to open up tonight yet, if she persevered. This may be unconventional, but it might be worthwhile in the end.

Blue moonlight flooded in through the large bare window, and she noted that the sky was almost clear now, a dark indigo. How quickly the sun set. It was getting close to the shortest day of the year. She could hear him on the phone, and a few minutes later he was back with a fresh beer. He refilled her cup. She felt relaxed for the first time in weeks.

"I ordered a pepperoni and a Greek. Figured I'd cover all the bases, and I can always use the leftovers," he grinned sheepishly, another cigarette pinched between his smirking lips, "… for breakfast."

Before long there was a thudding on the outer door. "Be right back."

She jumped up and grabbed her purse. "Let me get it."

"No, no. I've got an account, don't worry," his muffled voice came from the hall as he headed for the door. She heard him open it and then, "Hey Stu." Stu replied with equally colloquial greetings and bummed a smoke. "Thanks, dude." The door closed.

"I can't believe they deliver here."

"I'm a regular." He shrugged, and dropped the boxes on top of the cluttered coffee table. "Dig in. Oh, do you want a plate?" he asked, as an afterthought.

Kate thought about the likelihood of there being a clean plate. She waved a hand. They settled in to eat their pizza. Afterwards they sat, sated, sipping their drinks and enjoying the quiet.

"Tell me how you're feeling about D'arcy now. Do you think we can get back to work?"

"I dunno." Eli cast his gaze at the floor, pursing his lips. Then he glanced up at her, flashed a tight smile, looked down again, shrugging, and spun his wedding ring around absently.

She waited for him to say more. When he didn't, she ventured, "What has she done that's so upset you?"

"I'm frustrated. I feel like she's playing games with me. I hardly know her. I even thought she was sick, for a while. The things that she's gotten upset about —women, money, time— well... I know they look bad, but I haven't done anything differently than I ever did, nothing we haven't dealt with before." He shrugged and took a drag. "But lately she's so sensitive, so demanding."

He flicked the ash from his cigarette.

"I would have thought my big break would make her feel better. It may not be secure, but I've been bringing in a lot of money for the first time since I met her. I didn't expect her to flip out."

"Maybe she just wants to know that she can rely on you— to look out for her sometime. Maybe she's afraid that you don't need her anymore," suggested Kate.

"But, that makes me sound so mercenary. I've always needed D'arcy by my side, but not for the financial support. She's my soul mate. No one understands me like D'arcy does. I just want her to trust me. Is that too much to ask? I'm the same man she fell in love with seven years ago."

"Are you?"

He tossed his head. "Maybe more so. I'm a man. I want to be acknowledged as one. I want respect. Haven't I kept my part of the bargain? Haven't I worked my ass off? What more does she want from me?"

"Maybe she needs something from you that's a little more mundane. Or maybe she wants you to take care of *her*. Even modern women who work, and have financial independence, need a little reassurance once in a while. She may be tired of the burden of responsibility. You could try being the caregiver for a change. You could be her protector." Where had that come from? Straight from her insecure subconscious, she imagined. "Maybe I'm just old fashioned at heart, but I think there's a part of every woman that wants her man to put something on the line for her. To *risk* something. What are you prepared to give up?"

Eli gave a cynical laugh. "That's not who I am. I'm not good at all those details. I just take one day at a time, y'know? I'm an artist, for God's sake!"

Kate drew herself up, resolved. It was now or never. "Tell me about D'arcy's parents. What happened when you met them?"

Eli tossed his head back on the sofa with a gust of air. "So this isn't just a social visit?" he deadpanned, gazing up at the stained grid ceiling, then back at her, his expression grim.

She leaned forward, and looked pointedly into his eyes. "I want to get you and D'arcy back to where you were." Kate spread her hands like wings in a plaintive gesture. "I feel responsible for missing this issue with her family. I should have been more astute."

He looked at her keenly. "If D'arcy and I are going to make this work, we're going to have to do it without her folks. She has to decide where her future is."

"You can't mean that! You can't ask her to... to give up her family." Kate felt her words sticking together as she forced them past a tongue that seemed too thick. She hadn't meant to drink so much of the scotch. "Y'know she can't be happy if she has to choose." She reached across and placed a hand on his arm. She had to help him see a compromise was the only way.

Eli's chin was down, and his eyes flashed from under his dark brows. Even with his unkempt hair, and thick carpet of facial hair, he was still a handsome man. Dark eyes like pools burned into her own, shining like those of an animal, vulnerable yet dangerous. He seemed to be assessing her worth.

"Trust me. I won't tell anyone. I'll keep your secret, if I must. But help me understand what's wrong. I want to help you." They held each other's eyes, and she was uncertain who had fallen under whose hypnotic spell, for in that moment it seemed mutual. Jeez, she felt woozy. In the back of her foggy mind drifted the thought that this was so inappropriate.

He released a heavy breath, his shoulders sagging. "They offered me money."

Kate was suddenly alert.

"D'arcy's parents. When we went to meet them. To tell them we wanted to get married. The old man took me aside and offered me money to disappear from her life." He spoke in a monotonous drone, as though it were too painful to recall the facts with the emotions still attached.

Comprehending, Kate felt her eyes fill with tears. She blinked. "Oh, Eli!"

His face was cool, his mouth twisting in a bitter sneer. "It was a generous offer. I should have been flattered, I suppose. A hundred grand to pack up and leave, no explanations, never to be found again. 'Go study at the Sorbonne. Start your career in Paris, or somewhere else far away from my daughter, if you get my drift.' That's what he said. It was more money than I'd ever seen in one place, and they knew it. They assumed I was a gold-digger."

"Poor you."

He nodded again, lips tight. "D'arcy never knew, never understood the degree of their opposition, and I didn't have the heart to drive a wedge between her and her parents. When I declined his offer, they simply forbade our marriage, and D'arcy and I returned to Vancouver and did it anyway. Afterwards, they carried on as though I never existed. As though there was no marriage. It's been a very uncomfortable co-existence ever since."

"So, there's never been any acknowledgement? No apology?" Kate asked, incredulous. He shook his head. They were sitting very close together, shoulders touching. She looked hard at him for a long time, thinking. This had gone on too long. How could it be fixed? "D'arcy made her choice. She chose you. You have to tell D'arcy, and together challenge them. It's time."

He turned his head and looked at her in return. "I'm not a coward, if that's what you think. I was brought up to fight, especially against people like that. But I couldn't do that to D'arc'."

"They did it to themselves. You did the right thing. And you and D'arcy have passed the trial by fire. You can't let this come between you anymore." She gave his hand a squeeze. "It's time you took a stand. They've shown their true colours. They're not going to give up on their daughter. I'm sure they only wanted what's best for her, in their eyes, and are probably ashamed. Madame Duchamp found you an agent didn't she? Think of it as an olive branch. But still, they wouldn't be getting away with treating you like this if you didn't keep it from D'arcy. The secret's been festering too long."

This seemed to be what Eli needed to hear. His dark eyes shone with long suppressed tears, which clung to his long black lashes, and his lips curled and twitched involuntarily. He gave his head a violent shake. She reached toward him and patted his arm. This invitation was all he needed to release his pain and anger, and he wept silently for several minutes while she held his hand between hers.

At last, he sat up straight, wiping his dripping nose and eyes on the sleeve of his work shirt, and stared across the room, his mood distant. He sniffed and rummaged in his pocket for his pack of cigarettes, fishing one out and lighting it, drawing a deep breath. When he'd regained some control, he turned to her with a watery smile.

"Another drink?"

"Oh, God, no. I can't. Unless you have some tea?" She smiled back.

"No tea, but I could make a pot of strong coffee," he offered.

She normally didn't drink coffee, but she needed it tonight. And she wasn't quite through yet. "Even better, thanks." He rose and went to the small kitchen. She heard running water and cupboards and old wooden drawers squeaking. She imagined he needed a few minutes alone to gather himself and salvage some dignity. She waited, thinking of ways to resolve the issue.

She could smell the coffee aroma slowly permeate the stale, oily air. When he returned ten minutes later with two mismatched mugs of steaming coffee, she had a plan.

"I hope you like it black," he said. "I might be able to find some sugar, if you want, but I don't have any milk." He grinned awkwardly, his composure reclaimed.

"Black is fine, thanks," she said, taking a mug. "I think I've got enough toxins in my system for one night without adding sugar to the mix."

Eli guffawed. "You sound just like Simon, with your green tea and health food," he exclaimed.

"Oh, don't say that." She pressed her eyes shut, shaking her head, and looked down into her mug of coffee, smelling the strong black acidic brew. She took a bracing sip of the bitter liquid, and wondered if her stomach could handle it.

He sat down and lit another cigarette, extracting a chocolate bar from the pocket of his shirt, and made a good-humored offer by waving in under her nose. She laughed and raised a silent hand in protest.

"Seriously. What's up with you two?" he slurped his hot coffee like a parched man in the desert, and set it down, ripping open the wrapper on his candy and taking a huge bite. He spoke past a mouthful of chocolate, his words garbled, "Besides the conflict thing, why aren't you two all over each other? I can see it in your eyes as plain as day."

Kate felt her face flush hot, and glanced at Eli, blinking. She raised a hand to smooth her brows, her pulse fluttering. "I can't talk about this."

"Why not? Confidences go both ways, you know. After hours, it's off the record." He smiled gently, inviting her trust.

She sighed, and sipped her coffee again, seeking fortitude. How could she explain her obsession with Simon, her fear of him, to a client and a virtual stranger? She wanted him to trust her, but more than that, she felt she could trust him, and that their nascent friendship justified it.

She sat back with a sigh. "When Simon and I first met, we were just teenagers. Not unlike you and D'arcy, I guess. But I was in a very vulnerable place when I met him. I was suffering from a significant trauma, followed by a huge emotional loss. I was also young and idealistic. I transferred all my idealism and emotional neediness onto him, I guess. I imagine he broke it off because I became clingy, and not very interesting, after a few months. That's all there was, really, to our so-called relationship, though it was intense while it lasted."

Kate paused, and swallowed, thinking. How ironic to reduce her love for Simon, and all that it caused, to a glib summary. Eli leaned back, sucked on his cigarette, listening.

"The worst for me came afterwards. I couldn't let go of him— of the *idea* of him." She shook her head. How could anyone understand the way she had lost any sense of reality. "It went on for a few years, though I doubt he knew. We had one unpleasant encounter the last time I saw him— maybe fourteen years ago." That was one secret she would never tell another soul.

Eli looked up, his eyes sympathetic.

"You're not disgusted?"

He made a wry face and shrugged. "Everyone's got embarrassing moments in their past.

She continued. "After that, we lived our separate lives. I had to deal with depression, with very damaged self-esteem. There were a few years of counseling. Then..." She shrugged. "... a new life, a new career. I don't have any regrets. I wouldn't have discovered mediation if I hadn't gone through that. But... when he walked into the board room... I... " *I don't know what.* She shook her head, reliving the shock of that moment.

"Wow," he said softly. "I think I get it." He scraped a hand across his bristled chin.

She smiled into his eyes. "It's not easy, as you can imagine."

He thought a moment, then sat up abruptly and slapped his knee. "No. Life's too short for regrets. There's a reason you and Simon are together again. This was meant to be. I can feel it. You can't throw it away because of a little fear." He jabbed a finger in her direction, driving his point home.

"A little fear... " she chuckled under her breath.

Eli raised a hand and held her chin, lifting her face to look carefully into her eyes. "How would you feel, if you walked away, and never found out? This is something special. You need to go for it, take the risk."

How ironic was that? She cocked an eyebrow at Eli, her look full of meaning, and dipped her chin. He gave her a wry smile and a gimbaled eye. "I'll make a deal with you, Eli Benjamin. I will dig deep for the courage I need to, find out, as you say, if this is something worth fighting my demons for. But you have to promise me the same. You have to meet with Madame Duchamp. With or without D'arcy, that's your choice. But you have to let me set it up for you." She cocked her head at him, waiting.

They sat facing each other for several minutes, each of them searching their soul for the strength to commit to facing their worst fears. Then Eli offered his hand, palm open, and she slowly slipped her hand over his, and they squeezed. Her fate was sealed. *What have I done?*

sixteen

November 24, ----

Dear Roster Administrator;
I write in rebuttal to the grossly exaggerated claim brought for-
ward by the attorney, Sharon Beckett, that I misled both her and my
clients by failing to disclose knowledge of a former acquaintance
with...

Kate sat, eyes unfocussed, staring at the blinking cursor
on her computer screen. *What a stinking pile of emotional melo-*
drama. She couldn't do it.

She blinked, and hit the delete key until the screen was blank
again. Then continued to tap her fingers on the mouse pad for
several long, thoughtful minutes, gazing blindly at the balsamic
moon suspended like a slender sling in the clear night sky outside her vast windows. She heard the distant squeal of tires outside. A faint, faraway siren echoed.

Dear Roster Administrator;
This letter is in response to the claim by Sharon Beckett that I
allegedly withheld knowledge of my client's attorney when our past
relationship might have been disclosed at the outset. In retrospect, I
see that this may be true. However initially I was uncertain of his
identity and my hesitation led to avoidance out of embarrassment.
I convinced myself that the fact we had not seen each other in over
fifteen years...

She felt sick. Not sweaty, shaking, dizzy sick, like staring
into the dark chasm of her past tended to inspire. This was a
nauseous, tight swirling in her stomach. A burning behind her

eyelids. A heavy weight like a foot upon her heart. She knew everything she'd ever struggled with had finally come together in this one horribly painful moment and that her actions now would either free her or weigh her down for the rest of her days. Or maybe not. The society review board only needed to know enough to restore her good reputation, but Kate knew there was more going on in her heart. Even though she knew her error was a misdemeanor, Sharon's spitefulness still had her emotions roiling. There didn't seem to be an easy way out. She had to think clearly. Again she deleted the text.

What is most important to me? What do I value? What do I really want in life? What's really at stake here? Questions spun round and round in her head as she fingered her eternal knot pendant, flipping it over and over, asking for guidance.

These should be easy questions. They were ones she'd tackled before. Kate knew what it was like to be lost, not to know or trust herself. She also knew what it felt like to put herself back together, one brick, one cell, one idea at a time. Kate knew herself. She knew she cared about people and she knew her insight and skills could help people with problems that she understood. She understood human frailty, and she empathized deeply with people who had screwed up and deserved another chance at happiness.

Doing this had given her life focus and meaning and joy. She felt a deep sense of purpose and was rewarded by the life's work she'd chosen. This insight and commitment was what made her so particularly good at mediation. Better than the others. It was this ability to understand and help others that provided her with clarity and self-respect. Without this work she wouldn't be whole, would have so much less to offer. To her clients, to her friends and family, and certainly to Simon or Jay or anyone else with whom she might choose to share her life. Without that solid foundation, she would be so much less, incomplete as a person.

And yet, despite her focus on her work and career, she also wanted Simon's love. She had, on some level, always wanted Simon, and even when she questioned her own judgment, her own motives for wanting and believing herself in love with him, she still needed him with the very core of her being. As if her desire to be with him was a force bigger than her. Wanting him so much had loosened the stones of her foundation years ago and begun an erosion of her belief in herself, an avalanche of self-doubt that had nearly obliterated her sense of self. She had rejected the dependency this notion of romantic love had created in her. The weakness it implied. This was the reason she was so afraid to surrender to her attraction to him. This was why allowing herself to be near him was so terrifying. Simon somehow represented an abyss that might, should she venture too near the edge, annihilate all that she had become. All that she came to value about herself, and depend upon. Why was she so afraid? Did she really fear losing herself if she surrendered to love?

And yet she still wanted his love. She wanted Simon's love like no other. Her every attempt at a relationship had failed precisely *because* of the love she had experienced with him all those years ago and still carried inside her like a glowing ember, a flame that refused to be extinguished. Nothing could compare. God knows, she'd tried to love Jay. It always came out sounding like an enumeration of his good qualities, but in the most unfeeling, abstract terms, like a curriculum vitae for a job as husband and lover. He certainly qualified. But she just couldn't make herself love him no matter how hard she'd tried. Poor Jay. Poor Grant. Poor Thom. Poor...

Kate shook her head and picked up the letter from the Roster Administrator, re-reading the already painfully familiar lines.

Dear Ms. O'Day,
It has come to our attention... breach of professional conduct... failure to disclose former relationship with counsel for your client, a Mr. Simon Sharpe, esq.... Ms. Beckett's concern for her client... standards of professional ethics... etc. etc. opportunity to explain... Please respond by... Yours truly, Dr. Leonard Howard, Roster Administrator.

Kate knew that Rose, her mentor and councilor, saw everything that crossed Howard's desk. She'd been on the executive for years and practically ran the society. Kate closed her eyes, seeing Rose's familiar kind face, remembering the hours she'd sat in her office talking and crying her heart out. The bitter memories brought a fresh flood of tears to her eyes. She sat, wracked by silent convulsive sobs, reliving the painful exploration of her darkest days. She had had so much going for her, and so many things that she wanted to achieve, and had been brought so low in one, really it was just one, black stroke of fate. All the other stuff, even her convoluted dependency on Simon, all of that was just a complex emotional response to the first.

She felt the old anger burn in her core, the resentment that such a mindless act of brutality and selfish disdain could cause such havoc in a life. Her life. Yet part of her felt a contemptuous pity for the guy that triggered it all with his vile act. And she felt sorry for her young, helpless, idealistic self. It was time to rise above it and find some peace. But her scars were still tender, despite all that.

Those were tough times but she got through them and she'd thought it was all behind her. While she was glad she'd called Rose in October to ask her advice when all of this began, she knew that meant there was nothing she could hide now. Nor did she want to. Honesty and integrity meant everything to Kate.

If she valued her self-respect, her professional reputation, her peace of mind, her very way of life, the only way through this was straight through the gauntlet. She would tell the truth, take the consequences and piece it all back together on the other side. Even if that meant she had to face humiliation. She was certain hers wasn't such a terrible transgression that she would lose her license. Even if it meant she had to walk away from Simon. There was no other way. Determined, she returned to her keyboard.

To the Roster Administrator and Executive of the Mediator Roster Society of BC;

I cannot prevaricate. There are those among the executive who know enough about my past to make the truth unavoidable. Furthermore, my training in this honored profession has given me sufficient self-knowledge to be unable to deny the kernel of truth in this claim and still face myself in the mirror.

It was without a doubt unprofessional of me to avoid disclosure of the full details of a past relationship with the attorney assigned to my current mediation client, when I knew myself to be affected by his unexpected reappearance. I sought guidance from my mentor and we agreed I could move forward. In truth, I knew him intimately, and was emotionally involved with him for some time. These issues are clearly not fully resolved for me and my renewed and, I admit, not entirely unavoidable reacquaintance with him has brought that to the fore.

I can, however, commit to a deferment of this personal matter, however difficult, whatever the consequences may be, until my commitment to my current clients has been fulfilled. This is my first duty. Rest assured, I do have the self-awareness, confidence and discipline to carry out my responsibilities without allowing this matter to interfere any further.

Despite the above and the fact that these events have been a distraction to me and therefore may have compromised my efficacy as a professional, I maintain that there is not and has never been any conflict of interest or risk to my clients. I hold my clients' well-being, and my responsibility to serve them, above all else. If my confusion over this matter has allowed any errors in perception or judgment, and I do not believe it has, then it is within my power to correct these small lapses. I believe my understanding of the clients in this case is as insightful and accurate as ever and I remain committed to work to the fullest of my ability toward a satisfactory resolution to their case. At this point, I believe my clients' trust has not been compromised and that a mutually satisfactory mediation of their conflict is possible, even likely. They are now both fully apprised of the situation and have not expressed any desire to make changes to the arrangements.

Kate hesitated, reviewing her text, considering her next move.

I deeply regret that these circumstances have caused my esteemed colleague, Ms. Beckett, any concern for her client, and I respect her integrity in pursuing the matter through professional avenues. It is my sincerest hope that, with further understanding, she will be willing to let the matter rest.

That felt like a slight untruth. Not that Kate's remorse wasn't genuine, but in her gut she knew Sharon's motive to be less than honest, with not a small measure of vindictiveness and manipulation behind it. But since, short of making these unfounded accusations public, it would be the honorable thing to say, and since she knew a copy of the letter would be sent to Sharon, it served its purpose doubly well to give her the benefit of the doubt. It wouldn't do to provoke the woman considering what she had already done.

Feeling somewhat better, she proofread and printed the letter, signing it and sealing the envelope before she could change her mind. She might as well put it right into the mailbox, while she was in the mood. She stood and pulled on her coat and grabbed her bag.

A pair of lavender Fluevog Luna boots in the shop window on the corner had been calling to her for weeks. Tall, supple distressed leather with buckles top and bottom and chunky heels. They shouted power. *Those boots are made for walkin'. I am definitely going to buy them.* She lifted her chin, pulled her shoulders back, and entered the shop. A little recompense was due.

On the way out the door onto the street, she practically crashed into a tall, dark man hunched in a broad overcoat. Jay.

She felt herself shrink inward, the bubble of happiness her boots had brought her popping. This was the very last thing she needed right now. "Jay," she said halfheartedly.

She noted the minute wince that registered dismay on his handsome face. She was sorry that she couldn't feign enthusiasm she didn't feel.

"I need to talk to you," he said.

She stared at him, impassive.

"I'm not willing to let you go." His frustration had built, showing in the determined set of his jaw, his furrowed brow.

"I won't change my mind." It was harsh, she knew. But how could he press her?

He looked crestfallen. "I love you."

"But Jay, I don't love you."

"Give me a chance. We can be so good together. You'll come to love me in time."

"No. I won't." She was impatient to go. She didn't want to go through this again. "Why won't you accept that?"

"I'm as right for you as you are for me. You know it."

"If you knew me at all, you wouldn't say that. You don't know what I need."

The muscles in his jaw bunched. "I know it's only fear of commitment... You have to trust me."

"It's not about trust. It's not fear of commitment." She was starting to bristle with resentment.

His eyes pulled to the side, glaring down the street. "You don't know your own mind. You never could make decisions."

Kate tamped down her resentment. "That may be true, but at least my doubts are my own."

He grabbed her shoulders with gloved hands, pressing his face closer. "I'm sorry. I didn't mean to say it that way." His strong, handsome mouth stretched taut, quivering. "I miss you." His face came closer and he tried to kiss her, but she pushed him away.

"Stop it. I'm sorry I mislead you, Jay. You deserve better than this, but I can't be what you want." She squeezed her eyes shut, gritting her teeth. "I'm in love with someone else." She stepped back, noting the stunned, open-mouthed expression on his face. Her heart squeezed with remorse, her throat constricting with tears. She should have told him sooner. If only she knew it herself. Her last words were whispered. "Leave me alone, Jay. Please."

She was tense, sweating, jittery, and had the beginnings of a massive headache. Her nerves were shot. She stormed away toward the mailbox at the end of the street and slipped her envelope into the slot with a trembling hand. How much more could a person take in one day?

Kate was finally able to meet with D'arcy and her mother after waiting for almost two weeks. She was excited to resume reconciliation sessions, but filled with trepidation before the prospect of confronting the issue of her alleged professional misconduct with D'arcy and the formidable Madame Duchamp.

She had to be perfectly clear in her mind how she would address the issue of her relationship with Simon and believe her own story, or she would never come across as sincere. Securing their confidence was critical for her plan. She had to win over D'arcy's mother if she hoped to persuade her to meet privately with Eli. Kate had to make sure the meeting went ahead as planned or she'd need a new plan.

Her case files were spread out on the dining room table. Oscar leapt up and spread his mangy body out across her papers, flicking his bent tail and tossing her a feigned look of disdain. "Oh, you're not fooling me, you old baby," she crooned and gently plucked him off the files to curl him onto her lap, stroking him.

Only a few minutes had passed when the phone rang and, expecting it would be D'arcy with some question or change of detail, she answered it formally, but with a smile in her voice. "Kathryn O'Day," she said.

A moment passed. "It's Tuesday. I miss seeing you, Kathryn O'Day," said Simon in a gentle, playful tone.

Oh! Her heart rate shot through the stratosphere, sending

adrenaline through her veins. He was the last person on earth she'd been expecting. Kate had spent a good deal of time and energy thinking about Simon, but that was a far cry from being ready to talk to him. A fluttery feeling in her belly told her she wasn't prepared. In her astonishment, she actually forgot to reply.

"That bad, eh? I was kind of hoping you'd be glad to hear my voice," he said.

"Uuh." Glad to hear his voice? The sound of it sent her head spinning and her pulse racing. She was overjoyed to hear his voice, she wanted to leap for joy. But that was bad. On the one hand, she'd committed to postpone dealing with this relationship until the case was over. On the other, she remembered her vow to Eli, and tried to calm herself sufficiently to say something warm and friendly, and yet retain some dignity. What would he think if she suddenly came on like a schoolgirl with a crush, or an old lover keen to rekindle the flame? While she was in some respects both of these undesirable things, she certainly didn't want to appear so. Oscar batted her idle hand and she resumed scratching his chin.

"Kate?"

She put a hand on her heart to steady it. "Sorry to sound so stunned. I haven't heard from you in awhile and I'm afraid my mind was elsewhere." *I sound like a ninny!* She was trying to convey so much with just a few words and the tone of her voice, she could hardly think at all.

"I was only checking to see if you've made any progress with D'arcy and Eli. I'm afraid I've been quite delinquent for the past two weeks. I haven't even spoken with Eli since he walked out."

"Really? I'm surprised." She hadn't missed the dejection in his voice. Her recovery had been too slow; he had mistaken her hesitation for disdain. A weight settled to the base of her stomach.

"I'm off to meet with D'arcy this afternoon… " she paused, " … and her mother. They've just returned from Montreal together." She waited for his reply.

"O-oh?" He sounded uncertain. "And how are you planning to handle that?"

"We-ell. I don't know what to expect from Madame Duchamp, of course. But I'm going to try to get her to agree to meet with Eli."

"You're crazy. Eli won't go for that." Simon's voice held more than a hint of concern. "That'll be a disaster."

"You really are out of touch. Eli and I have an... understanding. It was his idea to meet her alone. He's going to confront her."

"About what?"

"About the $100,000 bribe they offered him seven years ago," Kate revealed this jewel with smug amusement in her tone, anticipating Simon's reaction. He did not disappoint her.

"Je-sus!" he breathed. "I knew there was something there. But I never imagined... " he tapered off.

"Yeah." Kate bit her lip, pondering her next words. "I really think this needs to happen to unlock this issue for Eli and D'arcy." She chose not to mention her concern over the complaint. She would deal with that on her own.

"I see... " The silence stretched out, brittle and uncertain. "Well, I guess you'd better get ready then."

Oh. She didn't want to let him go so soon. "I... uh... I'll let you know how it goes, okay?"

He didn't immediately reply. "Sure. That'd be good." Was it her imagination or did he sound despondent?

Say something else! Her mind screamed, though nothing came to her. "I'm really glad you called. It was nice hearing from you." That was pathetic. He'll think he's being dismissed.

"Yeah. Maybe I'll see you next Tuesday, if all goes well." His voice was tense and awkward now.

Instead of saying good-bye, she waited, undecided. "Simon?"

"Yup?"

"I... uh... miss seeing you, too," she finally gambled, her heart thumping in her chest. What if he'd reconsidered his interest in the last two weeks? She had been anything but encouraging, or genuine, for that matter. Maybe he was tired of her games and thought her ridiculous. "It's always nice to talk things over with you. You always understand," she added for insurance. *What a coward I am!*

His long silence did nothing to pacify her. "Okay. I'll see you then," he finally said, his voice thoughtful. He said her name softly, in a hopeful whisper. It felt like a caress. She set the phone tenderly back in its cradle.

Two and a half hours later she had reviewed her files, made a page of notes and outlined a rough agenda for the meeting. She took a deep breath, gathered her papers and her coat, and called a taxi. If the weather hadn't been so godawful all month, she could easily have walked over to the Hotel Vancouver, but the rain hadn't let up for weeks. She had begun to feel she would never see the sun again.

Twenty minutes later, she was in the elevator heading up to suite number ten. On the way, she'd struggled, not entirely successfully, to keep her focus on the case and not let her thoughts drift to Simon. She did, after all, have to be prepared to discuss her relationship with him with Madame Duchamp and D'arcy. If only it were simple. She could hardly answer her own questions about her feelings for him, let alone theirs. But she did know that she had them and they continued to overwhelm her. Whatever happened, they weren't through yet.

The broad corridor held the hush of an old world hotel in its thick, plush, bordered carpet, deep crown moldings and paneled wood doors, an impression they undoubtedly endeavored to maintain. She passed one discrete bellhop, who made himself silent and invisible.

When Kate knocked, D'arcy opened the door with a wan smile, and invited her into the deluxe suite. It was not overly spacious, the constraints of the old hotel's walls overwhelming any efforts to modernize, but these limitations were more than offset by the quality of traditional appointments. Darkly polished Louis XIV furnishings and heavy tapestry draperies, sparkling chandeliers, gilt trim and gleaming brass fittings created an old-world elegance.

"How nice to see you again." D'arcy moved aside, and gestured with a sweep of her limpid arm for Kate to enter. There was no sign of Madame Duchamp. "Mother will be out in just a moment."

Kate took a seat at the round mahogany table to one side of the sitting room, understanding that she was to wait for an audience. Some things never changed. She smiled at D'arcy.

"How was your trip?" She made a point of seeming relaxed, shucking her coat and tossing it over a chair and reaching for her briefcase. It occurred to her that D'arcy was perhaps the most tense of all of them and Kate should do her best to set her at ease. "Here, sit down and talk to me."

"Would you like a cup of tea?" D'arcy asked, standing awkwardly a few feet away. Kate studied her oddly shy demeanor. Her formerly cherubic but chiseled face was now just plain plump though her complexion much improved. She wore her usual dark shadow and eyeliner and thick long lashes, as well as shimmering rosy lipstick. The pale lips and dark eyes in the round, porcelain face brought the idealized beauty of Noh theatre masks to mind. Kate imagined she'd had a couple of weeks of good sleep and pampering at home. Odd that after six years of marriage, her parent's home might still seem more hers than the one she shared with Eli.

"No, thanks. Water's fine," she replied with a wave of her hand, noticing the cut crystal water jug and glasses standing ready on a tray. Before D'arcy came closer, Kate noted that she seemed heavier altogether and lacked a distinct waist. She wore a knee-length blush pink cashmere cardigan over a loose-fitting blouse, the crisp white collar points drawing attention to D'arcy's graphic features and gleaming dark pageboy, expertly cut. The hard edges of the shirt and hair almost succeeded in distracting from the ample femininity of her other parts. Her breasts, for one thing, were fuller, and the blouse could no longer disguise the swell of her abdomen beneath the pleats. A light blinked on in Kate's head, and her mouth dropped open with a gasp. "My God, D'arcy! You're pregnant! I can't believe it!" She shot to her feet, just as D'arcy had pulled out a chair.

D'arcy looked chagrinned as Kate embraced her, laughing.

"I guess I can't hide it any longer," she said meekly.

"Does Eli even... ? You must be months... " She stood back, gripping D'arcy by the shoulders and compelling her to meet her eyes. D'arcy's only reply was to shake her head and drop her eyes. "This is a much bigger muddle than I thought. Why did you keep it a secret?"

"I imagine that is a woman's prerogative, don't you, Miss O'Day?" interrupted a rich, sonorous contralto from the doorway to the adjacent bedroom, a voice she instantly recognized. Kate stiffened and looked up, curious and uneasy.

Kate corrected her posture. "Up to a point, Madame Duchamp, I suppose, depending upon the circumstances." She stepped toward the sturdy, round-faced grey-haired woman who had just entered the room, extending her hand. "How do you do?" Kate was stunned; not only did she sound like the Queen, she even bore a resemblance, less a decade or so. She might have laughed were she not so intimidated.

Lowering her heavy-lidded eyes in disdain, D'arcee's mother ignored the offering, turning to close the door, and swept haughtily into the room toward the table. "Please sit down." Kate had met other women like her before. She was of a certain generation, accustomed to privilege and power and her style reflected this. She filled a well-tailored short jacket in quilted, plum silk, and a coordinating wool skirt and silver blouse, like a seamstresses mannequin, generously padded and smooth. Kate'e eye caught on a large amethyst pin in the shape of a quail, with a coil of silver on its head, pinned to her lapel.

Kate was only too glad to get going. "Please, after you," she gestured for Madame Duchamp to take a seat and waited for both she and D'arcy before she took her own. She was determined not to be cowed by Madame Duchamp's dismissive manner and regal bearing and equally determined to take the bull, so to speak, by the horns.

"I'm quite certain you've had a full report from Sharon Beckett, D'arcy, and much as I'd like to launch right into our discussion about the mediation, especially in light of recent... " she dipped her chin "... developments, I sense a certain reticence on your part and I'd like to address your concerns around Sharon's complaint before we continue."

Madame Duchamp raised a perfectly penciled eyebrow and inclined her head ever so slightly. "That suits me, Miss O'Day. I trust you have your defense prepared."

Kate's breath caught, and she met D'arcy's eye, which was determinedly blank. Why did she put up with her mother's controlling ways? She continued to address D'arcy instead of letting the older woman take control. "On the contrary. I'd like to know exactly what you've heard, and then I'd be happy to clear things up for you." She would not to be drawn into a mock trial, as Madame Duchamp appeared to have her verdict prepared. She would take an entirely different approach. Still uncertain what the dynamic was between D'arcy and her mother, she kept one eye on D'arcy while waiting for her mother to reply.

"Your name came highly recommended to me, Miss O'Day, when D'arcy informed me of her desire to pursue mediation and it is with great dismay that I have learned of your unprofessional conduct in allowing your personal affairs to interfere with your representation of my daughter's interests."

So it's to be like that, is it? Well, Kate knew how to disarm such obtuse and pompous speech. She leaned forward on her elbows, meeting Madame Duchamps eye directly. "Please. Remind me in precisely which way I have behaved unprofessionally?"

Madame Duchamp's eyes widened but Kate had no reason to fear that she was too reserved to speak frankly when invited. "Why, you are alleged to be having an affair with the legal representative for the opposing side. You're completely biased. Please don't play games with me."

While inwardly she bristled, Kate leaned back and smiled. "On the contrary, I never play games. I'm so relieved to hear you use the word 'alleged.' It would have distressed me greatly to hear that Ms. Beckett claimed to have evidence of such an indiscretion, for truly, how could she, or anyone, know the nature and extent of my relationship with Mr. Sharpe?" Madame Duchamp leaned forward incrementally, her pencil thin brows flattening, poised for her next attack, but before she could leap at the deliberate lure Kate had dangled, she continued. "I will confess to one thing, however."

Kate enjoyed observing the sharp spark of triumph that darted fleetingly across Madame Duchamp's features, with a curl of her lips and a narrowing of her eyes in anticipation. "I admit to having a *prior* relationship with Mr. Sharpe, which I failed to disclose the day he walked into the boardroom at Flannigan, Searle, Meacham & Beckett. We hadn't seen each other for almost fifteen years and quite frankly I was shocked and embarrassed." She paused, and met D'arcy's eye, wondering if she would find an ally or opponent there. She'd been surprisingly mute, her smoky eyes darting back and forth. "I regret that now, though I still have no idea what I should or could have said in the moment. Perhaps a simple, 'Blow me away, it's my old lover, Simon,' would have sufficed, though the way Ms. Beckett has been carrying on, I strongly doubt it."

"Are you suggesting Ms. Beckett has been biased in her assertions, Miss. O'Day?"

This was a touchy area. Kate pursed her lips and met Madame Duchamp's eye steadily. "I'm not interested in retaliating with allegations of my own. I would only suggest that Ms. Beckett, too, has known Mr. Sharpe for many years and has, in my opinion, been overly eager in her attention to the matter, despite my reassurances."

Madame Duchamp's interest was piqued. "Handsome man, this Simon Sharpe?" she queried D'arcy for confirmation of this, a lively sparkle in her eye. D'arcy sat upright, an expression of feigned innocence on her face and shrugged.

Kate leaned forward, her hands open on the table, ready to make her case in earnest. "The point is, the mediation was entered into in good faith despite the erstwhile relationship. And in response to your assumptions, first of all, in mediation, there are no 'sides.' I am not a judge and I don't view D'arcy and Eli, or their legal counsel, as opponents. I'm a facilitator and I believe —and D'arcy can confirm this— that I've done an excellent job facilitating communication and reconciliation between them. Hence my excellent reputation. Mr. Sharpe may have been a distraction," she shook her head, concluding with her assurances in the spirit of confidence, "but there is no way possible his presence can have affected my objectivity or ability to work for my clients —*either* of them."

D'arcy spoke up finally. "It's true Mother. Kate's been wonderful."

"Yes, I see." Madame Duchamp acknowledged dryly, eyeing her closely, reluctant to give away her advantage. "And what of your relationship with Mr. Sharpe now?"

Kate pressed her lips together and shrugged. "To be perfectly honest, I really don't know. I can't deny that we have some… " she waved her hand vaguely in the air, "…unfinished business between us. But it's very complicated. I can promise you that whatever it is will wait until my clients' needs are met. To the extent that it is within my power, I can also promise that I will not see Mr. Sharpe privately or socially outside of our sessions until the case is concluded. You see, there is no *affair*." Kate had not planned this, but surely it was a commitment she could keep, and was worth something. A little more time to think and a bit of distance was probably a good thing. And her promise to Eli would not be broken, only postponed.

"That's not really necessary is it?" D'arcy said she was not worried about Kate's objectivity —that she had already proven herself. D'arcy petitioned her mother, "They're both such lovely people." Despite the sweet kindness of her words, D'arcy regarded Kate with deliberate intensity.

Kate didn't answer, but smiled wryly and eyed D'arcy and then her mother.

"And what of Ms. Beckett's complaint?" enquired Madame Duchamp.

Kate shrugged, making light of it. "Nothing for you to worry about." She smiled, knowing she herself had plenty of worry ahead.

"Hmph." Madame Duchamp appeared to be satisfied. "Shall we ring for tea, girls?" *Girls?* Kate interpreted this as a good sign.

While she waited, her thoughts drifted to Simon and how compatible they really were, how attuned and well-matched their tempers, how safe and comfortable she felt with him, despite her irrational fears, and they were irrational, she realized. Events and experiences from long ago affected her mind and her emotions, but had no bearing on what they had together. It was up to her to keep the past in perspective and to move beyond it.

She pondered his call this morning, and the tender feelings it triggered.

Already, her life felt dull and barren without him. She missed his erudition, his spiritual questing, the charmed and warm-hearted humour with which he regarded people, but most of all his perceptive insight into the human soul. If a relationship with him didn't pan out, she would miss his friendship, his companionship, and something more, something intangible she couldn't put her finger on, an irresistible force that defied words. She had a compulsion to slip out and call him, just to bring him somehow nearer, but realized this was a foolish longing. She had no reason to call, for the meat of the discussion was yet to occur.

Minutes later, room service having been bidden and D'arcy having made a visit to the toilet, they faced each other again as allies.

Once more, Kate resumed the discussion in the driver's seat. Using her summary notes, she guided Madame Duchamp through the key points of the case and the essential terms of the draft resolution. Normally, Kate would not provide such detail to a third party, but it was clear this woman played a pivotal role, and besides, Kate needed to butter her up.

It was evident from her comments and questions that D'arcy's mother was very loving and doting and, in her efforts to protect her daughter, this came across in hard-driving expectations with regard to Eli. It was no wonder he could never measure up. Kate didn't envy him membership in this dynasty.

"The bottom line, ma'am, is that D'arcy isn't a little girl anymore. She's a grown woman capable of managing her own affairs, despite her trust fund." Kate pulled back, precluding rebuke, as she drove her final point home. "But D'arcy and Eli can't make their relationship work unless you… " she paused, looking for the best word, " … agree to abdicate responsibility, so to speak." Eyes darting from Madame Duchamp to D'arcy and back, she resumed in an upbeat tone.

"I think what's needed is a fresh start. You got off on the wrong foot with Eli seven years ago, and…" Kate watched Madame Duchamp's eyes narrow suspiciously. "Well, he's more than proven himself worthy, but the present is tainted by the past." Even as the words left her lips, Kate reeled with the significance of her statement, which echoed in her head. She continued, determined. "You need to clear the air, and then, start again. I believe you and Eli need to meet, to talk, and come to some kind of understanding. After all, there's the baby to consider." This fact still stunned Kate as she looked pointedly at D'arcy but it occurred to her that it would likely work in her favour.

"And you, Miss D'arcy, need to tell your husband about the baby in question. I can't believe you've kept it from him, and from all of us, until now." She raised both hands, as if to contain the wonder in her head, and shook them.

D'arcy's expression was pained, but then she explained that she didn't want Eli to compromise out of guilt or a sense of duty. She was waiting for him to commit to her as an individual. She needed him to declare his love and devotion to her and to their partnership without that added pressure.

"I can understand that, but relationships are built on trust. I don't know what Eli's going to say or do when he learns of this. This adds a whole new dimension to our discussions. We'll have to tread carefully and you need to be prepared to accept an emotional response, to which… he is fully entitled." She reached for D'arcy's hand and gave it a squeeze. "Don't judge him too quickly on this."

Kate tried to understand D'arcy's position, but it was difficult not to view her secret as unfair and dishonest, not just with Eli, but with everyone. They had worked so hard, for so many weeks, and all the time she'd harboured this secret. It was astonishing. Thinking back, it seemed obvious now. All the signs were there, the changes both physical and emotional. All along, Simon had known something, had insisted that D'arcy was hiding something. She should have trusted his intuition, should have listened.

On D'arcy's agitated insistence, Kate promised to keep the

baby secret until D'arcy had found the right moment to confide in Eli, but urged her to do it soon.

"Eli has a right to know. He's not a child who needs to be manipulated, whose feelings can't be trusted." Kate challenged D'arcy on her own condescension toward Eli. She had no doubt of D'arcy's affections but noted that because of the power imbalance in their relationship, D'arcy had always judged him inferior or immature. Madame Duchamp showed a particular interest in twirling her wedding band and checking her diamond-encrusted wristwatch at that moment. "You have to accept that he is a grown man, as capable of understanding and responsible decision-making as you are. Give him a chance, and," Kate nodded, "he might surprise you."

"My, look at the time," came Mme. Duchamp's predictable interjection. "I'm afraid I will have to excuse myself shortly." Her armour remained intact as Kate pointedly raised her eyes to meet her adversary's.

"There's just one thing, Madame Duchamp, before we–"

"Call me Helen, please."

"Helen," Kate did not break her pace, "your work is not done, I'm afraid." Madame Duchamp, Helen, froze in place, her eyes locked on Kate's. She would not mention the bribe. It was not her place to share this secret with D'arcy. "If you care about your daughter's happiness and hope for a stable, healthy home for your grandchild, then you must commit to repairing your damaged relationship with Eli. It's up to you."

Her face tight and blanched, Helen seemed at a loss for words. Hesitantly, she sidestepped, "I expected you to resume your sessions first, assuming he… Eli… will agree."

"He'll come back. I can promise you that. He wants to as much as D'arcy does. He also knows that it's time to face his responsibilities. He wants to meet with you first, Helen. Alone. I said I'd make the arrangements." D'arcy appeared shocked and confused. Helen pulled her mouth into a tight line, and gripped a thumb with the other hand, rubbing it repeatedly. Her eyes closed on a long blink, and opened with a flutter. Kate could well imagine why she was ill at ease. Her past had returned to haunt her and here she was, cornered, forced to atone for her sins and without her husband beside her. Kate would have put money on the fact that she'd be on the phone to him the moment she was alone. After extracting a commitment to make herself available to meet with Eli within the next few days, Kate wrapped up the meeting and bid them farewell.

On her way home in the taxi, Kate stared blindly at the rhythmic swipe of the windshield wipers, almost as though they had contributed to her hypnotic trance. She thought again of her apropos comment to Helen and D'arcy.

The present is tainted by the past.

She missed Simon. The desire to find him and fall into his comforting arms, to tell him every detail of her day was so powerful her chest ached with it, and her head felt so light and woozy, she thought she might faint. Waiting until the case was concluded before pursuing her relationship with him was going to be excruciating. There was no denying it, she loved him. There was no other way to describe the overwhelming breathless feeling that swelled inside her when she thought of him. It was something more than that wild, pulse-racing flutter she felt when she was near him, more than the mindless heat she felt burn through her blood when he touched her. She loved him deeply, over and above being as much in *love* with him as she ever had been.

seventeen

Kate hustled past the Four Seasons Hotel toward the domed glass structure of the mall entrance just as pinpricks of snow materialized on the chill evening air, the first of the season. Dusk came early this time of year, and stores were staying open late already in anticipation of the Christmas shopping madness yet to come. She was glad she had only one or two more gifts to find.

The snow fell gradually, and picked up speed as she approached the mall. She stopped in her tracks, suddenly struck by the serenity of the scene. Tiny twinkling white Christmas lights twined around the reaching silhouetted branches of several small trees on the corner plaza, and contrasted against the deepening indigo of the evening sky with its screen of small snowflakes drifting gently in all directions, they were as yet so insubstantial, the air so calm.

Finding a bench under one of the trees, she perched for a moment, allowing the nascent snowfall to land on her upturned face and bare hands, enjoying their gentle, cool caress. She was glad of the snow, though in this mild maritime climate, the odds were it wouldn't be here when Christmas came around. But one could still hope.

Her mood was one of elation and optimism. Her mind was extra alert and active, with a sparkling, fizzing character to her thoughts, as she reviewed her week. It was almost as though some of those cold, spiraling ice crystals were dancing around in her head. After she'd waited by the phone for most of yesterday, Eli had called at last to report on his meeting with Helen on Friday. With Kate's help and urging, they'd managed to schedule a luncheon meeting in an acceptable location for Friday noon. Predictably, *she* would not go to his studio, and he would not set foot in the Hotel Vancouver. Kate had suggested a pleasant bistro they would both find acceptable, and finalized the appointment. Then she could do nothing but wait.

When Eli finally did call late last afternoon, she immediately sensed that it had gone, if not very well, then not too badly. Eli's voice was strange, filled with strain and substance, his words sparse and he announced gravely that they'd come to an understanding. Kate's impression was that it had been difficult for both of them. He seemed changed and, though he offered few details, she trusted him.

"Have you told D'arcy?"

He told her Madame Duchamp had promised to fill her in. "It'll be alright, Kate, don't worry," he had said with the weight of new authority that gave her a curious confidence. Whatever particulars had transpired, Eli was explicit in one thing. He was ready to resume reconciliation if D'arcy was. Kate was ecstatic and promised him to schedule a meeting for the coming Tuesday. She could hardly wait to tell Simon.

Lost in her evening reverie, only gradually did she become aware of the shoppers moving in silent, colourful pantomime through the glass of the brightly illuminated mall, like a scene trapped inside a snow globe, with the snow on the outside.

Busy shoppers bustled to and fro, laden with their shopping, emerging and disappearing from the mouth of the escalator like ants from an anthill, rainbow bright baubles and strands of green metallic tinsel suspended from the domed ceiling. She squinted her eyes. There was one very pretty family that her wandering eye kept returning to, they seemed so idyllic in their pose and delightful mood, perched as they were on the landing by the doors. A father in a toque and his young child sat on a bench with their backs to her, laughing and talking animatedly with the young and very beautiful mother, with her fashionable leather coat and tall boots, her long, shining chestnut hair. She bent to put something away and then turned to lift her little girl, for now Kate could see the brown pigtails, to give her a kiss and a tight squeeze, as though in parting.

Kate's breath caught in her throat with a hitch. It was at this precise moment that she realized she knew the players in this little drama only too well.

She watched, horrified and transfixed, as Simon rose, laughing, from the bench to pry Maddie's clinging arms from around

Rachel's slender neck and lifted her into his arms, allowing Rachel to button her coat and hoist her many bags into her arms.

When Simon bent to kiss Rachel on the cheek, and she moved away, almost as if in slow motion, and pulled her graceful gloved hand from his grasp, Kate felt a fragile perspiration clinging to her lip and brow, her stomach a churning, poisonous chemical brew.

Here she was again, on the outside, watching.

When ready, Rachel leaned in to kiss Maddie once more, and then exchanged words and nods with Simon at close quarters, their eyes meeting in common understanding. His family. They looked so beautiful together. Why couldn't they have stayed in Richmond, where she would never have to see them together like this.

Kate felt all the breath collapse in her chest, her heart shrinking and folding in on itself, and her vision narrowed, dark spots appearing at the fringes. More than panic, this was pain, deep and sharp, slicing through her, eviscerating her. This is what she had been guarding against with every new affair of the heart. But against Simon himself she had no defense. She stood frozen as darkness fell, clutching her fists to her ribs, shivering uncontrollably, convinced she would never draw a full breath again.

Rising and backing away from the glass, she had lost interest in any further shopping. Spinning on her heel, she hurried away into the deepening night, the swirling vortex of the falling snowstorm swallowing her. She strode fretfully away, trying to slow and deepen her breathing. Shanti-mukti-shanti-mukti.

On the way home, the image of Simon's complete family flashed again and again in her mind's eye. How could Kate mess with that? Though he had never hinted that he might yearn for a reunion with his wife, maybe that's what would be best for Maddie, and for him as well. What loving father, who had once worshiped and idealized his beautiful, clever wife, wouldn't? The fact that she still had the power to undo him, to drive him into a passionate fury or a melancholy funk was evidence enough that he still cared about Rachel. That was as it should be. Wasn't it? She felt a prickling sensation behind her eyes, and blinked it away furiously.

Was there a place for Kate in such a perfect picture? Is that what she wanted? Was it simply jealousy? It was a humiliating but undeniable truth that she could not, even at her best, compete with either the fantasy or the reality of Simon's exquisite wife. Even if she had character flaws, which she undoubtedly did, she was still his child's mother, the one that he had chosen.

Confused, Kate determined to keep her distance, and at least give him the chance to reconsider his duty to his family. Getting in the way went against everything she believed. It was the right thing to do. Despite her promise to Eli, she was perfectly capable of choosing right over expedient, however tempting the alternative might be. It was a heartening thought, though it left her feeling cold and hollow.

Around her, the snowflakes converged and coalesced, covering the darkening sidewalks with a fine blanket of white. If Simon wanted to be with her, he'd have to first be free.

Yesterday's pristine white city had begun to disintegrate, as pearly cloud cover moved in over the city, temperatures rising just enough to half-melt the freshly fallen snow. Slush lay on the sidewalks and roads, pushed into furrows by car tires, with inches of icy water accumulating next to the curbs.

Though it was still only early December, Kate had put considerable effort into decorating her loft over the weekend, and was glad to set a warm and celebratory stage for D'arcy and Eli's reunion.

She'd found a Grand Fir tree worthy of her high warehouse ceilings and had it erected in the corner of her space, filling the room with the fresh, pungent outdoor fragrance of evergreen forests. To this was added both colours and layers of rich aromas reminiscent of the season, the cinnamon and orange and brown sugar reflected in the reds, golds, russets and greens that signaled the arrival on her doorstep of all the bounty of the Silk Road.

It took her mind off the fact that her hopes with regard to Simon were muddled. She'd even considered going to spend Christmas in San Francisco with Mom, Dad and her brother's family, just so she wouldn't have to sit here alone, feeling like a castoff.

But she had to set her personal grief and disorientation aside, and be strong. This was a momentous occasion for Eli and

D'arcy. Eli had dug deep and gathered his courage, garnering tremendous respect from Kate. That Eli could rise to the occasion, and draw on some previously unknown inner strength to achieve what he had not been able to do for seven years, gave her a terrific boost in her faith in human nature. It reinforced her personal beliefs about people, and relationships.

When Simon arrived, Sharon and Eli were already seated with Kate, and D'arcy hadn't yet shown up. He took his seat, leaned in to help himself to an assortment of tempting Christmas gingerbread and shortbread from a platter, and accepted a cup of sweet-smelling hot, spice tea, catching Kate's eye and smiling in appreciation. She smiled shyly but quickly looked away, resisting the temptation of melting into the warm embrace of his familiar blue eyes.

Everyone exchanged polite greetings, and well-wishes, and somehow by unspoken consensus did not ask Eli for details about his meeting with D'arcy's mother, though of course they all knew about it. Nor did anyone make reference to Eli's angry outburst more than a month earlier, which seemed like old news and no longer carried any emotional punch. He hadn't said anything yet about the pregnancy, so she didn't raise it. It was a shy awkward reunion, and everyone was on their best behavior. Even Sharon didn't mention her complaint, which Kate was grateful for. An undercurrent of tension and expectation awaited D'arcee's arrival.

Eli had grown his hair longer, and wore it bound back with a ribbon, and also sported a thin goatee and mustache. It gave him a swashbuckling appearance, a la Johnny Depp. Instead of a leather tunic and a shirt with puffed sleeves, however, he wore a fine black turtleneck sweater and jeans, but was no less dashing. He also seemed to carry himself a little straighter, his shoulders squared and his chin proud.

When the buzzer sounded D'arcy's eventual appearance, they all jumped slightly, and then shuffled and squirmed to hide their unease as Kate went to let her in. She was back in top form, with precisely groomed hair, makeup and fingernails, and stylish clothing. She wore a bulky sweater and slim jeans under her thick winter coat. She said hello to everyone but had eyes for only Eli, and sank slowly onto the sofa, crossing her legs and twitching her pointed high-heeled boot.

As Kate sat down, she locked eyes with D'arcy for a long moment, and tried to sense the status of her big secret, to which D'arcy responded with rising colour, and looked away. Kate had a sinking feeling, and went on red alert.

She opened the meeting and spoke for a few minutes, recapping where they were when they were interrupted, and what new issues she thought needed discussing. She wanted everyone, Eli and D'arcy in particular, to ease back into the rhythm of the sessions without being put on the spot. She wove her discourse in and about the sticky issues that precipitated Eli's outburst and even made oblique reference to Eli's meeting with D'arcee's family without making either event seem too sensational or traumatic. She ended on a note of expectation meant to buoy everyone's mood.

Kate concentrated firmly on her methods. She had to work to avoid Simon's searching blue eyes. He kept attempting to catch her eye, and she could see that he was confused by her aloof manner. She didn't know how hard it would be. She had to remain cool, tried to send polite smiles but inside, she was crying, and could only manage fleeting eye contact.

At last, the discussion came around to the issue of family, and Kate invited comment. "Does anyone want to start the discussion in light of what I've said?"

Simon leaned in to speak, earnest, as though he'd been waiting for his opportunity to pick up where he left off a month ago. "I've maintained that every couple needs a supportive family network to help them through. It's even more important during difficult times. And if there are children, believe me, you need family even more."

"I absolutely agree," said Kate. You have no idea, she thought sadly, wishing she'd had the nerve to call him as promised to fill him in on D'arcy's condition. Now she realized she was the only one who was in on the secret.

"But what if there's a history of abuse? How can you support it then?" Sharon seemed poised to make an elaborate argument to defend her point, leaning forward, her face earnest.

"There are exceptions, of course." Kate kept her voice soothing. "In the case of absent or estranged parents, the counseling profession always advocates substitutes. That's how important a social support network is." Kate stopped herself, not wanting to stray too far from the key point. "Anyway, we're not talking about estrangement, only conflict that can be resolved. Is being resolved."

Eli nodded, and cast earnest eyes at D'arcy, who met his gaze directly, and her gratitude and love was plain for everyone to see. Eli visibly sat up taller.

"We've— D'arcy and I have always planned to start a family in a few years. It was just a matter of getting a bit settled first."

D'arcy was quiet for a too long moment, her eyes glazed in thought, then lifted her chin and said in a quavering but determined voice. "That's how this all got started. We can never have a family if there is no security or stability. That's what worried me. I was seeing success, but not responsibility."

Kate's sat forward, holding her breath in anticipation, one hand pressed over her mouth, allowing her clients to practice their newly honed communication skills.

Eli bristled. "Do we have to rehash that subject again? I've been working for years, D'arcy, with no reward. Can't you just give me a chance to enjoy my success? There's plenty of time."

In obvious frustration, Eli bared his teeth in anguish. He clenched his fists and pressed them to his knees, his chest rising and falling. In a softer voice, he pleaded. "I'm being recognized and appreciated for the first time in my *life*. Let me enjoy it. Give me time to get used to it."

Kate braced herself. This felt wrong. Eli gave no hint that he knew about the pregnancy.

D'arcy looked desperately at him, "I always recognized your talent. I appreciated you. Wasn't that good enough?" she trembled, her control faltering, and Kate expected the worst.

"No." Eli says quietly. "No it isn't enough. Can't you see that it's different?"

D'arcy was quiet. "I know. I understand. But it can't go on like this. We can't afford to be selfish anymore. I need you now."

"I just want this time. Can't you give me that?"

D'arcy's eyes filled with tears. She wailed, "No. I want to but I can't. I'm scared... " She shot to her feet suddenly, an uncontrollable sob escaping her lips, and rushed from the room. A moment later, they heard the sound of the bathroom door slamming, the only room in the place where she could sequester herself.

Eli tried to follow her wildly, and after a few halting steps, wheeled expectantly to face Kate, his dark, passionate eyes pleading with her to intervene. His anguished face seemed to express: *After all I've been through, how can this be happening?* Kate reflected that life often seemed unfair, and had a cruel sense of humour, especially with regard to the timing of important events. But she knew if they could get past this one last hurdle, Eli and D'arcy would be alright.

Eli threw up his hands, his voice rising indignantly. "What is it? Please somebody tell me! What is wrong with her, Kate? Why won't she talk to me?"

A tight knot twisted in Kate's belly, and a sense of foreboding crept over her. "Stay calm, everyone." Kate stood and gave Eli's arms a squeeze, her eyes meeting his still flashing ones with what she hoped was reassurance, and went after D'arcy. She knocked softly on the bathroom door.

"D'arcy? It's Kate, open up." The sobbing inside subsided gradually. Kate waited. After a moment, the door slowly opened a crack.

Kate pushed her way in, glancing around. D'arcy sat on the toilet seat, her shoulders hunched, her eyes sunken in smudged shadows, looking miserable. "Come sit with me in the bedroom." She led the way through the connecting door, and sat on her bed. D'arcy followed despondently, and slid down beside her, mopping at her streaked mascara and dripping nose.

Kate sighed heavily, her stomach dense as a heavy stone. "I was sure you would have told him, Darcy. I'm trying very hard to understand why you are so afraid to trust Eli with your news."

D'arcy kept her eyes downcast. "I... think... now I'm afraid of what he will do when he finds out I kept it from him for all this time. My reasons... my feelings are so complicated, so confused I don't know if... I'm just so emotional." She lifted her wet eyes to Kate's imploringly. "I've made such a mess of everything."

"I know D'arcy. I know. But you know how important this is. You've got to tell Eli... no matter why you kept it a secret, you *cannot* put it off any longer. Believe me. It's going to get better. You're doing so well. Really." Kate sat quietly, stroking D'arcy's back while she waited for her to regain her composure.

After a few minutes of silence, D'arcy stood up sharply, determination in her movements, and bent to examine herself in Kate's dresser mirror. "Oh my God! I look a mess." She licked the corner of a tissue and dabbed at her eyes, distressed.

Kate offered her make-up for repairs, and D'arcy patched herself up, and combed her hair sleek again. She stood up tall, smoothing her sweater over her swelling abdomen, and firmed her chin, though it quivered. They returned to the others in silence.

Kate broke the silence that awaited them like an empty theatre. "D'arcy has something important to say."

"Eli," D'arcy turned to face Eli, her fear palpable. "I've kept something from you, that you should have known long ago." Her voice quavered and she stopped.

Kate kept her eyes focused on Eli, who kept his face impassive, though she could sense his apprehension in his ebony eyes. The only sign of his tension was his Adam's apple sliding up and down his slender neck as he swallowed silently. She knew he feared something terrible, that D'arcy was ill, or wanted to go ahead with divorce, and felt sorry for him in his state of prolonged ignorance.

D'arcy bit her lip, hesitated, then whispered, her voice watery. "I'm pregnant."

After a moment during which Eli sat, his eyes vacant, his face blank, his reaction was sudden. Jumping up, he gasped "What? What? How could... ? D'arc..." He darted a furtive glance around, perhaps seeking refutations or reassurance in the surprised expressions of Sharon and Simon. When his eyes met hers, Kate gazed back steadily. She wouldn't pretend she hadn't known. "I can't believe... " he sputtered stepping closer to D'arcy.

Simon sat very still and tentatively glanced over to meet Kate's eye. Raising his brows, he nodded his 'aha.' He did not look exactly smug— but he seemed to feel vindicated. She recalled that he had maintained all along that D'arcy kept a secret; at last he was proved right. His instinct hadn't failed him. Kate acknowledged his insight with a tilt of her head and a small knowing smile. His gaze returned to Eli, who looked stunned.

Eli looked hard at D'arcy. "When? How?"

"I'm already four *months* pregnant," she said with emphasis. "I didn't plan it!"

Eli agitation was evident. His jaw moved, but no sounds emerged. No one made a sound. At last he looked hard at her— meeting her eye, his brows pinched together. "Why didn't you tell me?"

She sobbed again, shrugging. He also seemed overwhelmed, his face twitching uncontrollably while he processed the earth-shattering news.

"I– Excuse me." He said, his voice cracking like a choirboy's, and he spun and swiftly strode away, out the yellow door into the hall. Kate prayed he would go no farther. D'arcy crumpled and wept soundlessly, and Sharon quickly moved beside her to comfort her. Kate looked up sharply, widened her eyes and jerked her head for Simon to follow him.

While the men were outside, and Kate could only hope that Simon would work his usual magic on Eli, Sharon gushed her surprise and congratulations while Kate endeavored to calm the distraught D'arcy, who wailed that her fears were justified by Eli's reaction, and that all their hard work was for nothing.

All conversation came to a halt when Eli and Simon reentered the loft, and the three women looked up anxiously. Eli lifted his chin, smiled and strode with resolve over to D'arcy, and sat down beside her, calmly taking her hands in his and facing her. He leaned in and kissed her tenderly, whispering, "I'm so incredibly happy."

D'arcy visibly let go of the tension that held her upright, slipping into a softened posture, her face slackened with relief, like a balloon with a slow leak. Her chin continued to quiver through a watery smile.

Eli leaned back, draping his arm over D'arcy's shoulders. "Well. Where were we?" he said, his steady gaze directed on Kate.

Kate raised her brows slightly in response, casting her eyes from person to person around the room. She waited an additional few moments to be certain the hullabaloo was in fact over. Just like that.

"Okay. Well. I believe we were about to discuss the importance of family in a successful marriage, and, specifically, how you two would like to see that expressed." She smiled in invitation, a challenge to them all to embrace a more frank discussion than they had yet had.

She couldn't quite believe it, but somehow she knew, they'd crossed an invisible threshold of some kind, like the crest of an alpine ridge, and could see a new vista unfold and stretch out on the other side. The end was in sight.

This was Kate's chance to guide her clients into their future, stronger and better for having done the work of mediation. She felt both a sense of victory, and vindication.

From the corner of her eye, Kate saw Simon lean back against the sofa, folding his arms across his chest, his eyes roaming over her. She felt contentment radiating from him, and she shared the moment of elation, knowing that they'd accomplished something important together. Though she caught his smiling eyes from time to time, she did not dwell there, but somehow, without words, there was mutual understanding.

Alas, that understanding applied only to their shared work, and not their relationship.

eighteen

Kate was ecstatic over Eli and D'arcy's last session. Eli's reaction to D'arcy's shocking news didn't surprise her, at least not initially. What did surprise her was how quickly he'd pulled himself together and embraced such a profound change to his own life. But, that was the new Eli, or seemed to be. She still wondered what Simon had said to him in the corridor.

As for her, she could taste the end of the case. The rest was routine, really, although finalizing the agreement was a kind of long drawn out coaching process that gelled all of the lessons they had learned, and was important in its own way. The challenge for her would be to keep a cool, civil distance between herself and Simon, and this would achieve both her ends. Sharon, hopefully, would abandon her threat of pursuing a formal complaint with the Society once she had received a copy of Kate's letter, and she and Simon could delay addressing their relationship until the case was over. It would be hard. It was difficult enough to resist his warm, compelling eye contact on Tuesday when D'arcy's secret was revealed. She'd wanted to smile and throw her arms around him in her delight, and to acknowledge his sensitivity and insight. But that wouldn't do. At all costs, she must tamp down the aching sense of loss and longing that burned inside her ribs.

She sat at her paper-strewn desk suspended between joy and despair. The flat platinum sky pressed down heavily, obliterating any sense that Christmas was coming, making her exuberant decorations seem tawdry and falsely optimistic.

She stood up and moved to the window, staring absently through the rain-splashed glass at the view over the grey city. The buildings and the water beyond were partly obscured in the distance by low clouds, fog and falling rain. Mist obscured the condos across False Creek, altering the landscape until it was unrecognizable: close and claustrophobic. She placed her slender fingertips gently against the cold glass, and then pushed her palm against it for a moment. Turning back to her desk, pensive, she pressed her cold palm against her warm one, relishing the contrast. She picked up the Administrator's response that sat on top of the papers on her desk, fingering it thoughtfully and her eyes fell on her carefully worded response underneath. Sharon should have it by now.

Briiing. Briiing. Briiing.

Kate reached for the phone.

"Good morning, Kate," Sharon said.

What impeccable timing.

"Well. We're very nearly at the end of D'arcy and Eli's case. I never would have believed it, but it seems they're on the road to a true reconciliation," Sharon admitted.

Kate was suspicious. "Yes. I'm pleased, obviously. Eli came through in the end, despite the shock."

"And despite his unreliable and, in my opinion, untrustworthy character."

"You can't still believe that."

"I never felt comfortable around him. To each his own, I suppose. But D'arcy, now, that I never suspected. I was getting rather frustrated with her distracted, emotional behavior."

"She had her reasons, I guess." Surely Sharon didn't call just to rehash.

"I've even begun to wonder if the two crazy kids deserve each other, for all the mess they'd made of their marriage." Sharon's brittle laughter grated on Kate's nerves. "D'arcy seems happy, and Madame Duchamp is satisfied, too."

"I'm pleased to hear it. What can I do for you, Sharon?"

"Just a bit of unfinished business, Kate. You can't tell me you and Simon haven't been seeing each other all along. You're so adept at hiding it. But all those puppy dog eyes and coy smiles— I haven't missed a thing. If you thought I had, you were sorely mistaken. I really feel this flirtation is unacceptable."

Kate drew a slow breath. "I made my case quite clearly in my response to the Society. I believe–"

"Yes. I got my copy Tuesday afternoon. But I'm not sure you understand the problem."

"Which is?"

"Once the case is over, you still have to leave him alone."

WTF? Tension snapped through Kate, stiffening her neck, tightening her grip on the phone. She spoke through clenched teeth. "Do I?"

"Ever since this case began, I've been having a hard time persuading Simon to spend time with me. It's almost as though he wants to sever ties with all his old friends and acquaintances. I worry about him. I don't think he's really over the whole separation thing. I know he's terribly lonely, poor thing. No one in our circle of friends has known Simon longer, or understands him better, than I do."

Though Kate doubted that, it did concern her that he'd cut himself off. *Am I really the cause of that?*

"It's what's best for Simon. How could you know how vulnerable he is? You're an outsider. He's not ready for another relationship."

Echoes of Will's speech that morning at Simon's house. Everyone sure felt he needed protection from relationships with women.

Unless it's with you, I suppose. Kate kept her voice steady. "What do you want me to do, Sharon?"

"You must promise not to see Simon again once the case has concluded. *In toto.* You have to see that."

"Pardon me?" Even though Kate had vowed to keep her distance for now, she wasn't going to take orders from Sharon, or bow to her threats.

"If you give me your solemn word, I'll drop the complaint. It's simple. That's all I want."

Blood pounded in her ears. She could hardly believe what she'd heard. "That's blackmail, Sharon. I would have thought you were above that."

"Not blackmail. An understanding between friends. So… your word?"

"My *word* is… that I will continue to act upon my own council, as usual, and not be bullied by you. *That's* my final word." How dare she? Kate's hands trembled and she gripped the edge of her desk, struggling to take deeper breaths, to stay calm.

"You'd better hope the board executive can find it in their hearts to pardon you, for the sake of your reputation. Otherwise I imagine the whole interlude will be terribly embarrassing for you, especially with your award coming up after Christmas."

"Haven't you done enough damage?"

"Not as long as you and Simon insist on mixing business with pleasure. I found your response to the Administrator very enlightening. But I doubt very much he'll dismiss the complaint. You know he'll refer to the Executive now, don't you? Ethics are not arbitrary or negotiable. You can't expect to work in this business and write your own rulebook."

"Don't even pretend that you're concerned about ethics."

"I intend to see this through to the end. I'll be sending notice to the Administrator of my intent to proceed. In fact, the letter is sitting right here on my desk, ready to go. I wanted to give you one last chance."

"How considerate of you." Kate's voice had become hard and flat. There was a moment of silence, neither woman speaking.

Kate thought for a moment, and despite her misgivings, continued. She owed it to Simon to get this woman off his back, at least, even if she couldn't save herself. "You're sadly mistaken. I know it may have seemed like there was something going on from time to time, but Simon and I were simply renewing an old acquaintance, that's all. You can do what you want to me, but it won't matter in the end. You won't get what you want."

After a long pause, Sharon said, "What do you mean?"

"Simon can't be having a relationship with me. Or. You. Sharon. I have reason to believe he and Rachel are... or will soon be... getting back together." She swallowed, her throat suddenly dry and painfully tight. "That's what Simon and I have been talking about. I've been coaching him." It was a small lie, if it was for a good cause.

Sharon's response was quick and shrill. "They're nearly divorced! They've been separated for two years. You know that."

"Perhaps they were too hasty. People have second thoughts. They have a daughter. They're a family, Sharon, whatever their differences have been. That's no small consideration. I saw them together. They sure didn't look separated to me." As Kate elaborated on her fib, something she couldn't help but worry about, the less plausible it seemed to her. Kate could hear Sharon's quick breathing.

"You're lying. You're trying to dissuade me from pursuing this complaint. It won't work."

"Couples reconcile all the time, Sharon. Look at D'arcy and Eli. Look how bitterly they fought just a few months ago. But they love each other. People don't give up that easily on a commitment that's supposed to last a lifetime. After all, you were the one who told me Simon and Rachel were the golden couple, so ideally suited to each other. As their friend, you should be happy for them." Kate waited through another tense silence. It turned out, when motivated, she was a better liar than she though possible. She hated herself for feeling smug and satisfied at Sharon's discomposure. Kate wasn't a vindictive person, but this horrible woman deserved it.

"Well. If it's true, of course I'm very happy for them. But it won't change my decision to file a complaint against you."

Her eyes burned as tears of frustration welled. She held her voice as steady as possible for her parting words, knowing how true they were. "As you wish. There's nothing I can do to stop you."

The following Tuesday, Kate was uneasy —excited to be finalizing D'arcy and Eli's agreement, jittery awaiting a response from the Committee to Sharon's complaint. All things needing to be cleared up before Christmas, which was now only nine days away, heralding at least two weeks during which almost no business could be conducted. She was running hot and cold, her stomach churning, as though she was being *consumed* from the inside out. It was like enduring one long unending panic attack, and she felt as frayed as the old armchair Oscar favoured as a scratching post. Anything left unresolved would eat her alive by January.

And, if she was completely honest with herself, Kate was edgy, wondering what would happen between Simon and herself once all, or most, of the obstacles were out of the way. Would he still insist on being with her? Or would he realize his duty to his family and agree to work on reconciling with Rachel? Would he tell her to mind her own business? Still, first things first, and until then, she must try not to be distracted by him.

"Good morning, everyone," Simon said as he joined the others around her long dining room table, their papers spread out in front of them.

"What delectable flavours are you tempting us with today,

Kate?" Simon asked, eyeing the plate of cranberry-studded scones without shame, smiling broadly. She felt his energy pulling at her, as though their unspoken understanding kept them close. Closer than was wise. She could hear it in his alluring, warm voice, and had to resist the temptation of his compelling blue gaze or she would forget herself.

"You'd better be careful, Simon, or you'll soon be putting on as much weight as me," laughed D'arcy, patting her bulging middle. Eli, who sat very close, threw back his head to join in the laughter, and reached out to give D'arcy's rounded belly a loving pat, tossing a warmhearted, self-conscious grin at Simon.

Simon evaded D'arcy's teasing by changing the subject, accepting his cup of tea and addressing her. "You two sure don't look like you need us anymore, if you ask me. What are we doing here when we all could be catching up on our Christmas shopping?"

"Patience now. We're almost there," smiled Kate. "Today we're going over the final, *final,* resolution agreement, which will be an important tool for D'arcy and Eli in the coming years." She emphasized her point with a raised hand, palm out, like a vow, then shrugged. "Then I just need to meet briefly with them for signatures. You attorneys are scot-free after today," she teased, tossing a small smile in Simon's direction, "and are most welcome to go shopping, if it pleases you. As far as I'm concerned, you're only here for the baking, anyway."

"Busted!" mumbled Simon, past a mouthful of scone, grinning. He swallowed loudly, and Kate tore her eyes away from his bobbing Adam's apple, wishing she could press her mouth against his warm skin.

He continued. "What do you say, Sharon? Should we call up Rachel and head out for a shopping spree? She hasn't told me what she wants for Christmas. I'm sure she's confided in you." Sharon looked up sharply, a question posed in her eyes. He grinned idiotically at her.

What was that all about? Kate's assertion that he and Rachel were reconciling was compelling, but it was supposed to be a lie. Wasn't it? He seemed to be rubbing Sharon's nose in it. But what did he mean by it? The notion obviously troubled Sharon more than she let on. Kate could only hope her own misery didn't show.

"Perhaps next week, Simon. I'm already booked up this week." Sharon smiled stiffly, clearly unsure whether he was joking or not.

Kate turned away to read sections of the agreement for Eli and D'arcy to review, and Sharon paid rapt attention, though Kate detected her eyes sliding back and forth from Kate to Simon, curious and ever vigilant.

There was an undercurrent of tension between Kate and Sharon that seethed under the surface like a sleeping serpent, keeping Kate on edge, though they were both putting on a good pretense of indifference. Kate could sense Sharon puzzling over the notion of Simon and Rachel reconciling, and almost pitied her. If it weren't for her own insecurities.

Just as Kate read a statement about trust, D'arcy blurted.

"I have to say something." She cast her eyes hopefully around the table, waiting.

Kate looked up from her page. "Yes?" What new confession was this?

D'arcy hesitated, facing her audience like a firing squad, her hazel eyes wide. "I had a long chat with my mother."

Everyone's eyes drifted expectantly toward her.

"I knew I was missing something." She eyed Eli nervously. "I knew I was being shielded from something. So I confronted her."

Kate's eyes darted to Eli. His eyes creased thoughtfully, but he said nothing.

"I think she knew I wasn't going to be put off. Or maybe she needed to come clean." D'arcee's nasal voice dropped to a half whisper. "She confessed everything. She told me about the... the bribe, Eli." She turned to him sympathetically, her anguish at this discovery still evident. Eli winced ever so slightly, but held his tongue. "Oh, Eli..."

"I wish you would have told me, but I understand why you didn't. She and Papa have regretted it for years. Long before we had difficulties, they knew they'd been wrong about you, but what could they do? They feared you." She reached for his hand, and squeezed it. "They thought you would tell me, of course, and when you didn't right away, they felt..." She hesitated, her shoulders twitching slightly in a tiny shrug. "They thought I'd be so angry that I would disown them, or something. Mother was in tears, if you can imagine."

Kate couldn't.

Eli gave his head a minute shake. "It's all over now, cher," he said, his tragic eyes belying the nonchalant tone of voice he sought. "They love you very much. They were trying to protect you, that's all."

"Don't defend them! What they did was unconscionable. You're my husband. I'm their daughter. Somehow, there needed to be an expression of faith, and it never came until you had the courage to face her and force the point."

Eli's gaze darted to Kate, then back to D'arcy.

"She now realizes that you have too much integrity to ever have used that information to drive a wedge between us, that you bore the weight alone all these years. She begged my forgiveness, Eli, but it is you whose forgiveness they need."

"Don't worry, cher. Your mother and I have an understanding. It's okay now."

"She respects you very much. Eli, I respect you very much." There were tears glistening in D'arcy's wide mossy eyes and she placed the palm of her hand against his shadowed cheek. They gazed at each other intently, oblivious to the others. Kate's throat ached, her eyes stinging with unshed tears. A hush descended.

"Excuse me, I'm going to put some more water on," she murmured, and quickly slid out of her chair and strode away.

Sharon seemed to understand that the two of them needed a few minutes alone, and excused herself too, heading for the bathroom.

Simon stood up without a word as Kate escaped into the kitchen, leaving the hushed sound of D'arcy's tears, and Eli's muffled voice behind her. Deeply moved by D'arcy's words, Kate stood perfectly still, one hand on the empty kettle, the other dabbing at her nose and eyes with a tissue.

Simon's voice behind her was spoken softly, so as not to startle her. "There, you see? Anything's possible."

She whirled around, her eyes wide, a hot flush rising up her neck. "Oh. It's more than I could have dreamt."

He rested his fingertips lightly on either side of her ribs. "Perhaps there's still hope for us."

Oh. She thought she could avoid this. She slowly lowered her eyelids, shaking her head. "Please. Don't. You don't know—"

"Yes, I do know," he insisted. "Sharon phoned to gloat about her evil machinations. That's how I learned about my rumoured reconciliation with Rachel." A corner of his mouth pulled up.

"Well, then," she whispered. "You shouldn't even—"

He laid the back of his knuckles gently against her cheek. "We have to spend some time together. I miss you desperately. It's time for us to exorcise a few demons of our—"

She pulled away. "No. We can't. You're just giving her ammunition. Besides…" Kate felt hot tears rising, and she turned brusquely away and filled the kettle, slamming it onto the stove and hurrying out of the kitchen, leaving him standing with his eyes closed, clearly frustrated. Another moment with him and her emotion would be impossible to hide.

Kate resumed her seat at the table, trying to smile at D'arcy and Eli to cover her own distress. Simon came in and sat down, and Sharon joined them a moment later. Before long, the kettle's whistle pierced the air insistently, and she realized that she had forgotten to light the stove. Simon must have done it. She shot him a curious glance before rising and picking up the teapot.

"I'll be right back with fresh tea."

When she got to the kitchen she made the tea, and then noticed a note resting on the countertop that hadn't been there before. She squinted at the familiar, angular handwriting.

I can't stand this. I know you're worried about Sharon, but the worst is already done. We'll deal with it. We have to find a way to talk. I need to understand what's going on between us. I want to see you. This is so important to me. Please. When can we meet?

A tremor dashed down her spine and arms. She paused a moment to calm her agitated, shallow breathing. *I am so confused! Why can't he just wait a couple of weeks?*

When she returned with the teapot, Simon was busily bent over his document as though unaware of her discomfort while Sharon read aloud to D'arcy and Eli with her suggested revisions.

Kate set the teapot down with a thud in front of Simon without looking at him, and picked up her papers, her stomach roiling. "I'm sorry. Could you repeat that, please, Sharon?"

They went back and forth, clause by clause, discussing various additions and deletions, marking up their copies. Her mind wandered.

What should I do? Just ignore him! What else can I do?

They'd moved on a couple of pages, back on the subject of career, income and education, and Kate hunched over her draft, industriously making margin notes. She read out a proposed change, directing her attention primarily toward Eli and D'arcy at the other end of the table, her voice low.

"I'm sorry, I missed that," Simon said.

She turned her head and stared at him, his expression puzzled and hesitant under her fierce glare. She frowned at him, unsure if she was more angry or bewildered.

Simon seemed to shrink back, as though regretting his rash words, or dreading her reaction. She looked pointedly into his worried eyes and said, "Here. Read my notes," deadpan, handing him a page of her draft agreement, and returning her attention to the others. He took it, his eyes screwed up, and reviewed what she had written in the margins, nodding, glowering.

He handed the page back, and almost didn't notice the small scrap of paper that fell onto his draft in front of him. He jerked suddenly and set another page quickly atop her reply, returning her page with a sharp look.

She felt like a schoolgirl passing notes, and glanced nervously at Sharon, a proxy for the stern schoolteacher, ready to rap their knuckles.

"Thanks." Kate avoided meeting his eye. She was aware of him surreptitiously reading her quickly scribbled note, undetected she hoped, since everyone's head was bent over their own pages, jotting notes or reading.

Stop this nonsense! she had written. *Just leave it alone. I promised I wouldn't "see" you while the case is still open. Don't you get it? She's watching us like a hawk. It's too risky, and furthermore, I don't want to get mixed up in your family situation. You don't even know whether you want to be married or not. You need to focus on your family first. Forget about me.*

She saw him scowl over his papers, his breath slow and ragged.

Please, Simon, she begged him silently. *Stop playing games!* They could not ignore the professional ethics claim. He could ruin everything for her by behaving this way. Sharon's accusations couldn't be given any further validity.

She sighed and shut her eyes as she saw him pick up his pen.

She knew he'd written her another note, but he just sat stiffly, his blunt fingers tapping impatiently on the tabletop. The discussion continued, and Kate almost came to believe she was mistaken, or that he'd changed his mind. They were discussing career and education at length when he spoke.

"Oh, that reminds me..." he stopped abruptly, realizing he'd interrupted, "Sorry... I'm sorry, I just remembered something. It'll wait. Please, carry on." He waved a hand at Sharon and

D'arcy who blinked and frowned at him like he was off his rocker. Eli smirked and gave him a wry, suspicious smile that baffled Kate.

She could barely concentrate as they listened to D'arcy talk about her interest in political affairs, and how she had always wanted to go back to school to study more political science and international affairs and possibly work as a lobbyist.

When the topic seemed to be nearly spent, and Sharon was suggesting a new clause or two in expectation of future career changes and educational opportunities, even after the family was started, Simon suddenly turned to Kate and spoke in a stage whisper, just loud enough for the others to hear what he said. "Uh. I remembered the conversation we had about Mediation and I... uh... was wondering if you had found that program brochure from the Justice Institute. I think you said... " he paused expectantly, and she could see what he wanted in his sharp blue eyes, "...that you had it somewhere."

She could just as easily have shut him down, but it would seem rude to just brush him off. Instead, she put on a polite sardonic face, and turning, said. "Yes. Of course, I still have it. Let me find it for you." Rising slowly, she went to a file cabinet against the window, and bent to throw open a drawer. After riffling through, she extracted a file, returned and set it on the table, opening it and flipping through until she found what she wanted. "Here. This will give you some idea of what's involved— the course-work, etcetera. It would be different for you, of course."

It would have been too easy if no one else had picked up on his McGuffin. Eli raised his eyebrows curiously. "Changing careers, are we, Simon?"

"Well... " he shrugged. "No... Maybe." He was flustered, obviously unprepared to defend himself. "Just curious." He made a show of leafing through the brochure until Eli's attention had drifted back to the main discussion. Kate too, forced herself to turn her attention away. Eventually he passed the brochure back to the table in front of her, pretending to lose interest in it, and she understood that another note awaited her.

She lifted the brochure's cover and could not stop herself from twitching slightly upon finding his note, slyly shuffling papers as she discretely read it.

Okay. Alright. I don't want to do anything to jeopardize our rela-tionship or your reputation. But you have to promise me—it's not over. Don't shut me out! Promise you will see me when the coast is clear. I will wait. I promise. It's worth it to me. You're worth it to me. I know what I and my family need. Trust me. Please give me a chance.

Oh my God! He acknowledged what she'd been saying and he was still insistent that he wanted to… to whatever. Did this mean that he wasn't… that he wouldn't… ? Oh, she didn't know what it meant, but her internal organs were twisting and clenching, despite her willful desire to push down the flutter of hope that made her tremble and perspire, that made her heart trip and clatter like a box of china teacups.

Simon sat with his eyes cast down, and she could feel his tension. He really didn't know how she would respond, or how she felt. But despite her fears and reservations about their past, she realized she wanted to find out more. She had changed. She cast her eyes about the table, not pausing to look at anyone, but moving from face to face, making certain she was not being observed, then let her eyes rest on him.

He slowly raised his eyes to hers, burning with an intense blue light.

Their gaze met, and she felt herself flush hot and cold, and her eyes burn with a multitude of emotions, a swirling mix of affection and annoyance, anxiety and anticipation. Whatever she thought he wanted or needed, she couldn't resist him. She loved him.

Their eyes locked for several long moments, hers straining to express all that she was feeling in the absence of words, or touches. Recovering herself sharply, she felt rather than saw Sharon studying them in a smug way and Kate was left to wonder what she thought she knew and how much damage she could wreak in a week or two.

nineteen

It was impossible to concentrate. The work was tedious despite the encouraging progress. Follow-through with details had never been Kate's strength, but she knew from experience that this process helped her clients move forward.

Her emotions were a ship at sea, tossed on the waves of a turbulent storm.

Kate wasn't convinced that Simon knew what he wanted. Even if he were attracted to her, he seemed to be of two minds, since he was clearly reluctant to cut ties with his wife by finalizing the divorce, while behaving like a lovelorn fool with herself. Well, *she* wouldn't be fickle, rushing headlong into another mistake. She had some common sense, and a very good idea of how badly it could go if you fooled yourself into believing you were in love, and were disappointed.

The trouble was, she *was* fickle, and weak, particularly when it came to Simon Sharpe. Against her better judgment, she wanted to swoon at his pleading note. How could she say no? She stole a glance at his profile while he bent his head to read, fingers of energy radiating off of him, calling to her. How she wanted to reach out and touch his strong angled jaw, stroke his bow-shaped mouth that always hid a smile, tuck his soft blond waves behind his finely shaped ear. She wanted him so much she burned with it, was tempted to throw caution to the wind, and give in to him even under the eagle-eyed scrutiny of Sharon.

In a perverse way, she was grateful to Sharon. Without her interference, and the pressures of the case, Kate would surely have been lost and unable to save herself long ago, before she was able to temper her desire with mature common sense.

Perhaps she could avoid him demolishing her heart again, if she put a stop to their entanglement now.

She could even understand and forgive herself for indulging in a little fantasy. How could she not succumb to the charms of a man she had been crazy about as a girl. But if it was going to end, now was the time, before any real damage was done. Her very satisfactory life would go on without Simon in it, as it had before, and perhaps she would be a little wiser. Trouble was, just the thought of that made her heart squeeze painfully, and her eyes scald with unshed tears.

Blinking, she glanced at her watch. It was past noon. According to her house rules, no one worked through lunch. "It's after twelve people. But we're very close to the end of the document, I think another hour should do it, but I don't want to push anyone. Are you feeling hungry or tired? Can we continue?" She looked around, waiting, while everyone consulted stomachs and watches.

Sharon shrugged, apparently accustomed to working through the lunch hour without ill effect. Eli seemed a little restless.

"Eli, are you hungry?"

"Oh, a little. But I need a smoke break." He stood up and bent to kiss D'arcy's ear, and groped in his jacket pocket on the back of the chair. He clutched a pack of cigarettes when he stood up. "Where can I... ?" He glanced around.

"I wish I had a balcony, but... wait a minute. It's such a beautiful day..." Kate thought it would be worth the intrusion, if Lena were home. She raised a hand, and picked up her phone.

"'Allo?"

"Lena? It's Kate."

"Kat-ey! 'Ow are you, dahling?"

"I have a favour to ask. Can I send a client over to have a smoke on your balcony? It's so lovely out."

"Why of course, of course."

"I'll send him over." She hung up.

"There. Across the hall, my neighbour Lena has a bit of balcony you can access through a French window. The view will be great today." She grinned at Eli, who was grinning back, clearly pleased with the prospect. "She's expecting you. I'll forewarn you, though, she's eccentric." She twitched cautioning eyebrows.

Eli moved to the door. D'arcy stood up and scurried after him, conspiratorially. "I want to come, too."

"Are you hungry, D'arcy?"

"Well. We're always hungry, you know." She rubbed her belly with a sheepish smile. She had finally given up attempting to hide her pregnancy, and now wore a snug fitting black sweater with a narrow band of fur trim, and wide trousers with high-heeled boots.

Eli and D'arcy went to the yellow door.

"Take your coats, you two, it's cold out there. And don't be too long. I'll see what I can find to eat. I didn't expect us to take so long today. Sharon, Simon, what about you?"

"I can always eat, but don't trouble yourself," he quirked that self-deprecating, one-sided smile that made Kate's heart melt. "But I've got to call the office if I'm staying longer today." He pulled out his cell phone and drifted over to the far side of the room.

"I really must talk to a couple of clients, too, Kate," said Sharon, glancing around hopefully, peering down the corridor towards Kate's bedroom.

"Um, do you need privacy?" Kate gestured toward the closed door.

Sharon nodded, "Yes. Ideally. Would you mind?" She grudgingly smiled her thanks, darted a suspicious glance after Simon, and headed toward the closed door, already dialing.

"Just hold on one sec," Kate said, chasing her. "I'll check if it needs tidying. It's my private space." Egad. She'd never been in this situation before. Did she really want Sharon poking around in her bedroom?

Sharon paused her dialing and waited expectantly by the large window while Kate ducked into her bedroom. She cringed. Of course she never tidied here. No one ever came in, least of all work colleagues or clients. Even the decor and color scheme here was different... personal. The rumpled, unmade bed looked like sand dunes at sunrise, the blend of mauve, peach and pale gold soothing and feminine against the carved antique headboard and soft grey walls. It was a side of her that few people saw.

She kicked a litter of discarded clothing and shoes into her closet and closed the door, and raked a couple handfuls of freshly laundered bras and underwear from the bed to shove them into her bureau drawer, sliding the drawer shut with the side of her leg while she scanned the room. Jeez! She scooped and dumped loose cosmetics into a bag, catching a glimpse of her harried self in the beveled oval mirror, rolled her eyes, tucked her hair behind her ears before tugging and smoothing her duvet, plumping her pillows.

The slightly drooping bouquet of roses Jay had sent her still sat on the bedside table, dropping wilted petals artfully, and she wished she'd kept his note to throw Sharon off the scent, but it was long gone. The entire operation took about three minutes. It was not perfect, but...

"Well?" Sharon's head poked through the door.

"Okay. Excuse the mess. Come on in." Kate glanced around one last time, trying to see her space with a stranger's critical eye. Not terrible.

Leaving Sharon to her calls, Kate went into the kitchen, wondering what she could scrape together. At least she'd been to the bakery for some nice fresh bread. Maybe she could find something to make a few sandwiches. She rummaged through the fridge and pantry still puzzling over Simon, wondering if he could ever be happy in any relationship, given his predilection toward romantic idealism, and herself, with her utter terror of intimacy and rejection. *It's not as if I'm discontent with who I am as a person.* She could happily live alone. But whenever there was the possibility of love, her history came back to haunt her. No amount of counseling could ever completely rid her of her trust issues. And now, in spite of her doubts, he claimed that he wanted to be with her again. Him! Simon. Her ghost and her nemesis. Her heart of hearts.

She was mixing mayonnaise into tuna, lost in thought, when she sensed him behind her. She stopped her movements, held her breath, but didn't turn. He moved closer, she could hear his slow even breathing, smell his skin, warm and clean and masculine. Still he didn't speak. Then she felt his warmth next to her body like the sun, radiating heat, and felt his hot breath on her neck.

He gently lifted her hair, and bent over her, inhaling deeply into the soft crook of her neck, sending a shiver through her, and then gently nuzzled her ear and neck with a small hungry sound deep in his throat, like a whispered moan. She sucked in her breath, and willed her heart to still its frantic beating.

"Simon... " she sighed breathlessly.

"If you say my name like that, I won't be held accountable."

"Is Sharon–?"

"Still in your room on the phone. I can hear her voice."

She turned around to face him, pulling her neck out of his reach, but he moved even closer, and took her head between his hands, his startling clear blue eyes blazing into hers, captivating. Then he lowered his mouth hungrily onto hers. She heard a squeak, and a moan, and this time it was herself. How could she keep a clear head when her body was throbbing with the heat of his touch. Just when she thought she might slither, spineless to the floor, he released her, breathless.

"You can't tell me you don't feel anything for me, Kate," he whispered against her mouth.

"I never said that."

"We have to work through the fears and questions that are keeping us apart. I have to be with you. I know I promised, but–"

"No! We can't… " Her thoughts were scrambled. She had to stop…

"Yes, Kate. Shh." He reached for her again, his hands at her back, tugging her into his body, hip to hip, his unspoken need darkening his eyes to indigo.

She forced herself back, shaking her head, and whispered helplessly. "Stop toying with me. You know I feel something. I can't resist you. I can't *stop* feeling…" Her hands formed tight fists to stop herself from pressing her hands against his muscled chest, and she felt her throat constrict with the pain of confusion and desire. With an iron will, she stiffened her spine and raised her chin in defiance of his power over her. "You mustn't tease me when you're still involved with someone else, that's all. It's cruel."

His eyes widened. "Who am I involved with?" The wry smile returned to his face. It occurred to her in that moment, how much he had changed over the years. He was still the same Simon she knew and loved all those years ago, and yet, there were differences. His bones were more rugged though fine, and he carried himself with the same silky grace. His eyes, the same stunning sky blue, were wiser, creased at the corners. His smile, still teasing, still sardonic, was a little sadder. There were layers to Simon now, complexities, nuances. More to love… more to lose.

"You're still married to Rachel, of course," she whispered.

He laughed without sound, his unruly blond brows knitting. "I thought you started that rumour, to confuse Sharon."

"It's confusing me!"

"What is?"

"Please don't treat me like an idiot. I saw you together… the whole family thing." Why was she scolding? She had no right. She opened her hands, palms on his chest, patting and pushing him away at the same time. "But it's good. She's your wife. She's Maddie's mother. You should be with her. You don't owe me anything. Just… just don't mess me around." She mixed her hands through the air.

Simon's face registered his confusion and exasperation. He raised both hands, palm up, pleading. "She's not my wife. Kate, I'm not seeing anyone else. I'm especially not seeing Rachel. You've got to be kidding. I'll admit, I've dragged my heals with the divorce, but it's only custody issues. I admit I want Maddie to have a mother. What's wrong with that?"

Kate swatted away his arguments like gnats on a summer day. "I'm not capable of surviving a reckless affair. I can't deal with it, especially with you." She jabbed his chest with an angry finger. "Please respect my needs and stop playing with my feelings."

"You're out of your mind! Why are you throwing up obstacles between us? It's not rational. Haven't I made myself clear? I'm not interested in light flirtations or affairs." He gripped her shoulders, pulling her closer, bending his head to plant a tender kiss on her brow, and touch his forehead to hers. "Kate, I've fallen in love with you. I want to be with you. Only you." Kate's heart skipped a beat and her lips tingled. Her eyes, despite herself, were drawn to his mouth as he leaned toward her. She felt herself drawn to him.

The front door closed with a thud, and they heard a clatter of voices, feet and laughter, and both jumped back. Sharon was suddenly there too. How long had she been back from the bedroom? What had she heard? Kate's eyes flew open in shock, her mind a whirl. *Oh my God!* With a strangled low sound, she grabbed the bowl of tuna salad and shoved it unceremoniously into Simon's hands without explanation. He was going to have to think on his feet. She turned to the counter and pulled the bread out, preparing to make the sandwiches, her hands flying, the blood pounding so hard through her veins that her teeth were vibrating, her head hot with mortification.

Cool as summer linen, Simon turned to the open doorway, laughter in his voice. "Hey, you're back. Hope you like tuna sandwiches, 'cause that's what you're getting." She heard the sound of the fork clattering against the sides of the bowl, as if he really had just been helping in the kitchen.

"Kate!" D'arcy's voice sailed high, giddy. "Eccentric isn't the word. That woman is downright peculiar!" She giggled.

"What did we miss?" Simon enquired, laughing obligingly.

"You wouldn't believe the place," Eli offered. "It's piled to the rafters with brass Buddha's and prayer beads, stacks of paper everywhere... Incredible. And Lena... wow."

Kate pulled herself together, forcing a laugh and raising her voice. "I warned you guys. What do you expect from a woman who spends half of every year trekking around Nepal with a Sherpa, and the other half hermitted away with her mail order business?" The jarring odour of cold winter air, incense and cigarettes wafted about Eli and D'arcy as they shucked their coats and hung them up, snickering and whispering, heads together.

Kate stole a glance in Sharon's direction. Fortunately, the upheaval seemed to have distracted Sharon, who was watching D'arcy and Eli curiously, intrigued by their adventure. If she'd seen or heard anything in the kitchen, she wasn't letting on. Kate's breathing slowed ever so slightly, and her pulse calmer.

"She's lived quite the life. We almost had to stay there for lunch, she told stories..." D'arcy shook her head, meeting Eli's eyes, sparkling with shared delight.

"Lunch will be ready soon," said Simon, turning back to the kitchen, and looking into Kate's eyes with silent laughter, communicating his shared embarrassment, affection, and so much more with the intensity of his starry gaze. The smile she'd forced onto her face fell away as she realized how much he could convey with those eyes, so much meant just for her.

Kate pointedly avoided his gaze while serving a platter of tuna sandwiches and coffee and more Christmas cookies. Once they were all seated, he turned, pensive and preoccupied, nibbling half-heartedly on his tuna sandwich, his glazed eyes fixed on the shimmering mirrored baubles slung across the Christmas tree in the middle of the room.

Kate tried to keep her attention on what D'arcy was saying. " ... hair dyed flaming red, who knows what colour it was... "

"It's probably snow white now. I'm sure she's not a day under seventy." Eli interrupted.

"I'm sure Lena's not that old. I took her for sixty, maybe," Kate said, incredulous.

"I'm not so sure. You should have heard some of the stories she was telling, of growing up in England," Eli contradicted.

D'arcy shook her head vigourously, plucking another sandwich from the pile. "But she's French. Surely she's French, with that accent."

"No, no, no. I think she's originally from Bulgaria or someplace. She lived in France for many–"

"Good heavens, she sounds very colourful, anyway," Sharon interjected. "And she actually makes a living importing statues of Buddha?"

"And you wouldn't believe what else!" D'arcy exclaimed. "You really had to see the place to believe it Sharon. Piles of boxes and heaps of stuff. All sorts of religious artifacts from Tibet, China, India…"

"That would interest you, Simon, wouldn't it?" Sharon turned to him, jogging him out of his personal train of thought.

"Hmm?" He blinked.

"What's the matter? You don't seem to have your usual appetite." Sharon scowled at the half-eaten sandwich that hung suspended in his hand.

"Preoccupied, Sharon, that's all." He glared at her for a moment and shook his head. "Not hungry, I guess." He set down his sandwich, glancing at Kate. "I… uh… have to make another phone call, actually, excuse me." He pushed his chair back and stood up, moving away from the table while he pulled out his cell phone.

"He's awfully quiet today," commented Sharon.

"Must be work," mumbled Eli.

"Or his daughter?" D'arcy softly speculated.

"He's such a devoted father," offered Sharon in an undertone. He disappeared behind the carved privacy screen, and his cell phone rang in his hand.

"Hello?…Right, I was just about to call you."

"Excuse me for a moment." Kate stood up, taking advantage of the fact that the others were eating and still talking about her crazy neighbour.

"I did want to go over that with you," he was saying into his phone. "Thursday might be possible, but I'll have to check with my secretary later today, when I'm back in the office."

He glanced at her.

"I think there's a precedent for that, yes," Simon said distractedly as she moved past him to the bathroom, following her with his eyes.

A moment later, as Kate opened the bathroom door, he stepped through the door, nudging her back into the room, still talking on his phone. "I've gotta go now. Bye." He hung up the phone abruptly, and rather rudely she thought, and closed the door. "It's just my brother," he explained, but that didn't explain at all the previous chatter about secretaries and precedents.

"Ssss... " Kate caught herself before she exclaimed loudly, but not before he silenced her with a fervent kiss. "Mmmm." She gasped, her eyes wide, recovering and pulling away with her hands against his firm chest. "What are you doing? Are you crazy?" she hissed.

"Mmm. Crazy for you," he murmured, his hot and needy eyes raking over her body.

"Looks like you've got more than talking on your mind today. This is ridiculous. We can't be in here together. You promised." Kate stood with her arms akimbo, a strangely aggressive posture given the fact that she was whispering.

He grinned, and raked a hand through his hair, drawing a breath. "It's only that I'm so damned frustrated playing these stupid childish games. Agree to see me and maybe I can relax." He was begging, becoming belligerent. He pressed on in an urgent whisper.

"Shhh." She opened the connecting door into her en suite drawing him through, separating their voices from eavesdroppers by one more door.

He closed it, glancing through to her bedroom over her shoulder. "If at the end of this, you send me away, then fine. I'll go. But not without understanding something. I can feel... something between us that's overpowering me. I know you feel it too. And it's not just shared memories of our old affair. It's more. There's a bond between us that we can't ignore."

"How can I ignore it when you won't leave me alone?" she sighed, exasperated.

"You can't tell me you don't feel anything, Kate. That you don't want to see me ever again once this case wraps." Simon grasped her shoulders and squeezed, stroking her arms in frustration. He gazed deeply into her worried eyes. "I need to be alone with you."

"I don't know. I only know we cannot do this while we are

trying to work together. I'm in so much trouble already." She felt her face threaten to crumble as tears welled again. This was too much. She couldn't deal with it.

He sighed, and brushed a hand over his eyes. Then he framed her face with his palms, slid them down to cup her shoulders, squeezed reassuringly. "I know. I know you're worried. I'm confident Sharon's complaint will come to nothing, but I understand you're concerned. She's got no foundation. It'll be dismissed. It'll be okay, sweetheart, I promise. "

He wrapped his arms around her and hugged her, pressing his face against her neck, cheek to cheek.

"How can you say that? Look at us." She lifted her hands to illustrate, and ended with them against his cotton smooth back, rubbing up and down. He smelled so good.

"Okay. Not now. Let's have dinner." He paused to think, pulling back to push her hair back from her face. "Saturday. We'll just talk. I promise."

"That's what you said last time," she replied, meeting his eye apprehensively. Why was she even considering this given her earlier resolution? "Can't you wait a week or two until this case is resolved and I hear back about the complaint? I'd just like to know where I stand before I flaunt our... whatever... in public."

With one bent finger, he touched her eyebrow lightly, traced a line down her nose, dragged a fingertip across her bottom lip, making her shudder. "Please, Kate. It won't hurt. I can't think about anything else. I feel like you're rejecting me, and I can't–"

"Oh, alright. But not... out anywhere... Here, at the loft. Just stop talking to me now. Please." She shoved him gently away. "We can't stay here. They'll come looking..." She sliced the air with an agitated hand, and marched out of the room before she surrendered completely to his persistent touches.

twenty

K ate's stomach sickened with worry. She awoke early and lay in bed, spread-eagled, body and soul too weighed down with inertia to move. She had been filled with a vague aching sense of loss while she imagined Simon reconciled with Rachel, or moving on to a new relationship, as though she'd let something unimaginably precious slip through her fingers, although this was offset by a sense of its inevitability. Although she still had doubts about his conviction and the intensity of his feelings since their encounter on Tuesday, now she was worried for different reasons. It was almost easier if there were insurmountable obstacles. No matter which way things turned out, she was thrown into nadirs of emotional turmoil that threatened to engulf her.

Then, yesterday, just as if it had been preordained, she had been punished for agreeing to have dinner with Simon on Saturday. At least that was how it felt to her. A letter from the Mediation Roster Society had arrived in the mail. She should be relieved, in truth. The complaint could have gone to a formal review. On the other hand, the whole matter might have been dismissed. She knew Rose MacIlhaney was behind it. In retrospect, she was grateful she'd taken the trouble to consult with her mentor back in October. Kate remembered exactly what she'd said in reply.

"It's a very grey area, Kate. You no longer have a relationship with the man, and haven't seen each other for a very long time. It's not likely to affect your judgment regarding your clients, so it's up to you to decide if your performance is negatively affected in any way by his presence. Only you can answer that." Affected by his presence, indeed.

Clipped to the Administrator's letter announcing his referral of the matter to the Practice Advisory Committee was a hand-written note from Rose.

Dear Kate,

I'm sorry I could not shield you from this. However, your thoughtful and sincere appeal made a favourable impression on several members of the executive, myself included. You are capable of working through this difficulty, and both you and I know that you need to. This is an opportunity for you to dig a little deeper and sort these ghosts out once and for all. You won't regret it, I promise.

Affectionately, Rose.

Hmph. If Sharon's claim had come as a surprise to Rose, she might have been shocked and disappointed in Kate. As it is, Kate knew she was being subjected to a test. Only Rose could take this situation and make it even more challenging for her. She was reminded of her commitment to Eli. Hopefully she would get only a reprimand, but still, it was humiliating, and it was still possible that, on presentation of the facts, the committee might recommend disciplinary action, even temporary suspension of her license. They had the power and at that point, it was out of Rose's hands. Her stomach and heart squeezed tight at the thought, as though they had become molten and fused into a solid mass in her middle, like a lump of cooling magma. She slipped one hand out from the duvet and pressed a tight fist against her aching chest. *I cannot live without my work.* Nevertheless, Rose had raised the stakes.

Oscar twitched in his sleep. She lay listening to the rhythmic wheezing emitting from his coiled body nestled next to her, waiting for his anxious predatory dream to find its resolution before stirring. Her own dreams had been fraught with worry, her nerves shredded.

Bweeeeeeh. Bweeeeeeh.

What the hell? She glanced at her bedside alarm clock. 6:34. Who was ringing her buzzer at this hour?

She tried to gently shift Oscar, but he jerked awake and jumped off the bed, freeing her to run to the intercom. "Hello?"

"Kate. I've got Starbucks." It was Alexa, presumably on her way to the office.

A moment later they were sprawled on her sofa with *vente lattes* and almond croissants. "Hey. Thanks."

"Nmpmffm," Alexa replied with her mouth full.

"Nice to see you. What's the occasion?"

Alexa swallowed and rinsed her mouth with coffee before replying. "It's ages since I saw you. I've only got an hour before work."

They grinned at each other.

"How's everything?" Alexa asked between bites.

Kate didn't know how to answer her. She recounted the news of her letter from the Executive first, as that seemed perhaps the most pressing of her worries.

Alexa chewed and swallowed. "That's a drag," she admitted, but said no more.

She filled Alexa in on the progress of Eli and Darcy's case, always careful not to reveal personal details, and the fact that Simon was pushing to spend more time with her, even though the timing was especially bad.

"Anyway, the other bit is… " she glanced at Alexa, contrite. "I gave in and agreed to have dinner with him on Saturday night," she added quickly, "at my place." She winced, anticipating Alexa's reaction.

She shrugged and took a sip of her coffee.

Kate continued to stare at her, waiting for a response, a scolding, something.

Alex looked up. "What? You want me to warn you that you're setting yourself up for temptation, what with you being all Martha Stewart-y cooking a nice meal at home?"

Kate wrinkled her nose. Is that what she was doing? Seducing Simon?

"Why is this so hard?" Alexa said. "If I thought this much about a relationship before I got involved with someone, my sex life would be non-existent."

"I'm not talking about sex, Alex, I'm talking about love."

Alex rolled her eyes and took a long slurp of her latte. "Love shmove."

Kate smacked her friend's arm, almost spilling her coffee. "That's your idea of help?"

Alexa gave her a wry smile.

"What I've been thinking about is, this whole obsession thing. How the mind works."

Alexa sipped and munched and nodded.

"I've never spent so much energy thinking about another man."

"I know."

"So. Is it that there's something inevitable about me and Simon? Am I destined always to love him? Is it fated, or something?"

Alexa's eyebrows went up dramatically.

"Don't answer that. I know you're skeptical about my spiritual meanderings."

Alexa huffed through her nose in acknowledgement of this truth.

"Or maybe I'm utterly deluded. What it comes down to is the nature of truth, the nature of knowledge. It's a metaphysical question. How am I ever to know? What criteria should I use? And does it even matter when you're talking about emotion?"

Alexa crossed her eyes at Kate, and Kate retaliated by thumping her with a cushion.

"Remind me why we're best friends again," Alexa said.

Kate pursed her lips. "Because we're good for each other. If we were the same, we'd both be impossible, with nobody to contradict us or call our bullshit."

"I'm calling your bullshit, sister. If I have a bullshit card, I'm playing it now. I've never heard you indulge yourself in your metaphysical mumbo-jumbo quite like this before. And if I have to listen to much more, you're going to owe me bigtime."

"Shut up and listen," Kate replied. "I need to air these thoughts before they drive me mad."

Alex set down her empty coffee cup and reclined, putting her feet up on the spool coffee table that she loved to hate, feigning boredom.

"Over the years, I convinced myself that my obsession with Simon was based only on a reality that existed inside my own head." Kate spiraled a hand around her head. "Some kind of unfulfilled, doubtless neurotic, need. Romantic, yes, but delusional. As you know, Simon wasn't a part of my life, and as far as I knew, he never would be."

Alexa closed her eyes and laid her head back. "Go on."

"I learned to survive and to rely on myself. But a part of me never forgot that love I felt. No other experience could compare to it. He haunted my dreams. And so… I guess, I could never really be happy with anyone else. Never happy without him, or the construction of him that I carried in my mind."

Alexa opened her eyes and glanced at her phone. "I have a meeting in a half hour, honey."

"I'll be quick."

Alexa smiled, indulgent.

"There's the rub. I want to be whole and feel complete without him. Without anybody. Not just independence. Not just love. But wholeness. Somehow, somewhere along the road I left a part of myself behind, and now nothing feels right."

It was her nature to believe in abstractions, however unrealistic. Even her emotional life was fueled by ideas. She could be moved to agonizing or passionate tears by music, art, drama, nature, acts of kindness, and even random events. Hers was the type of personality that looked for and found deep philosophical meaning in ordinary things. Her world was not material or existential but spiritual, intellectual. She couldn't help it.

"So the question I'm asking myself is, is this real because I *feel* it, or do I feel it because it *is* real? "

Alexa sighed. "You don't really expect an answer, I hope."

Kate sighed. "I don't know what to do, or even what to think. The foundations of my carefully reconstructed world are threatening to crumble— have been crumbling ever since Simon crashed back into my life in October."

"Remember what I said last week? I don't know how you come up with this stuff, but what if all your focus on finding the perfect mate is an excuse to avoid making a commitment because of your fear of intimacy and commitment?"

Kate groaned and flung herself back against the sofa cushions. "Why can't I be normal? Surely most women don't go through this."

"I guarantee it. But because Simon is Simon, the man you've always wanted, you have to dream up extra complicated reasons why you can't have him."

"You're right. Thank you."

"Hey don't mention it. That's what I live for." She grinned and stood up, preparing to leave.

Kate knew it was the years of obsession, the grief, the depression and the healing that had taught her to intellectualize and analyze her feelings to death. Ultimately there was no answer to whether Simon was her true soul mate, if such a thing existed, despite the appeal of having one person to provide her with validation, to know her and love her for her essential self. But in the end, it was no help. You were left with your gut feelings. With fear, with love and with trust.

Because their attorneys had already initialed the document, and she needed only D'arcy and Eli's signatures on the final resolution agreement, she was meeting them at their condo apartment on the West Side. Five copies of the lengthy document weighed down her briefcase and gave her mission a satisfying sense of finality, offsetting in some small way the weight of worry she carried as well. Afterwards, she was meeting Alex for a much-needed girls' lunch, the first in awhile. If she couldn't figure out what to do, Alexa was usually able to help her see straight.

She couldn't be happier with the case, despite the setbacks. D'arcy and Eli had worked through some trying challenges, and she knew they were going to reap the benefits for years to come. It would be challenging, but then, what marriage was not?

Not that I have any first hand experience, she thought wistfully, *commitment-phobe* that I am. All things considered, she seemed to have gotten a slow start in life. By the time she'd sorted through her psychological difficulties and her career, her school friends had already gone through a couple of waves of settling down and having families. Except, thankfully, for Alexa. *I'm thirty-four years old!* Was there romance and a family life still ahead? Or was she too burdened with fears ever to make a relationship work? That's what she'd told Jay. The truth was that life with Jay would always feel like a compromise. And she didn't think she was the type to settle.

Eli greeted her at the door with his now-familiar grin of contentment. It looked somehow out of place in his swarthy, unshaven face, as though it hadn't yet decided whether to stay, as though his happiness was a source of embarrassment or surprise. She could hardly wait to see him as a proud father. He was as like to burst at the seams. "Kate! Good to see you. Come in." Instead of his uniform of jeans and leather jacket, he was comfortably clad in baggy sweatpants and a t-shirt decorated with holes and paint splatters. She wouldn't be surprised to learn that he had slept in them. His feet were bare, despite the cold season, and his long hair unbound and unruly. He took her coat.

She followed Eli upstairs and into a sleek, contemporary interior with modern furniture. The lines were clean and the colour palette subdued and neutral, in black and tan. It was tasteful and it somehow suited both D'arcy and Eli.

D'arcy shuffled in from another room, glowing. "Hi. How are you?" D'arcy leaned across her swollen belly to kiss Kate's cheek.

"Good, thanks," she replied, smiling at D'arcy's glowing complexion. "You look great."

"Thanks. I feel pretty good, too." D'arcy gestured ahead of her toward the open living area. "Come in, sit down."

Kate moved toward the glass dining table, and stood, smiling and waiting for them to join her.

"Cup of tea?" enquired Eli.

"You own tea bags?" teased Kate.

"Hm." He smiled sheepishly. "We knew you were coming, eh?" It was nice to see him in their comfortable, domestic setting. He seemed at ease.

"Thank you, yes." She pulled out a chair and sat down, hunting in her case for the documents. Turning to D'arcy, she said, "Well. This is it." She thumped them down on the table.

D'arcy's full lips puckered thoughtfully, the corners curling up slowly, and she nodded.

"Are you glad you chose mediation?"

"You know I am. I don't know where we would have ended up without your help."

Kate shook her head. "You two did all the work, believe me."

Eli joined them and set a mug of tea down in front of Kate, the tag of the tea bag dangling over the side. "Hope that's okay."

She looked up, offering him a smile of thanks and lifted the steaming mug to her nose. Once he'd taken a seat, she walked them through the final changes, opened the agreements to the final page, and turned them around, indicating where to sign. "I guess you have figured out by now that in cases such as these the document ends up being more a symbol of the process that you've worked through. Just a reminder, even if you never pull it out of the envelope again." She studied them pensively. From now on, they were on their own. She felt like a mother bird tossing her chicks out of the nest. They would soar or perish, but there was no more that she could do for them.

"You've got to be kidding. You know I'm going to have to shake this in Eli's face to get him to cook dinner once in awhile," laughed D'arcy.

"There's a better way, you know," said Kate.

Eli looked alarmed. "What's that?"

Kate looked pointedly at him and replied, "Stop feeding him."

"Ah," he laughed. "But you know what that leads to."

Kate pressed her lips together, remembering. "Well pizza, beer and chocolate may do well enough for you and I, but now you have a family to feed." They chuckled together.

D'arcy's brow furrowed. "What are you talking about?"

Kate answered. "I had the great pleasure of dining with Eli at his studio last month," she laughed. "It was most—interesting."

"My sympathies. I had to hire a backhoe to shovel it out." D'arcy's grimace said it all.

"That reminds me, Kate," Eli angled a sharp eye on her, suddenly sober. "What about our pact? I've kept my end of the bargain. You're not backing out are you?"

Kate remained silent, pondering. Yes, Simon was coming for dinner on Saturday, but what then? She'd given in to his persistent urging, but with the case ending, would she agree to see him again? If only she didn't feel so ambivalent. Finally, she spoke. "I'm in so much trouble I don't know what I'm going to do."

She stared intently at D'arcy. "You mustn't let on you know. Especially to Sharon. Even though this is basically over. But I'll tell you, since you know so much already, Eli."

They both leaned in.

She waffled and then confessed in a subdued voice. "I said he could come for dinner Saturday. To talk." She threw both hands up in resignation.

"Hah!"

Eli's eyebrows shot up as D'arcy's lowered in a scowl. "Simon, I suppose you mean? What kind of trouble?" she asked.

"Sharon has filed a complaint against me with my professional organization—claiming conflict of interest and breach of standards of conduct. I don't know what will happen now. Disciplinary action is still possible."

"That bitch!" Eli muttered

She didn't mention the cover note from her mentor, who sat on the executive. Rose was apparently concerned about her. Reading between the lines, it was clear she might have been dealt with more harshly without Rose's intervention. It still remained to be seen whether she would be found guilty and disciplined, or not.

"How long has this been going on?" D'arcy asked.

"The complaint or the affair?" Eli joked.

"There is no affair!" Kate felt her colour rising.

The smirk on Eli's face argued otherwise. "He's coming for dinner?"

"Stop it. You're horrible. I meant the complaint, of course." D'arcy slapped softly at him.

"Since mid-November I guess, about a week after we broke off sessions. Remember I told you she had suspicions."

"Based on what, though?"

Kate shrugged. "Just feelings. There really hasn't been much going on at all." She pulled a face in response to Eli's skeptical expression. "A—a lot of tension mainly. I think she's been watching Simon pretty closely though. She seems to claim some sort of proprietary interest."

"*I* knew it, though. I mean, I don't mean to make your case worse," Eli hedged. "But I had a feeling right away that Simon had something… " Eli waved a hand vaguely in the air. "…going on with both you and Sharon. I spoke to him about it. That's when he confessed you knew each other back in college."

D'arcy shook her head. "I never saw a thing."

Kate was disheartened to hear that Eli noticed the strange attraction between she and Simon almost immediately. It was no wonder then, that Sharon had noticed it too, and become… jealous? Is that what it was? It dismayed Kate that she'd hidden her emotions so poorly. Hardly the objective professional she prided herself on being.

Eli shrugged. "Call me a sensitive guy."

D'arcy elbowed him, shaking her head. Turning to Kate, she sobered. "Is there anything we can do to help?"

"Not right now, but thanks. We'll see what the Practice Advisory Committee comes back with. If I'm suspended you can have me for dinner."

"We'll do that anyway," laughed Eli.

"Eli, how can you be so cruel? Why do you think this is *funny*?" D'arcy scolded.

"You'll see. It's not funny. I'm just… encouraged. Everything will work out just fine. It was meant to be." The smile he gave Kate was warm and knowing, almost conspiratorial.

"How can *you* be so sure when I *'m* not?"

twenty-one

By the time she was through meeting with D'arcy and Eli, Kate had to rush to meet Alexa on time, striding briskly the few blocks to *Emile's* on Broadway. The weather was changeable. She squinted at the indecisive wispy and tumbled clouds that pulled apart in all directions like candy floss, moved by unseen forces high in the stratosphere. Despite the early hour, a band of clear sky to the Western horizon showed tints of mauve and orange with a cool white sun hovering low in the winter sky like an alabaster bowl.

In spite of everything, Kate felt oddly buoyed by D'arcy's sympathy and Eli's mulish encouragement.

When she arrived, Alexa was waiting for her at the restaurant on the corner, a small atmospheric French bistro that Alexa favoured on the nights she came home late from the office.

The place was narrow, as French bistros ought to be, lined in gleaming varnished wainscoting with old posters from the French stage pinned above, interspersed with charming *objets,* such as taxidermy grouse and cracked crockery. The *maitre'd* nodded in their direction, and after allowing a few moments for them to settle, sidled over with menus and a warm accented welcome in a voice as slippery and gravelly as Georges Brassens. She slid into a chocolate leather banquette behind a veil of thick crisp white linen, smiling at him and glancing around.

Other guests were sparse but there were a few business types nodding over papers, and one solitary well-heeled middle aged woman, who looked to be a friend of the maitre'd, for he stopped by her table frequently and exchanged more than a few hushed words in French, his sonorous voice rumbling like a truck.

The aromas of bacon fat and delicately stewed meats reminded

Kate of long-forbidden temptations. She scanned the menu *du jour*. It seemed almost a crime to order quiche when there were so many other fabulous choices, yet Kate knew no one made it better, and she craved it today.

After ordering a carafe of white wine and their food, they sat for a few minutes in silent appraisal of each other's mood.

"Well," Kate said. "How goes it with 'the partner'?"

Alexa sighed and shrugged. "Oh, he's gone back home this week, apparently." She said this without conviction.

Kate shook her head, feeling cross with Alexa's stagnant romantic life and low expectations. "You're wasting your life on that deadbeat. Time to cut him loose and find yourself a real relationship."

A slow sardonic smile spread across Alexa's face. "Like you, for example?"

Kate found herself fidgeting, and squirming, not quite able to hold Alexa's gaze.

"Okay. Let's have it. Are you worried about that letter?"

Kate filled her lungs and let out a long, slow sigh that crested on an almost-whimper in her throat. So many things were compounding at once, she could hardly find the words. "Yes and no. But that's not what's bothering me. I just came from the final meeting with my clients, and they said something…"

Kate related the meeting with her clients and their inexplicable support and empathy with her and Simon. "It's almost as if hubby's cheering us on." Alexa's reaction was equally enigmatic, regarding Kate through narrowed hazel eyes. "It's rather ironic given the ethics complaint."

Alexa took a thoughtful sip of her wine, and jabbed her grilled pate with her fork, waiting. Jane Birkin warbled softly in the background, filling the lull with the whispered innuendo of her melody, an intimation of longing and melancholy. Kate frowned. The French had a way of making everything so trenchant.

"How well do they know you?"

Kate open her mouth to reply, then shook her head. They didn't really, did they? But for that one evening with Eli, she'd not shared anything personal with them. As was often the case, she ruefully considered, she knew so much about her clients that her empathy gave the sense of intimacy, when in truth there was none. "Oh, Alex. Maybe it's just wishful thinking. Maybe I need to hear people saying, 'Oh, you're so perfect for each other! I'm so happy for you,' to justify my own irrational feelings."

"Is that what you want me to say?" Alexa asked.

Kate ignored her and focused on her salad and quiche for a few minutes, chewing slowly, savouring the creamy, rich texture. Was that really it? Could she trust the opinion of virtual strangers who knew nothing of her relationship with Simon, or her painful past? How could they know what was going to make her happy?

"Anyway, I've been having second thoughts about having him over for dinner." She glanced at Alexa. "And third thought, and–"

"Just do it, already. Stop thinking so hard."

Kate ploughed ahead. "Am I supposed to stay single forever? Where will I ever find a man as good as Simon again? Who will understand me if he doesn't?"

"Shut up about that already! How is that going to make your life any easier? Have a go with Simon. Enjoy the moment. If it doesn't work out, so what? You're a beautiful, intelligent and still young woman, Kate, and there are, contrary to what you seem to believe, still lots of fish in the sea."

The pressure to make sensible choices made her anxious. Kate almost anticipated a familiar dizzy, fainting spell, but took a deep breath and realized she hadn't had one in a while. In fact, she really was getting a handle on her overwhelming emotions. "But what if–" A faint buzzing in her head drowned out the music and she froze mid-sentence.

Alexa made an exasperated sound in her throat. "I love you Kate and I'll always be here for you, but you're driving even me completely nuts. Instead of analyzing everything to death, just go forward, swing with the punches, live and see how things turn out. Have a little faith that you'll be able to judge as you're going along. It's just dinner, for goodness sake. He's not proposing marriage."

The buzzing grew louder, more insistent, almost like it was coming from outside her head, not inside. Kate consciously slowed her breathing. *Shanti-mukti-shanti-mukti.* But what of love? *What of my undying love for Simon?*

The buzzing finally took the shape of the muffled insolent refrain of Alexa's silenced cell phone. Kate shook her head in confusion.

Alexa pounced at her bag, plunged her arm into its depths, and removed a plastic bottle of spring water, her car keys and a hairbrush before emerging with the phone, tucking it under her dark hair. "Yes?" A pause. "Oh, hi, Krystof." Her eyes darted to Kate and down at her plate. Alexa fingered her knife, turning it over and over, it's polished surface glinting in the sunlight. Alexa's colour rose. "Tonight? Sure, sure I can. Okay." Alexa closed the phone and set it down, her eyes meeting Kate's. Kate lifted her eyebrows in sardonic query. "He wants me to work late." Alexa's shoulder jerked up, and the shadow of a sad apologetic smile skipped across her face.

Kate pressed her lips together.

Alexa continued. "Do you remember our first conversation about this back in October, after Simon had surfaced, and you had your first panic attack? I think I was more excited than you were. Even though we trashed him that day, I was kind of hopeful that you'd hook up." Alexa's gaze drifted to the street scene out the window, her throaty voice softening to a purr. "I spent so many years watching you worship him, and..." she raised a clenched fist, "...hoping it would work out for you, I think I lost sight of reality, too. You made a beautiful couple, and seemed so much in love, even though it ended up short-lived." Alexa lifted her glass and sipped wine, pensive. "You know I'm not romantic, but who wouldn't wish your dreams to come true, most of all me? You know I love you like a sister."

"You're contradicting yourself. On the one hand, you say follow your dreams, and on the other, go with the flow. What about your thing with Krystof? He's married, has a kid. Do you not have hopes that your relationship with him will become something more?"

Alexa shook her head. "Nah. That's what I mean. We're just biding our time together, enjoying each other's company. I don't think about what it means or how long it will last. I don't care. In fact, I know it won't–"

"But...

"It's for the moment. If feels good. I know I'll be all right. I don't have to have all the answers. You need to be more like that. If being with Simon, or just thinking about being with Simon, causes you all this stress... well then, don't do it. Just drop it."

Kate's heart squeezed. "I'm not like that."

Alexa set down her glass and reached across to grip Kate's

hand. Kate looked down, fixing her gaze on the wide amber and silver ring that Alexa always wore, strong, bold and uncomplicted like her friend. "I've been a poor friend these past few months. This has been an earth-shattering event in your life, and who could understand that better than me? But I've been preoccupied." She slowly rocked her head back and forth, her moss-smoked eyes shot with gold sparks intent on Kate's. "I don't blame you for slipping back into your old fantasies."

"I'm not fantasizing. I'm trying to deal with my life."

Alexa wiped her mouth and stuffed everything back into her bag. "Well, whatever makes you happy. That's the best advice I can give you. It's just that you always seem to make yourself suffer. It's not necessary."

"I still need to decide what to do."

"If you can't deal with it, then cancel the dinner—it'll only confuse you more. You have the strength. You don't need him. It's not supposed to be this hard. Let it go, Kate."

Can't deal with it? Alexa made it sound like Kate was both immature and weak. Is that what her best friend really thought of her?

"Do I *have* to walk away from Simon to prove that I'm strong?" That sounded almost like a cliché. In a roundabout, paper-bag-princess sort of way. But it wasn't that simple.

She'd show her.

She was strong. And if she was a little crazy for love, well, who wasn't? Even Alexa couldn't extract herself from a destructive affair with her married boss after three years of getting jerked around like a puppet, despite her protestations. She was in no position to give relationship advice. It seemed Kate would have to figure this one out on her own. Kate wasn't like Alexa and she'd have to rely on herself to know what to do.

Kate finally understood there was no one she could turn to who could help her decide what to do about Simon.

She'd held off calling him to cancel their dinner date. *There's no rush. I might as well think it through.* He would understand, wouldn't he? Her emotions frayed, she'd gone to an hour and a half long yoga class Saturday morning in search of serenity, but found herself less than satisfied at the end of it, tears somehow held just at bay, as though the meditation had allowed deeply buried feelings and thoughts nearer the surface. With nerves that felt raw, she reached for the phone.

It rang just as her hand closed over it.

"Hello, honey! How are you?" came the familiar distracted voice.

"Mom." She tensed, her defenses going up unconsciously. Her voice always came out sounding tight and strangled when talking with Mom.

"I'm fine. Busy, of course. How are you?"

"I'm super, honey. I'm so glad I caught you. Can you join us for dinner tonight? I'm making lasagna."

Ah. The moment of truth. She sunk into a chair. "Uh. Thanks, Mom. But I'm have a friend for dinner." Well, at least for the moment that was still true. *I can still change my mind.*

"Oh! Is it with that nice tall architect, what's his name...?"

Like she forgot his name for just one minute. Mom had been hinting about Jay for almost two years. Why didn't she just come out and say what she was thinking? *Hurry up and get married you social deviant. I want more grandchildren before it's too late!* Kate sighed heavily. Mom didn't need to know the details. "You're thinking of someone else. Nope. I'm not seeing Jay-the-digital-artist."

"Oh. I see. Well, okay then." How is it her mother was able to inflict guilt with so few words, like little poison darts. "We don't see much of you, honey."

"I'm pretty busy with work. I've just brought a really great couple to reconciliation," she announced hopefully, twirling the fringe on a placemat.

"Uh huh. That's nice. Did you get the email from Stuart with the kids' Christmas wish list? Are you planning to come to San Francisco with us for Christmas?"

More guilt. She stood up, tapped her foot. "I don't know, Mom. Probably not. I can't leave... " she let her excuse trail. Mom wouldn't understand her anxiety over the Executive review, and she sure wasn't going to open that can of worms. She straightened the placemat, lined up a haphazard stack of mail.

"Yes, of course. Your clients need you. Would you like us to take a package for you?"

Kate nibbled her fingernail thoughtfully. "No, it's okay, thanks. I shipped it. Well, I'd better go. Say hi to Dad for me. Call me before you go." Kate hung up the phone and sighed again, her fingers tapping an uneasy tattoo on the tabletop. It wasn't too late to call Simon and cancel the dinner. He'd be disappointed, perhaps even angry. But she could always say she'd come down with a cold and just postpone it until… Or maybe after her disciplinary hearing, she would feel… Aah! *Will I ever know my own mind?*

Part of her was soaring with happiness in expectation of his visit, his comforting companionship, perhaps even his renewed attentions. Was that the naïve and deluded part? But there was still that small helpless creature cowering inside of her, fearful, insecure and uncertain. And it couldn't be ignored. It was whining so loudly it made her chest hurt. She had to *do* something. She picked up the mail and moved it over to her desk.

She drifted to the kitchen and browsed through menu ideas. It wasn't that she'd decided one way or the other, but she ought to be prepared, just in case. *Oh. Who am I kidding? I want to see him. Of course I do.* She wanted to spend that longed-for quiet time with him, all alone, away from prying eyes. She ached for it. Therein lay the trouble. Longing for Simon became an obsession, an illness that had debilitated her. She couldn't allow herself to want him and not feel somehow that it was a weakness, a dependency. How could she trust herself?

She opened the fridge and stared with indifference at its contents, her sight turned inward. But perhaps that was the answer. Since he insisted on spending time with her, she might as well indulge herself. If she focused on being objective, the illusion would undoubtedly pale. She was no longer a naïve nineteen-year-old girl. She would be able to see him for himself: just an ordinary man. She might even get bored or irritated, like she had with other men. The more she thought about it, the more it seemed like the solution to her dilemma. An antidote. As long as she didn't get carried away, and as long as she didn't lead him on, of course. That would be dishonorable. She had to stay cool. Observant, open, but cool. Yes, that was it. It would be a kind of test. She felt her shoulders relax, and looked forward to the evening with a new sense of resolve.

After running out to shop and stopping for a quick lunch, she hurried home to prepare dinner. There was barely enough time left for a shower and change of clothes. Her gut told her he'd arrive around seven, though they hadn't specified a time.

She stood in her faded jeans and bra and nodded at her favourite pretty blue and violet sweater on the bed. There was no need to dress up and yet she wanted to look nice. Nice, but not sexy. Well, not too sexy. But not frumpy. *Crazy woman.* Her hair was barely dry, and she just managed to dash on a little make up when the buzzer sounded. Her heart pounded as she looked at the red numerals on the alarm clock beside her bed. Six forty-four. She pushed the button to unlock the door; her stomach knotted and she felt a bloom of perspiration on her freshly washed skin. Irritably, she applied more deodorant and a spritz of cologne for good measure and yanked the sweater on, buttoning its dozen tiny buttons with trembling fingers. A quick glance in the mirror to assess the results revealed wide anxious eyes and tight drawn lips. Pacing and wringing her hands like the accused before the jury's verdict for the four or five minutes it took him to arrive upstairs, she forced herself to take pranayama breaths, trying to bring back the focus of her morning yoga and her earlier sense of purpose. But now she just felt agitated and excited.

Opening the door at his tap, she found… "Jay?" *Oh. My. God!*

He hunkered in the door, lifting his arms in appeal. "Hey, Kate." He took a tentative step forward and exhaled with force. "Wow, it's good to lay eyes on you."

"What are you doing here?"

He walked past her, his eyes narrowed. "Were you expecting someone else?"

She went rigid. "You shouldn't be here." She bit her lip. How quickly could she get rid of him? He stopped at the hall table, lifted a book, fingering its spine, and turned around to face her.

"I want to apologize for pressuring you. I've been thinking—"

The door buzzer sounded loudly and she flinched, the hair on the back of her neck prickling. Oh God Oh God *Oh God!* This was not good. Kate stood indecisively in the doorway, her eyes flitting between Jay and the empty hall, wishing she could disappear.

"You are expecting someone," Jay said, scowling. He set down the book.

Moments later, Simon bounced to the top step, wearing his sheepskin coat, both hands behind his back, his face flushed. He strode to the open door and offered her one of his lopsided, bashful grins, and she thought, *Calm down!* of her rapidly beating heart. He definitely got very high marks for unassuming charm and just plain breath-stopping handsomeness. She couldn't help but return his shy smile. She shot a nervous glance at Jay, standing now with his brows knit, realization dawning.

"Hope I'm not too late... or early?" Simon said from the doorway, unaware of Jay's presence.

"Hi. No, well, maybe a little." She backed away, her heart pounding.

His eyes were cast down as he spoke. "I know this isn't technically a... er... date, but I brought a bottle of wine for dinner, and— " one arm swung around, presenting a brown paper bag choked by his leather gloved hand, "—and this doesn't count as flowers, since it's so close to Christmas," his other arm presented a freckled pink potted poinsietta. He stole a cautious glance up into her eyes and she found a twinkle of mischief there. *Oh God. What am I going to do now?*

Laughing nervously into his eyes, she said, "Riiiight. Thank you." Her eyes flicked to Jay, who stood rigidly, his face darkening.

Simon was looking down at the floor again, or rather, following his gaze, at her feet. They were bare, and she had thankfully had a pedicure. "Charming," he said to her pale pink toenails, which wiggled self-consciously, and his smile returned. "Aren't you going to invite me in?"

"I... uh, sure. There's just..." She looked at Jay desperately, drawing her lips between her teeth. The contrast between the heavy sense of dread Jay's arrival had brought, and this thrill of excitement now as she regarded Simon was marked, and she could hardly conceal it. Poor Jay!

Jay shrugged ominously and stepped forward, his jaw tight.

Simon looked up then and saw him, stopping short, his shock and confusion evident.

"Oh! I–"

Oh, God, no! Her scalp tingled. She turned to see Jay's handsome, chiseled face arrested in a muddled expression of concern, confusion, hurt and irritation.

"What's... " His dark eyes pulled away and locked in astonishment on their target. If looks could kill, she thought.

"Jay..." she hissed. She could try to explain either or both of them away, but who was she kidding? She faced Simon. "Jay just stopped by... unannounced. He's leaving now."

Simon stepped through the door, his jaw hard, his unwavering blue eyes as cold as ice. "Are you alright?" He set the wine and poinsietta down on the oak hall table with a solid thunk, his hands lingering on them, his eyes sliding back to Jay's. "Good evening," he said, a tight smile pulling at his cheeks. His head swung in her direction. "If this is a bad time, I can—"

Kate swallowed hard, looking from Simon to Jay and back again. Their eyes were fused in a silent dual, shooting daggers and unspoken threats.

She had to say something. This was unbearable. "Uh, Simon? I've told you about Jay. Jay, this is Simon." She laid one hand lightly on Simon's arm, claiming him. "He's just arrived for dinner." The explanation felt pathetic, and Kate reeled at the tension in the room. "Jay is…" she stopped, uncertain what to call him.

"The man who hopes to marry Kate," he said grimly, his eyes unwavering.

"Jay, please. We've…we ended our relationship." She shook her head slowly, her throat thickening. "Please don't—"

"Don't what, Kate?" His gaze met hers darkly, and she cowered under his accusing glare. "What's going on here, exactly?"

"It's none of your business anymore. Please leave." Kate fought to stop her chin from trembling.

There was no sense dissembling. Jay had to understand. She held her breath and lifted her chin, her eyes on Jay's face, as his dark hazel eyes flitted from her face to Simon's again and again in disbelief. She could see the veins pulsing in Jay's temple and a hollow twitch in Simon's tightly clenched jaw. Her blood roared in her ears, drowning out all sounds but the rapid drumbeat of her pulse. It felt to her as if an hour passed.

Finally, thankfully, she saw resignation and acceptance dawn on Jay's face. He squared his jaw and jutted his chin, a cool, knowing expression settling into his eyes like a shroud and she felt him withdraw from her emotionally, as though he'd constructed a wall around himself, brick by brick, as they stood there by the door. She felt her heart squeeze painfully in sympathy, like a cold hand tightening around it. He didn't deserve this humiliation. He'd been a wonderful friend and lover to her. He'd done his best. It just hadn't been enough.

"Congratulations, Simon. You've won yourself a grand prize indeed." Jay reached out a hand toward Simon, ever the gentleman, though his chauvinistic words irritated Kate while they attempted to compliment.

Simon's eyes narrowed, still holding Jay's steady gaze without flinching. He didn't take Jay's offered hand.

"I hope you know what you're doing," Jay said to Kate, tight-lipped. He turned and went out the door without another word, without another glance in Kate's direction.

Several tense moments passed after Kate silently closed the door on the sound of Jay's footsteps retreating down the stairs. She ventured a look toward Simon's face. "I'm sorry. He just dropped in. Terrible timing."

Kate watched Simon slip out of his coat and hang it up. His trim, broad-shouldered frame was accentuated by a fine grey cashmere crew neck sweater. She realized she was ogling the contours of muscle on his arms and back, and pulled her admiring eyes away.

He stepped forward and wrapped her in a warm hug, squeezing and releasing her, stepping back to dip his head and study her expression. He peered at her, unspoken questions in his shadowed blue eyes.

Her breath was still shaky. "I need a drink."

"Yeah, I imagine. Try that. I'm sorry if it doesn't go with your food. It's an Australian cab-sauv."

"That will be perfect. It's Italian. The food I mean. I'll get the opener." She was grateful for something to do, and took the bottle in a bag to the kitchen. She popped the eggplant Parmigianino into the preheated oven while she was there, ditched the bag and carried the wine and opener back to the table. She was twitchy again, despite her best efforts to stay calm, and fumbled with the wine opener, unable to coordinate her trembling hands.

Simon sidled up and gently covered her hands with his, pulling the wine and opener from her, deftly opening the bottle and pouring into the glasses, then set the bottle down and handed her one glass. She smiled awkwardly and gestured toward the sofa and he led the way.

He chose a seat that faced her massive Christmas tree, tilting his head back to take in the lights and sparkling ornaments that climbed up to its lofty peak. She was grateful not to have to meet his eyes.

"I can't remember if you told me how you got this monster in here."

She laughed softly. "I have a couple of strapping young contractors that help me out."

He raised a suggestive eyebrow at that. "I'm glad you didn't say Jay."

She lowered her eyes. She wasn't ready to explain. She hadn't expected Jay to turn up, or to put up a fight. It had shaken her up.

"Do you want to talk about it?"

Kate swallowed salt, feeling tears stinging the back of her eyes. "Not really." Her voice shook. She shook her head to clear it. "I... he's having trouble dealing with the break up. I really hurt..." her chin trembled, and she stopped. "I'm sorry." She covered her face with her hand.

His fingertips stroked her hair gently, soothing.

"I'm really sorry to have put you in that position."

She sniffed, getting control. "It was only partly you. It had to happen anyway. But he really is a decent guy."

He looked back at her tree. "You put all those lights and things up yourself?"

"Of course." She smiled, grateful at the change of subject. It was just another example of Simon's sensitivity, in contrast to Jay's self-centeredness. She didn't want to compare him to Jay, but the thought pushed itself into her consciousness anyway. "It's ambitious, I know, but it's worth it. It's my favourite part of the holidays. I could forego the rest, just for the lights."

Simon grunted. "Food's important too, though. Wouldn't be the same without the food." His blue eyes twinkled with humor.

"You're quite the foodie, aren't you?" She smiled. It was a natural introduction to a conversation about their respective family traditions, and anecdotes collected over the years. Soon the encounter with Jay was all but forgotten, and they were laughing together. He got more high marks for being a warm and easy conversationalist, and for not pushing her on the subject of Jay. They always seemed to fall naturally into a comfortable camaraderie. There was nothing forced or uptight or false about their times together.

Simon cleared his throat, compelling her to turn and look at him questioningly. "Now that the case is over..." he said. Kate's stomach fluttered with a surge of panic. "What's been happening with Sharon's claim?"

She released her breath in a flood of relief. Kate filled him in, explaining how her mentor at the Justice Institute was probably responsible for avoiding a full hearing. She quite consciously left out the part about Rose being the one who counseled her through the roughest patches in the past. There was nothing Rose didn't know about Kate. That was one reason this episode with Simon becoming public was so humiliating for her. She sighed heavily. "I suppose I should be grateful. I expect I'll hear from them before Christmas. I hope so anyway. It's killing me, the waiting."

Simon reached to gently push the hair from her eyes with a finger. "I'm sorry you have to go through this. And I'm really sorry for my part in it. But I have a good feeling about it."

Kate prayed he was right, but she couldn't be so confident. She sighed and rose. "I'd better check the oven." Almost an hour had passed, and yet it felt like mere minutes. She was trying to keep her cool, but instead it felt as though she were being carried on a bed of clouds, her feet not quite touching the ground.

Simon's voice carried in to her. "Do you mind if I put on some music?"

"No, go ahead. Whatever you want." Moments later, the joyful twang Cindy Church singing "It's Christmas" from her Quartette disc floated onto the air. Oh! He'd chosen her favourite Christmas album. But that meant nothing, of course; it had been on top of the pile.

"That's nice. Dinner's almost ready." Her voice sounded thin and reedy in her ears. Kate stole a moment alone in the kitchen, trying to sooth herself. She wet a tea towel, and dabbed its cool edge on her temples and on the back of her neck. This wasn't going according to plan at all. Not only was Simon being a perfect, kind, adorable, and sexy gentleman but she was a wreck! Not at all the cool objective critic of his shortcomings she'd planned to be.

She strode to the table, setting down a large bowl of salad, and lit the candles, hoping Simon didn't see her unsteady hands.

He was beside her. "Do you always eat by candlelight?" His voice was warm and teasing.

The familiar lines from another Christmas song wove themselves into her consciousness with images of cold winter weather, and a couple alone together. She felt the heat of his body next to her arm, and willed herself to stay calm. "I do actually. Even when I'm alone. It stops me from snarfing my food."

She laughed, and cringed inwardly at the nearly hysterical note she heard.

"You're quite the romantic." He was facing her, but she resolutely examined the table setting, correcting the placement of forks and napkins as the lyrics of the song painted a picture of lovers spending a winter night embracing by a fire.

"You are too, I think," she ventured. Her stomach fluttered with nerves, and she gripped the back of a chair for support.

"You know I am." She felt his hand on her shoulder. He turned her to face him, and she forced herself to look serenely up into his face. His look was kindness itself, not threatening, and yet the heat that lay beneath his tender expression caused his eyes to blaze. He brought his knuckles up to caress her cheek. It was an incredibly intimate gesture that threatened to turn her knees to butter. "Thanks for doing this."

There was nothing she could do to alter his course. Not that she wanted to. Her arms and legs were petrified, and she could feel a tremor surging upward and through her, ready to take down her foundation and topple her. She was held captive in a trance while a part of her observed his face bend close to hers. She wondered if her pounding heart was visible through her sweater. Of their own accord, her eyes fluttered closed as she felt his lips brush softly against hers. She adored his gentle kisses, pent with controlled passion. There was nothing she could have done to prevent her body from responding to his touch, feeling herself sway toward him. Sensations washed over her one by one as heat flooded her body. Her thighs tingled and tightened, her breasts prickled and warmed, and her breath quickened alarmingly. Objectively indeed! She had a very powerful bias toward this man, and couldn't imagine ever becoming bored or irritated by him. He wrapped an arm around her back and pulled her closer.

But, a voice inside her head shouted, *This is not what you want!* She forced herself to pull away from his embrace, shaking her head. Is it? Wordlessly, her unsteady legs carried her to the kitchen to retrieve their dinner before it burned. When she returned with the Parmigianino, he hadn't moved, and stood considering her with a quizzical expression, his head tilted slightly.

"Parmigiano de melanzane," she announced in a quavering voice as she set the steaming hot dish down on the table. At least she knew she could distract him with food—for a while.

"Lucky me," he exclaimed, eyeing it with interest. Was that a hint of sarcasm in his tone?

"I'll be right back with the bread." When Kate returned, Simon had refilled their wine glasses and stood poised behind his chair, waiting for her to sit. She almost overturned the breadbasket as she set it down and recovering, moved to her chair. She smoothed her hair with fluttering hands. "Please, sit down."

They both sat. She offered him bread, and he helped himself, breaking it and eating it slowly, sipping his wine and gazing at her overlong, his eyes serious though that private amused smile lurked just below the surface. She felt her cheeks grow very warm, and busied herself to avoid looking directly at him. Kate served them both, and then raised her glass. *"Buon appetito." I'm behaving like a ditz,* she observed critically. He'll think I'm a fool.

The corners of his lips quirked up and he raised his eyebrows and dug in. He paused, a thoughtful expression on his face and went back for another forkful, and another, before stopping. "This is amazing. It's the best I've ever tasted."

She couldn't help beaming in pride, her chest expanding, and her face stretching in a grin. "You exaggerate."

"I do not. You've found the key to my heart. Between your muffins and this, I'm determined to have ten children with you."

She looked up sharply, the heat rushing to her cheeks. "You're joking. What a thing to say."

He smiled roguishly. "I may be embellishing, but I'm not joking really, no."

Her smile failed her while her mind whirled desperately. Was he just teasing her? How could she remain objective under such an onslaught? If she wasn't already hopelessly in love with him, surely she would fall in love tonight. The effort of holding back her natural responses bled her. She felt her breathing come short and shallow and her senses throbbed like something soft and alive, some pulsing organism, a sea anemone perhaps. She wouldn't get through the evening at this rate, she felt so light-headed. She had to break the tension, move, change something. She grabbed the salad bowl and thrust it at Simon. "Salad?"

Simon took the bowl from her with a wry smile. "Thanks."

He seemed to sense her anxiety. They passed the remainder of dinner without further propositions or flattery. Instead, Simon ate heartily, and artfully steered the conversation toward D'arcy and Eli, and how they were doing on their own, together again.

When they'd finished eating, they sat awhile, staring at each other. She still felt tense, but better, easier than that paralyzing moment earlier. After a few awkward minutes of fidgeting, she gathered the dishes, and he sat, following her movements with his eyes, but otherwise sitting perfectly still, his fingertips steepled in front of his chin. He was very cat-like, and she imagined him patiently eyeing his prey, his tail swishing. She detected a hint of a smile teasing one corner of his mouth.

Stopping, she gazed at him, questioning. "And just what makes you think there is any desert?" She couldn't help but smile.

He broke into a grin. "I know you. And moreover, you know me." His eyes had darkened to indigo and were twinkling with humour.

She shook her head, suppressing a smile. "Might I suggest you take a breather, after three helpings of dinner? Perhaps in a few minutes you'll be able to do justice to the p-i-e."

He lifted his eyebrows, nodding, a smile playing at the corners of his mouth, and finally stood to help her clear the dishes. Ooh. How could he be so annoyingly cool and coy at the same time? He was torturing her. After tidying up and putting away the leftovers they took the remaining wine and sat together on the sofa again, contemplating the tree. Kate really wanted to dim the room lights and bask in the twinkling multi-coloured glow of the Christmas tree, but she knew it would seem too... well, just too.

Apparently, he needed no such encouragement, for Simon slipped his arm comfortably around her shoulders and they continued sitting quietly gazing at the tree. Holding herself back from sinking into his embrace, Kate was anything but quiet on the inside, although part of her wanted to relax and relish the moment. Staying cool was proving to be impossible. So far she was ranging from very warm to sizzling hot. Her neck and shoulder were on fire with the touch of his arm, making her efforts to appear nonchalant ridiculous as she took a sip of her wine. Naturally, she dribbled wine over her chin, and had to wipe it away, gasping in embarrassment.

He shifted his weight and she froze. "Tell me something." She could feel his soft warm breath against her hair, and knew he had turned to face her. She felt her breath catch, waiting for him to continue. He reached toward her face and gently wiped a spot on her chin. "Can you honestly explain to me why we should not keep on doing this 'til the end of time?"

Kate's eyes were drawn to his like magnets. She felt as though he could see into the depths of her soul, and know her darkest secrets, though with her mind she knew this was not so. She made a feeble attempt to diffuse the tension by laughing, saying, "You mean gaze at the Christmas tree and slobber wine down our selves?"

He withheld his smile. "Don't try to hide from me, Kate. You keep negating our feelings. I came here to sort this out."

She was incapable of speech, robbed of breath. Her eyes slid over his shoulder.

"Look me in the eye and tell me you don't feel the same way."

She did as he asked, and knew he could see both her fierce love, and her naked fear.

"I know you're afraid. But I don't really understand why?"

She shook her head and felt her lip quiver with the tears that choked her and pricked at her eyes.

He reached for her face again, but this time he cupped her cheek softly in the palm of his large hand, caressing her with his thumb, gently wiping away a fugitive tear. "I've fallen in love with you. With my eyes wide open." He shrugged helplessly, dropping his hand. "Perhaps unfortunately for you, this time I'm not afraid of what that means. I want to love you completely and forever, and somehow we can't even get started. I'm very frustrated, trying to understand. Please, let me, Kate." His voice broke on his last beseeching words and she could see the lights of the Christmas tree reflected in his glistening eyes. "Is it Jay?"

Oh, how she wanted to surrender to his love! Kate felt every cell of her being yearning for him, reaching, electrified, aching. What would life be like with Simon there beside her, every day and always? "Oh, Simon, I… " She didn't know what to say. How could she explain to him her convoluted fears? "It's not Jay. He… he asked me to marry him, but… " She shook her head, realized how unfair it was to have held on to him. "It wasn't meant to be."

"Tell me then…"

Kate raised her left hand to knead her furrowed brow. "I want to believe you."

"You don't? You don't think you're worthy of my love?"

She cringed. "I know you're sincere. I mean I know you believe it." She licked her lips, praying for the right words. "I don't really know what you're looking for, and…" She chewed her lip. "…

and I really don't know what I need." She paused in response to the look of hurt on his face. "No. Don't take that the wrong way. I want to be honest with you. There have been plenty of very nice men in my life, even those declaring their love for me, and no matter what happens, I always find, in the end, I spoil it. I can't give my self completely to them, however much I admire them. "

"How is it you've brought so many men to their knees?" His lips pressed into a straight line. "And always end up alone?"

"My heart is guarded. It's damaged." She clenched her fist, then opened her hand toward him. "But you're different. I want to give it to you, Simon. I really do. This time." Why did she add those last words? It was as though some devilish part of her wished to drag every ugly fact of her past out to show him, inviting him to examine and prod her wounds, like some soft creatures in a tide pool. "I'm..." she shrugged "...afraid."

"What is it? You don't trust me?" She became aware that his back was up. His mood took on a sharper edge, and she could feel his exasperation mounting.

She shook her head. "I don't trust myself. I don't want to need you too much. I feel I'll lose myself. The life that I've built."

"Is that why you throw yourself into your work? At what cost? Maybe if you accepted love in your life, and trusted me to be here for you, you could relax about your career instead of driving yourself so hard."

She could only stare at his face, frowning. Every thing that he said resonated, each piece straining to fit into a whole explanation. He was trying so hard to understand her. But what could she tell him? How could she explain?

Simon gazed at her, his eyes remote, shifting, seeming to deliberate for several beats. He paused, the muscles in his jaw working, his eyes on the tree. "You don't make sense. I don't want to push you, Kate. I can give you as much time as you need. But I have to see more of you. We have to give this a chance. Whatever is bothering you, we can work through it, or..." He jerked his shoulder abruptly. "...learn to live with it." He didn't seem overjoyed with this last option. "Just don't kick me to the curb out of fear. Please."

Kate was overcome with guilt and grief. He truly was a wonderful, kind and caring man. How could she explain that the problem was her, not him. She chose her words carefully and forced herself to say them, despite the knifing pain she felt in her heart. "It's not your fault, Simon. You deserve to be with someone whole. It isn't fair to continue dating you until I've dealt with my own baggage. It might be easier… better to work things out with Rachel. She can't be any crazier than me." She choked back a sob.

She saw him flinch, a spark of blue fire in his eyes. She thought for a moment that she might have pushed him to the edge of his temper at last. A tense silence stretched between them, unspoken words and threatened trust hanging thick in the air like a noxious gas cloud.

He growled through his clenched teeth. "I don't love Rachel, damn it. I love you." He gripped her shoulders and shook her once as he said them, and the dark, wild look in his eyes, hooded as they were by furrowed, bushy brows, was frightening and familiar, cutting like cold steel through her heart, despite his words. His voice dropped to a whisper. "Even if you are crazy."

She heard herself gasp and sob as more hysterical tears escaped and sliced across her temples. Her heart fluttered wildly at his words, a dove straining at the bars of its cage. Mindlessly, she thought, *I want you to fight me. Prove me wrong. I want you to win!* And yet, she cowered, turning her face aside, her shoulders shaking, her hands flying up to cover her face.

He sucked air through his teeth, trying to bring himself under control. He squeezed his eyes shut and wrapped his arms around her, tight and hard as iron bars, for a brief moment before releasing her, in slow motion, tender and contrite. "I'm sorry."

Motionless, Simon stared glumly into her face. He kissed her between the eyebrows and said again, "I'm sorry," shaking his head. They both knew there was no point in pursuing it any further tonight.

Kate wasn't sure what had been settled, if anything. Her insides felt like a knot of twisted wire, sharp and tangled and raw. She wiped furiously at the tears drying on her face, the echo of her frightful sobs still quaking her bones.

Simon drew a long slow breath and released it. "What are your plans for Christmas?"

Perplexed, she stuttered without thinking, "I… n-nothing, really. Probably just hang with Alexa. My family… th-they'll all be in San Francisco but…"

"Good. Then they won't miss you. I want you join me and

Maddie for Christmas Eve dinner. I'm cooking for Will and a few friends. Bring Alexa." His air of reassuring lightness was obviously forced, but still, just what was called for. He lifted her chin with one bent finger. "It'll be good, you'll see."

Kate felt a final shudder run through her. Without another word, Simon pulled her into his embrace and held her tightly, caressing her back and hair until she was calm, warm and still. Finally, he pulled away from her and held her at arm's length, holding her eyes, his crooked half smile teasing her. "You know I'm not leaving without pie."

twenty-two

Kate had insisted that Alexa detour downtown to pick her up for Christmas dinner at Simon's house, arguing that she was, under no circumstances, arriving there alone to fend for herself among strangers, intimates of Simon's no less. Alexa thought she was being a baby for needing moral support, but came to get her anyway.

"Relax and enjoy the evening. Don't worry so much."

Alexa had been reticent, initially, about the idea of spending Christmas Eve at Simon's. But then, with a twinkle in her eye, she'd agreed.

"So. You must be relieved. What did the letter say, exactly?"

Thankfully, Sharon's complaint had generated only a brief formal letter from the society president. She was still stunned at the outcome of all those weeks of worry. "Oh, he very diplomatically reminded me to make full disclosures in the future to avoid triggering this kind of misunderstanding."

"That's a really nice Christmas gift," Alexa said. "I'm so glad."

Kate agreed. However much of a relief the formal letter was to receive, even better was the long, compassionate, personal note from her mentor Rose that accompanied it. Amazingly, there would be no serious consequences affecting her career, or her award and presentation at the annual meeting in January. She could still barely believe that she'd been so lucky.

But though she was relieved, and had been ecstatically dancing around her loft yesterday, at the moment her mind could not focus on work. This moment was for Simon. Simon and herself.

Despite her apprehension, Kate was determined to do this, to spend the time with Simon that he wanted. Not least because of her commitment to him, but also because of her pact with Eli. It was really a promise to herself. To keep no more secrets. To peel away any defensive mask of deceit. To stare down her demons once and for all.

Simon's house was festooned with colored lights when they arrived, with a lush festive wreath on the green door. A stout Christmas tree stood sentinel in the front window among the silhouettes of milling bodies visible through the veil of drapery. She turned to Alexa, seizing her arm in a death grip.

They paused on the porch a moment in rising clouds of their own condensing breath and she shivered in the cold, crisp air. Scant dry snowflakes drifted down as she stood gathering her resolve.

"Take a deep breath. No hurry," Alexa said, turning to offer her a reassuringly steady gaze and a wry grin.

Unexpectedly, the green door with the wreath swung open wide, spilling warm golden light over the deck of the porch and blinding them temporarily while threads of a sprightly Latin version of *In Excelsius Deo* plucked on a classical guitar rode out on a bubble of warm air.

"Don't stand there hemming and hawing," bellowed a blond giant who filled the frame of the door, making Kate step back to stretch her eyes up to his broad face. He grinned at her. His accent was unmistakably from Newfoundland.

She stood gaping. Where was Simon? The giant turned.

"And you mus' be Alexa. Come in, come in, come in." Suddenly Kate was grabbed by a massive paw and hauled in through the door like a rag doll.

In what felt like no time at all, she found herself at the table squeezed between Simon's brother Will and his lawyer friend Casey, the large blond Newfie. She had the vaguest recollection spinning in her head of a string of introductions as she had slurped down her first glass of white wine. She looked around at the friendly and attentive strangers that surrounded the table, wondering if she'd remember everyone's names.

The inviting atmosphere was warm, and filled with the fragrance of evergreen and Asian spices emanating from Simon's kitchen. He'd popped out for the briefest of hello's and returned to his cooking, giving her the thinnest of lifelines with a second's meaningful eye contact. Alexa was no help, seated at the far end of the long table, already embroiled in some kind of red-faced debate with another friend she vaguely recalled from university days, a slovenly, bearded guy named Bruce. In Simon's relative absence, Will had adopted a kind and protective manner, at odds with their one hostile encounter on the front step weeks ago.

Across from her a tall, hunched big-boned woman, with a large, concave face like a serving platter, and skin as white and soft as pastry dough was asking her a string of questions about how she knew Simon. Her androgynous voice was nasal and sibilant. Kate recalled her introducing herself as "Alberta Lowell, call me Bertie." She had the hunched and twisted back caused by severe scoliosis, but for all that she was a powerful presence, and reminded her of Julia Child.

"He'll be here shortly, don't you worry. It's quite a production, this feast of his, every year, but he insists on doing everything himself."

"Every year?"

Bertie nodded.

"Well, it'll be the first time I eat Thai food on Christmas Eve." Kate wondered if she'd be able to eat anything after almost throwing up from anxiety on the ride over.

The children apparently had been fed earlier and relegated to the basement playroom. Kate was surprised, therefore, when Maddie dashed into the room. "Michelle! Emma spilled her juice and Jack says he won't clean it up and she's crying!"

"Oh, dear. Excuse me, please," Casey's wife Michelle, a thin, angular woman with over-large glasses said in her high-pitched voice, and slipped away.

Simon launched the meal bearing a soup tureen, announcing it was Tom Yum to wisecracking all around, setting it down and serving everyone, passing bowls. He stopped and narrowed his eyes at Kate halfway down the long table. "What are you doing sitting way down there?" he mumbled. She shrugged, but she didn't miss the slanting glances and pressed lips from those around her. Simon rolled his eyes and smiled. It was plain she'd been absconded, but for good or ill was the question.

"Casey, would you do the honors?" Simon sat down expectantly.

"Aye. Aye." Casey folded his huge hands together like two great Christmas hams and bent his flaxen head. "Lord, t'ank you for bringing our friends together this night, on the eve of your birt', to share in your bounty. Watch over our loved ones near, far and departed. Bless this food to our use and us to your service. Amen."

A chorus of Amens led immediately to a cacophony of clattering cutlery and chattering voices as everyone simultaneously ate.

The fragrant soup was followed by spicy green mango salad, steaming coconut rice, shrimp on sticks, deep fried tofu and curries in several colours. Finally, Simon carried in a large platter of Pad Thai noodles to a chorus of compliments.

Before he took his seat, Simon walked up behind her and gave her arm an affectionate, reassuring squeeze. Bertie asked about Simon's parents, who were on a cruise, while Kate gazed at him, wishing he was sitting beside her.

"Simon, boy," called Casey. "Come here a minute, will you."

"Excuse me," Simon touched her shoulder and moved around the table. The warmth of his fingers inexplicably infused her with courage and contentment. Kate's eyes followed him as he exchanged affectionate words with Casey, and then stood by Bruce and Alexa for a few minutes, listening then laughing with genuine amusement.

Bertie smiled at her with a knowing look. "His folks like to seek out warmer climes. Simon got his travel bug from them, I suppose. Are you a traveler too?"

"Yes. I guess I am."

Bertie nodded. "That's good. I've often wondered if Simon would find another woman to share his life. Whoever settles for him would have no regrets."

Kate gasped. "No. He's an exceptional man in every way."

"Yes, he is."

"Ah… you've known him long?"

"Since he was a youngster. I was a neighbour and babysat the two boys for years. He's always been so good to me."

"Oh, really?" Kate said. "Has he changed much?"

"Yes and no. He's… mellowed." Bertie's face sobered thoughtfully. "He's had a heavy heart." Bertie leaned toward Kate, nodding and smiling broadly. "Or he did, after Rachel. I've noticed a change in him of late."

Kate felt her face flush with heat.

The laconic Bruce heaved himself to his feet and raised his beer. "A toast to our favorite chef, a most generous and talented host, our Simon." His podgy face harbored glittering dark eyes as sharp and devious as a fox's. She remembered him being almost as thin as Simon. Kate smirked, noting he was keeping a keen eye on Alexa, who was now pointedly ignoring him.

Simon flashed a grin at everyone, but it was Kate's eyes he sought and held, and they sparkled with pleasure. She felt herself warm in response. He dipped his head in acknowledgement, then rose from his chair and raised his glass. "I'd like to add a special toast. Congratulations to Kate, who's just had some good news with regard to her career. She's survived a potential crisis," he grinned and winked at her, "and will be receiving a special award in the New Year. To Kate."

"I'll drink to that," Alexa said.

Kate felt her face heat while everyone raised their glasses in salute, wondering what, if anything, Simon had told his friends about their embarassing work-place flirtation.

She was soon engrossed in conversation with Will, Casey, Bertie and Lily, coyly fielding their questions, as she relished Simon's amazingly flavorful dishes. Again and again, she felt Simon's gaze on her like hot darts and her eyes slid over to meet his. Inevitably, his mouth curled into the familiar half-smile that undid her, and she felt herself soften and warm under his affectionate sensual stare. She had wanted to experience him in his own element, thinking that perhaps what stirred between them would wither or feel awkward, but her experience was quite the opposite. In the warmth and security of his home, his friends and traditions, she felt entirely welcome, entirely connected to him.

"Kate? Katie, girl." Casey's voice intruded.

"I'm sorry, what?" She looked at him blinking and noticed he and Bertie standing and gathering empty plates. "Pardon?"

"By God, where've you been, girl? I was saying go wit' Michelle and see the kiddies until we gets the dishes done."

"Oh, no." She stood up. "I'll help, of course."

"No, you won't. Go on wit' you." Casey led her away from the table. "You too, Simon, boy. No dishes for you, either." He ushered Will and Bruce toward the kitchen. "C'mon boys."

Simon shrugged and, slipping his fingers between hers, gently pulled her along behind Michelle, ducking through a door in the hall. Down a narrow staircase opened a carpeted basement room brightly lit and scattered with colourful toys. The children sat side-by-side watching the end of The Santa Clause, the littlest girl half asleep.

Michelle stooped to pick up her daughter, who curled against her neck, and she sat down in a nearby armchair.

"Daddy!" said Maddie jumping up. "Is it time for ice cream?"

"Not yet, sweetie. Dishes first." He lifted her and gave her a kiss, setting her down again.

"Awww." She assumed a serious expression, her cupid's bow mouth pouting at Kate. "Did you like Daddy's dinner?"

"I sure did. He's a very good cook, isn't he?" said Kate.

"S'pose. I don't like Thai food. It's smelly. Wait 'til tomorrow. He's making turkey."

"Oh. Well I'm sure that will… be very… " Madison turned away to speak with Michelle, instantly forgetting her. She shook her head, smiling after her.

"Why don't you stay?" Simon hesitated, wincing. "Unless you have plans, of course. Join us tomorrow too. It would be just us and Will," he whispered.

"I couldn't intrude. Really, I…"

"Please." His eyes lit up and he lowered his voice, a sudden heat evident in both. She looked into eyes that burned into hers, the vivid blue shadowing to cobalt under his earnest brows.

She sucked in a breath. "Oh, I…" She turned her head to the side. Her response was visceral and immediate, heat arrowing through her core at his suggestion. She felt a shudder run through her. Her lips felt dry, and she swallowed, licking them. What was she supposed to say? *Yes, I'd love to sleep with you again?* She shot a nervous glance over at Michelle, who was animatedly talking with the children about the movie they'd watched.

Simon raised a hand to smooth his brow. "I'm getting a bit ahead of myself. But stay until the others are gone, please?" Color rose into his neck and ears. "I'm sorry. I didn't mean to…"

"It's okay." Kate felt herself flush, raising a hand to cover her face. "I… I…" She felt ridiculous and giggled stupidly. Oh my God! This was it. She couldn't hide any longer. She wanted so desperately to love him. She *did* love him. She respected and admired him more than any other person she had ever known. And he was lonely and vulnerable too, just like her. She knew that now. She also knew she could trust him not to hurt her, not to reject her again. Not intentionally anyway.

"Quite frankly, I can't wait for them all to leave," he whispered, stroking her cheek with his knuckles, his eyes lowered to her mouth, "…so we can be alone." An expression of self-deprecating exasperation flickered across his face and made her laugh.

He turned away and dropped to the floor next to the little boy with glasses strapped to his shorn head, leaving her standing helplessly, thinking about the kiss that wasn't, her lips tingling with need. "So, Jack. What will Santa be bringing you in the morning?"

Jack threw himself onto Simon's lap. "Pirates!"

"Arrh, pirates?"

"Lotsa pirates. An' a big pirate ship. And a dead-man's skeleton and a monkey that climbs up to the top of the mast."

Simon laughed. "Is that so? What else?"

"A package that come from me Aunty Sheryl. But I already know it's a knitted sweater. T'is same every year." Jack shook his head sadly, and Simon's expression of sympathy hid his amusement well enough.

Kate squatted down next to them. "How about you Emma? What's Santa bringing you?" Kate shot a glance at Michelle, who smiled and gave Emma a little squeeze of encouragement.

Emma squinted suspiciously then appeared to decide Kate was trustworthy. She slid off her mother's lap and waddled over, leaning toward Kate, pressing her pudgy hand to Kate's cheek and whispering loudly in her ear. "Ith a thecret. I getting a baby." She backed away grinning, her eyes wide with anticipation.

"My goodness, aren't you a lucky girl?" said Kate, as Emma turned and sat down on her bent knee. She couldn't help thinking how lucky Michelle was to have two beautiful plump children.

"Do you haf a baby?" asked Emma, gazing up at Kate in fascination.

"Um. No, I don't. But I'd sure like one some day," Kate said, and realized how true this was, hugging the tiny, adorable Emma and deeply inhaling her sweet vanilla-scented hair. *Oh, yes, I do!*

"You kids wait right here. I think there's one more present for you here somewhere." Simon rose and went to a cupboard, returning with two brightly wrapped packages and handing them to Jack and Emma, who squealed with delight.

"Oh, Simon, you spoil them," said Michelle.

Simon waved her objections away and wagged a finger at the children. "You can't open them until morning. And don't forget to write your aunt Sheryl a thank you note. She makes those sweaters for you with her own hands and she loves you both a lot."

"Yes, Uncle Simon."

Kate exchanged a knowing glance and smile with Michelle, who cast fond appreciative eyes in Simon's direction.

"Anyone down there ready for ice cream?" Casey's call from above was met by a chorus of cheers and they thumped upstairs after the children.

It wasn't long before Will and Michelle were helping Simon serve dishes of fried bananas and coconut ice cream, to the delight of the children and sighs of satisfaction from the adults. He called them Thai banana splits.

Simon shifted to a chair next to Kate, forcing everyone to shuffle, and sat watching her eat while slowly sipping his coffee, seemingly preoccupied with sprinkling toasted coconut on his ice cream.

He checked in with her often, to see if she liked her desert, to ask if she wanted more tea, as she chatted about her travels with Bertie and Alexa. Kate's thoughts were in turmoil, trying to come to terms with both past and present. Every time she caught him gazing at her, she felt her face flush and pulled her eyes away.

"Si-mon, boy."

He dragged his eyes from Kate to respond to Casey. "Hmh?"

Casey simply looked at him questioningly, let his eyes slide over to Kate, and back again. She felt herself blush. Were they that conspicuous? Shaking his head, his teasing smile spoke volumes. "Ar, what are we going to do with you?"

Simon blinked. "Did you... "

"Never you mind, then. I was asking for the peanuts, but it seems you've got your head wrapped up in other t'ings."

Lily, Will's shy date, a student from Hong Kong, passed the peanuts over, an unspoken question in her eyes.

"His head's in his pants, if you ask me," said Bruce, to guffaws of laughter from the men.

"Leave him. I think it's adorable," said Michelle.

"Enough," hissed Simon, his ears burning bright red, glancing again at Kate, who's face heated at hearing the lewd comment, despite assiduously pretending she hadn't. "That's enough of that." He pressed his lips together, chagrinned.

Casey threw his head back and slapped his thigh, letting out a whoop of delight. He peered closely at them again, grinning. "There's another explanation, boy."

Simon's smile failed him, his Adam's apple sliding up and down as he swallowed.

Michelle saved him. "Let's do the gift exchange now."

Simon heaved a sigh and stood up, now avoiding Kate's eyes. "Great idea!"

They all shifted into the living room, some with drinks in hand, where Michelle had laid out a number of brightly wrapped packages in odd shapes and sizes on the coffee table.

"Oh, you didn't tell us about this," Kate moaned.

Michelle explained, "It's a tradition for everyone to bring a small, inexpensive, and preferably amusing gift without labels, which we then randomly choose–"

"And ruthlessly trade," cut in Bruce.

Simon gave her elbow a squeeze as she passed by. "Don't worry. We always throw in extras."

"But beware," warned Will. "Being a rookie will not spare you from ridicule."

"I should say not," chuckled Bertie, sinking heavily onto the sofa beside Kate and giving her arm a friendly pinch. "Ooh, my back. Think of it as a test of your mettle."

Casey shook a matted Canucks toque, passing it around so everyone could draw small numbered pieces of paper from it, while Michelle attempted to explain the rules of trading with numerous interruptions from Will and Bruce as they argued the finer points.

"It's all in fun. And it ends in mayhem every year regardless of the rules," said Simon, who nestled a drowsy Maddie on his knee. Kate studied the cozy pair discretely from under her lashes, still astonished at the sight of Simon as a nurturing father.

"Can I play too, Daddy?" came Madison's halfhearted plea.

Simon pressed a kiss on her soft flushed cheek and held her closer, whispering into her curls. "You'll get your presents in the morning."

"Alright. Who's first?" asked Michelle.

"Tis me," replied Casey stepping forward, and drawing a small rectangular package. He withdrew a book and read the cover. "Ar. 'Tis a wee book of Haiku's by... uh... Koba... uh ... yashi Issa."

"Oh, read one," urged Alexa.

Casey flipped the pages, scanning and considering his options. "Truth be told there's many t'ings I understand, but poetry isn't one of 'em. Here: 'love-struck cat/down into Wolf Valley/he goes.'" He screwed up his face.

"Oh, that's easy. The cat will risk everything in search of love," Lily said.

Bertie said,"And since I've got number two, I'll take it from you. I do enjoy haiku." Kate watched this trade with interest as Casey stood to choose another gift from the pile. This time it was a package of caramel corn.

"Look out Casey. I've got number eight, so if nothing better turns up, you might still lose it to my sweet tooth." Simon grinned and slowly eased from his chair with a now sleeping Maddie drooping in his arms. He bent and laid her gently beside the Christmas tree, propping her head up on a cushion and tucking a throw over her. Kate observed his caring ministrations with wistful interest and was surprised to see him slip from the room as Bruce stood up.

"I'm next," Bruce said, picking up a small flat package. His face screwed up as he opened it, puzzling over its contents. He looked up, shrugging, and handed it to Lily, who sat nearby. "You're the expert."

Bertie rocked and rose stiffly. "Ah, too much sitting for me. Excuse me." As Kate watched, Bertie hobbled out to the hall assisted by a walking stick, her broad hips causing her peasant skirt to swirl. Simon returned and leaned in the doorway.

"Ah." Lily nodded sagely, speaking with her thick Chinese accent. "Very lucky gift. This Ho Shou Wu. Ancient 'elixer of life'. Mix this with wine and is very rejuvenating. It restore youth, make hair grow long and black and also improve virility. Very valuable."

There was a general chorus of laughter. Simon slumped into Bertie's spot next to Kate, sliding his arm over her shoulders and sinking down into the cushions. Warmth suffused her and longing to curl into him like a cat, she glanced around to see if anyone had noticed their comfortable intimacy.

"That'll help with the beer belly, old man."

"Be nice," protested Bruce.

"Not to mention with the ladies," Michelle said.

"Who said I needed any help?" Bruce rebuffed, scowling.

Lily turned the package over in her hand. "Is tempting to take it from you, but I think you need more." She nodded soberly and handed it back to Bruce with a twinkle in her dark eyes, getting into to spirit of the game.

Simon slipped a folded piece of paper into Kate's open hand. "Remember this?" he whispered into her hair, and she shivered as his warm breath tickled her neck.

Looking up, she saw his earnest expression and shy smile. Curious, she unfolded the paper. Three handwritten lines that seemed strangely familiar lay scrawled on the old scrap of foolscap. She silently read, *'Dewdrop licks petal/dusky eyes reflect my soul/moonlight touches us.'* Her heart lurched as the memory of his romantic haiku, scribed one romantic night during their long ago affair, flooded back and, drawing a sudden breath, her eyes darted up to find Simon watching her intently. "You kept this?"

He nodded.

Their eyes locked for long moments, during which nothing existed but their shared memories and she was filled with a sense of longing and, at heart, belonging. He reached to caress her arm with his free hand, leaving it there, and tucked his head down to kiss her cheek tenderly. She felt tears welling and burning at her eyelids and blinked them away, biting her lip. Simon smiled contentedly and drew his eyes away, snuggling closer to her and squeezing her shoulder.

Lily opened a large flat box, frowning slightly.

"Oh! It's a vintage classic Twister game!" Michelle shouted. "I used to just love that. Perhaps you're too young to remember, Lily."

"I guess I'm next," Alexa stood up, finger to her cheek, perusing her options. "Here, this one's got my name written all over it." She picked up a perfect cube and ripped it open. She opened the box and withdrew a sphere. "You see? One architectonic shape inside another."

"It's a Magic 8-ball! Here, here, let me see it," said Will, reaching out a hand. He turned it over, and rolled his eyes to the ceiling with mock concentration. "Will Bruce get laid tonight?" He got elbowed as he turned the ball and peered into it. "'Outlook not so good.' Gee, sorry buddy. Maybe you could take the elixer and try again." He guffawed, his eyes dancing around the room, inviting general laughter. "Ow!" he exclaimed as Bruce punched him affectionately.

"Let me try." Alexa took the ball back with a sly glance in Kate's direction. "Will I leave here alone tonight?" She turned the ball over and read, "Cannot predict now.'"

"Just wait until Bruce tries the elixer," said Will, to more hilarity.

"Who said I was thinking about him?" said Alexa with disdain, avoiding Kate's eye, but digging her elbow into Kate's ribs.

"Alex!" Kate reprimanded, feeling her face flush hot. "My turn, and I'm taking that away from you before..." Kate plucked the 8-ball out of Alexa's hands, tossing it onto the sofa beside her.

Alexa jabbed her playfully and leaned over to choose a small package. Opening it, she found a small polished brass compass. "Oh, it's lovely. It looks like an antique." She swiveled it round and tipped it, studying the bouncing needle as it settled on the enameled N. "It seems to work perfectly. Don't you dare take this from me, anyone. I'll fight you for it."

"There you go. Something to show you the way that you can trust," said Simon soberly, and Kate glanced at him wondering if he understood her fears.

The game concluded quickly amid further teasing and laughter.

"Okay, my turn." Simon stood and struck a thoughtful pose, gazing longingly at Casey's caramel corn.

"Hold onto your poppycock, Casey."

Simon laughed. "I've thought it over and I've decided that Casey is the far better qualified attorney when it comes to bombast, gibberish, gobbledegook, Jabberwocky, piffle, hooey... and horse-feathers. So he can keep his poppycock." He paused for effect, and was rewarded with laughter. "Whereas I, on the other hand, being of sober mind and domestic inclination... " He slowly turned, squinting in turn at everyone in turn and flipped imaginary hair over his shoulder, "...have always wanted long black tresses." He reached and plucked the Chinese elixer from Bruce, "*And* ten more children." With this he winked mysteriously at Kate.

Her smile froze, and she felt hot prickles and tingles climb up her breasts to her cheeks.

"Besides, you can't be trusted with children, you buffoon," he said to Bruce and fell back onto the sofa, laughing, and Kate thrilled with the physical energy of him touching the side of her disconcertingly responsive body.

"Will you people leave me be," groaned Bruce, standing to choose yet another gift. Kate observed Bruce wistfully, her mind on Simon and his coded communication. She took his meaning perfectly well when he referred to their dinner last Saturday, and she hid behind dropped lashes.

Bruce ripped the wrapping paper off. His face lit up with delight like a child on Christmas morning. "At last!" He held up a hockey jersey with a large number '19' and the name 'Naslund' emblazoned across it. Seeing Will's expression, he growled defensively.

"Alright!" shouted Will, leaping from his chair and lunging toward Bruce on the loveseat.

"Hands off!" yelled Bruce.

"No way, you loser. I'm next. It's mine!" With this he pounced on Bruce and yanked at the jersey, but Bruce was unwilling to concede and fought back. They wrestled each other over the back of the loveseat and onto the floor, where the others, laughing, could only hear their grunts, muffled curses and thumps. At last Will stood up, his shirt askew, a huge grin stretched across his face, and held aloft his prize. "Yes!" He punched a victorious fist into the air.

A moment later, Bruce emerged, his face as dark as a thundercloud, his hair and shirt equally disheveled. "This just isn't my night."

Michelle's voice cut through the clamor. "It's Twister time!"

Simon turned and earnestly addressed Michelle with hands on her shoulders. "Sorry. Twister is not in the stars tonight. Please take your children home."

Everyone bid Casey and Michelle a good night and a Merry Christmas, and they bustled out the door bundling their sleeping children, gifts and bags of leftover food. They were soon followed, after swift kisses and hugs good night, even for Simon, Kate noted with interest, by Alexa, who had offered Bertie a ride. "Merry Christmas, Katie, love," she said. Shortly afterwards the lonely and downtrodden Bruce left.

"She didn't even ask if I needed a ride," Kate said as the door closed behind them.

"She's an astute woman," smiled Simon.

"Hmph."

Lily stood on the front porch in her long quilted parka, stomping booted feet. "Let's go-oo, Will."

Simon gripped his brother's hand. "Thanks for your help tonight, bud."

Will turned toward his brother, looking up and shaking his head. "I was such a jerk. I was sure you'd get your ass kicked again." Kate frowned, confused, scanning Simon's face for clues. Simon smiled and hugged him roughly, thumping his back. "Thanks. I might yet."

Will pulled away, grinning and shaking his head, darting a glance in Kate's direction and lowering his voice. "I'm envious. Even Mom never looked at me like that."

"That's 'cause you're the ugly one," Simon teased. "G'night."

Will shuddered theatrically and led Lily out into the hush of thickly falling snow. "Huh. I hope you know what you're doing, bro."

twenty-three

They were alone at last. Kate waited on the sofa, gazing at the empty disordered room, pretending she hadn't over-heard Simon's touching, if confusing, exchange with his brother. Despite Michelle's efforts to tidy up, the living room looked like a bomb went off. There were dirty mugs and glasses here and there, bunched up giftwrap, sofa cushions and throws in disar-ray. The almost barren, soiled dining table sat in the background awaiting another opportunity to stage a laughing crowd. Kate could almost hear the echo of laughter and loving voices, and felt a warm sense of completion and contentment. Closing the door, Simon padded silently to the living room and leaned on the doorframe.

"Well, we both survived," he said.

"I can't believe you put yourself through that every year."

His smile was tentative. "They're not that bad, are they?"

Kate grimaced. "That's not what I meant. They're all lovely. Colourful, but lovely. I meant the work, the preparation and cooking. It was amazing."

"Thanks. I like to do it for them. I realize they're a tad eccen-tric. But they're my orphans and I take care of them."

"Your *orphans?*"

He snorted. "It started years ago. First time Mom and Dad went on a trip, I felt I had to do something for Will. And Bertie. After her husband died, she had no one. Bruce, too, is kind of uncomfortable with his family, so the holidays are hard. Then I met Casey through work. And he and Michelle are so far from their families. It just..." his shoulder jerked up, "...evolved."

"And now you've added me and Alexa to your list of orphans?"

"I was thinking maybe adoption in your case." His eyes

creased, twinkling, and Kate felt a shiver of heat and anticipation. "But first I have to tuck this girl in." He turned to the sleeping bundle under the tree and peeled away the blanket to reveal the adorable Madison, her round cheeks flushed under a disheveled brown mop.

"It's a miracle she slept through it all."

He chuckled and knelt to gently lift her limp form. Gazing at her sweet face, he bent to brush his lips across her silky pink cheek, and his intense love for her was palpable. He stopped and peeked at Kate over his shoulder. "Come with me?"

Kate rose and followed him up the stairs and into Maddie's room. He set Maddie on her bed and, with the expected awkwardness, patiently extracted her from her wrinkled party dress and tangled tights. She remained as limp as a rag doll while he wrestled her limbs into her nightgown and pulled the blankets up around her shoulders. She'd worn herself out; she didn't move a muscle. He bent to kiss her forehead and stood. "She'll be up early. I have to be ready."

In response to Kate's questioning look, he beckoned with one finger and led her into the darkened hallway, where he slid opened a closet door and pulled down a large lumpy bag from a high shelf.

Back downstairs, Simon added several brightly wrapped packages to those already arranged under the tree. "She knows some of the gifts are from me, but there has to be a surprise element or it spoils the Santa logic," he explained.

Kate smiled in understanding, then brightened. "I almost forgot. I have gifts for you and Maddie." She looked around. "Where did I put my bag?"

"Is that yours in the front hall?"

She retrieved it and set it down, opening it and rummaging until she extracted two parcels, both wrapped in elegant silvery blue paper with matching ribbon the same shade as her sweater. Her eyes shied away from the small pouch bearing her toothbrush and a change of clothes, her stomach doing a little gymnastic flip as she closed the flap on her bag. She set the gifts under the tree, glancing over her shoulder to beam at him.

He stood looking her up and down, his admiration evident. It was mutual. She flushed hotly, wondering if he might be thinking similar thoughts to hers.

He held her eyes and moved silently toward her, taking both her hands in his to lift her up, and bent toward her. He held back hesitantly. Kate had to tilt her head back to maintain eye contact, and she did so, gazing thoughtfully into his eyes, the barest hint of a welcoming smile touching her lips. It was evidently enough encouragement for him. He kissed her once, tentatively, and pulled away, still searching her eyes. For what? He kissed her again, more quickly and said, "Just one more thing."

She watched him wordlessly as he fished two stockings from his bag, hung them from hooks on the mantelpiece, then proceeded to fill them with small packages, mandarin oranges and chocolate. He turned toward her, hesitant, and lifted a beautiful quilted stocking embroidered with an angel and silver stars on a navy blue sky. "I have a spare. Shall I hang it for you? Or would you prefer a cold, lonely taxi ride home?" He tried to make light of it, pouting in a hammy way, though she knew he was perfectly serious.

Well. This was it. Decision time.

Searching her eyes again, he moved towards her, holding her arms in his hands. "I'm so glad you're here. This is all I want for Christmas. Just you." He stroked her cashmere sweater, running one fingertip gently along the scooping neckline next to her skin, over the tops her breasts. He drew in a ragged breath. His voice sounded strained. "Make me even happier. Let me wake up tomorrow with you in my arms. Please."

Kate's breath left her, her throat constricting. "I… I'd like to say yes, Simon. I would… " She hesitated, feeling the too-familiar crawling, fearful sensation that had preceded her anxiety attacks of late. Consciously distancing herself from the anxiety, she observed it, named it, knowing that she had to move past the irrational fear. She turned away, out of his embrace, concentrating on her breathing, and reached a hand to grasp her knot pendant, silently asking for strength from whatever force in the universe meted out her fate. At the same time she knew, it was up to her.

Stepping up behind her, he said, "Is it my imagination that you've had a change of heart?" He turned her toward him again, dropping his voice. "I've fallen in love with you Kate, all over again. Tell me I'm not crazy to think you might love me too."

She kept her gaze cast down, too afraid to meet the earnest expression in his eyes. She wanted him. She knew what she needed to do. She only needed to give herself permission to feel the love she had for him, and put her fears aside. Simon lifted her chin gently with his fingertips.

"Tell me, Kate. I won't hurt you. I promise. But don't be afraid of my reaction, either. I know Will thinks I'm made of glass. Whatever you have to say, I can take it. Tell me the truth."

Kate peered uneasily at his creased brow, aware that his eyes glistened with fear of his own, and wondered. He didn't deserve this. After all he'd been through, Simon should never have to doubt that he was loved.

"Have I got it all wrong?"

"No. Simon, I..." Her voice was a whisper, and she dug down deep for the courage she needed to face her own truth, and to open her heart to this man, who meant everything to her.

"Tell me what it is? What's the matter? Is it a fear of commitment?" His frustration was unmistakable. His voice dropped. "Is it Maddie? Are you worried about... having to step into a mother's role?" Simon released her and stood with his hands out, palms up, beseeching. "Tell me."

Kate shook her head emphatically. "No! Absolutely not. Put that thought out of your head." She swallowed, gathering her thoughts. "I have... I suppose you've noticed how I've been." She sighed heavily, on a frustrated grunt. Where to begin? "When I saw you again, something happened to me. A kind of... relapse."

"Saw me?" Disbelief ratcheted Simon's voice up a notch. Without a word, he wrapped his arms around her and pulled her head against his chest, stroking her hair and back. He gently pushed her away and asked his question again, this time with only his pleading eyes, waiting patiently, trusting her to explain if she could.

She could. She must. Kate breathed a deep and quivering sigh and raised her eyes to his. She turned inward, searching for the words to explain. "There is... a part of me that has never stopped loving you. Even when you didn't love me. Even when you weren't there, I obsessed over you. And I had to go on with my life." She squeezed her eyes shut. She shook her head for a moment, opened them and continued with a quavering voice, pushing the words past the blockage in her throat. "I had to make sense of that. Why couldn't I function? Eventually, with help, loads of help, I came to understand that my love for you was a kind of unhealthy attachment that arose from a void inside of me. I had no self-love, no sense of self worth. I was so ruined by what happened to me, by... by what I finally *realized* happened to me..."

"Wait. You're losing me. I still don't understand what you're talking about."

Of course not. Kate stopped speaking and closed her eyes, breathing slowly and deeply for a long time, reaching for the strength to continue.

"How could you love me and still be afraid?" Simon asked. "Love is a wonderful thing. A joyous feeling." She could hear his confusion and hurt, and see a brooding darkness descend over his face. "You know you can trust me, Kate. Please explain. Tell me everything so we don't have painful secrets between us. I want to really know you."

Kate slowly raised her eyes to his, and they came into focus, piercing and penetrating. "I do *love* you, and I trust you. But I don't trust... myself?"

"You don't sound certain of that." He frowned, clearly perplexed.

"I know. I've been trying, but I still can't find the words to express this fear," she clenched a fist and pressed it into her middle. "This feeling inside me that says, I can't have this. I don't deserve this kind of, of... happiness. Fulfillment. Security?" She shrugged.

"Don't deserve...? Why?"

Kate pushed her hair back from her face, tucked it behind her ear. "That's not even right." She tried to calm her thoughts, and sink down deep, quiet the noise and wait for the truth, the words she needed, to surface. Because she needed them. Now. This was her moment of truth. It was now or never, and Kate was not prepared to let this moment pass. She knew she stood on a precipice, her future lay in her own grasp. It was time to let go of the past, and embrace a future that was, unbelievably, a dream come true. For better or worse.

Even if she and Simon didn't work out, in the long term— because who really knew what the future held? She deserved to give it a chance. To give them a chance. It's what he wanted. And it was what she wanted, too, in her heart of hearts. Kate was not a bad person. She had not made such terrible mistakes. And limiting her whole life because of one unfortunate incident, punishing herself, and Simon too, because of something so far in the past, out of their control, was foolish.

She would never have the closure and redemption that confronting or punishing her attacker might provide. If indeed that wasn't a myth. But she refused to continue to punish Simon for the actions of another. Or to punish herself.

If in the end they moved on, well so what? That would be a decision born of the true circumstances of the life she was living now. She'd survive. She'd be okay.

How could it be worse than what she'd carried around for years? An unrequited compulsive love for a man that didn't even exist outside of her imagination. Kate realized she had obsessed over an ideal, a hollow man, not a real man. A crutch to lean on, something to buttress the dark abandoned mine shafts of her heart all these years, something to keep real love at arms length.

Kate had been lonely. So lonely. She had always been waiting for him. Not to rescue her, but to fill that space that only he could fill. Her man with heart, even though she knew that what she had been missing was a part of herself. Even so, she had known a profound connection once and, having tasted it, would never be satisfied with anything less.

Simon stood before her, his face aglow with compassion. She saw his warmth and solidity, his patience and yearning. She would give Simon her love, with no strings attached. She could not deny him or herself. But first, she owed him an explanation.

"I do love you, Simon, I do." She caressed his cheek with one hand. "But there's something I have to tell you, before… before…" She shrugged, and turned away to stare out the picture window at the still night.

No wind disturbed the lush snowflakes on their slumbering descent. Muted streetlights, ringed by diffuse halos. Coloured lights trimming neighboring houses muffled now under a thick blanket of fallen snow. In the pool of ice blue light from a streetlight, something shiny, red and sharp gleamed in the neighbour's front yard, like a blade, cutting the surface. A forgotten bicycle perhaps. She smiled.

"The moon on the breast of the new-fallen snow, gave the luster of mid-day to objects below." Soon, the falling snow would completely obscure the red bicycle, until only a soft, blurred outline could be detected, the gash healed over, only a scar.

She turned to Simon, reconciled to tell him everything.

"I didn't want you in my life. I was grieving–"

He was clearly puzzled. "In October?"

She smiled, shook her head, and continued. "It wasn't me that crashed into your dorm, drunk as a sailor at three in the morning, banging on the door and begging to be let in." She could remember the upheaval like an earthquake. He had turned her world upside down then too.

"Are we talking about college?" he looked doubtful, embarrassed and confused.

She looked up from his chest into his eyes. "Yes. Please listen." She paused, smiling weakly and shifting uncomfortably. "I don't know why you wanted *my* miserable company." She sighed and squinted up at him, determined to get it over with. "Let me tell you what you never knew. You may remember, when we met, that my boyfriend had just dumped me. I don't know if I told you. What you *never* knew was that... I was still in trauma from a... a rape in the last semester of high school."

"What?"

She held up a hand. "Not Ben. I was on a school trip... we were out drinking. We met some touring American soccer players..." she shrugged. "And after it happened... you just don't know... I felt so... soiled, so worthless." She again turned her eyes to the soothing view outside.

"Why didn't you tell me? We were close enough."

"The thing was... I didn't know it exactly. Not that I was in trauma– well, that too. I mean, I didn't remember the rape. Had totally blocked it out. A kind of selective amnesia caused by trauma-related stress. The memories didn't come back until about ten, eleven years ago. I guess I was finally ready to face it. I don't know. I'd heard of that happening to people, but you can't imagine your own mind playing such tricks on you."

"Not playing tricks. Protecting you from pain." His voice was barely a whisper.

"Well. I felt the pain, only much later. But I was so... broken. I was a mess when I met you. A much bigger mess than I even seemed on the surface. I didn't even understand it myself, because I'd dissociated from the memory. I was withdrawn, depressed, passive and needy. And you kept coming back, cheering me up, drawing me out, until I came to depend on you, until all my hopes and dreams hung on you, my savior. My knight in shining armor."

Now, she loved a real man, and though a part of her feared he would never measure up to the dream, the thought was com-

forting in a strange way, trickling into her tortured consciousness like a tonic, softening and sweetening her suffering. This
was complicated and messy, but infinitely better. She had lived
through violation, rejection, pain and self-loathing and put
herself and her life back together again, stronger than she was
before. She could never sink that low again. She would survive.

"And I didn't know a thing."

Anger surged through her, suddenly, and she wanted to strike
out. Her fists tightened and shook with violence. She didn't
know the pent up anger and resentment had been bottled up
inside her. She glanced down at her hands. Painful memories,
like overripe fruit ready to burst, surfaced, overwhelming her.

"And you took what you wanted without giving anything in
return," Kate said, knowing it was wrong. She shook her head,
negating the words. Yet she couldn't stop the flow of bitterness.
"Then when you figured out how messed up I was, you bolted."
What a horrible, mean thing to say. What had happened wasn't
Simon's fault. She stole a wary glance at him, blurred through
her tears.

His face reflected the shock she knew he'd feel. "I never knew
this about you. What promise did I break? I was *nineteen*."

"I'm sorry. That was wrong. That came from a dark place." She
placed a palm on his chest, over his heart. "It's not true. I just
have this residual anger inside of me, for that nameless, faceless
man that took what I didn't offer, and my innocence and faith,
too, without consequences. And maybe even at society for leaving me with decades of psychological garbage to deal with. But
I shouldn't direct it at you. Nothing that happened to me was
your fault. I know that."

"It's okay to feel anger. It's right to feel anger at what happened to you. I'm angry too, that some lowlife asshole could vio-
late you that way. It makes my blood boil."

Kate heart swelled at his declaration. The fact that Simon rose
to her defense comforted her a little.

He continued thoughtfully. "But, you're right, in a way. I was
selfish. And immature. And stupid. I knew you better than you
think. I'd fallen in love with you too, in my limited way... I
understood, on some level, that you needed compassion, that
you were hurting. But I didn't have the words to express it, or
the life experience to deal with your pain, Kate. The closer I got
to you, the more I felt it. It scared the hell out of me. So I shut it

out. I shut you out." His blue eyes glinted sharply, skipping like a flat stone across the surface of his memories.

"I was too young, and too accustomed to being selfish to be so... so needed. I was weak. I didn't want to have to work at a relationship, never mind make a commitment. We were so young." Simon's jaw worked as he contemplated the scene out the window. "I didn't mean to hurt you. The last thing I would have wanted was to make things worse for you." He reached out and caressed the side of her face with the knuckles of his hand, letting it rest there. Her eyes welled with tears and she felt them spill over and slide down her cheeks. He brushed them away gently.

She slowly shook her head, her mouth twisting downward. "It wasn't your fault I came unglued. You just showed up in my broken world at a time when I needed something to hold onto. I expected too much from you. And what we had was so... " she sucked in her breath, her voice breaking, "...so intense..."

He pulled her gently toward him until she was pressed against his body, wrapped his arms around her and laid her head against his collarbone, stroking her hair softly. "It was. We had something extraordinary, despite all that."

She forced herself to continue. "Simon. That's not all of it."

"Shh. Enough now."

"No. Listen. I can't stop until you know the rest." She pulled away, and strode woodenly toward the fireplace, staring unseeing into the dying flames.

"What else is there? Every time we bumped into each other on campus, I couldn't wait to escape. I felt guilty, and I'm ashamed of it now."

Shame. She knew about shame. "Simon, we didn't bump into each other. Oh, maybe once or twice. But it's a big campus. Didn't you guess?" Her voice was a hoarse whisper. She wrung her hands, twisting her fingers painfully. This was the hardest part to confess, but she didn't want there to be any more secrets between them.

"What do you mean?"

Kate cleared her throat. "Simon, I looked for you! I followed you, and... and memorized your class schedule, your routes. I made sure I was there to bump into. I basically stalked you!"

"Really?"

"I've never felt more ashamed of anything I've ever done in my life. It's the most pathetic thing I ever... I was so lonely and so full of self-hate that I needed to validate my misery in some concrete way."

Stepping up close behind her, he placed his hands on her arms. She could feel his warm breath on her neck like a balm.

"Don't torture yourself. It's all in the past. You've worked through it. You understand what brought you to those acts of desperation. It's over." He slowly turned her around to face him, searching her face.

"I was so obsessed with you." She shook her head. "No, not even you, because what did I truly know of you? Just the idea of you… that I could hardly think of anything else. I went on for years, on some level, maybe two or three years, hoping, yearning… until… "

"I know." He raised his hand, palm outward, grimacing. "Oh, I get it now." Then he clenched it into a fist and pressed it against his lips, his eyes glistening in anguish. "Don't remind me. I was truly heartless that night. I… I was more than heartless; I was cruel. The things I said, the way I behaved… I can hardly bear to recall."

"You couldn't know."

Simon searched her face. "Even so, it was inexcusable, to use you that way. And I never saw you again. I never knew what happened to you. Why did you leave without… In the morning I could have…"

She sucked in a deep breath. "I was filled with horror at your contempt of me. I couldn't face you." She closed her eyes. "That… encounter… seemed to slash through the wall of my repressed memories. The anger of it echoed… I tumbled into a profound depression that went on for a year, more than that."

Simon's face reflected her pain like a shadowed mirror. He opened his mouth to speak.

She raised a hand to stop him and continued; now that she'd started, she had to finish. This was part of her and he had to understand. "I think that was why I was so needy. Before that I was sensible, independent and ambitious. Afterwards, I felt worthless. Un-loveable. And then, there you were. We probably would have gone our separate ways eventually. But I *couldn't* let go. You were my lifeline."

"Right place, wrong time." A sad smile tugged at the corner of his beautiful, sensual mouth and a light sparked in his eyes. "So you were never really in love with me at all."

She offered him a weak smile. "Sure I was. You were beautiful. I lost myself in you. But like you, at that age, I should have been able to let go and move on." She sighed. As she spoke, the revelations of her therapy and self-analysis took on a deeper meaning than they had ever done before. She understood, at last, what Rose had been saying. "Right man, wrong kind of love. For the longest time, I needed you to validate me. As if, if I could have the love of a man I thought was so perfect, so ideal, then I would be ok. I would be clean and whole again. Your rejection was more than I could bear and, for years after, I wouldn't give anyone the chance to reject me again. All I could feel was the self-hate and even that I didn't understand. But I don't need you to validate me. I don't want to need anyone."

"Of course you don't."

"It was only by accident that I stumbled into therapy. I knew I needed help." She frowned at his chin and then closed her eyes.

"You're wiser than you know. To ask for help is the hardest thing."

She gazed into his eyes. She felt suddenly so tired, as weary as an ancient crone. "I'm sorry. I'm sorry to drag you back into those terrible times. I spoilt what we could have had. If I weren't so needy... I'm so humiliated that you knew me then. Try to imagine how I felt when you walked back into my life in October. I hate that I'm still so... I thought I'd worked through it all. I've been afraid you couldn't love me when you knew how dysfunctional I was." He pressed a finger to her lips, and shook his head slowly, his eyes full of gentle compassion.

"You've been afraid of rejection, because I rejected you before. You thought you weren't worthy. But I promise you, I see you and love you as you are– and I'm not going anywhere. Not this time."

He leaned toward her and pressed his lips softly to her forehead. "We are each of us an island. But we don't have to do it alone, Kate." His eyes drifted to the flickering embers. "I'm sorry for your suffering." He paused, pensive. "But, I'm not sorry I knew you then. And I'm glad you've shared this with me. We understand each other. We're stronger. Now we can go forward together without games or secrets. We can make something together that's better than either of us have ever had before."

He put his arm around her and drew her closer. Tongues of flame licked at the embers, burning low now, glowing red in the semi-darkness. "From where I stand now, it's crazy to imagine a couple of teenagers being able to deal with any of these issues, isn't it?

He turned to her again and wrapped her in a comforting embrace, bending his forehead to touch hers. She stood, limp, empty as a deflated balloon, her arms hanging at her sides, tears drying on her cheeks now that she had unburdened herself and they had each reached toward forgiveness. Then, slowly, tentatively, she slid her hands around his back, and held him tightly, heart to heart, the safest of harbours. A few silent minutes passed. He let go then and looked down, cupping her tear streaked face in his hands, searching her eyes intently. Then he bent his head and touched his lips to hers, as lightly as a butterfly's wing. They sank onto the sofa, piled with blankets and cushions, and he turned to stare at the glowing coals, pressing his lips together, then spoke softly, under his breath, so she could hardly hear him.

"You aren't the only one who was obsessed with an ideal and pursued it relentlessly. I had the same notion when I was young. For different reasons, obviously, but I searched and sampled and moved on, hurting people along the way, no doubt, until I thought I'd found it. That's why I married Rachel so young. She seemed, on the surface, to meet that image." Simon closed his eyes for a moment and shook his head woefully. He faced her and gazed into her eyes with such sober honesty that Kate's heart ached.

"How wrong I was. I was arrogant and foolish. It was a hard lesson. At first I thought... you seemed similar... but getting to know you... Now I see that no one can meet an ideal. I didn't know what was important."

"How can anyone, without living?"

"But I was so arrogant, and so wrong. Despite your insecurities, you are everything I want... have ever wanted." His uneven smile was soft and endearing, and she reached out and touched the curling corner of his beautiful lips with a fingertip. "But I could never have *imagined* you. I had to discover you and myself, too. You weren't so very crazy. But I am sorry for your pain, my love."

She wanted him now, so desperately, with her body and soul, but she had to learn to want him gently, to put away her fear of needing him so much. She held back the urge to kiss him, afraid she would devour him, lose herself completely in him.

"Kate?" She lifted her gaze into his penetrating blue eyes. "What about now? Are you still afraid I'm not who you think you love?" He shifted his weight, his hip pressed against hers, thigh to thigh. "There's nothing wrong with holding up ideals, as long as you don't let them get in the way of true happiness when it's staring you in the face. Do you want me in your life now?" He took an expectant breath. "Tell me you need me too, as much as I need you."

She opened her mouth to reply, to try to find words to express the overwhelming feelings that swept over her, and leaned toward him.

This was it. She knew that what she'd yearned for lay beyond this moment. "I can surrender now. I can love you with all of me."

"You make love sound like a sacrifice. True loving takes nothing away."

"I know that now. I don't mean sacrifice, but acceptance."

"And loving will make you stronger."

Then he kissed her powerfully, opening his mouth on hers and pressing so deeply their teeth clashed and she thought their skin would break. He plunged his tongue into her mouth, searchingly, longingly. She felt the power of her desire and his overtake her and jolt through her breasts and womb and thighs like a river of molten lava unleashed after millennia of longing. And at last she did let go and kissed him back with all of her, opening the floodgates of her love and passion like a volcano, ripping open and spilling its banks. At long last they paused for gasping breath.

She laughed nervously, under her shuddering breath. "I haven't felt this consumed since I was... nineteen."

He chuckled softly and kissed the end of her nose. "Mmmm."

"You have quite the way about you."

"You still don't get it, do you? It isn't me. It isn't you either; it's us together."

Simon pulled the pile of fleece blankets and quilts onto the floor in front of the fireplace and laced his fingers with hers, slowly kneeling and pulling her down onto the soft mound. He lay her back gently and leaned on his elbow beside her, kissing her again, slowly, languorously, tasting her, nibbling her lips, and then feathering kisses across her eyebrows, and the line of her jaw until he reached her earlobe and suckled it slowly, licking. Currents of heat coursed through her body where his skin touched hers, but she hesitated, pulling back.

"Maddie?" she whispered, remembering the little girl upstairs.

"Very heavy sleeper," he murmured, continuing his gentle onslaught.

She lay quite still, her eyes following his movements at first, and then slowly closing, so that she could feel only him, her lips slightly parted, her breath ragged. His hands roamed across her body, stroking and caressing her shoulders, arms, back and thighs as if he would have all of her at once until she was trembling with tension and anticipation. Her body arched toward his, yearning to touch every part of her to every part of him. She could feel his arousal pressing against her abdomen, and a surge of molten desire shot through her, emptying her mind of all but one thought, to envelope him, to be one.

twenty-four

When at last Kate let go, she experienced a flood of sensation and emotion unlike any she had felt before. Kate's liberation rendered her uninhibited, intense and ardent, the expression of her love boundless and wild in a way that evoked the first time.

All her worries were annihilated by the here and now, of her connection with Simon, her need for him. His achingly familiar scent, the wiry strength of his long, lean limbs and arching body drove her mad. She was carried away on the floodwaters of their shared desire, inundated and bewildered by the intensity of her own feelings. When she reached for him it was as though all the power of the universe was unleashed through her, her fingertips and lips and eyes and the very core of her womanhood astonished by the force of their connection and electrified by it. In that moment, she could believe their bodies and souls mingled in some cosmic dance, as though their love subsumed their individual selves. Falling into his shimmering flame-blue eyes, she saw everything and nothing. And she felt timelessness and weightlessness and selflessness so absolute it was near unbearable and she was submerged in him like death and rebirth. Simon's muted roar and wracking sobs echoed her own sensations.

"I love you so much," he said, his voice quavering. "Words just can't…"

"I know. I know," she whispered hoarsely, her eyes closing. "I… " she drifted away, utterly spent.

Kate awoke in Simon's bed the next morning. She watched his peaceful slumber, the sheets tangled around his beautiful long limbs, her heart squeezing joyfully. Here she was on the other side.

Slipping out of the bed without disturbing him, she did sun salutations at the foot of the bed, truly filled to brimming with gratitude. She was just coming down from upward dog when she heard his voice.

"Kate?" he said tentatively, the panic rising in his voice. "Kate!"

"I'm here," she replied from the floor. Simon sat up, peering over the edge of the bed, his eyes wide, to find her contorted on the floor, one knee up under her nose, her arms outstretched.

He sat up to watch. "Aah. Yoga?"

"Mmhmm. Sorry. I waited for you, but you were sleeping so soundly."

"What do you call that?"

"Eka pada rajakapotasana."

"Huh?"

"Pigeon pose," she mumbled to the carpet, smiling, then pulled back, her arms in the air.

He lay back in bed, sighing. "You have beautiful breasts."

They had staggered upstairs to his large white bed and made love a second time, slowly, dreamily and unhurriedly and fallen asleep again.

Simon's face reappeared over the edge of the bed. "Oh my God! What's that?"

"Downward dog," she said, laughing breathily from her inverted position.

"Are you trying to kill me?" He rose from the bed and stood behind her as she stood up.

She was grinning over her shoulder, her eyes cast down at his brazen erection. "Merry Christmas."

He grinned back, stepping forward, ready to pounce. The tip of his cock was just poised at her entrance when his delirious grin twisted into a grimace.

"Ah, damn. Maddie will be up any moment. I'll deal with you later." He lightly slapped her bottom and planted a possessive, hungry kiss on her mouth. "Come down when you're ready." He sighed, pulling on sweats and a t-shirt and hurried downstairs.

Kate had a quick shower in Simon's ensuite and, curling her nose at last night's wrinkled clothing, wrapped herself in his plaid flannel robe. Toweling her hair dry, she wondered how Maddie would react to finding her still in the house. She slipped downstairs to find Simon busy in the kitchen again. She plonked herself down on a bar stool and grinned at him a little sheepishly.

"Merry Christmas again," she said.

He licked his lips and smiled wryly. "Merry Christmas to you, ma'am." He set a large cup and saucer in front of her. "Lose your clothes?"

"Should I have dressed? I was worried what Maddie would think." She took an appreciative sip from the steaming mug of tea. "Mmmm. Chai. Perfection."

Simon made a face, shrugged, and turned his attention back to his waffles. "Kids are adaptable."

"You're cooking breakfast?" she enquired. "I would have thought you'd have had enough of playing chef after last night's dinner. It was a spectacular feast, Simon. I'm amazed at your skill, not to mention ambition."

"Thanks." He shrugged, his back to her, and continued his work. "I like to be in the kitchen. It's relaxing and gives me time to think. Besides, my daughter has expectations."

She sighed and took another sip of her tea.

He shot a quick glance over his shoulder. "What?"

"Oh. You know." She laughed, teasing, "I was just thinking how you're just about the most perfect man I've ever met."

"Is that so?" he replied.

"Mmhmm. Almost… ideal, as a matter of fact."

"Almost…" He laughed heartily at that. He bent to place a waffle in the warming oven and turned his attention to whipping cream. She gazed out the French doors, thinking how different the atmosphere felt between them this morning, all tension and reserve evaporated. Despite colder temperatures, the bright sunshine softened the shallow blanket of snow that coated the lawn and flowerbeds. The reflected glare was intense, making her squint. The stone terrace and larger shrubs were already half bare, and glistening wet, shimmering.

Kate turned when Madison shuffled sleepily into the kitchen wearing her rumpled pink flannel nightgown covered in tiny white snowmen. She stood and took in the scene, blinking blearily.

"Daddy." She yawned.

"Morning, sunshine," Simon said to her, in a laughing voice. She was incredibly cute. It was obvious she hadn't yet remembered the occasion.

"Hi, Kate," she smiled sleepily. "Did you sleep over?"

"Yes. I wanted to be the first to wish you a Merry Christmas, Maddie," Kate said, smiling and meeting Simon's eye warily. He smiled.

"I'm glad." Madison yawned. "Oh!" she squealed, remembering, suddenly wide-awake. "Was Santa here? Can I open presents now, Daddy?" The questions tripped over each other in her enthusiasm.

"In just a few minutes, sweetie," Simon said as he set their plates on the bar. "Let's have a little breakfast first, okay?" He turned back to the stove.

"I don't want breakfast. I can't wait."

"I'll tell you what," Kate suggested, raising her brows and looking at Simon. "If it's okay with your Dad, you can open my present to you right now, then after breakfast you can tear into the rest."

"Oh, Daddy. Can I? Can I? Please?"

"Hmmm," Simon seemed to consider "I suppo-ose. But hurry, the waffles are ready." Kate went into the living room without another word and returned with the oddly shaped, soft parcel she had brought, handing it to Madison. She clutched it in her tiny hands, her eyes as big as saucers.

"Go ahead. Open it up." Kate grinned at Maddie, expecting her to tear into the paper. They both watched her, with her bouncy brown curls mashed into an adorable nest, her round cheeks flushed with excitement. Simon pressed his lips together in amusement as Maddie knelt down on the floor with the parcel between her knees and carefully pulled off the bow and ribbons and attempted to peel the paper neatly away, her little brow frowning when it tore. Finally she revealed a long-legged rag doll with a mop of brown hair just like hers.

"Ooh. Kate. It's beautiful," exclaimed Maddie. The giftwrap fell to the floor and a small suitcase bounced out. "What's this?" asked Maddie as she picked it up. Simon served the food, observing the exchange.

"It's a suitcase full of clothes for her to wear, so you can dress her," replied Kate, sliding off her stool to crouch next to Maddie. Her face lit up with delight. "Let's have breakfast and then I'll help you." Maddie threw herself around Kate's neck with a huge bear hug, and Kate had to force back inexplicable tears.

"Thank you soooo much."

Simon and Kate burst into laughter at this delightful display of innocence and goodwill, their eyes meeting over Maddie's head. *Thank you,* he mouthed.

They ate breakfast, all perched around the high kitchen bar, Maddie and Kate 'oohing' and 'aahing' over Simon's culinary skills. "You can't go wrong with waffles, strawberries and sausages with a four year old," he said, setting a small glass of milk down in front of Maddie, and refilling their tea mugs.

"Works at thirty-four, too," said Kate through a full mouth.

"Drink up your milk, Maddie, and we'll go open the rest of our gifts," he said. It didn't take long before they were all settled in the living room around the tree. The tiny colored lights glowed weakly in the strong sunshine that angled in through the front windows. Simon put on a Diana Krall CD.

Maddie went first, opening her new toys and games carefully, though with increasing enthusiasm as time went on. Finally she opened a large square box and let out a delightful squeal.

"Oh Daddy. It's just what I always wanted," she cooed, looking it over. "What is it?" She lifted her innocent enquiring eyes to the adults, waiting expectantly for an explanation. After they recovered from a bout of hysterical laughter, wiping tears from his eyes, Simon replied, "It's something I loved when I was about your age, Maddie. I thought you would like it too. It's a kind of building kit." Maddie's smile twisted into an uncertain scowl.

"You can't play with dolls all the time, Maddie," said Kate. "This will teach you how to be clever and solve problems. It will help you become a smart lawyer like your Mommy and Daddy."

"I don't wanna be a lawyer," dismissed Maddie with a toss of her curls. "When I grow up I'm going to be a Mommy. I'll take my babies to the park to play and give them baths and hug them all the time."

Simon blinked. "That sounds lovely, sweetie. Just remember that Mommy's have to be the cleverest of all. Mommy's know how to do everything."

Maddie giggled. "Oh Daddy, that's not true. Mommy can't cook anything." She flapped a dimpled, dismissive hand at the suggestion. Simon pulled a chagrinned face and glanced at Kate, who was biting back her laughter.

"She didn't have to because I did," said Simon. He drew a breath, held it and let it go with a huff. "Daddy's have to be clever, too. Your turn." He hefted a large rectangular package to Kate, dropping it in her lap, and sat back to watch.

She carefully opened the heavy gift to reveal a large format Thai cookbook, with gorgeous glossy photos of the people, countryside, markets and villages of rural Thailand. "It's spectacular! Thank you," she gushed, leaning in to kiss him.

He looked over her shoulder as she flipped the pages, stopping here and there to comment on the gorgeous colors and interesting details that he remembered from his travels. "The Thai people are the happiest, most peaceful people I've ever met on my travels. I'd like to take you there someday."

She nodded enthusiastically. "Well on that note, open mine," Kate said. "There are some places I'd like to take you."

He stood and retrieved the blue package with curiosity. It was also rectangular and heavy, but more squat than hers. "Hmm. Could it be a book?" he teased.

"Perhaps, but not just any book." Their eyes met, full of fun, and she felt her face crease in a grin to match his. "Go on."

Simon ripped away the paper and ran his fingers over the cover, which was embossed with gold on brown leather and bordered with delicate tracery and foreign script. As he realized what it was, he grinned and slid his eyes over to her coyly. "The Illustrated Kama Sutra?" he nodded. "Ve—ry nice. Thank you." A chuckle erupted from his throat. "Well, we'll have to read it together, won't we?"

"Whats it Daddy?" asked Maddie.

Simon glanced up, his ears suddenly reddening. "Nothing you'd be interested in, sweetie. Grown up... ah, it's a ... how-to manual, I guess." Maddie harrumphed and forgot them again. He turned to thank Kate with a long, deep, lingering kiss that aroused a deep, thrumming response in her. They were listening to the strains of *You're Getting to be a Habit With Me,* and Simon sang along briefly, off key, pressing his face into her silky hair until he made her laugh.

After their gifts, they relaxed in front of the fire sipping tea, nibbling on mincemeat tarts and tossing benign glances at Maddie industriously playing with her new toys and dolls. The doorbell buzzed suddenly, and Simon jumped.

He sat up straight, yanked at the front of his wrinkled t-shirt and surveyed the room. It was a mess, torn gift-wrap, Mandarin orange peels and dirty dishes everywhere. He grabbed a plate, scraped some debris onto it, glanced around desperately, catching Kate's puzzled frown, then sighed, laughing nervously, and set it down again.

"I'll be right back."

"Who is it?" Kate sensed his agitation.

The look he sent her was pitiful. "I think it's Rachel," he grimaced and shrugged, looking around helplessly. *Ah.* She understood his discomfort. Then he straightened his shoulders and headed for the door.

It wasn't Rachel, after all, but his elderly neighbor with a small gift for Maddie and a tin of cookies, to thank him for helping with a contractor earlier in the year. "Thank you, Mrs. McCall. Merry Christmas." Closing the door with a sigh, he returned to the living room, laughing, and set down the gifts. "I don't know what I'm so nervous about. She will show up eventually."

"Who?" asked Maddie.

"Mommy, Maddie. She always comes to wish you a Merry Christmas around lunchtime."

"Oh, yeah." Maddie seemed unmoved by this news.

He stood awkwardly a moment, hands on his hips, taking in the scene of intimate domestic ease and Christmas chaos, obviously still uncomfortable with the impression this would have on his wife. "Maybe we ought to get dressed," he suggested, raking his hands through his disheveled hair.

Just then the doorbell rang again and they all jumped this time. Simon looked at Kate again and sighed, closing his eyes for a moment and heading for the front hall again.

He paused briefly, before opening the door. It was Rachel this time. She strode into the front hall like a fashion model, her long leather coat hanging open to reveal a slim black velvet pantsuit and tall high heeled boots. Her long mane glowed chestnut, draped around her hirsute collar, a wild and shaggy horse in a snowy Siberian landscape. She ignored his *déshabillé,* a starlet's smile pasted on her shimmering face. She was stunning, Kate thought, and obviously on her way somewhere, judging by her attire.

"Simon."

"Rachel."

Rachel didn't notice Kate curled up on the sofa in Simon's robe as she barged past him into the living room, setting her bags down, slipping out of her coat and tossing it on a chair near the door. Okay this is weird. Kate caught Simon's eye over Rachel's shoulder, and he pulled a face.

He gestured towards Kate. "Er... Rachel I'd like..." but she was oblivious.

"Madison, sweetheart, Mommy's here!" Rachel called out.

Simon stood in the doorway observing her performance. He rubbed the back of his neck and folded his arms over his chest, tucking his chin in and watching with raised, twisted brows.

Kate held her breath and hunkered down silently, half hidden by the visual clutter of piled boxed gifts and shreds of gift-wrap, hoping beyond hope that Rachel's ignorance would extend through her entire visit. As if.

Maddie was cool and a trifle befuddled as she glanced over at Kate, trying to put the pieces of her new world together. Now this was definitely getting freaky.

"Hello, Mommy." She held her doll upside down by one leg and rummaged amongst the clothing options that spilled out of the suitcase and over the floor.

"What have you got there, Maddie? A new doll from Santa?" Rachel asked.

"No, Mommy. It's from Kate," Maddie replied matter-of-factly. "Who?"

Maddie pointed at the sofa where Kate sat. Her stomach dropped like a stone. *Oh shit.* "Her."

Rachel whirled around, her brows knit, "Who?" her eyes widening as she took in Kate's attire. Kate felt her face stretch into a tight smile, and tucked the robe around her knees.

Simon stepped in. "Rachel, this is Kate O'Day." Simon made the awkward introductions. Rachel said nothing, her face frozen in surprise.

"How do you do?" Kate tried for a warm friendly voice, though it quavered a little. "I've heard so much about you."

"I'll bet," Rachel replied sarcastically, standing up. "Simon. Do you really think this is appropriate?" she said caustically, turning to him and ignoring Kate. Kate felt the muscles of her chest and neck and face draw up and tighten into a mask.

Kate saw Simon stiffen. "I do," he replied calmly. "Maddie

knows Kate well. We've known each other for many years," he said, smiling wryly at Kate.

"Really?" drawled Rachel. She seemed to gather her thoughts, her lips pursed. Turning to Madison, she said, "Maddie, why don't you get dressed quickly and Mommy will take you out for a little walk to the park. Put your snowsuit on."

"I don' wanna go now. I want to play with my presents for awhile," whined Maddie, looking up at Rachel with solemn eyes. "Can we go later? Pleeease."

"Hmph," Rachel said, her lips pressing into a thin line. "I can't stay that long. I have to catch a plane. I brought you a Christmas present, Maddie. Do you want to open it now?"

Maddie looked up. "Okay." Rachel stooped down to pull a beautifully wrapped parcel from her bag, handing it to her. Maddie pulled at the ribbons, but they were knotted, frustrating her. Rachel, flustered, reached out to help her. Together they wrestled the wrapping off, but not before Rachel snagged a nail and shook her hand, swearing under her breath. Maddie pulled the box open. It was upside down, and the contents slid out in an avalanche of tissue paper. Maddie lifted up a black velvet jumper and looked briefly at it, then put it aside and rummaged amongst the tissue paper searching for something else. She found a pretty blouse with embroidered collar and cuffs. Her face fell when she realized there was nothing more.

"It's clothes again," she said finally.

"Yes, Maddie. Mommy brought you a special outfit from New York. Isn't it pretty?" Rachel's voice was falsely bright, hiding her discomfort and disappointment.

"Yes, Mommy."

"What do you say, Maddie?" Simon prompted quietly.

"Thank you, Mommy." Madison stood up, put her arms up. Rachel suddenly embraced her tightly and kissed her cheek, leaving a bright red crescent of lipstick.

"Merry Christmas, baby," she said and stood up, smoothing out her jacket with well manicured hands, nails painted dark red for the holidays. "Well. If we can't go to the park, I guess I'd better be going, then." Maddie blinked up at her mother. Rachel looked at her and forced a wide smile on her features, then turned to pick up her coat and headed for the front hall. "Nice to meet you, Kate," she said with a distracted air.

Kate said nothing in reply, merely lifting her eyebrows skeptically.

Simon frowned thoughtfully.

"Bye-bye, Mommy." Madison stared after Rachel for a few moments and then turned her attention back to her new doll, struggling to pull on the doll's dress. It wasn't going well and she looked discouraged. Suddenly she stood up and ran to Kate, hurtling onto the sofa and curling up next to Kate.

"Help me dress her, Kate, it's stuck," she insisted, shoving the dress into Kate's hand. Kate took the doll from Maddie, keeping her eyes cast down, terrified that this trusting gesture would throw Rachel into a fit of maternal jealousy. Nothing happened.

Simon followed Rachel slowly and paused at the doorway to look back at Kate and Maddie, his brows pulled together. He sighed. Kate watched him turn and exchange a long, significant look with Rachel, his Adam's apple sliding up and down his lean neck. Kate was embarrassed for them all, and wished she wasn't there to witness the painful scene, and yet her eyes were drawn like magnets to the couple standing stiffly in the hall, her ears straining for every soft-spoken word.

Rachel pressed her glossy red lips together and shook her head slightly. "I should be happy for you, I suppose, but... "

"But?"

"I don't know. It makes me sad somehow."

"I understand."

"I know I've been a dreadful mother. But I don't want to lose Madison."

He paused. "That's up to you."

Rachel chewed her full lower lip thoughtfully. She nodded, as if to herself. "I've got to get to the airport."

"Just a minute, then, I have something for you." He turned and went down the hall, and the few minutes he was gone felt like a thousand hours to Kate, who looked at Rachel, who was not looking at her. He returned and handed a manila envelope to Rachel without a word.

"What's this?"

"Your Christmas present."

She slit the envelope open with a long, sharp fingernail and pulled out a sheaf of papers, scanning them. Her face opened, "I never thought... I'm... shocked."

What?

"It's what you want, isn't it?" *Ah. The divorce papers. He'd finally relented.*

"Yes, but… "

Simon shrugged. "Call us when you're settled in Toronto."

After a long moment, she slipped on an expression of cool indifference along with her leather coat and turned to the door that Simon held open.

"Merry Christmas, Rachel," said Simon quietly.

"Merry Christmas, everyone," said Rachel with brittle brightness and strolled away. He stood watching her go, and Kate said nothing, waiting.

Kate studied Simon's face as he turned toward her. "Was that what I think it was?" she asked him as he returned to the living room.

Simon stood looking pensive for a long moment. He nodded thoughtfully, then blinked and returned her gaze, smiling weakly.

She frowned, concerned. "Are you okay?"

He threw back his head and laughed suddenly, grabbed Maddie, swinging her around above his head and fell onto the sofa beside Kate, tickling and wrestling with Maddie, who giggled and squealed like a piglet yanked from the teat. "I'm better than okay," he said. "I feel wonderful." Leaning over, he kissed Kate enthusiastically then smothered Maddie with kisses too. "Are we still going skating today?"

"Da–ad." whined Madison.

"Ma–ad," Simon mimicked. "We agreed we'd do it this afternoon. Remember? Come on, it'll be fun."

Maddie sighed and stood up.

He reiterated his question to Kate with his eyes. She smiled and nodded. "I'll have to stop at my place to get skates and change my clothes."

"What are we waiting for?"

twenty-five

His scuffed and cut up hockey skates were the same vintage as Kate's, a pair of figure skates that hadn't been seen in stores for twenty years. It made her want to laugh and cry at the same time. They really were two birds of a feather and her chest squeezed at the thought of all the years they'd missed... but what was the use of thinking like that? They had the future.

Stumbling around the ice together with Madison between them on her tiny pink skates they found their balance as a unit. Soon they were laughing and forgetting the encounter with Rachel. They exchanged jokes and greetings with the others who were enjoying themselves, too, and Kate felt a joyful sense of celebration and optimism bubbling up from deep within.

Simon frolicked on his skates, circling Kate and Maddie, gliding backward holding Maddie's hands and whirling her around. His face was stretched tight in a smile of pure joy, and his eyes sparkled like sunlight in the sky. Seeing him so joyful and relaxed filled her with perfect pleasure. She recalled Bertie's words from the night before, that he had been lighter lately, and she was glad. He deserved every bit of it.

Kate was a competent but not a brilliant skater stumbling and wobbling about from laughing so hard. "I'm more of a hindrance than a help for Maddie. I'll take a little break; you go." She released Maddie's hand and coasted off to the side, stumping to the bench where they'd left their boots and falling back in relief. She smiled and waved to them as they set off again.

She watched them circle around the oval rink, Simon guiding Maddie, steadying her.

Maddie was tiring too, so he picked her up, wrapping her legs around his torso, and took her for a few breakneck laps around the rink to her squealing delight. "Faster, Daddy, faster!" she urged as they passed Kate again and again.

While Kate watched Simon and Maddie skate away yet again, they stopped across the rink, and he held her as he spoke to her, their faces close together.

"Kate. Merry Christmas!" came a shouted cheer.

Looking up, she saw Eli and D'arcy approaching side by side, each holding steaming Starbucks cups. D'arcy was bundled in her black faux fur, her head and neck swathed in fuzzy white angora, her increased girth visible under her bulky cover. Eli still wore the battered brown leather jacket he wore back in the fall, though he'd made the concession of adding a navy blue knit stevedore's toque and gloves.

They had barely exchanged greetings when Simon and Maddie glided up beside her.

"Hey, Simon!" Eli greeted him cheerily. "Merry Christmas," D'arcey said. Grins and hugs were exchanged all around. There was a general babel of chatter for a few minutes as everyone spoke at once, exchanging news and greetings.

"And how are you, gorgeous girl?" said Eli, chucking Madison under the chin. He reached into his jacket pocket and pulled out a small candy cane, which he held out. "I have something for you that's bigger than this, but you have to help me get it from the car." He addressed Kate. "We were planning to drop it off at your loft anyway. This is awesome. Do you mind?"

"Can I, Daddy?" Madison squirmed down from his arms and took the candy cane from Eli.

"Sure." He shrugged, looking at Kate and D'arcy with their heads together. "The women won't even notice you're gone," he added.

"Oh, no. I need Darc' too," Eli's brow creased. He tugged at her arm. "C'mon, cheri, let's get the stuff." D'arcy turned an indulgent smile toward him and nodded. Simon quickly changed Maddie into her boots and the trio were off down the plaza hand in hand, leaving Simon and Kate, for the moment, alone.

The dome of overcast sky formed an ethereal bluish light, and though it was only mid-afternoon, the overhead lights flickered on, amber and disorienting, like the glow of gaslight in a

Van Gogh painting. The idyllic moment smote Kate. *Is this really happening to me?* A quintessentially Christmas dreamscape: children and couples gliding around the rink, smiling parents looking on from the sidelines, dozens of snow-capped evergreen trees stepping up the terraces bordering the plaza, sparkling with tiny red and green lights. Faint tinny music played, broadcast over speakers suspended from the domed roof over the ice. It was Johann Strauss' "Blue Danube Waltz". She looked up and caught Simon's eye and they laughed.

"I'm having an out-of-body experience," said Simon, grinning. "I feel compelled to fulfill my role here." He pulled her gently but insistently onto the ice to skate together while Maddie was occupied. Simon took her hand and wrapped one arm around her, propelling her forward, leading her in a synchronized dance around the edge of the rink in time to the waltz. Kate imagined that they were like the tiny characters in a wind-up Christmas ornament, circling the frozen pond. All those years of hockey had made him a confident skater and he wove them among the other skaters with ease. She closed her eyes for a moment, allowing herself to trust his lead and glide effortlessly across the ice.

"We're like pawns in a very big game, Kate. I feel like there is something inevitable about the two of us." Simon stopped speaking, waiting, perhaps, for her to indicate her understanding of his metaphysical musing. She glanced up and he searched her eyes.

"I think I know what you mean," she answered. "It's as though no matter how much we try to mess things up, there's something bigger, a force, a plan. All we have to do is open ourselves to it's... it's fit. It's goodness."

Simon took both her hands in his and skated backwards, facing her, gazing intently into her eyes. "Yes. That's it exactly. There's a word I like... *Syzygy.*" At her puzzled expression, he explained, "It means union. Alignment." He squeezed her hands. "Kate. My Kate." Her heart thudded at his tender words. She felt as though she were in a dream, an unreal world where fantasy and reality blurred. Simon bent toward her and kissed her slowly but ardently, his blue eyes smoldering. They gradually coasted to a halt.

They drifted to the center of the rink, and spun in a slow-motion arc. He gripped her hands, his mouth quirked into that beguiling, self-conscious half-smile. She regarded him as though suspended in time, long moments of confusion and speculation and wonder swirling around them.

"I adore you Kate. I love all of you. I love your strength and idealism. I love your hot temper and your passion. I even love your fears and insecurities. Without your weaknesses, your unique history and idiosyncrasies, you wouldn't be you, and it's you I've come to need. You are my heart's reflection. You complete me Kate."

Tears welled in her eyes as she gazed up at him, waiting for the fear, the doubt, the uncertainty to overtake her. But it wasn't there. There was nothing but joy and anticipation at what their future might hold. Nothing but her whole heart filled with love for him. Her chin quivered and hot tears spilled over, coursing down her cold-reddened cheeks.

"Pinch me. Am I dreaming?"

"Forget your dreams. It's time to stop dreaming and start living," Simon replied, his face tilted up.

"What does that mean?"

"What do you want it to mean?"

Kate knew what happy endings her dreams harbored. But a crust of skepticism still clung to her old wounds. She whispered, "I'm afraid."

Simon sobered, moving closer, pulling their joined hands up between them, their faces so close she could feel his warm breath on her icy cheeks. Tipping his forehead to touch hers, peering intently into her eyes, he nodded. "Okay. Let's be afraid together. One step at a time. How about Boxing Day? Can we be together tomorrow?"

She didn't hesitate. "There's no place I'd rather be."

"How about the next day? Do you think we can spend the twenty-seventh together? Just you and me, and Maddie." His eyes twinkled with humor.

She smiled back, teasing. "Yes. I think so."

"And all the rest of our tomorrows?" He stretched and pulled something out of his front pocket. "That wouldn't be so bad, would it?" She looked down, confused, as he held up a fine antique gold ring, its emerald-cut diamond enveloped in tiny, filigreed claws and curlicues of white gold that glinted in the lamplight. It was stunning, a promise held aloft in Simon's long fingers.

"Simon?" She peered at him, questioning. "Are you… is this?"

His smile was enigmatic, but his eyes burned with feeling. "That would be rash, don't you think? Forgive me for rushing ahead. I just need to claim you for my own. Let's call it a promise for now. Can we do that?"

She felt her heart squeeze, stealing her breath and her voice. She pushed out the words, "I hope so. I...I would like that."

"Well, good! That's certainly what I was hoping, since I've made a bit of a scene here." He laughed softly, making a show of glancing around.

She mimicked him and saw that skaters and bystanders stared at them. Simon's smile was so broad it threatened to crack his face. He bent his tall frame to kiss her firmly on the lips, then slipped off her mitten and slid the ring onto her finger. "This was my grandmother's. It's old and precious, like our love."

Kate gazed down at the antique ring on her finger. "It's beautiful, Simon."

"I found you once, but the time wasn't right. This time I'll never let you go."

"Is this some kind of cosmic love story? A fairy tale?" she asked in disbelief.

His smile softened. "If you like. Yes. I suppose it is. Am I your Prince?"

She nodded slowly, smiling. "You bet."

"What does that make you? Cinderella?"

She shook her head. "No. Must be Sleeping Beauty." She paused to let the feeling of joy overtake her. "I'm awake now."

Just then, Maddie galloped toward them, "Daddy, Daddy," she squealed, slipping on the ice. Simon caught and steadied her, lifting her up into an embrace. Before he could reply, Eli and D'arcy caught up, carrying a shopping bag and large, flat rectangular package.

"Hey you two," teased Eli.

D'arcy beamed. "I've never seen such big grins. It looks like you both got what you wanted for Christmas."

"Me too," offered Maddie, wrapping her arms around Simon's neck.

Kate was overwhelmed by everything that was happening. Her chest swelled and her throat tightened, until she could no longer contain her joy. She quickly brought a mittened hand to her trembling mouth to suppress a sudden sob.

"Whoa," laughed Simon, wrapping an arm tightly about her

shoulders and squeezing. "You're not reneging on me now, are you?"

Kate gazed up into his clear sky-blue eyes and saw the naked love and trust revealed there. "Not on your life," she managed to sniffle and felt her face stretch into a smile of pure joy.

"All right then," said Eli, grinning. "I have just the thing. It's sort of a Christmas present, but mainly, it's a little something to express our thanks." He handed the large flat square parcel to Simon, who set it down on his skate and turned to face Kate, eyebrows raised.

"Not so little," said Simon.

"Thank you both so much," added D'arcy. "You saved us from ourselves." She reached for Kate with leather-gloved hands and embraced her with a quick kiss on the cheek.

"Open it," urged Eli.

"What, right here? Now?" asked Kate. She had a pretty good idea what the parcel contained and was thrilled and honored to have one of his paintings, but still was curious as to Eli's selection. She hesitated, then grabbed the edge of the brown paper and tore it away. She drew in a breath, awestruck, as the image on the large canvas emerged. "Oh, Eli! It's the Magdalene." Kate felt tears well up and overflow. Tears of joy. Tears of fulfillment. Tears of acceptance.

epilogue

So... to my fellow mediators, despite your particular skills and methods, your vast experience and excellent communication skills, I would ask you to remember this... That behind every proud and stubborn facade, underlying every position, is a human heart in need of understanding, forgiveness, and love."

The room broke into enthusiastic applause.

"Thank you."

Kate waited at the podium for the applause to die down. She glanced again at the beautiful cut crystal trophy resting beside her hand, and cast her gaze around the elegant ballroom, acknowledging the smiles and nods of her familiar colleagues and their partners.

"Thank you very much."

At last, she gripped her award, picked up her loose notes, and stepped down from the podium. Already people were rising and moving toward her. She shifted her award to her left hand in order to accept handshakes, a giddy thrill running through her as her eyes fell on the antique ring on her left hand, a sparkling treasure even more precious to her than the cut crystal trophy, and harder earned.

"Ms. O'Day. That was wonderfully inspiring." A younger woman pressed closer. "I loved that quote about the light. What was it again?"

Kate turned to her. "Ellis French, isn't it?" The young woman beamed and nodded. Kate smiled. She was a bit of a celebrity tonight, at least among her peers. "It goes *'The wound is the place where the Light enters you.' By Rumi.*"

"Lovely metaphor. So true."

"I agree," murmured a grey-bearded middle-aged man to her other side. "Human beings are rather fragile creatures who carry the battle scars of their lives with them as they venture forth."

"Yes, but…" the keen young mediator jumped in.

He held up his hand, silencing her. "Don't think I'm contradicting Ms. O'Day." He turned to Kate, pressing her hand with his. "On the contrary, your speech was an important reminder that human beings are rather strong and resilient, and somehow do manage to carry on no matter how much damage they have sustained. In doing so, they build up walls around their hearts, and don a formidable armour to protect them from further damage."

"Yes, we do, sir. Unfortunately it's these protective barriers that often keep us apart. Apart from others, and apart from knowledge of ourselves, even though this is not in our best interests."

"This is the what Rumi meant, Ms. French. Knowing this gives us a way in, a way to help them find forgiveness and redemption. As you have so consistently done, Ms. O'Day. Congratulations. Well-deserved."

"That's a great compliment coming from you, Dr. Howard," Kate said. "Thank you so much."

"Let the girl breath, Leonard."

Kate's eyes touched on a smiling Rose McIlhaney as she approached and swept Kate into a soft mother-bear hug. Her familiar, comforting voice rumbled in Kate's ear.

"Well done, my dear. Well done."

"Thank you so much, Rose. For everything. I wouldn't be here without you."

Rose tutted and shielded her as she guided her back to a round table to the left of the podium. Kate's eyes came to rest on Simon waiting patiently while she enjoyed her moment in the sun.

His grinning face was suffused with pride, his clear blue eyes shining with a love so clear and unconditional, it could not be denied. He stood and swept her into an embrace.

"Congratulations, my love."

"Oh, you feel so good." She squeezed her arms tighter around his warmth and solidity.

He pulled back and touched his lips to hers, chastely, but she felt the magnetic pull of his desire for more. "How soon can you escape your fans?"

Kate's cell phone, sitting by her place on the table, buzzed. Simon picked it up, glanced at it and shot her a sly grin. "There. I don't have to beg you to leave. Alexa is doing it for me. She says, *'I'm so proud of you, honey! Hurry up and join me for a drink to celebrate.'"*

"I promised, didn't I?"

"You did. But I wish we could go straight home and celebrate by ourselves." He leaned down and kissed her again, more deeply this time.

"Mmmm. Me too."

He sighed. "Tonight is for you. And I have a sitter. I don't want to short-change you. There'll be plenty of time for that later."

"If we're still awake."

"Well, there's always tomorrow. Or the day after that." He kissed her again, the corner of his beautiful mouth pulling up in a teasing smile. "Or the day after that."

"I can't wait until I can move in and we can be together every night."

"It won't come soon enough for me. Then we can get to work making babies so we'll never have to go out again."

"Gah! You don't mean that." She swatted him. "Let's go meet Alex before you have me barefoot in the kitchen."

"Never! Your people need you. I'll have to learn to share." His laughter warmed her down to her toes, and seeped into every crack and crevice in her heart, healing her, filling her up.

Her heart swelled with joy, gratitude and a love so deep, she could no longer doubt that this was her new reality. That when she walked away from this podium, this special night, Simon would be beside her, and they would take their next steps, and the ones after that, together, hand in hand.

The End

subscribe & follow MACS!

To receive exclusive updates from M A Clarke Scott and to be the first to get news, please sign up to be on her personal mailing list!

You'll get instant access to cover releases, chapter previews, exclusive offers and great prizes!

SUBSCRIBE:
www.maryannclarkescott.com

Facebook:
https://www.facebook.com/maryann.clarkescott

Twitter:
https://twitter.com/maclarkescott

Goodreads:
https://www.goodreads.com/author/
show/15160160.M_A_Clarke_Scott

acknowledgments

This book has been around for a long, long time, and so the list of people to whom I owe thanks is long indeed.

To all my teachers and mentors, to all my writing peers from whom I've learned so much and who welcomed me into the most supportive tribe imaginable, to the Halloween Writers who were my first critique group, the Marvelous Mountain Mavens, Michele, Donna & Joanna, who have supported me and championed my career, to my Atta Girl partner Kyla with whom I can discuss, apparently, anything, and who dares to push me that extra little bit, and to my family, who have allowed me to be the eccentric writer in their midst, neglecting them and burning dinner with regularity– Thank you.

Thanks also to the first editor of this manuscript, Elizabeth Lyon, and the last editor of this manuscript, Eileen Cook, both brilliant and insightful ladies, as well as all the contest judges and beta readers who offered constructive criticism through the years – you helped me so much, and made the story better and better with each iteration. But of course, any shortcomings in the story remain my own responsibility in the end.

book club discussion questions

1. Kate fails to completely disclose the details of her former relationship with Simon, playing it down to avoid embarrassment, and the need to discuss it with her clients or with Sharon. Ethically, this is a grey area. *Do you think she handled it properly, or should have revealed all? Was she wrong to keep the case?*

2. Eli also keeps a secret for seven years, fearing the facts would cause a rift between D'arcy and her parents, and wishing to avoid her getting hurt. *Do you think he was right to do so, or that he created more problems in his marriage because he kept silent?*

3. Kate struggles to decide whether she should commit to Jay or search for something more in a relationship. She feels that he lacks some qualities that she values, despite being a very nice man. *Do you think she could have been happy with Jay if she'd chosen him? If you've been in a long-term relationship, did you have the kind of compatibility Kate and Simon have, or not? How did this affect your relationship over time?*

4. Kate originally planned to study Urban Planning, but veered into counseling after benefiting from it herself. *Do you think she is drawn to mediation as a way of compensating for her own fear of commitment and intimacy, and unfulfilled needs?*

5. D'arcy keeps a secret of her own while in the midst of divorce proceedings and mediation. She has her reasons. *What do you think they are, and would you have done the same under the circumstances?*

6. Kate struggles throughout the book to decide whether the feelings she has for Simon are "real." She's concerned her memories are confusing fact with fantasy, and doesn't trust herself. *Do you believe that it's possible to fall in love with the same person twice? How can this be, and how might the two sets of feelings differ?*

7. Have you had any experience with mediation before? *Do you think this is a valuable process for couples struggling with complex issues before leaping into divorce?*

8. Kate claims that she had repressed memories of a trauma earlier in her life, and that certain events triggered the return of these memories. The author's research convinced her that repressed and recovered memories are possible, and even logical responses to traumatic or stressful life experiences. Memory is a complex thing, and there are many mechanisms at work. *Do you believe that this can happen to victims of violent crime or other painful experiences? How do you think repressed or fragmented memories of trauma could manifest, or impact a person's life?*

   NOTE: for further reading, go to: http://www.jimhopper. com/child-abuse/recovered-memories/ or http://www. psychologicalscience.org/journals/cd/12_1/McNally.cfm

9. Sharon takes the high road regarding professional ethics and conflict of interest in the mediation case. *Do you believe her interference was purely professional in nature, or that she had other, more personal motives?*

10. Kate's best friend Alexa is the first person she goes to, to share her feelings and fears, even though she didn't tell her everything about her past before. Alexa is by turns supportive, protective and critical of Kate's judgment and ability to cope. *Do*

you think Alexa is a good or a fickle friend? Does she give Kate what is needed moment by moment, or should she have tried to help her in different ways? What is your responsibility when your friends face a dilemma and ask you for advice?

11. Simon's friends and family are very protective of him, and cautious about accepting Kate. Darcy's mother also plays a controlling role in her life, though Simon later encourages a stronger bond with family. *Do you think they are over-protective? How do you feel about families and friends that interfere or pass judgment on potential mates? Do they sometimes know us better than we know ourselves? Do you think it important to take their opinions into consideration?*

12. Sharon and Rachel, and to some extent Alexa, are portrayed as unsympathetic, hard career-focused women. *Do you think it necessary for an ambitious career woman to make sacrifices to their personal lives or do you think this is a myth? Can you Lean In and Have it All at the same time? Do you think some women project a harder image in order to compete in their professional environments or is it that serious ambitious women are perceived as bitches? Is this fair?*

13. Rachel seems resigned by the end of the book to surrender her marginal role as mother to Maddy, at least for the time being. *Do you think her moving away will negatively affect Simon's daughter? Do you think Maddy is better off with a full time step-mother than a distant mother?*

14. Alexa, Sharon and Rachel all get their own stories later in the Having It All series. *Which of these four women (including Kate) do you most identify with? Whose story would you most like to read?*

about the author

M A Clarke Scott's early loves included two things: books and art. In her world-view, blank white pages, canvasses and even walls, are begging for her creations.

Neither of these passions have waned, despite all the other adventures she's had in the meantime. She wrote her first romance novel at the age of nine, but soon abandoned both writing and drawing for a career in architecture, then an academic career in environmental gerontology. Tiring of both, and still none the richer, she has returned to her first loves, writing and art.

Her geeky fascinations include wormholes and time travel, archeology, European history, French films, neuroplasticity, metaphysics, Jungian psychology, using big words ;-)

She loves to write about young women on journeys abroad who discover themselves and fall in love while getting embroiled in someone else's problems... and professional women struggling to balance the challenge and fulfillment of their career with their search for identity, love, family and home. She also loves to weave dramatic relationships into close-to-home sci-fi adventure plots, particularly in the steampunk and cyberpunk sub-genres.

You can read more about M A, her books and ideas that strike her fancy at www.maryannclarkescott.com

M A lives with a small menagerie of large men and small mammals on the beautiful West Coast of British Columbia, and though she knows she lives in paradise, still loves traveling the world in search of romance and adventure.